GRAY WITCH

HAILEY EDWARDS

Copyright © 2022 Black Dog Books, LLC

All rights reserved.

No part of this book may be reproduced in any form or by any electronic or mechanical means, including information storage and retrieval systems, without written permission from the author, except for the use of brief quotations in a book review.

This is a work of fiction. Names, characters, businesses, places, events and incidents are either the products of the author's imagination or used in a fictitious manner. Any resemblance to actual persons, living or dead, or actual events is purely coincidental.

Edited by Sasha Knight
Copy Edited by Kimberly Cannon
Proofread by Lillie's Literary Services
Cover by Damonza
Illustration by NextJenCo

GRAY WITCH

Black Hat Bureau, Book 5

Famous monsters are resurrecting across Mississippi, each one recreating their own gruesome deaths through new victims. Every time Rue pins down one horror legend, another appears with its own bloodthirsty agenda. The summoners raising these vengeful spirits save their best for last, a cruel gift that shatters Rue. But she's not the only one whose heart gets broken.

Once her father realizes what the summoners have done, who they've awakened, there is nowhere they can hide where he can't find them. After this final betrayal, there are no limits on how far he's willing to go to bring down Black Hat, the director, and anyone else who gets in his way.

Including his own daughter.

1

A funk reminiscent of dead mice decomposing in the walls and unwashed armpits ripening under the hot Alabama sun wafted to my nose and kicked my tear ducts into high gear. Had it been summer and not a tepid February day, I might have retched at the macabre trophies mounded before me in a precarious stack.

Death fogged their eyes. Bloody hair caked their foreheads. Mouths gaped on their final roars.

And then there were the spines. So many spines. So, so many spines.

Beyond that, on the killing field, the daemon performed a victory dance he'd learned from Mystic Realms.

Around me, in bleachers constructed from the weathered bones of challengers past, loomed daemons.

Fangs. Horns. Wings. Fins. Tails. Claws.

The appendage combinations alone threatened to drop my jaw upon entering the otherworldly arena.

The entire coliseum existed inside a magical construct adjacent to Hael. A pocket realm with a dedicated purpose and set location you could reach via a gate anchored to the arena. Or, if you were fancy like me, through a doorway you carved yourself.

Odds of an ambush were slim but never zero. Why chance it? There were seven challengers vying for the throne without the daemon making himself a target by arriving with the veritable rainbow of spectators.

All of whom had set aside their differences and united today with one desire.

To witness their prince slaughter usurpers who coveted his crown with extreme prejudice.

"Pleat my skirt and call me a cheerleader." Clay, back from plundering the concession stand, plunked down next to me in the royal family's box. "Got pompoms? A megaphone?"

The crimson mohawk he rocked was an impressive two feet high, and yes, he measured it before we left the house. The tee with the daemon's grinning face made me wish I had ordered one when Clay offered. The black rosettes stenciled down his arms were cute, but he had abandoned the set of temporary fangs after swallowing one.

"Do I look like a spirit store to you?" I coughed as I caught a whiff of his snack, a greasy paper bag of what resembled fried pinkish crickets in hot sauce. "What are those?"

"A daemon delicacy." He held one out to me. "Try it."

"No thanks." I did my best not to gag. "I'm trying to cut back."

"I have an idea." He bit it in two then offered me the top half. "Now try it."

"Yeah." I shoved away his hand. "Still no."

"It works when Ace does it." He popped out his bottom lip. "Is my spit not good enough for you?"

"No one's spit is going to make me eat that." I sniffed the bag. "That's not hot sauce, is it?"

"Nope." He tossed the reject into his mouth and crunched down. "You don't know what you're missing."

"You don't know what you're eating."

"Mmm." He ate another one. "Zesty with a hint of *what the hell did I just put in my mouth*."

"I worry about you." I inched farther away from him. "You'll try anything once."

"You're not wrong." His grin flashed twitching legs caught between his teeth. "What did I miss?"

"Somebody got disemboweled. Then beheaded. Somebody else got torn in half. Then beheaded."

A subtle clap-stomp clap beat through the ranks, which I echoed, but it was hard to rah-rah for senseless violence. Even if the participants volunteered for slaughter in droves, as if it weren't a death sentence.

"I was gone ten minutes." A not-cricket fell out of his mouth. "Tops."

"The daemon has a guild thing with Colby in two hours. He wants to hurry up and get home."

"Oh, yeah." He retrieved the snack from where it landed on his thigh. "They're raiding the Tunnels of Tumult."

"Mmm-hmm."

No matter how often Colby explained Mystic Realms to me, I couldn't wrap my head around its nuances. The details held my interest about as well as when I gushed to her about my newest book with subplots galore.

All I needed in order to support her was knowing that gaming was to her what reading was to me.

A happy place.

A much happier place than the one I was currently in.

Screaming, roaring, the crowd surged to their feet as the daemon wrenched his opponent's hip from the socket, tore off one of his six legs, then beat him to death with it. *Classic*. Why bring a weapon when you could make your own? Next came his finishing move. A quick twist of his wrist, and off popped the head.

"Are the challenges always this hardcore?" I indicated the crowd with my chin. "And so well attended?"

"Yep to the first." He skimmed the gathering. "Nope to the second."

As a frequent attendee, Clay was the authority here. This was my first time witnessing the spectacle in its glory. Or should that be *gory*? A front row seat to watch the daemon fight for his—and Asa's—life wasn't my idea of entertainment. I had avoided my debut for months, but I was all in with Asa now. If I wanted him—and I did—I had to stake my claim for all to see.

Grateful for the cooler Asa packed for me, I dug out a bottle of chilled water. "What makes today special?"

"Stavros is the only person who pulls in these numbers." He patted my head. "Until you, apparently."

"Lucky me."

"Hey, friend." Eyes on my drink, Clay wet his greasy lips. "Can I have a sip?"

"You have roach legs stuck in your teeth, so no. I don't want your backwash."

"They're crickets," he corrected me then examined one. "Probably."

Heaving a sigh, I surrendered one of the precious bottles for his use, to pollute as he saw fit.

"Rue."

The daemon bounded over with the oozing head of his latest kill and presented it to me on his palm.

"For you." He dropped to one knee and extended his arms until ichor dripped onto my pants. "You like?"

All eyes followed the prince, and the gazes of every daemon in the stands now bored holes through me.

"It's the best one yet." I ignored the foul stain spreading across my jeans. "My new personal favorite."

"Rue claps for me." He swung the offering to show Clay too. "Claps help me kill faster."

Clay choked on a laugh he blamed on a cricket leg going down the wrong pipe.

"Well—" he coughed into his fist, "—you are half fae."

The nod to the Tinkerbell effect made me smile, but the daemon tilted his head to one side.

"There's a play called *Peter Pan*," I explained. "When Peter's best friend gets hurt, the audience is asked to clap if they believe in fairies. Tinkerbell, his best friend, is a fairy. So, the claps save her life."

The whimsical idea appealed to him, if his bright eyes were any indication.

A crackle filled the speakers overhead before they squealed in an earsplitting screech then fell silent.

"Ruger of Agonae," the announcer boomed, then a heartbeat later. "Face your doom."

Interest perking at his classification, I kept my eyes peeled for my first look at another Agonae daemon.

A male swaggered onto the field who was the equivalent of the daemon on steroids. His features were a perfect mixture of hard angles and sharp edges, his fangs thick and white, his lips full of sensual promise. He wore his silky black hair in four Dutch braids tied at his nape. Strands escaped to frame his pretty face, drawing attention to the perfect arches of his eyebrows and his coal-black eyes.

"Jason Momoa called," Clay broke into my thoughts. "He wants his eyebrows back."

"Yes." I couldn't put my finger on it before, but he was right. "He's got a Khal Drogo vibe."

"Who are you, and what have you done with Rue?" He recoiled. "She never watches TV."

"Ask Colby how much trouble she got in when I caught her watching the Dothraki wedding episode."

A shrill whistle left his pursed lips, and his grim expression confirmed I had been right to flip my lid at the graphic nature of the show. The guild had been watching together, which was no excuse for Colby diving in with them. Mentally, she was ten years old. She always would be. The others were aging up, but Colby wouldn't. I ached for her, for that forced stasis, but she knew better. She just didn't want to feel left out.

During the two weeks that followed, she *really* felt left out with no internet access.

"Lady Witch," Ruger called, yanking my attention to the field. "Will you grant me your favor?"

This guy was throwing off some hardcore renaissance faire vibes. Mmm.

My kingdom for a fried Oreo. Oh! Or a fried Snickers bar. Or a fried Twinkie.

Really, anything that didn't make me want to hose it with bug spray or step on it first fit the bill.

"Why would I do that?" I scrunched up my face, playing my part. "I want a champion who actually wins."

The crowd erupted into laughter, the daemon puffing up with pride, but Ruger only doubled down.

"Will you be mine, beautiful darkness, if I win?"

The daemon scoffed as if it was the most ridiculous question he had ever heard. "Rue mine."

"Let the wicked lovely speak, half breed."

A hush fell over the spectators as the insult landed, or maybe it was the faint buzzing in my ears.

"Call him that again." I let him see his death in my eyes, how much I would enjoy it. "I dare you."

"Lay a finger on him," Clay warned me out of the side of his mouth, "and Ace forfeits the match."

And I would have let my temper write his, and the daemon's, death warrant.

"I applaud your willingness to overlook his deformities, but you could fuck me with your eyes open."

The daemon swung his head toward me, lips screwed tight over his fangs, a furrow dug across his brow.

"Are you still talking?" I appealed to the eavesdropping crowd. "Are you guys bored too?"

The overwhelming answer was *yes*.

Indulgent smile on his lips, Ruger executed a courtly bow to me then pivoted on his heel.

Any concern on the daemon's part vanished, and he pounded a fist over his heart. "Rue love me."

"You really are a sad thing, aren't you?" Ruger rolled out his shoulders. "Barely comprehensible."

The buzzing turned into a full-on roar as Clay slung an arm around my shoulders to restrain me.

"Don't do it." Clay held on tight and forced my head onto his shoulder. "Don't give him what he wants."

As far as I could tell, what he wanted was to die horribly. By my hands. Wrapped around his throat. With that stupid smirk etched on his stupid face. *Forever.* Because after he was decapitated, I would shave his stupid hair and shrink his stupid head for a rearview mirror ornament to brighten my drives to the shop.

"Can this guy die already?" Leaning into my pose, I faked a yawn. "I'm falling asleep over here."

As far as my fellow spectators were concerned, it was the right thing to say.

Their prince's arm candy was bloodthirsty, ready to kill for him, and they ate it up with a spoon.

A chant began in the row behind me and picked up speed as it swept through the stands.

"Fight."

"Fight."

"Fight."

"Ruger of Agonae," the announcer thundered over the ruckus. "Fight or forfeit."

The daemon settled into a ready stance, but Ruger grinned over his shoulder—then ran straight at me.

"Dreams do come true." I touched my wand through my pants. "I can defend myself, right?"

For such a bulky daemon, the guy was moving fast. He also wasn't deviating from his collision course.

"Oh, hell yes." Clay tossed his snack to a nearby daemon. "You absolutely can."

That was when I realized Clay had ditched his food, and it wasn't to help me.

"Let's get physical," he belted out. "Get down, get hard, get mean." He clapped in rapid bursts. "Let's get physical and beat that other team." He stomped as the daemons joined in. "Go, Rue! Go, Rue! Go, Rue!"

Six feet away from the royal box, Ruger leapt, claws out and fangs glistening.

I let him come, let him see I had no fear, let him register just how big the mistake was he had made.

As he started pinwheeling his arms, desperate to halt his descent, I unsheathed my wand.

Magic percussed the air when I tapped him on the quivering nose, and he burst into powdery ash flakes.

"Anyone else?" I fanned the gray flurries away from my face. "Or can I get back to watching the show?"

Whoops and whistles erupted in the crowd, and they picked up Clay's chant, lifting it until my ears rang.

The two remaining challengers slinked to the forest's edge then disappeared into the shadows.

Muscles tensed in the daemon's calves, the instinct to chase riding him, but he allowed the cowards to flee with a disgusted grunt.

An orange-skinned daemon with flaming yellow hair jogged out to greet him dressed in a red leather suit with black shoes. A gold lavalier mic flashed at his collar, and a bodypack transmitter bulged at his spine.

"The winner and still champion," the announcer roared, "Astaroth Xan Stavros, High Prince of Hael."

Grinning like a fool, gore smearing his face, the daemon allowed the announcer to thrust his fist into the air.

After the obligatory grandstanding ended, the daemon jogged over and vaulted into the box with us.

"Congratulations, big guy." I raked my fingers through his stiff and sticky hair. "You kicked butt today."

"Rue okay?" He crushed me against his chest. "Ruger not hurt Rue?"

"Oof."

Lungs screaming for oxygen, I coughed out a garbled answer.

"She's fine." Clay wedged us apart. "Or she will be, if you let her breathe."

Glee sparking in his eyes, the daemon bounced on the balls of his feet. "You have fun?"

In no universe would I ever consider him fighting for his life *fun*, but he was high on victory, and the final event did brighten my day. Really, I didn't feel bad fibbing to keep a bounce in his step. "It was a blast."

"Literally." Clay wiped his face. "I need a tissue to blow Ruger out of my nose."

"Crybaby." I used the hem of my shirt to wipe my face clean. "Snorting daemon never hurt anyone."

Fast as a blink, the daemon scooped me into his arms and leapt to the grass, setting me on my feet.

"Me next." Clay held out his arms. "I want to be carried everywhere I go too."

The daemon rolled his eyes in a Colbylike gesture then turned to me. "Go home now?"

"Sure thing." I worked to contain my relief. "We're done here."

Heaving a sigh, Clay jumped the railing and landed beside me with his second pout of the day.

About to tease him for it, I tensed when flames ignited as the daemon exchanged one body for another.

Hair in grisly tangles, Asa wore the daemon's black leather pants and onyx piercings, but that was it.

Worry trickled through me at the unscripted switch. Asa had explained before we left that he would hold his daemon form to please the crowd. They weren't big on fae. Princely or otherwise. It was dangerous to swap now.

"Rue—"

That was all the warning Asa got out before I noticed the crowd parting around a newcomer.

From the sudden hush, I decided he was a high-ranking daemon wearing human glamour.

But his face, if it was truly his, set my heart pounding in recognition of who approached us.

Orion Pollux Stavros, Master of Agonae, High King of Hael.

Asa's father.

They could have been brothers. *Twins.* The centuries spanning between them were as nothing.

Except for the steel of his eyes, sharp as honed daggers, the opposite of Asa's jewel-toned warmth.

"Son." Overlooking Asa, he fixated on me. "You weren't leaving without saying goodbye?"

"Father." Asa kept his voice smooth and even. "I wasn't aware you were coming today."

Had we known, Clay wouldn't have left my side to indulge his culinary curiosity at the concession stand.

Suddenly, Ruger's bid to go out with a bang made a lot more sense. He had been performing for Stavros. Or, possibly, acting on Stavros's orders. Had Clay not warned me, I would have accomplished what none of the challengers had managed: I would have killed the daemon.

"You requested an audience with me." Magnanimous, the high king spread his hands. "Here I am."

"Here you are," I agreed. "Lucky thing you caught us before we left."

"Fortunate indeed." He smiled with avarice that chilled the marrow in my bones. "You must be Rue."

"That's what they tell me." I returned his frank appraisal with zero interest. "You're High King Stavros."

"You will soon be family, so I'll allow a degree of informality. You may call me *Your Highness*."

Determined to play nice, for now, I bit my tongue until it bled. "Thanks."

"Perhaps you prefer *Master*?" He studied my mouth. "I would like to hear it fall from your lips."

The thinly veiled order made my knuckles itch for an introduction to his jaw. "I'm good."

"Of that, I have no doubt." He cocked an elbow in offering. "Please, join me for a walk."

Amputation was preferrable to touching a man who had assaulted a woman as he had Asa's mother.

"*We* would love to walk." I threaded my arm through Asa's instead. "Thanks for making time for us."

"Of course." His throat bobbed as if swallowing my dismissal required actual, physical effort. "Shall we?"

A subtle shift on the edge of my vision told me Clay would maintain a polite distance, unless we needed him.

"I understand from my son that you wish to be rid of your *y'nai*."

"Yes."

"Our people will expect a certain amount of cultural tolerance from you."

"I'm prepared to honor Asa's daemon heritage, as well as his fae heritage, in equal measure."

A tendon flexed in Stavros's neck, but he kept walking, taking time to nod to his loyal subjects in passing.

"Yet here you are, black witch, proving yourself a liar. You can't afford to shun *our* customs, Rue."

"What of my customs? I am, as you say, a black witch. Where is your cultural tolerance?"

"You are a fascinating creature, but I have yet to be convinced you're a proper match for my son."

Way to sidestep a question yet still give me an answer loud and clear.

"You have no say over who I mate." Asa delivered the line with the ease of a person used to repeating an old argument. Often. "I'm a person of mixed heritages, and so is Rue." White witch, black witch. A smidge of daemon. "We each must do our best to honor the differences between us."

Amused by Asa's show of good faith, his father shook his head as if indulging a precocious child.

"How about I keep the *y'nai* with the stipulation it can't harm anyone without my permission?"

"That defeats the purpose of *y'nai*," he said, gracing me with the same patronizing look.

"I would appreciate leniency in this matter." I swallowed my pride. "Your Highness."

My pride threatened to come back up and spill all over his shoes, but I managed to choke it down.

"I would appreciate it if you removed the wards blocking the *y'nai* access to your property."

Yup.

I should have upchucked on his fancy leather shoes.

Hold on a minute.

The wards.

Finally, he was making me want to not claw off his face, air-dry it, and use it as a smoothie coaster.

Hmm.

Lots of daydreaming about curing flesh into jerky-like stiffness today.

I knew I should have eaten before we left the house.

"The wards stay." I brooked no argument. "Any daemon too weak to cross them isn't my problem."

The air of a challenge left Stavros grinning and earned me a warning glance from Asa.

"Why agree to a meeting," Asa interceded, "if you never intended to grant our request?"

"How could I resist an opportunity to meet your lovely *potential* mate?" Stavros, who was never getting another *highness* out of me, quit walking. "By all accounts, Rue, you are clever, wicked, and cruel. You're aware my son shares none of those qualities? His mother spoiled him. Emasculated him. Ruined him."

That high-pitched whine returned, filling my ears, deafening me to whatever he said next.

"Your father was a remarkable black witch. Legendary. Even among our kind. Mixing my blood with your heritage can only result in cunning offspring with the potential to crush other worlds under their heels."

Had the director taken the same no-nonsense approach with Calixta? Or had breeding been her idea?

You know what? Scratch that. There are things kids don't need to know about their grandparents.

"Sever your fascination with my son." He smoldered at me. "Together, we will topple empires."

Apparently, history really did love repeating itself. Me? Not so much.

"As much as I would love to never in a million years take you up on the offer, I'm with Asa."

"Allow me to castrate him, and you may keep the boy." He smirked. "A gift to my future bride."

White noise screamed in my head. Tension coiled in my muscles. The world bled into shades of crimson.

As the chains began to drop away from my black witch core, I knew—I *knew*—I was going to attack.

And I would kill him.

But that would put Asa on the throne, so...

Priorities.

With great effort, I leashed my worst impulses, smoothed my features, and sank back into my skin.

"Look at the time." I checked my bare wrist. "I have heads to put on pikes at home, so we'll be going."

"Think on my offer." Stavros smiled then, hot and honey sweet. "I'm twice the daemon he is."

"Biologically? Yes." I toyed with a lock of Asa's hair. "But he's dae. The best of both worlds."

A soft breath parted his lips, telling me no one had ever stood up to this bully for him.

Their loss. He was mine now, and I wouldn't let anyone hurt him. Especially not his dillweed of a father.

"Thank you for your time, Father." Asa slid his arm around my waist. "We'll be going now."

"Perhaps I'll visit." His father's eyes simmered where Asa and I touched. "To test those wards."

The warning was plain for me to hear, and the threat to me and mine made my blood boil.

"Heads don't pike themselves." I tossed him a wave. "We'll send you a card at Christmas."

Subtle tension quivered through Asa when we turned our backs on his father, but I tapped his thigh with my wand, assuring him I was armed. We were going home. If we had to go through his dad first, so be it.

"Please tell me he put the moves on me as some misguided fatherly test of my love for you."

"You said *love* without frothing at the mouth or your eyes rolling back in your head."

"*Hey.*" I elbowed Asa. "I'm not that bad."

He kissed my temple, and I felt his smile against my skin.

"Father doesn't believe *no* applies to him. *Consent* is not in his vocabulary."

"What I'm hearing is, there's a good chance I'll get to teach your father a few new words."

"I wouldn't have invited you today if I had known he would be here."

"You've met my family." I leaned into him. "It's only fair I meet yours too."

Mine was a boatload of crazy manned by a crew of the criminally insane, Aedan being the exception. Guess that made him the captain.

"Father aside, how did you enjoy the spectacle?"

Had he really not heard the answer I gave earlier? Or did he want one tailored to him?

I wasn't sure how deeply he slept when the daemon was ascendant, but they each had moments they kept for themselves. They didn't share everything. Thank the goddess. The daemon must have held on to that one. Proof I accepted him, that I was proud of him for surviving.

"I enjoyed the fights more than the concession stand offerings," I hedged. "Clay might not agree."

"Those..." Asa wiped a hand over his mouth, "...weren't crickets."

"I don't want to know."

"Tell me later, Ace." Clay met us halfway back to the bleachers. "Have a nice chat with Papa, Rue?"

"Stavros wants to knock me up in the hopes of birthing the next apocalypse."

"I miss all the good stuff," he grumbled. "Did you at least kick him in the nards for the insult?"

"No." I regretted it too. "I was trying to be good."

"Sorry FIL was an assclown." Clay pinched my cheek. "And that he wants to raid your ovaries."

"Pinch my cheek again," I growled at him, "and see what happens."

"Which cheeks would those be?" He pitched his voice low to match Stavros's. "Wanna polish my scepter? Ride my throne? Lick my crown?" He doubled over laughing until he wheezed. "The last one's a keeper."

"How about I erase your *shem* then donate your body to Mrs. Gleason to use as a scarecrow?"

"I'm not scared." He smoothed a hand down his chiseled abs. "I look good in plaid."

Thanks to his (literally) sculpted physique, he wasn't wrong.

An urgent ring from his pocket shut us up as he brought the cell to his ear. "Kerr."

As Asa listened in, he pressed his lips into a hard line, but I was stuck waiting.

"Yes, sir." Clay vibrated with glee. "We'll leave now."

After ending the call, Clay all but skipped to our private exit and waited for me to activate the portal.

Only after we stepped from the bustling arena onto the quiet driveway in the exact same predawn hour as we had left for Daemon Fight Club, thanks to the pocket realm's distorting time, did he hold still long enough to explain.

"The Boo Brothers are back." A slow grin spread wide. "Three guesses who gets to hunt them down?"

2

"The Boo Brothers." I must have misheard him. "As in Malcom and Emmett Holmstrom?"

"The very same." Clay practically skipped to the front porch. "Can you believe it?"

"I thought they were dead."

"So did I." He held the door for us. "They've got to be in their fifties."

About to check on Colby, I froze as her battle cry rang out and then about-faced so as not to distract her.

The last time I got her killed in Mystic Realms, she refused to talk to me for a month.

Okay, she did speak to me. *In elvish*. It might as well have been Klingon.

"You're sure the director wants us to hunt down a couple of humans?"

This would be a cakewalk compared to the caliber of cases usually assigned to us.

"Well, no, but what the director don't know won't hurt him."

"Then who handed down the order?"

"Parish," Asa answered, having overheard the call. "Do you know him?"

"Jai Parish?" A chill skittered down my spine. "The Dragon?"

Parish was an ancient fae of undetermined species who smelled like brimstone and death. Smoke spilled from his nostrils when his temper spiked, resulting in his affectation of being a smoker, but cigarettes were an amusing prop. He had been known to carry the same one in his pocket for years before replacing it.

As many fae did, he resembled a beautiful man in his midtwenties, about Aedan's age.

But you only had to stare into the midnight-blue pools of his eyes to glimpse eternity.

"He's the Deputy Director of the Black Hat Bureau," Asa confirmed. "Took over right after you left."

"The director killed Mikkelsen," Clay added. "Used a nasty spell to rip out his spine."

"Why?" I aimed for the fridge. "Not that he needs a reason to pitch a hissy fit, but still."

Mikkelsen had been his right-hand man a century or more, but no one was safe in the Bureau hierarchy.

"Mikkelsen was there the night you took down the Silver Stag. The director wanted his proxy present on such a high-profile bust, but Mikkelsen didn't even get out of his car. The director was pissed, looking for an outlet. He decided if Mikkelsen had gotten his shoes dirty with the rest of us, he would have figured it out, that you were planning to defect, and been able to stop you. That was his reason. Insubordination."

Hard to believe Jai had accepted the promotion, but, much like Stavros, the director wasn't a man who heard *no* often.

Where had the director, who had been hunkered down for months, gone that required Jai to step in?

Possibilities wedged under my skin like splinters, persistent and irritating, but I couldn't pick at them yet.

"Drink." I grabbed two cold water bottles for Asa. "The blood of your enemies can't be that quenching."

With a murmur of thanks, he downed the first one in a single gulp then reached for the second bottle.

He maintained eye contact with me while he drained it too, making my mouth go dry and throat tighten.

"Ouch." Clay whistled low. "Swap bodily fluids, and he stops needing to swap, well, bodily fluids."

As weird as it was to admit, I did miss that obsessive drive to share food with Asa, but it was fading.

"You're so right." I leaned into Clay's conjecture. "Let me tell you how we—"

"Lovers need their secrets." He clamped a hand over my mouth. "Keep yours to yourself."

"What else should I know about the Boo Brothers?" Asa wiped his mouth with the back of his wrist. "The fact Jai sent us after them makes me wonder what I'm missing. We're a high-value team. This sounds like one of the cases assigned to rookies to dip their toes in Bureau waters."

"This is a dream assignment." Clay scoffed at his ignorance. "These guys are legends."

"You can't ask for their signatures then kill them," I said slowly. "You get that, right?"

"Kill?" He flattened his palm to his chest. "No one said kill."

"Mmm-hmm."

How else he imagined a showdown with two hunters of the supernatural ending, I had no clue.

"These 'legends' are human?" Asa leaned around me to dig in the fridge. "Are you sure?"

Nudging him back when he grabbed for water, I exchanged his pick for two bottles of tasty electrolytes.

"They tell people they're half human and half angel but not Nephilim." Clay made the sign of the cross with his fingers. "Those are evil."

"Here." I pulled a wooden chair from the kitchen table then shoved Asa down. "Sit."

I shouldn't have been flustered when he tugged me onto his lap, but everything was different now. Even this, maybe *especially* his casual affection. I was still adapting to the portions of a committed relationship that happened with our clothes on.

Stupid feelings.

My inner black witch hissed in my mind that I was weak, pathetic, unworthy of respect or love.

The rest of me, well, it tended to agree. But to keep him, it was willing to throat punch my doubts.

Asa's warm breath skated up my nape, banishing my turmoil and settling my worries.

For now.

"They have a divine purpose." I picked up the story. "They're *special*." I leaned back against Asa's chest, stuck to it, then suffered a pang of guilt for not feeling as remorseful as I should have, given why he was dirty. "They believe ridding the world of the paranormal blight is their God-given right. That it's not murder, if the victims aren't human. They're big on the slaughter of innocents, murder of sympathizers, and theft."

Holy crusades, as history had proven, cost a fortune. Their money had to come from somewhere. Why not punish nonbelievers and pad their bank accounts at the same time?

"If they're not Nephilim," Asa wondered, "then what are they?"

"As far as anyone can tell," Clay drawled, "they're half human and half hot air."

A laugh spluttered out of me, but he wasn't wrong.

"They're truly mortal?" Asa circled my hipbone with his thumb. "Human?"

As warmth spooled through me, I began an exploration of the inside of Asa's thigh with my fingertips.

"*Hey.*" I flinched when Clay popped my hand. "No fair." I slung the sting from my fingers. "He started it."

"Let's break this up before someone—say, I don't know, *me*—upchucks."

"If you do, it's not our fault." I scowled at the level of his hand-crafted navel, a cosmetic alteration he was oddly proud of. "It's all those crickets you ate."

"Okay." He shook his head. "No more Mr. Nice Golem."

Rocking forward with preternatural quickness, he snatched me from Asa then sat back with a grunt.

"Now." He plopped me onto his lap and locked his arms around me, immobilizing me. "Let's get back to the case."

"The Boo Brothers have a patron, or patrons, who may or may not be para." I farmed my memory for more details. "They gifted the brothers magical artifacts and filled their head with stories of angels and demons. Their peak popularity was fifteen years or so ago." I attempted to get comfy, but Clay wasn't built for snuggles. "Do you remember the interviews? Goddess, those were the absolute best. Each a true cinematic gem."

"How could I forget?" Clay explained to Asa, "They did talk shows, local news, commercials."

"That's how they came by the catchy moniker *Boo Brothers*. A talk show host forgot their names during a live broadcast. He blurted that instead, and it caught on. You could tell it wasn't an act for them. They were true believers."

"Totally cuckoo," Clay agreed. "Viewers loved it."

"There was cosplay. So much cosplay." I chuckled recalling it. "Really, they were minor celebrities."

"That will work against us," Asa pointed out, "if they seek shelter with their fans."

Prove to their rabid followers they spoke the truth, and we kick-started a full-scale witch hunt.

One that spawned yet another wave of talk shows, news coverage, and televised specials.

Basically, the worst of all possible outcomes, given how far technology had come since their debut.

"You're not wrong," I agreed. "This has the potential to out the paranormal community globally."

Huh.

Maybe Parish hadn't let us off as easy as I first thought.

"What happened to them?" Asa leaned forward, fully invested. "How did they disappear?"

"The Boos vanished at the start of filming a special on how to hunt demons. Everyone blamed a publicity stunt, but then word got out that the much-anticipated series was canned. Fans were *not* happy." Clay pointed at his chest. "To save face, the network aired a special on hunting the Boos instead. Their disappearance was all over the news by that point, so they cashed in with everyone else to recoup their investment."

"Conspiracy theorists were convinced demons killed the Boos to keep their weaknesses from becoming common knowledge." I shifted on Clay's lap, but my butt was falling asleep fast. "No one knows what really happened to them."

Our job, it seemed, was to figure that out and then put a stop to their latest whackadoodle scheme.

"The director allowed this?" Asa rubbed his jaw. "He let them spread that much propaganda?"

"They were an overnight sensation," Clay explained. "One day, they were just *everywhere*."

"The other thing to remember is, they were really, *really* bad at their job. The artifacts would have killed paras in droves, if the brothers used them instead of wasting time on religious ceremonies they invented for the sake of ego. They also 'redeemed' more humans than paras, so they went to jail for breaking and entering, kidnapping, and aggravated assault. Their victims were branded as nonbelievers, of course."

Yet the Boos always slipped those charges. The brothers were Teflon. Another gift from their patron.

"The director was choosing his moment to strike," Clay added, "but they vanished before he gave the order."

"The timing pointed toward them having an informant inside Black Hat. A high-ranking one." I couldn't help but add that to the reason for Parish's assignment. We had been working rogue cases. This was starting to fit the profile. "The director was furious, but he never found a source. Not as far as I know."

A shiver coasted down my spine at how Asa was staring at me, a glimmer in his eyes I couldn't pin down.

"Granted," Clay fussed, drawing my attention, "they could have taken master classes from Rue."

"Yes, yes, I know I'm a terrible friend and unworthy of you or your wig collection."

"Hey, you said it." His lips hitched to one side. "Not me."

"The director was content with that resolution?" Asa scooted forward. "He didn't verify their deaths?"

"The downside to commercializing their work," I said, wrapping up Asa's debriefing, "was people viewed their disappearance as more of a series finale than an actual missing persons case. Hardcore Boo fans let their freak flags fly, but the average viewer? They flipped the channel and moved on with their lives."

Quicker than a heartbeat, flames erupted in a fiery aura around Asa as the daemon claimed his skin.

Mid-transition, he lunged, glee bright in his eyes, his clawed hands grabbing for me.

A clash of titans might have been fun to watch, had the titans not clashed in the living room.

With me stuck between them.

"Rue mine," the daemon bellowed as Clay leapt to his feet and dodged his lunges. "Give back."

"Rue was mine first." He held me over his head like I was a surfboard. "You'll have to take her."

"Rue is going to murder you both," I wheezed, "if you don't put her down *now*."

"Uh, guys."

The guys paused their game of hot potato to crank their heads toward Colby.

"Aedan found a message in a bottle in the creek." Her antennae quivered. "Can we open it?"

Behind her, on the monitors dedicated to property surveillance, Aedan waved to the camera.

"Yes." I cradled the excuse with both hands. "That's a great idea. Let's go do that."

The daemon slumped with disappointment, and Colby soon mirrored his posture when he told her game time had been postponed. I'm sure orcs the world over heaved a sigh of relief for a momentary reprieve. Good thing they bled pixels. Otherwise, the faction would be facing extinction via bloodthirsty moth-girl.

Clay, thankfully, had the sense to prop me up while feeling returned to my extremities.

"It's like the *new* pirate expansion pack for Mystic Realms." She fluttered. "What if it's a treasure map?"

"Don't think I didn't hear the emphasis on *new*, smarty fuzz butt. Christmas was two months ago, and we don't celebrate Valentine's Day." I sighed over Clay's sharply indrawn breath. "What? We wait until the day after then stock up on cheap chocolate and cute plushies. We're not total heathens."

The reminder of the upcoming holiday broke me out in a cold sweat when it hit me that Asa was my first boyfriend/potential mate. He might have expectations for the day that were different than mine.

Thanks, fascination, for hitting me with a holiday tailored to emotional paranoia.

"Phew." Clay clutched his chest. "There for a second, I thought you had forgotten all my teachings."

"The point I was trying to make is this. You're going to have to spend *your* coin if you want to upgrade." I noticed her worrying her hands. Never a good sign. "What did you do?"

For her to be dropping hints so hard they crushed my toes, she must be in dire financial straits.

"There was this sale on dragon eggs..."

"*Colby.*" I swear my heart stopped a beat. "You spent hundreds of *real* dollars on *virtual* dragon eggs?"

Granted, I had given her most of the money, and I had agreed to let the guys give her the rest, but still.

Mystic Realms developers must be rolling in cash. Actual money they skipped to an actual bank to deposit.

"They're a good investment," she argued. "They just take time to mature."

"She can resell them for four times what the eggs cost her." Clay came to her rescue. "The catch is, it will take months to hatch them." He offered her a commiserating glance. "Until then, her coin's not liquid."

As hard as it was for me, I put my foot down. "Then you'll have to wait for it to liquify."

Hands clasped in front of her, she turned her pitiful face toward Clay.

"No, ma'am." I slapped a hand over his eyes. "You're not suckering him into it either."

Slowly, she turned her face toward the daemon, searching for an ally.

"Nope." I marched over to the daemon. "Don't count your dragons before they hatch next time."

"Fiiine." She launched into a glide in a sulk. "Can we go check the bottle now?"

"Yes." I flicked a wrist toward the front door. "Let's go."

The daemon lumbered after Colby, the pair discussing pirate ship names, while Clay walked with me.

"You're good at the parenting thing."

"Yes, well, I was lucky." A hoarse note crept into my voice. "I had a fairy golem father to teach me."

"Aww." He slung an arm around my neck and reeled me in for a kiss on the cheek. "You love me."

"Yeah, yeah." I shoved him off me with a laugh. "You already knew that."

"Still nice to hear it." He bumped shoulders with me. "How many nieces and nephews should I expect?"

"Why are you so obsessed with me procreating?"

A shudder rippled down my spine when his comment reminded me of Stavros's offer.

"Mostly, I'm curious how much weight you could gain. Like, is there a record we could beat?"

We?

There was no *we* in stretch marks, labor, or postpartum weight loss.

"You want to use me…to break a record for the most pounds gained during a pregnancy?"

"Or maybe I just want to do this and not get caught."

Wary, I cut my eyes toward him. "Do what?"

"Tag." He thumped me between the eyes. "You're *it*."

Using his head start, the jerk took off at a sprint, cupping his hands to yell to the others, "Ahoy there."

"I'm an aquatic daemon," Aedan said dryly, "not a pirate."

Devious Clay might be, but he was a lot of golem moving at a high rate of speed on a downward slope.

Hot on his heels, I tripped him, and sent him sprawling. He shoved up on his forearms, spitting grass as I stepped over his legs to join the others at Camp Aedan to inspect the peculiar bottle in Aedan's hands.

An odd aura surrounded it, giving it a faint rainbow sheen. "You found that in the creek?"

The glass was thick, handblown, and a deep azure like the vintage kind locals stuck on bottle trees.

"Yeah." He handed it to me. "Water would void any nasty spells on it, right?"

"In most cases, yes." I shut my eyes and rolled the glass between my palms. "There's something..."

"Smash for Rue?" The daemon, still high on adrenaline, looked hopeful. "I like smash."

"I know you do, big guy, but there's magic in there." I sniffed the cork. "Ah."

A pungent whiff of copper and decay told me who sent it, and it spoke volumes about Dad's power that its trip down the creek hadn't washed away all traces of his signature.

"Rue safe?" The daemon's fingers twitched, eager to snatch and crush. "I smash?"

"I got it." I bit the cork—like a lady—and yanked it out with my teeth. "What in the—?"

A coin too wide to fit down the bottle's neck popped out of the opening and landed in Aedan's palm.

"That's gold." Colby's eyes rounded. "Like *real* gold."

"Pirate booty," the daemon agreed. "Like Mystic Seas expansion pack."

"I just had an out-of-body experience," I told Clay. "I thought I heard a commercial fall out of his mouth."

"You're laying it on thick, Shorty." He wiped the smile off his mouth. "You heard Rue."

"I didn't say anything." She blinked at him, all wide-eyed innocence. "I was admiring the coin."

Most of the time, I could forget Colby was—or had been—a ten-year-old kid prior to her death.

And then she pulled something like this.

I ought to nip it in the bud, but I was too grateful she still had that spunk and sass to punish her for what kids the world over did to their parents and guardians. She was testing me, pushing her boundaries. She was proving the bright spark that saved her life burned brighter than ever within her. So what if I wasn't traditional mom material? What Colby and I had defied labels, and that was okay.

"Go read." Clay nudged me back toward the house. "We'll catch periwinkles and give you a minute."

Visions of daemon crabs danced in my head. "What are those?"

"Tiny aquatic snails with spiral shells."

"I have those?"

"Most creeks do."

Nodding my thanks, heart a knot in my throat, I trudged back to the house and plunked onto the porch.

The parchment crinkled in my hand as I withdrew the neat roll. I broke the thick wax seal, opened it with care, and blinked away the black motes sparkling in the ink as the letter shed the magic used to create it.

Dearest Daughter,

I dare not write what concerns press on my mind, but I promised you letters, and this is the first.

Forgive me for my clumsy attempt at reconciliation. I was wrong to involve your cousin. Your mother was the diplomat. I preferred to stand at her side and intimidate people into giving her what she wanted, not that she required my assistance. No one could say no to her, least of all me.

I will keep this missive brief out of concern your wards prevented you from receiving it. I enclosed a payment for your cousin, for his service. It is my understanding he lives on your property. It was him I hoped would find this and carry it to you. As you trust him, so will I.

If you find a spare moment, write back to me. No expectations. We can go—or not—from there.

All my love,

Your Father

"Are you all right?"

A discreet distance away, Asa waited for my reaction to this first contact.

"Nothing earth-shattering." I handed it over. "More of a trial run for his delivery system."

"A stamped envelope is too conventional," Clay said, joining us. "Hiram is a master of the black arts."

And he had used that talent to send me a message in a bottle, as if I were still a kid who would fish it out of the water with a squeal of delight and rush to the smudge that remained of Mom in my memory for a hand with the cork. It was…charming. More than that, it was whimsical. It made me wish I could tell if he and I had exchanged secret notes this way when I was a child. If this was a test, I had no hope of passing.

The director had stripped me to the bone, stolen every memory his grasping fingers could pluck from my head, the better to mold me in his image. Impressions lingered, vague sensations, but nothing concrete.

I never hated him more than when I struggled to recall anything of Mom or Dad but found nothing.

Nothing beyond the stories I had been told, the pictures I had been shown, the memories I had spun from wishes and slivers of truth.

"He paid Aedan in gold for sitting in the creek, really?" Clay's eyes bulged as he read over Asa's shoulder. "Forget Black Hat. I'm buying a float, tethering it to a tree, and saving up those coins for retirement."

As if the director would ever cut him free.

But it would take someone crueler than me to remind him of that.

"You're already filthy stinking rich." I admired his financial savvy, though at his age, it would be a shock if he hadn't managed to amass at least a modest fortune. "How about save some for the rest of us?"

"You're going to mate a daemon prince, who will one day be king. I don't want to hear it, *Princess*."

Acid burned a path up the back of my throat, but I locked down my muscles to avoid flinching.

"Would I look sexier on a red float or a gold one?" Out came his cell, and Clay started shopping online. "I have a red wig that's to die for, but it's so hard to color match online. Yellow isn't my best color, but you know I'm a sucker for a theme. I could always use that shimmery bronzer, the one with a hint of mica."

"Now that we've solved the mystery—" I cut Clay off as he used voice controls to search for speedos, "—we should get packing." I reclaimed the note. "I'll update Aedan, if you guys want to get a head start."

Happy to wander off, nose to the screen, Clay made his way into the house.

The last mutter I caught was *gold lamé*, and that was traumatic enough for me to ignore the rest.

"You guys are leaving again?" Aedan met me halfway. "You're barely home these days."

"Re-upping has been like clearing a backlog of cases after a vacation." I rubbed my face. "A long one."

Ten years' worth, not to split hairs.

"Is it always like this?" He tried for a joking tone. "Or are you guys just special?"

"We're something, all right. I'll tell you what after I figure it out."

"You don't have to tell me." He stuffed his hands into his pockets. "I don't have to know."

"It's mostly family drama," I attempted to explain then stopped myself. "Not your side of the family."

A wide smile blossomed when I included him in my family grouping, and I hated we came from people or situations that made even the most tenuous connection swell our hearts with gratitude to finally belong.

"You mean your dad."

"Yeah." I wished he wasn't burdened with the knowledge Dad was alive, but there were no takebacks in the information game. "I'm still absorbing the latest implications, but I'll share more when and if I can."

"Almost forgot." He flipped me the coin. "That's worth about two grand. Keep it. For room and board."

The coin, having been spelled to pay Aedan, flipped itself right back to him.

"I think it likes you." I chuckled. "Besides, you don't owe me anything."

"Your dad sent this to me, right?" He smoothed his thumb over the design. "For playing mailman?"

"That," I allowed, "and I think he feels guilty about the whole kidnapping thing."

"Can you ask him not to pay me again?" He closed his hand over the coin. "We're family too, right?"

That I expected nothing from him in return for allowing his continued existence, let alone that I provided him with supplies to camp on my property rent-free, had been a revelation to him. *That's what family does*, I told him, and it was a lie. I wanted it to be true. I knew, for a lucky few, it was. But not for him. Or me. Be that as it may, the person I wanted to become felt that family, blood or chosen, wouldn't set a price on their help when it was needed the most.

As much as I based my ideal better self on those who embodied the qualities I wanted to share, I viewed those people as innately good. I wanted to copy them, yes, but I wasn't sure I could *be* them. For Aedan, who had known kindness only from his younger siblings, to model his ideals after me in any small way...

Before my emotional allergies got involved, I crushed him in a hug. "My family is your family."

Aedan buried his face in my neck and held on for just a moment before awkwardly stepping back.

"I wouldn't want Asa to get jealous." He cleared his throat. "I also don't want to get my butt kicked."

These days, he got tossed around by Asa on the regular, but it was all in service to the greater good.

The guys' self-defense classes were wildly popular in town, especially with teenage girls, which I'm sure had nothing to do with the hot instructors. It made me glad Asa intimidated people. I don't think, at this point in our fascination, I would handle him handling another woman well.

Considering how Arden was hit-or-miss in her attendance, she must have felt the same about Aedan.

Goddess bless, I did *not* want to think about what a catastrophe that pairing would be.

"I'll call the girls and give them a chance to yell at me instead of you."

More and more often, they were shouldering the burden of running Hollis Apothecary on their own.

"I'll keep an eye on them," he promised. "And the shop."

From his tone, I heard he would watch over the town too, which was a weight off my mind. I don't know how I ever did this without him. If I hadn't known he was here, I couldn't have left Samford half as often.

"Keep an eye out for yourself too," I warned him. "You are not expendable." I honed my glare. "Got it?"

"Got it," he said softly, ducking his head to conceal the vulnerability he couldn't quite hide.

Back at the house, the guys had finished packing. Colby was mostly done too. She had gotten distracted by turning her dragon eggs in their incubation cave, which was apparently a time-sensitive deal and part of the reason why no one wanted to raise their own dragon horde when they could buy hatched adults.

One good thing about frequent deployments? We always kept a half-packed suitcase on standby.

All the last-minute items were perishable. Fresh pollen granules or bottles of sugar water. To prevent container theft—*cough,* Clay, *cough*—I started leaving the set I used to transport moth grub in the luggage between jaunts. As I grabbed for them, I discovered they had made an unwelcome friend.

Lounging on top of my bras, the grimoire lazed in my suitcase as if it had every right to be there.

"Will you bring it?"

Never taking his welcome for granted, Asa leaned against the doorframe.

A quick shower had left his silky hair too damp for his shirt, but he already wore his Bureau-issued pants and shoes. His piercings from the challenges matched nicely, so he left those in. The black stud in his ear tempted me to nibble his lobe until he made that rumble low in his throat that never failed to melt my knees.

"The wards on the house would keep it safe from the average threat, but from someone like Dad? From one of the other authors?" I hated to admit it. "They could peel back the layers like onion skin."

"Then you should take it." Asa noted the book's nest and cocked an eyebrow. "How will you secure it?"

A finger pressed to my lips, I rose and dragged him into my room then shut the door behind him.

With Asa and I splitting time between each other's bedrooms, I had magically soundproofed both.

One way only.

Little moths had no business hearing about the birds and the bees, but I had to keep an ear out for her. And Clay. Honestly? Mostly Clay. She might be the instigator, but he was her willing partner in chaos.

"I have a nasty pendant that belonged to a djinn once upon a time." I pushed Asa down on the bed then knelt before my open closet door. "It's a classic case of bigger on the inside than on the outside." I cracked open the safe where I kept my dark artifacts hidden. "The djinn had an entire estate in there. It's empty now, of course. He's dead."

"You killed him?"

"Me? No. I found the necklace in evidence and added it to my collection. He murdered his masters by shrinking them to the height of a pencil, cramming them into a mason jar, then letting them suffocate."

Jewelry on my mind, I removed the mistletoe necklace Asa had given me and placed it on my dresser.

"What about the three wishes lore?"

"A trick to lure the unwitting to their dooms, as far as I can tell." I held up a ruby the size of my pinky nail set in a gaudy baroque-style frame that added ounces to its already hefty weight. "However, djinns have a rare and peculiar type of magic. What they desire, they can manifest. That's how they trick people into believing they have the control. The 'master' asks for a thing, and the djinn gives them the thing."

"Thus the lore is proven correct in their victims' eyes."

"A djinn is confined to its chosen vessel for life, so it gets bored. They play with people to break up the monotony of their existence, and to get fresh air, until they decide they've extroverted enough for one decade and kill their 'master' in the gruesome fashion that most of them spent the last ten years devising for giggles."

Those were the cases that had slid across my desk, anyway.

"How does the pendant work?"

"In theory, I read this inscription backwards, and it banishes the book inside the stone." I showed him on the chain how the spell was written across the links, glossing over how the clasp fused after I latched it. I might also have skipped over how decapitation of the wearer was the only method of removal for the pendant, should the wearer refuse to relinquish ownership of it. "Then I read the incantation forward to release it. The big question is whether the banished object must be alive. The grimoire has some degree of sentience. So does the pendant. I can't guarantee it'll work, but I've got a hunch they'll be BFFs."

No black magic artifact would refuse a chance to grow in power, even if it meant combining its power.

"Worst-case scenario?"

"The book will be bound to the pendant. Forever. Or until we destroy them both."

"Do you think it's worth the risk?"

"The book is a knowledge-hoarding brat. I'm happy to let it decay in there. Alone. Unused. Forgotten."

That last part I said while staring at the book, ensuring it heard the threat.

Which proved it was getting under my skin.

Books don't have ears.

"The important thing is," he pitched in with me, "it would keep the grimoire out of the wrong hands."

"I'm not thrilled with the solution, but it's not like I can call Dad to get a second opinion. The message in a bottle schtick is cute, but we don't have time to test how long it takes for him to receive and reply. We must verify that he's receiving as well. Until then, I can't risk more than the same niceties he sent me."

I ought to write him before I left, to confirm receipt if nothing else, but I wasn't sure what to say.

"What if the pendant decides it would rather have you for a new guest?"

"Then you better get ready to rub until I pop." I cut him a sly smile. "Out of the stone, I mean."

"Oh," he breathed, his voice soft, "I knew what you meant."

On my knees, I walked to him, rested my chin on his thigh, and gazed up at him.

"It's not too late to run." I locked my arms around his calf. "I would hold on, so it would be awkward, but you could try, and I would fully support that." Then I sat on his foot, wrapping my legs around his ankles. "The thing is, I love you. So, it's kind of your fault we're in this situation. I want the best for you, and I'm not sure that's me, but I'm also pretty sure I would viciously murder anyone who tried to take you, so..."

"It's my fault that your affection manifests as veiled murder threats?"

"What veil?" I grew my fingertips into talons I raked down his bare chest. "There was no veil."

"Forgive me," Asa murmured, eyes twinkling. "I interpreted

pretty sure as wiggle room."

"The only wiggling in this room will be me, on top of you." I rubbed my cheek along his inner thigh. "Or you, on top of me." I nipped him. "Any variation that involves you, me, and wiggling is okay in my book."

"It was too late to run—" he speared his fingers through my hair, "—the moment I saw you."

He lowered his head, his gaze intent on my lips, and kissed me slowly.

Melting at his feet, I was inching my hands down his waist when his tongue clinked against my teeth.

Desire muddying my senses, I wrote it off as my imagination.

Until the next sweep of his tongue clacked hard enough I couldn't ignore the sensation.

"What is that?" I drew back to examine him. "What did you do?"

"Nothing." A flush warmed his skin under my fingers. "It was done to me."

"You're blushing." I cupped his jaw and pressed my thumb inside his mouth. "Show me."

Cheeks pink verging on red, he stuck out his tongue, and it *glinted* at me.

"A new piercing?" I pried his jaw wider. "Is that…an *actual* diamond?"

Lifting his tongue, I examined the bottom of the barbell, but it was a simple daub of platinum.

"Yeth."

"Oh." I retreated with a sheepish grimace. "Sorry about playing dentist."

"I don't mind you in my mouth."

Now it was my turn for heat to flood my face, and other areas, and my gaze dropped to his parted lips.

"When?" I fished my brain out of the gutter. "I've been with you all day."

This morning, prior to the arena, he hadn't been sporting new oral jewelry.

I would have, *ahem*, noticed it.

I swore I heard the splash as my brain jumped off the high dive right back into the gutter where I found it.

"I have no memory of it," he confessed. "It must have happened prior to the challenges."

"You expected this?" I wasn't sure what to make of it. "I just…" I tilted my head. "Why?"

Had Asa not anticipated it, the daemon wouldn't have sought it out. He wasn't vain. Much.

"Rite of passage." He tugged on an earring. "The stone is mined from the cavern under the throne room. It symbolizes my sexual awakening and increases my libido. It stimulates my sensuality, ramps my desire, and lowers my inhibitions in bed."

"As opposed to out of bed?"

The flat look he shot me forced a chuckle out of me.

"Does it work?" I couldn't hide my grin. "Will you spontaneously ravage me now?"

"You're always in danger of spontaneous ravaging. This changes nothing."

"I wouldn't say that." I bit my lower lip. "I wonder how it will feel when you—?"

"Rue," Clay yelled through the door. "I know you're in there being a pervert."

"How does he do that?" I kicked my feet. "Just when we were getting to the good stuff."

Laughing at my tantrum, Asa captured my mouth with his in a bruising kiss that left me tingling.

Walking my fingers up his thighs, I tapped the waistband of his pants in invitation, willing to ignore Clay.

"Ace." Clay pounded on the door. "Be the responsible one. Put your pants back on."

Defeated by responsibility yet again, I thumped my head into Asa's lap, and he grunted, which, yeah.

Oops.

"How is it that the more I have you," Asa murmured, "the more I want?"

"Easy." I raised my head, ignoring the bulge in his pants. "You have a lot of making up to do."

"If sex was what I wanted, I could have had it." He smoothed his thumb over my bottom lip. "No, it's you I can't get enough of."

"I'm going to write down all the sweet things you say and publish it as *A Witch's Guide to Taming Dae*." I chuckled darkly. "I might even release an illustrated edition with a chapter titled 'Twine and You: It's Not Just for Turkeys.'"

"I'm counting down from five," Clay bellowed down the hall. "Then I'm coming in, ready or not."

Bracing my palms on Asa's knees, I pushed to my feet with an evil grin.

"Five."

I moseyed over to the door and leaned against the wall beside it.

"Four."

Quietly, I flipped the lock.

"Three."

Careful not to rattle it, I gripped the doorknob.

"Two."

I twisted hard…

"One."

…and threw it open wide.

Shoulder braced to smash the wood, Clay sailed across the room and pinged off the opposite wall.

"Can we help you?" Asa leaned forward, elbows on knees, hiding the tent in his lap. "You look to be in a hurry."

"Jeez, Clay." I folded my arms across my chest. "Learn to knock."

Clay, who had left a dent in the drywall, faced us with a thunderous scowl. "I know you heard me."

After dusting off his shoulder, he paused to check the shaggy brown wig replacing his mohawk then resumed his huff.

"I was otherwise occupied." I made goo-goo eyes at Asa. "All I heard was my name on his lips."

"You are a dirty liar who lies." He jabbed the air in front of me. "Know how I know?"

Willing to play along, I asked, "How?"

Clay set his index fingers to either side of his head. "No horns, no horny daemon."

Thanks to a nifty spell I sourced through an old contact, Asa was managing that condition, but Clay didn't need to know that. "Maybe they shrink when—"

"Let's leave my horns out of this." Asa rose, my attention slid to the front of his pants, then he sat again. "Ruc is packing." He shifted his weight on the bed. "We'll be out in fifteen minutes. Then we can go."

"I'm setting a timer," Clay warned, "*and* I'm leaving the door cracked one inch."

Tempted as I was to ignore his ultimatum and climb Asa like a tree, I couldn't risk Colby flying in on us.

After Clay left, I checked with Asa. "Care to play lookout while I work my magic?"

That accomplished two goals.

It secured the book for the trip.

And, most importantly, it took Asa out of range of my grabby hands.

"With pleasure."

Even the word *pleasure* from his lips made dirty thoughts pole dance in my head.

I had it bad.

So bad.

Goddess, it was terrifying.

A measure of understanding for the animus vow Dad struck after Mom died trickled through me and left me with the certainty that not only were feelings dumb.

They were downright lethal.

3

For better or worse, the grimoire had change of address labels to order.

The book came to me when called from the pendant, and it returned to its static oasis when banished.

Both of which made me highly suspicious.

The grimoire wasn't known for doing what it was told, and I hadn't had luck forcing my will on it either.

"Are you going to spend the whole trip scowling at your boobs, Dollface?"

A moth-sized cackle reached me as Clay's fan club of one encouraged his bad behavior.

Hand rising to my throat, I touched the pendant through my tee. "I'm not scowling at my boobs."

A loud sigh told me he had plugged Colby in so he could broach more adult topics.

"Now you're fondling yourself. Ace not doing it often enough for you?" Scooting forward, he pressed lips to my ear. "P.S. That's not the problem, and we both know it. I've got permanent blind spots seared onto my retinas from walking in on you two lust birds in the kitchen. *With the twine.* So, spill. What's wrong? You've been twitchy ever since we left."

Guilt thickened my tongue, but I couldn't admit the whole truth to Clay. Anything he knew, the director could compel him to confess. As a servant, he had no choice but to answer his master. Bad enough he knew about Dad and the grimoire, but that I couldn't help. All my grandfather needed to learn was that I possessed contraband dark artifacts. Let alone that they could amplify one another.

"I brought the grimoire." I lifted the necklace, ready to skate the truth. "I spelled it into this pendant."

Better to give up the grimoire's location than to confess to my stash of dark artifacts.

"That's a neat trick." His eyebrows winged higher. "You must have been working on that for a while."

"That's what Asa and I were doing earlier." *Skate, skate, skate.* "I needed a second set of hands."

"From what I've seen, that's the last thing either of you need. You're already like octopuses. Octopi? Whatever." He flicked my earlobe. "Eight-armed grope machines that leave suction cup marks all over each other."

"I'm not thrilled to have a new accessory, but it seems prudent."

"You're worried your dad isn't being transparent about his reasons for visiting you."

"No one is worried about Calixta breaking out of the swamp, which is weird, but okay. I get that the only way out for her is through the self-sacrifice of a relative, which leaves Dad and me. It's a safe bet neither of us will off ourselves to set a total stranger free to wreak havoc, but I expected more than a solid *eh* across the board. It makes me wonder, you know?"

Out of everyone, I was the most concerned about her future potential for mayhem. Maybe the only one.

"Perhaps it was an excuse," Asa offered. "Given the lethal nature of the animus vow, he knew it was cruel to show himself when he couldn't survive the confrontation with his father. Perhaps he allowed himself to be swayed into visiting you, by telling himself someone ought to warn you off Calixta."

Calixta Damaris, former High Queen of the Haelian Seas, and my grandmother.

As rough as my childhood had been, I had to wonder at Dad's, if he was content with leaving his mother to spend eternity in a watery cage. Between that, and Aedan's upbringing, I was pretty sure I should get my tubes tied before I risked adding to the catastrophe of being related to me.

"I'm not sure I do," I admitted, "but I want to believe that."

"We all do." Clay tweaked my nose. "For your sake."

"But I can't." I shifted forward in my seat. "What does that make me?"

Immediately, I began worrying the stone through my shirt, proving the compulsion on the pendant had a hold on me. *Fantastic.* It was burrowing into my subconscious, begging me to use it. The worst part? Not knowing if it was the tactile nature of the djinn's former vessel urging me to rub it or simply the grimoire taunting me.

I didn't want the grimoire digging its claws into me through prolonged exposure. The cage ought to contain it, but *ought to* was flimsy when it came to evil books bent on worldwide destruction seeping into your thoughts and influencing your actions.

"Until we know his motives," Asa said, "it would be foolish to trust him fully."

"That doesn't mean you can't be psyched to have your dad back." Clay settled back. "Who wouldn't be?"

"Yeah." I allowed myself a breath to be grateful. "I only wish it wasn't so complicated."

"Eh." Clay checked in on Colby. "You'll figure it out. You always do."

"Are you guys done yet?" Colby tossed off her headset before he could answer. "I have to tell you this."

"What?" I glanced over my shoulder. "And it better not be another paid ad for Mystic Realms."

"The Boo Brothers burned down a Waffle Iron." Her antennae quivered as she read off her phone. "Looks like yesterday or the day before."

"Heresy." Clay pinned the back of his hand to his forehead. "To think, I used to admire them."

"But—" she cut Clay's hysterics short, "—they also kidnapped a customer. A teenager. Samuel Todd." She glanced up at me. "They claimed he was a demon."

"Like an actual daemon?" I tilted my head. "Or hellfire and brimstone demon?"

"Probably a human enjoying their pecan waffle demon," Clay muttered. "This is sacrilege."

There was a *slight* chance this wasn't the Boos at all but imposters hoping to cash in on the sensation.

Fifteen years had little or no effect on a paranormal body, but it was significant to humans.

These guys weren't in shape to pull the crazy stunts of their youth without popping ibuprofen like candy afterward. Even if they were fit, even if they were yoga enthusiasts, the wear and tear on a human was evident when they pitted themselves against creatures who lived the next best thing to forever.

Then again, maybe the fact they pegged humans as "demons" nine times out of ten was for that reason.

Easier to capture, easier to kill, easier to pat yourself on the back for ridding the world of evil later.

That would make them sociopaths, not folk heroes, but they were master spin doctors.

"This is not good." I skimmed the first case to announce the Boos were back. "They're on a roll."

"More kidnappings?" Asa drummed his fingers on the wheel. "Or more arson?"

"Murders." I rubbed my forehead. "Four of them so far, all of them public."

"They want our attention," Asa surmised. "They want us to come for them."

"They do seem to be waving red flags in front of bulls," I agreed. "But they're not hanging around for the press. They're not awarding interviews. They're not printing T-shirts with their faces on them. They seem to be in hiding." I rolled that around in my head. "That's not like them. They lived for the spotlight."

"Someone helped them disappear at the height of their popularity." Clay made a thoughtful sound. "The Boos have paranormal benefactors. Makes sense they would step in to pull the Boos' feet away from the fire before they all got burned. Maybe disappearing was the cost of the Boos' freedom?"

"Then why allow them to stir up trouble again?" I shut my laptop. "Unless the Boos are rebelling?"

"Or they're setting a trap," Asa mused, forehead tight in thought.

"The benefactors or the Boos?"

"The benefactors were never identified," he reminded me. "Their artifacts weren't recovered either."

The Boos, wherever they had gone, almost certainly took their hunting gear with them. I bet the director was more pissed about losing a potential treasure trove of black magic trifles than the Boos themselves.

"That reminds me." I should have asked before now. "Where is the director?"

"Parish didn't say." Clay tapped his foot. "He pretended not to hear me when I asked that very thing."

"You are highly ignorable." A smile crept up on me. "I block you out five or six times a day, minimum."

"The director strikes me as the type to make his stand behind impenetrable walls."

"You're not wrong," I agreed with Asa. "He built the compound to protect himself, and his vision."

Few things had tempted him out of the manor when I was a child, and I doubted that had changed much over the years. Then I had blamed it on his being a workaholic. Now I wondered if he was afraid to leave my father without his direct oversight. Perhaps even wary of leaving me for long periods in case Dad had recovered enough of his magic to summon me to him. With Dad escaped, and seeking revenge for Mom, the safest place for the director was in the facility he had built himself. So why abandon his stronghold?

"He's also prideful." As if Clay had to remind me. "He slipped when he let you see him vulnerable. You're a mirror that reflects your parents' actions back at him. Paranoia others noticed that weakness might have gotten the best of him. He might have gone hunting your father before your father comes hunting him."

As much as I hated to admit it, "That would explain why Parish is in the driver's seat."

The director rarely handed over the keys, even to his second-in-command.

"For now, we focus on the Boos." Asa squeezed my fingers. "Can you get a warning to your father?"

"I'm not sure." I chewed on my bottom lip. "I couldn't decide what to write, so I left the bottle at home."

"Would any bottle work?" Colby wondered. "Gas stations still sell those old-fashioned Cokes."

"Good thinking." Clay high-fived her. "We can pick up a few the next time we stop for snacks."

"If all else fails," I pitched in, "Aedan can write the note and drop it in the creek for me."

Really, that might be the safest option. I was pretty sure, given Dad anticipated Aedan acting as mailman for me, the bottle would accept him sending it bon voyage without a hiccup.

"I booked us rooms in Raymond, Mississippi." Colby flitted to my shoulder. "It's a short walk from the Amherst Inn to the Waffle Iron fire. The other Boo scenes are concentrated within a ten-mile radius."

"We have to start somewhere." I kissed her forehead. "Good work, smarty fuzz butt."

As the most recent crime scene, evidence would be the freshest at the Waffle Iron.

"What did we ever do without you?" Clay gathered her in his wide palms, then he placed her beside him on the seat in front of her computer. "Oh, wait. That's right. *I* did the grunt work."

"I was the junior agent," I reminded Clay. "*I* did the grunt work."

A smile flirted with Asa's lips, but he wasn't as quick to throw Clay under the bus.

We really had to work on that.

Our *hotel* reminded me of a baking show gingerbread house that had collapsed on its way to the judges' table. The architectural details were stunning, or would have been, twenty years ago. Rot, time, and the owners' neglect had taken its toll on what had once been a true beauty.

"This isn't the picture they use on their website," Colby protested. "This place is a dump."

"This place is a bed-and-breakfast." Clay stepped out for a better look. "Not a mere hotel."

"All hotels serve breakfast." Her brow furrowed. "What's the difference?"

"There will be floral sheets, busy wallpaper, and a musty smell that lingers long after you've gone."

"That sounds icky." She kept her spot in the SUV, away from prying eyes. "I'll cancel the reservation."

A pang struck me for no good reason, and I found myself swaying on the precipice of doom.

"We're not going anywhere," Clay told her. "Rue caught feelings about this place."

"There's probably some little old lady at the check-in counter, praying she earns enough to buy groceries and her prescriptions this month." I shut my eyes. "I can't believe I'm saying this, but it's just one night."

"It's very nice of you..." Asa leaned over to kiss my temple, "...to show kindness to strangers." His warm lips slid to my jaw. "I'm sure the owner will appreciate your patronage." His teeth scraped my chin. "The world ought to have more people like you in it." His mouth claimed mine. "You're a good person, Rue."

"Don't get too excited." I withdrew to find Clay and Colby in *see no smooches/hear no smooches* poses. "I'm easily persuaded by a free homecooked breakfast. That's all." I crossed my arms. "I'm still evil."

"Evil as a marshmallow," Colby mumbled under her breath, squeaking when I approached the SUV.

"Take it back." I jabbed a finger in her face to hide my real target. "I demand an apology."

Careful not to hurt her, I tickled the spot where her wing joined her torso, and she exploded into giggles.

"Okay, okay." She rolled out of reach. "I'm sorry that your heart is as squishy as s'mores filling."

For show, I waggled my arm, groping the cushion for her.

"Lies," I hissed. "My heart is stone." I growled. "Granite even."

"Maybe until you met Asa," she cooed. "Now it's all ooey-gooey."

"Do you hear the disrespect coming out of her mouth?" I clutched my chest and slumped in my seat, her laughter contagious. "I'm going to the nearest chain hotel." I snapped my fingers at Asa. "Right now."

"I'm not eating stale cereal so you can make a point," Clay weighed in. "I say you confess to being a softy and check us in. Then you can ask about the breakfast menu so I can be prepared with my order."

"Traitors," I grumbled, unable to hide my smile when I saw how much Asa was enjoying himself.

Clay blocked the backseat while Colby climbed into his jacket pocket and settled in. Then we braved the crumbling path up to the crooked front door, which swung open and hit me in the shoulder. A guy who might have been in high school greeted us wearing star-spangled wizard robes straight out of a cartoon, complete with a pointed hat sewn from the same midnight fabric.

"Welcome, weary travelers." He opened his arms wide, bells tinkling on his sleeves. "Enter, if you dare."

"This is the Amherst Inn, right?" I noted the scraggly white beard slipping down his face. "We have a reservation, but if this is the wrong place, we're happy to go." I took a step back. "We might anyway."

"Markus," a breathless girl chastised as she shoved him out of the way. "Stop harassing the guests."

"I'm Trinity." She beamed. From within her silver foam helmet. Which matched her silver foam armor. I noticed a sword, a real one, in her hand and took another healthy step back. "You're at the right place." She lifted a gauntleted hand at us. "You'll have to forgive us. We have a LARPing thing."

"LARPing." I heard the faux-comprehending tone I used when Colby mentioned Mystic Realms. "Cool."

"Live Action Role Playing," Markus explained. "We act out scenes from our favorite books and games."

A quiver in my hair told me Colby was bursting with excitement over the idea.

"That a big thing around here?" I decided to play clueless. Because I was. "LARPing?"

"There are sixty-one members in our club," Trinity bragged. "We're one of the biggest in the state."

"We lost a few members last night, after the Waffle Iron incident," Markus reminded her, then confided in us with a wink, "Some people lack the constitution for the wizarding business."

The crimp of her lips told me she wasn't impressed with him correcting her.

Either way, we might have lucked into a pair of eyewitnesses for us to cultivate.

"That sounds like a good spot for dinner." Clay jumped in with both feet. "The food any good?"

Never one to miss a trick, Clay's thoughts must have aligned with mine.

"They're decent." Markus straightened his beard with mixed results. "Mostly, they're cheap."

"You can't eat there anyway." Trinity led us to the check-in desk. "It burned to the ground."

Usually content in the background, Asa stepped up beside me, and the girl almost started drooling.

"Has anyone ever told you..." she exhaled a dreamy sigh, "...you've got the bone structure to be an elf?"

A laugh caught in my throat, and Clay had to turn his head to hide his smile.

"Your hair is gorgeous." She reached out. "Have you thought of bleaching—?"

Snatching her hand out of the air, I turned the move into an awkward handshake.

It was that or let the *y'nai* chop her off at the wrist for the insult of touching Asa's braids.

"It's been nice meeting you." I released her. "Do you guys work here? Can you give us our keys?"

"Sure." Trinity flushed bright red. "Our parents own the inn. We work here after school."

"We slave away on weekends too," Markus added glumly. "Obviously."

Hard to believe it was still Saturday with everything we had seen and done already.

"Half days," Trinity muttered, rubbing her thumb over the desktop. "We have twenty minutes left."

"She's sorry about the hair," Markus told us when his sister kept her head down. "She's very handsy."

"I make wigs. For the other LARPers." Excitement bubbled up in her. "Everyone wants to be a Legolas or a Thranduil, so I study men with long hair." Her cheeks pinked. "Can I take some reference photos? Would you mind?"

Para photos in the hands of humans were a big no-no, but I wasn't sure how to beg off her request.

"I'm a bit of a wig aficionado myself." Clay removed his hair du jour with care. "I didn't bring any super long ones, like you mean, but I have a shoulder-length wig in brown. I can let you inspect it later, if that sounds good to you. It's handmade, and the stitching is phenomenal."

"That would be amazing." She bounced, and her visor thumped shut. "Thanks."

"No problem." He resecured his hair. "We can meet here at the desk later tonight."

Visor shoved up again, Trinity bit her lip. "I'm not sure if…"

"I'll come too," I volunteered, "if you're concerned about being alone with a stranger."

"Yes," Clay said wryly, "because two strangers is so much better than one."

"I'll come three." Markus quirked his lips at Trinity. "You have been promising to help me with my beard game."

Delighted to have found like minds, Clay handed each of them one of his cards. "Happy to do it."

"You're with the FBI?" Markus's jaw dropped open. "For real?"

"For real," Clay lied. "Just call when you're done with your thing, and we'll set up a time."

"Are all of you FBI?" Trinity looked straight at me. "Are you working a case?"

"We are all FBI," I confirmed, "and we are working a case."

"We should get unpacked." Asa offered Trinity a tight smile. "Can we get our keys, please?"

"Oh." Her cheeks flamed again. "Yes." She dropped our keycards twice. "Here."

To keep Trinity a safe distance from Asa, Clay took the cards and passed one to Asa.

"You head on up." Asa gave me the card. "I'll grab our bags."

Once he was out the door, Trinity goggled at me. "You're together?"

"They're engaged." Clay's eyes sparkled. "She just met her future father-in-law."

Aware it would hurt me more than Clay if I smacked him, I had to settle for plotting revenge.

"That's so romantic." Trinity clasped her gauntleted hands. "Fighting crime together."

That made us sound like superheroes, but we were antiheroes at best.

"Yes." I gritted my teeth at Clay. "Very romantic."

While they fell into a debate on real versus synthetic hair, I aimed for the staircase that curved up to the spacious second floor. On the landing, I paused to scan the ceiling, half expecting to find it cracked in two, but it was in good repair from this vantage. There weren't many rooms, maybe four down each hall. I located mine and pushed in the door, braced for what Clay had described.

Minimalist furniture. Pale blueish-gray walls. Bright-white sheets. Modern bathroom.

I was still standing in the doorway, debating if toxic mold in the walls caused this hallucination, when Asa entered the room and set our suitcases on the brushed nickel racks near the closet. He glanced around, cocked an eyebrow, and pivoted to soak up my reaction as if he required confirmation as well.

"The interior doesn't match the exterior." I shut the door. "Why renovate the inside when the outside looks like one good storm would blow it over?"

Flames tickled the corner of my vision, and the daemon claimed Asa's skin, sniffing and huffing the walls.

"Magic." He glanced over his shoulder. "Smell like flowers."

"A white witch cast a glamour in here?" I held out my palm and homed in my senses. "You're right."

Sure enough, there were traces of a glamour. It was old, very old, which had dulled the smell. Magic this settled into the bones of a building had been an ongoing project for a good decade or more. The owners must renew it every so often or else the illusion begins to fade. But which was real? Interior or exterior?

After Charleston, and the chain reaction that led to our rental there, I was happy to embrace paranoia.

The teens had no magical signature I could detect, so I would wait for the parents and question them.

Better safe than ridden by a boo hag. Or a Boo Brother, in this case.

"We need to talk to Colby." A pit opened in my stomach. "There must be a reason she chose this place."

The daemon crossed to me, planted a big kiss on my cheek, then nodded his agreement. "Bye, Rue."

"Later…" I tripped over a fundamental aspect of every person's identity. "I'll see you later."

The daemon didn't have a name.

How hadn't that occurred to me before now?

He was simply *the daemon*. The flipside of Asa's coin. The other half of his personality.

Asa considered the daemon an extension of himself, so it made sense why he didn't name him. The line dividing them was thin, almost transparent, which explained why no one else had either. But me? I held no doubts whatsoever that he was his own person, with his own thoughts and goals, likes and dislikes.

That he shared a body with Asa meant a name was the only recognition of self he could hope for in life.

Switching one skin for another, Asa took his turn behind the wheel. "You look troubled."

"I just realized something." I decided to keep that something to myself, for now. "Ready to go?"

Asa flicked a glance down himself, at his tattered shirt, and sighed at the waste. "Yes."

For a trip across the hall, he didn't need to look put together, though it was his preference.

We found Clay and Colby in a room identical to ours, except theirs was more grayish blue in tone.

"I'm going to sleep in the wardrobe," Colby announced, "like a real moth."

That stumped me for a beat, but then I remembered my question. "Why did you choose this place?"

"It's a block from Wattle Iron."

"That's it?" I watched her closely. "There's no other reason?"

"I *might* have also recognized a modified Mystic Realms emblem on their website."

"What does that mean?"

"One of the teens designed it," Clay speculated with amusement. "I doubt it was altruistic, if they added the subtle nod to their club while they were at it. Since it's still there, the parents haven't noticed it yet."

The idea had merit, given how tech savvy kids were these days compared to most of their parents.

"Reminds me of the symbols travelers used to carve into the siding or gate posts of homes who had been kind as a favor to those who came behind them who were also in need or food or shelter."

"That doesn't sound very appreciative." I frowned. "Defacement of property, which is disrespectful, and leaving a message that guarantees they would have a stream of visitors who would deplete their stores. It's a slap in the face to hospitality." I noticed everyone staring at me. "Anyway... LARPers? Website?"

"Colby?" Asa turned his attention to her. "What do you think it means?"

The spotlight shining so hotly on her choices made me itch to leap to her defense. I was used to being the one to call her out, but Asa had the right to ask. Not on the grounds of our relationship, which he would never abuse, but as an agent on a case that had taken a slight detour into Coincidenceville.

"That a Mystic Realms Live Guild meets here?" She emphasized the *G* in Guild. "Lot of guilds have weekly IRL meetings or game together. Everyone is in the same room but on their laptops. This guild, the West Field Wastrels, is super active." Her wings drooped down her back. "My guild lives too far apart to meet." Her antennae sank to half-mast. "They would also think I was a giant freak if they saw me in person."

"You're not a giant or a freak." I scooped her in my arms for the unwanted hug she needed nonetheless. "The way these kids run around playing dress-up as characters, they would faint to meet the real deal."

"You really think so?"

The fragile hope in her voice broke me.

"I know so." I kissed her forehead. "Next time, though, tell me if you're playing double agent, okay?"

There was no harm in it, this time, but all agents required permission for covert missions.

"Okay." She cuddled in close. "Does that mean I can stay here and live vicariously through the LARPers?"

As much as I longed to hand down a firm *no*, I couldn't clip her wings.

"As long as you stay moth-sized and out of sight." I stroked her back. "If you see anything weird, I expect you to fly like the pirate expansion pack has been released and the only copy is in my back pocket."

"It's an online download," she pointed out then mimed zipping her lips. "Yes, ma'am."

With her living in a virtual world, I shouldn't be surprised online games no longer came with hard copies. It showed my age, though. I might look like a pink-cheeked college kid with her whole life ahead of her, but I was a cranky old witch who appreciated purchasing items I could reach out and touch.

Before long, I would be shouting *get off my lawn* to neighborhood kids.

Asa cupped my nape, slid his thumb up the column of my throat, and my knees wobbled under me.

The supportive gesture made my gut clench and my mind pivot away from worries about Colby.

"Be safe, Shorty." Clay made it an order. "Don't fly into any flames, you being a moth and all."

"I'll try to resist temptation." She rolled her eyes. "Are you guys leaving now?"

"Did you feel that?" I rubbed my butt. "I swear I felt someone kick me to the curb."

The three of us left Colby to trail the kids into the woods for their LARPing.

I won't lie.

I wasn't happy.

More than protective instincts were to blame for the knot in my gut. There was a very real threat to her. But for her to stay in the field, I had to trust her to assess danger and react as we had been training her.

Fly away. Take cover. Make contact the second she was clear.

What happened in Charleston wasn't her fault, but it was a wake-up call for me. Sorie almost killed her. It wasn't the first time someone wanted her as a snack, and it wouldn't be the last. As her guardian, I had to do more than step up my protection game. I had to let her practice self-defense too.

The girl who begged me to save her, who clung to life with such ferocity of spirit, deserved to know that she would never be that vulnerable again. She had power, and the smarts to use it wisely.

Once we piled into the SUV, Asa cupped my jaw. "Are you okay with this?"

Sweat dampened my palms, and I wiped them down my jeans. "Sure."

"Colby can handle herself." Clay leaned back, rocking the vehicle. "She's a powerful kid."

"As long as she stays in the forest," Asa soothed, "she has plenty of places to hide."

Both the physical connection of his skin against mine and the determination in his voice let me relax into my seat. Fascination was a powerful force. I wasn't thrilled to be afflicted with emotions, but I had to admit, I had grown more and faster with him than I ever had without him.

"You're both right." I made myself believe it. "Let's go examine our first crime scene."

4

The Waffle Iron was a burnt shell with nothing to indicate it was once a favorite local dive. Charred beams had cracked in half against the metal skeleton of the building. Glass speckled the parking lot, and melted plastic trays lent pops of color to the blackened remains. Only a gnarled tree jutting through the asphalt had survived the blaze.

"Still smells like grease and burnt toast." Clay rested a hand over his stomach. "Maybe I'm just hungry."

"There's a memorial." Asa stood beside a teddy bear holding flowers. "For a kidnapping?"

"There was a cat." An old man stepped out from behind the tree, which had been too small to conceal a person of his size. "A familiar."

"Familiar," I repeated, thinking on his sudden appearance, "as in a witch's familiar?"

Cat plus *familiar* equaled witch in everyone's mind, right?

Thanks to books and movies, most everyone was, well, *familiar* with the term.

Now to figure out if that made him a fiction junkie or a fellow creature.

"What other kind of familiar is there?" He scratched his balding head. "What are you three doing here?"

"We're with the FBI." Clay watched the man closely. "We're investigating the Waffle Iron arson."

"If you're FBI, I'll eat my hat." The man wheezed a laugh. "Don't think you fool me, golem."

Definitely not human.

"You have us at a disadvantage." Asa dipped his head at the man. "I'm Asa Montenegro."

"You've got fae in you." He brightened. "I'm Wilbur." He gestured to the puny tree. "I'm a dryad."

"My mother is Aos Sí," Asa agreed, leaving it at that. "This is my mate, Rue Hollis."

My mate, my mate, my mate.

A herd of elephants stomped my stomach flat as a pancake. More of a crepe, really.

I opened my mouth, but nonsense words fell out, which earned me a soft laugh from Asa.

"Good of you to take pity on her." Wilbur clicked his tongue. "Poor girl must have dabbled too long in the dark arts. She's an incoherent mess." He shook his head. "She's a pretty thing, though. I see why you kept your vow. I sense her power. She'll give you fine children. Perhaps a nanny might ease—"

"No one is easing anything," I snarled, that buzz filling my head again. "Asa is *mine*."

"Bursts of clarity only make it worse." Wilbur squeezed Asa's shoulder. "I'm sorry for your loss."

Beside me, Clay was laughing so hard, his entire body bounced with each breath-stealing chortle.

"I'll take care of her while you work." Clay dissolved into giggles, slung his arm around my shoulders, and forced me to bear part of his weight. "A walk will calm her."

We hit the discolored sidewalk leading into town, leaving Asa behind to interview the crochety dryad. We had gone a few blocks before Clay caught his breath and stood on his own. Wisely, he didn't let go.

"Before you break into a car and drive off into the sunset to escape the word *mate*, let me explain what I know about dryads." He clenched his grip on me. "They despise black witches for thwarting natural law."

An ice cream parlor still in the process of opening beckoned him with promises of its classic flavors made fresh daily. This wasn't the first time we had eaten ice cream for lunch. With the right toppings, you could almost hit all the major food groups. The gummy version of them anyway.

"There's a good chance Wilbur would have attacked you once he satisfied his curiosity about Asa." A bell tinkled above the door when he shoved me through it. "Dryads are rarer than ever the last several decades. Pollution and deforestation are killing off a beneficial species we depend on to keep Earth hospitable. It would be a pity to kill one."

"Especially since he emerged at the scene," I slathered on the sarcasm, "and he might have valuable information he can pass on?"

"Ace claiming you made the dryad hesitate." Clay ignored the gibe. "It gave us time to get out of there."

"What I'm hearing is, I made a fool of myself for no good reason."

"You're in fascination, so you're allowed." He ordered a scoop of every flavor to be served in waffle cone bowls still warm from the press. "You do understand mating is the end goal?" He hesitated. "If you can't see yourself crossing that finish line at some point, you need to let Ace know you can't make that type of commitment."

Arms loaded with his plethora of treats, we backed out of the shop and claimed an empty table outside.

"I'm not saying I won't cross that line, but I'm not sprinting toward it." I set down my half of the goods, plopped into a seat, and promptly stole a waffle bowl from him. "There's a tiny problem that will have to be addressed first."

"Colby?" He spooned a glob into his mouth. "Oh." He dribbled when it hit him. "The bond."

"She and I are already bound for life. It's my duty to protect her." I poked the ice cream with a spoon. "Asa is stuck in a loop of endless challenges. It's not that I doubt his ability to hold his own, but I can't make that choice for Colby. It wouldn't be fair of me."

Attending my first challenge cemented the hazards of Asa's station and his tenuous grasp on his crown. Someone was always smarter, stronger, meaner. We were lucky the daemon hadn't met them yet.

"I'm sorry." He flicked a sprinkle at my forehead. "I shouldn't have pushed."

"You're used to me needing it." I couldn't fault him for that. "Before Asa, I wasn't exactly in touch with my feelings."

"That's not true. You beat them into submission on the regular." He was quick to defend me. "Locked 'em in chokeholds then slit their throats after they passed out. All very humane."

The look I cut him would have cowed a lesser man, but Clay was not one to moo.

"Seriously, you're getting there." He picked out a gummy worm and held it out as a peace offering. "Look how much progress you've made in Samford. You have a life. A *good* life. Friends. A business. You have it all."

The list he rattled off felt more like attributes belonging to someone else. The life of a different Rue Hollis. The apothecary owner had collided with the Black Hat agent, and the resulting crash had broken some things, like my bucolic paradise, and dented others, like Camber and Arden's innocence.

"For a long time," I said, eating the worm, even though I didn't like them, "I didn't have you."

That was the easier route, the one less likely to earn me a cheering up I wasn't sure I deserved yet.

"Or Ace." He made kissy noises. "We both know he's the real prize."

"I wouldn't say that." I kicked his foot under the table. "True friends are rarer than boyfriends."

"But not rarer than mates." He held up his spoon to forestall my argument. "*Potential* mates."

"Would you believe me if I told you I loved you both equally, but in different ways?"

"Not for a minute." He polished off another bowl. "But I'll leave it there."

Ten minutes, and at least as many waffle bowls later (for Clay), the wind blew the mingled scents of juicy green apples and cherry tobacco to me, causing my heart to squeeze.

Asa borrowed a chair from another table to join us, and I pushed my cookie dough cup at him out of habit. His tiny little smile as he picked it up told me he missed the overwhelming tug in his gut too. But it was redundant, I supposed, as much spit as we swapped the old-fashioned way these days.

"Well?" I selected a deep crimson one next, hoping for red velvet cake. "Get anything out of him?"

Twirling his spoon, he watched me as if expecting me to bolt. "I'm sorry I called you my mate."

Goddess bless, what a mess.

"Clay explained it was in our best interests." I regretted my first bite was fruity rather than cakey. "I overreacted." I shoveled in another spoonful, certain this was cherry cordial. "I won't next time."

Probably.

Leaning in, Asa pressed his lips to the underside of my jaw. "Thank you for understanding."

"Just so you know," I demurred, "if we have kids, and you hire a nanny, I will end you."

Hidden in the kiss, he sank his teeth into the tender skin of my throat. "That will never be an issue."

"The kids or the nanny?"

"The nanny." He sat back and dug into his treat. "Kids can come later or not at all."

"You don't have a preference?"

"I wouldn't mind a few more Colbys flittering around, but I don't think our biology works that way."

That he held her up as his golden standard melted my heart faster than two scoops left out in the sun.

"Well, I hope you're happy." Clay scooted back from the table. "Now I'm too nauseous to finish."

"You ate like four pints' worth." I gestured to his stack of empties. "Your stomachache is your own fault."

"No." He gathered everything and dumped it. "You did this to me. Both of you. You should be ashamed."

Asa, polishing off his bowl, offered me the last bite on his spoon, which I took while holding Clay's gaze.

"See?" He mimed gagging. "You're both disgusting." A shudder rippled through him. "So gross."

As a sister figure, I could sympathize with him. As a woman in love for the first time…not so much.

"One day," I promised Clay, "you'll meet a nice woman who isn't a homicidal maniac." I rested my chin on my palm. "Then you'll be the disgusting ones, and I'll be ready to mock you every step of the way. Every kiss, every smile, every touch, every sweet word, I'll be there. Complaining. Loudly."

"I don't mind homicidal," Clay said philosophically. "It's the maniac that always gets me."

Sensing that line of conversation could only get worse, I asked Asa, "What did Wilbur have to say?"

"The Amherst family owned the Waffle Iron."

"The Amherst family, as in the Amherst Inn."

"Mrs. Amherst ran the restaurant, which they franchised, and Mr. Amherst runs the bed-and-breakfast, which he inherited from his mother, after she passed two years ago."

"Mrs. Amherst must be the white witch," I surmised, "since her familiar perished in the fire."

"The Amhersts are a white witch family, but the familiar wasn't theirs. Wilbur claims the Amhersts didn't have much in the way of magic. The cat belonged to Mr. Amherst's mother."

"Odd that Mrs. Amherst brought it to work with her," I mused. "That has to be a health code violation."

"According to Wilbur, the cat was a sphynx."

"One of those naked cats that look like a rotisserie chicken?"

"Yes." Asa did a poor job of hiding his amusement. "Breed is beside the point."

"Okay, okay." I got sidetracked by that mental picture. "You were saying?"

"The current Mrs. Amherst is allergic, so they dumped the cat at the restaurant in the hopes it would become a mouser. It must have found a way in, maybe during the panic, and it couldn't get out again."

Locals must have recognized the cat as the former Mrs. Amherst's pet and cobbled together the memorial.

"Did he have the inside track on the Boo Brothers?" Clay butted in. "Did he actually see them?"

"He did," Asa allowed, his brow pinched. "He identified them from a photo I showed him."

"What am I missing here?" I reached out and poked him. "You sound like you're stumped."

"Was that a dryad joke?" Clay snickered then smoothed his features. "If so, it's in poor taste."

"Which is why you're laughing."

"Which is why I'm laughing," he agreed. "Anyway, Ace, out with it."

"Wilbur claims the Boos were…dead."

"Revenants again?" If so, I wanted to *nope* right out of this case. "Those are so icky."

"No." Asa pushed around his ice cream. "Not ghosts either."

"They were definitely full of enough hate and fervor to get stuck on Earth with unfinished business," I mused, "but if they're not ghosts or revenants, then what are they?"

"There's a full spectrum between ghost and revenant," Clay pointed out. "Poltergeists, zombies, vengeful spirits, wendigos." He pursed his lips. "Do vampires fall between the two? Dead like ghosts, but still feasting on the living, like revenants?"

"Vampires are more undead than unalive."

"What?" Clay twisted his mouth into a corkscrew. "Did you hear yourself just then?"

Ignoring him, a favorite hobby, I added to the pile of questions. "Why are the Boos here of all places?"

As far as we could prove, they had never stepped foot in Raymond during their lives.

"They were born in Maine, so there's no familial connection." Clay checked their file on his phone. "They have no living relatives on record. They crusaded down the East Coast into the Southwest, but there's no mention of this town in their exploits."

"Then either their deaths were connected to Raymond," I surmised, "or someone raised them here."

Given their MIA status for the last decade and change, we couldn't afford to rule out the possibility they sought refuge here. Though, if they were dead, we might never learn what made them pick this town to disappear in. For all we knew, they keeled over while passing through on their way someplace else.

"Assuming the burial site is here," Asa wondered, "what happens if the black witch decides they want to take their toys and leave? I can't imagine them going through the hassle if they can't use the Boos for more than a ten-square-mile radius."

"You would need an object imbued with meaning to a particular person to raise their spirit." I could only speculate so far without knowing what, exactly, the Boos had become. "A token with sentimental value, or a button off the shirt they wore when they died. Something along those lines. It stands to reason if they were attached to an item, it could act as an anchor. Move it and move them."

"We need to talk to Mr. and Mrs. Amherst." Asa tossed his trash. "Find out what they know about the Boos and the black witch." He took my hand and helped me stand. "Clay can question the kids tonight."

We had already encountered a white witch family and a dryad, so it stood to reason there were more creatures here than met the eye. Paranormals who were *not* in the Black Hat database. Assuming none posed an imminent threat, I would leave it that way. But if we located a practicing black witch, one dabbling in the realm of necromancy, I saw no choice but to add a pin to the map for the protection of everyone here.

And if we did have a black witch with an affinity for the dead on our hands, we had problems.

Necromancers had cornered that market, and they would kill to protect their monopoly. There was good money in bringing humans back from the dead as vampires. Even more in resuscitating pets who crossed the Rainbow Bridge before their owners were ready to let them go. All it took was cold, hard cash.

Semi-famous or not, ghosts like the Boos didn't make bank. Exorcisms paid peanuts, so did seances, but still. Just because necromancers didn't want to do those jobs didn't mean they would take kindly to learning someone else was doing them for free.

Oy.

If we were right, this had all the hallmarks of an inter-factions incident.

For all our sakes, I really hoped we were wrong.

5

Anxiety had been nipping my heels since I left Colby behind at the inn, and soon the nips turned to sharp bites I could no longer ignore. She had yet to check in, and Clay had a wig to unbox for the Amherst kids, so I nudged the guys into returning to the inn before my tendency to helicopter parent caused me to takeoff.

>*How's it going?*

Okay, fine, so maybe my rotors were whirling too fast to stop cold turkey.

>>*This is the coolest thing I've ever seen in my whole life.*

A pang shot through me as it hit home she would never participate in a group activity like that one.

>*I'm glad you're having fun.*

Thumbs poised above the keys, I debated ordering her back to the room until we got a lead on the Boos, but I couldn't pull the trigger. She might never experience this again, and we would be back there in ten.

>>*Can I stay out a little longer? They're about to summon the undead.*

A chill of foreboding prickled the skin on my arms, but I forced myself to remain strong.

>*Thirty minutes.*

That was all I could allow her without breaking into hives.

>>*Thank you, thank you, thank you.*

I glared at my hand until it cooperated and put away the phone to prevent me from hovering via texts.

Sure.

Yeah.

Blame my hand. Not my heart. Which ached and feared for her in equal measure.

A blip of time later, I stood on the lawn in front of the inn, puzzling over the purpose of the glamour. The Amhersts might have tried camouflage to hide from the black witch, hoping they would keep on driving. I hated to tell them, leaving a fresh magical signature behind was akin to loading cheese in a mouse trap.

"We need to ward our rooms." I studied the building, searching for cracks in the illusion. "Since this is the Amhersts' home, they'll notice the casting. We need to get in contact with the parents ASAP and explain we're not in cahoots with the black witch so they don't panic."

Asa's shoulder brushed mine. "How sure are you they know about the other witch?"

"If a baby gazelle is sharing a pen with a hungry lion," I drawled, "do you think it will notice?"

The allusion left me salivating, and I hated the instinctive hunger that rose in me every time I thought about the taste of fresh meat, the pull as it tore away in my teeth, and the boost of power that followed.

I'm not that person. I'm better now. I'm not going to break. I am stronger than my weakness.

Without a word, Asa slid his hand into mine and squeezed my fingers in solidarity.

Here I was, imagining punching my fist through the chests of our hosts, and he was worried about me.

He really must be in love.

"I'll go ahead and call Trinity." Clay whipped out his phone. "You told Colby thirty minutes, right?"

"Yeah." I packed away those thoughts. "That leaves me twenty to ward our rooms."

If the kids were practicing too, they might get a tingle as I worked my magic. I didn't want to spook them before I got a chance to speak to their parents and assure them I hadn't come for a family meal deal.

I hadn't gotten that vibe off the kids, but I had been wrong before. The biggest reason white witches were facing extinction was their elders' refusal to train the next generation. Unless they unlocked their power, they weren't a tempting target for people like me.

People like I *used* to be.

Asa walked ahead, but I touched Clay's arm to hold him back. "Thanks."

"For what?" He ran his fingers through his hair. "My sudden urge to talk wigs? As if I need a reason?"

"For ensuring Colby doesn't miss a thing." I hooked my arm through his. "This is a big deal for her."

Head resting on his shoulder, we strolled into the inn, and I set to work protecting us in our beds.

♥

"Incoming," Clay called, nineteen minutes on the dot later. "Moth at three o'clock."

Since they were roomies now, Clay had left their window open to make it easier for Colby to return.

"Does that mean you're heading down?" I crossed the hall. "Do you need help with anything?"

"You promised to chaperone, remember?" He held two wig boxes tucked against his chest. "Let's go."

Asa appeared in the doorway to our room, his shirt unbuttoned, and I heaved a sigh.

I might have sneaked in soundproofing while I was at it, but we wouldn't get to use it yet.

Pity.

Heedless of the possibility of being spotted, Colby sailed through Clay's window to smack me in the face.

"Oomph." I staggered back, peeling her spastic body off me. "What's wrong?"

"Rue." She ducked into the neck of my shirt and hid there. "They did it."

Cradling her through the fabric, I held on while approaching the window. "What did they do?"

Not since that first year had she been so shaken that she retreated into my shirt to hide from the world.

"Who are *they*?" Clay braced a hand on the sash and stared below us. "The LARPers?"

"Y-y-yes." She quivered against me. "They s-s-summoned the undead, like in Mystic Realms, b-b-but the Boos came."

"The Amherst kids," I said slowly, making sure I understood, "summoned the Boo Brothers?"

With the sun overhead? How was that possible? It wasn't, I decided, without a firm anchor.

Say, their bones.

"The Amhersts cast a spell, but it was a *real* spell, and the Boos showed up, and they played paper, rock, scissors, and the winner *ate him*." Her feet tucked into the space between us, tickling my stomach. "He swallowed him. Whole. Like a snake with a mouse." She sobbed against my chest. "It was supposed to be pretend, but it was real. It was *all* real. He's dead, Rue."

"Do you mean Markus?" I cast about for anyone else she might have meant. "Talk to me, sweetie."

"Sam." She peered out of my shirt. "His name was Sam."

Sam.

Why did that ring a bell?

"As in Samuel Todd." I pinned down the name. "The teen kidnapped from the Waffle Iron, the one the Boos claimed was a demon."

"The Amhersts are on their way." Her eyes pleaded with me. "We need to leave before they get back."

Had she not just reported a murder, I would have left with no more questions asked, but we didn't have that luxury. We had to investigate her claims to make sense of them, and we had to act like nothing was wrong if we wanted the Amhersts to incriminate themselves.

Forget cultivating them as witnesses. Thanks to Colby, we had found our killers.

Abandoning me, she glided onto the bed and wrapped herself in the green blanket Asa had knit her.

"We have to go downstairs." I slammed the window shut. "It will look suspicious otherwise."

"I'll stay with you." Asa sat beside Colby. "No one is going to hurt you."

Snuggling against his hip, she buried herself in her blanket, breaking my heart clean down the middle.

"We'll be back as soon as we can," I told her, then warned Asa, "Keep an eye out and your phone close."

"Be careful." He stroked her back. "Make your excuses and break away if anything is suspect."

"Come on." Clay picked up the wig boxes I hadn't noticed him set down. "I hear voices."

Out in the hall, the door shut behind us, I regained my composure and watched Clay do the same.

Voices drifted up the stairs as Markus and Trinity talked about dinner, some movie, random kid things.

Certain they weren't going to confess to murder where they might be overheard, we started down.

"Business is slow this week." Trinity rounded the check-in counter. "We may need to advertise—"

"Hey." Markus cut her off with a grin that looked natural, not forced. "Are those the wigs?"

"They are indeed." Clay clutched them to his chest when Trinity swooped in. "But first, would you like to join us for linner? We had ice cream in town, but we're starving. You do have pizza delivery here, right?"

Ah, linner. The meal between lunch and dinner. One of his favorite excuses to sneak in an extra meal. He wouldn't hear me complain. I enjoyed the ice cream, but my belly was convinced I had room for more.

"That would be awesome." Markus stole a notepad off the counter. "Give me your order, and I'll call down to Marco's. They can charge it to us, and we'll add it to your tab."

"Sounds good." Clay rattled off our usuals then glanced around. "Where do you want to do this?"

"This way." Trinity indicated for us to follow. "My craft room is back here."

The room was narrow but long. Plenty of space for a crafter. Based on the dated bolts of fabrics hung on the wall, I figured she took it over after her grandmother passed and had yet to clear out the reminders. A table had been built across the rear wall. A yellowed sewing machine took pride of place, but hairclips, wigs, and shears littered the remaining surface. The floor would have been at home in a barber shop. One that didn't require sweeping between customers. Like, ever.

Clearly, she enjoyed the creative process more than the tidying up afterward.

"Let me clean a space." She flipped on several longneck lamps. "I don't want to get them grubby."

This kid showed zero signs of remorse for what she helped do, and no fear of getting caught either.

"Will your parents mind if we feed you?" I leaned against the wall. "Should we ask permission first?"

We really needed to feel them out, decide if they had any idea what their kids were up to in the woods.

"We're not supposed to tell anyone." She paused in her tidying. "Since you're FBI, it should be okay."

To draw her eye, Clay shifted the boxes in a subtle prompt to get on with it before she got distracted.

"They're not here," she explained. "They left Markus and me in charge until they get back."

"Where did they go?" I kept it light. "A romantic weekend getaway?"

"No." She measured me. "They're settling the insurance claim on the Waffle Iron."

"Your parents owned it?" Clay, who was the better actor, faked surprise. "Why didn't you say so?"

"It's all anyone is talking about." Her fingers twitched on a lace cap. "We're tired of the questions."

"Markus made it sound like the food wasn't that great," Clay teased. "Who was the bad cook?"

"Mom." A faint bitterness shone through. "I'm surprised the place didn't burn down sooner."

Had I imagined the faint wistfulness in her tone? Hard to tell with her distracted air.

"I need to use the restroom." I shoved off the wall. "Be back in a minute."

"Down the hall and to your right." Trinity fell on Clay's wigs like a kid at Christmas. "Next to the check-in desk."

Ready with a lie about being lost if I bumped into anyone, I cracked open as many doors as I could, wary Markus would catch me.

The downstairs rooms were lived in, a tad messy, and dotted

with family photos. This must be where the Amhersts lived, which meant anything good was going to be here.

Choosing a room at random, I let myself in with a tiny spark of magic only to discover I had found the master bedroom. Neat as a pin, it fit the story the teens told us. I searched under the parents' bed and in their closet. I checked their bathroom and the linen closet. The latter held an elaborate shrine to Hecate, complete with a kneeling bench before her statue.

Most witches, black arts or white craft, prayed for her blessings. She was the goddess of the night, of the moon, of ghosts, and of necromancy. That might sound grim, but she was also the goddess of witchcraft.

To disrupt a sacred place of another witch was in poor taste, so I looked and kept my hands to myself.

Everything was as I expected it to be. Nothing scandalous. Nothing hinting at black magic use.

Though a light coating of dust made me question whether this was another remnant of the late Mrs. Amherst.

There was nothing for me to do but try another room and hope I had better luck there.

I shut the closet, making sure I left everything as I found it, then exited the bedroom.

"Oof." I bounced off Markus and hit the wall. "Hey, I'm glad I bumped into you."

His gaze flitted behind me to his parents' door, but I was striving hard for innocence.

"Trinity gave me directions to the bathroom." I hooked a thumb over my shoulder. "That wasn't it."

"No." A hard light entered his eyes. "It wasn't."

"Sorry about that." I flashed him a smile that showed too many teeth. "I'm terrible with directions."

"No problem," he was quick to assure me. "It happens all the time."

The obvious lie in his voice set my teeth on edge, but we both pretended everything was hunky-dory.

Markus wasn't the smooth liar his sister was, and I sensed he had a nasty temper eager to ignite despite his wide smiles, easy jokes, and good-natured attitude. He wasn't the actor in the family, for sure, but he'd fooled me at first. The mask wasn't fitting as well as it had earlier. If I had to guess, I would blame the high of his recent kill for exposing his true face now.

"What's the ETA on the pizza?" I worked to thin the awkward silence. "I'm starving."

"It'll be about thirty minutes." He thawed a bit. "You must eat a lot of takeout."

"We live on it," I confirmed, happy for a change in topic. "We live on the road too."

"Ah." He nodded once. "That would explain you hooking up with a fellow agent."

"Um, yeah." I wasn't about to discuss my personal life with a teen. "How did your LARP go?"

"Productive." He reached up as if to stroke the beard he no longer wore. "Practice makes perfect."

Within the confines of Colby's eavesdropping, he left me with goose bumps down my arms.

"Let me walk you to the bathroom," he offered. "I'll wait for the pizza at check-in."

No longer trusting him with my food, I allowed myself to be shuffled through the correct door.

Certain he would wait to escort me back, I went through the motions of flushing and washing my hands.

Sure enough, Markus was on his phone when I exited, and his gaze flicked up to mine. "Done?"

"Yeah." I turned back toward the craft room. "Mind walking me back?"

Might as well ask rather than fumble through another awkward exchange. He was coming either way.

"We wouldn't want you getting lost again."

At the door to the craft room, he saw me inside then shut it behind me. I almost checked to see if he locked it too.

"Was that Markus?" Trinity had her phone in hand. "I thought I heard voices."

"I bumped into him outside the bathroom," I fibbed. "He was nice enough to escort me back."

"That's him." She didn't glance up from the photos she was taking. "Nice."

"How's the wig inspection coming along?" I walked up behind Clay and peeked over his shoulder. "Looks like you two are getting serious." I caught his gaze and let a hint of warning touch my eyes where Trinity couldn't see and then mimed plucking a hair from her head. "I can't remember Clay ever letting anyone touch one of his wigs. He must endorse your noble quest."

"Try it on." Clay poured on the charm. "You know you want to elf yourself."

"Are you sure?" She examined the cap. "I don't want to hurt it."

"Here." He took it from her. "Let me help."

From a pile of bobby pins in a bowl, he selected two and seated the wig. As he secured it, she flinched, her back going stiff. But Clay's smile was guileless, and his self-deprecating laugh authentic.

"Sausage fingers," he muttered. "Sorry about that." He flicked the ends of his hair, tucking the stolen strands from Trinity in his collar so he could show her his hands were empty as he placed them on his lap in clear view. "I just glue and go, so I'm out of practice."

"No problem." The crease of her brow smoothed when he held up a mirror for her. "Oh wow."

"Right?" He chuckled. "The guy who makes my wigs is a magician."

Technically, he was a witch, but I wasn't here to split hairs. Just steal them.

A buzz in my pocket drew my attention to my phone.

\>\>*This is your excuse to leave.*

>*Thanks.*

>>*We need to get Colby out of here.*

A lump formed in my throat that I did my best to ignore.

>*We'll be there in ten.*

Eyebrows on the climb, Clay watched me with a question in his eyes.

"We have to go." I wiggled my cell. "We've got a lead we need to hop on while it's fresh."

"Okay." Clay rose with regret painted on. "Tell you what." He lingered. "Why don't you keep those?"

"Really?" Trinity stroked the longer of the two. "You're sure?"

"I have an extensive collection." To say the least. "I can afford to lose a couple in service to a friend."

"Thanks." Her smile faltered. "Guess you guys will miss out on pizza."

"Rain check." I anchored an answering brittle smile on my face. "We'll be out the rest of the night, but we should be back sometime tomorrow."

"The door's always open." She settled onto her seat. "Do you mind if I stay here?"

"We can see ourselves out."

On our way to the staircase, we bumped into Markus, who got to his feet. "What's up?"

"Duty calls." Clay gusted out a dramatic sigh. "Sorry, man, but we've got to go."

"Brutal." Markus homed in on me. "Guess we'll catch you later?"

"We'll be back late night or early tomorrow." I hit the stairs. "Enjoy that pizza."

"We will." Markus watched us go. "Enjoy your hunt."

Glancing back over my shoulder, I promised him, "We will."

6

Figuring Asa wouldn't have moved Colby, Clay and I returned to their shared room.

Sure enough, Asa was propped up in bed, Colby *and* her laptop settled across his knees. She was a bundle and a pair of antennae. That was all I could see sticking out of her green blanket. I couldn't tell if she had been teaching Asa how to play Mystic Realms or if he had only been watching her. Either way, she was much calmer now than when I left.

Based on the angle, and her degree of swaddling, I wasn't sure she noticed us enter.

"The rooms have been warded and soundproofed," I reminded them. "We can speak freely in here."

After checking that Colby was plugged in, Asa said, "We need to examine the woods behind the inn."

With her headset on, she was oblivious to the topic of conversation, but she must have felt the vibration of Asa's voice move through her. She peeked over the top of her screen, spotted us, and attempted a smile before settling back against him.

As much as I didn't want to prod her about this, we needed more answers.

And I needed to be sure she was okay.

Death is always a shock. Violent death even more so. Poor kid. She had been having so much fun too.

The mother hen in me wanted to cluck about how this was why she wasn't allowed to play with kids IRL, but I had had enough salt rubbed in my wounds as a child to know that wasn't productive. And it wasn't like it was her fault. I couldn't cast blame on her, or let her blame herself, without diminishing her.

That, I would never do.

"Are we leaving?" Our bags hadn't been unpacked yet. "Or are we surveilling?"

"We need to find out what happened in those woods for ourselves." Asa flicked Colby a glance. "She can't talk about it."

Another flashback to our early years had me tasting bile as I recalled her shutting down, going mute, when anything reminded her of the Silver Stag or what had been done to her.

Loud noises. Bright lights. Murmured conversation. Absolute darkness.

The huge swing in what curled her into a ball made shielding her impossible, but trauma never did follow a set pattern.

"For now, we take the laptops and any sensitive materials," Clay decided. "We'll drive into town and park at a supermarket. We'll lock those in the SUV, and you can ward it. We'll leave our suitcases. Proof we'll be back, in case anyone wants to set a trap for us while we're gone."

"What do we do about...?" I rubbed my arms. "She doesn't need to see more if this is triggering her."

"We get another hotel room." Asa aimed the comment at Clay. "You stay there with her, protect her."

"While you and Rue go have all the fun," he complained. "How do I always draw the short stick?"

"Colby loves you best?" I punched his shoulder and then

regretted it. "And, with one of us on Colby duty, I'll need Asa and the daemon for this if things get weird."

"I'm joking." Clay's amusement gave way to concern. "You know I love that kid."

"I know you do." I began gathering our critical items. "If you didn't, I wouldn't ask."

As much as Clay hated being left out of the action, he was a nurturer. He would make more headway with Colby than either Asa or I would while she was still smarting from her ordeal. The truth was, when it was her and me, I had been her only choice for comfort. That sucked for her, since I was a direct link to that traumatic experience. Clay was a blank slate, a warm shoulder to cry on, and he was good with kids.

He was an antidote she might not realize she needed for the festering wounds from her past.

Loaded up, I waited for Colby to shrink to moth-size and climb into Clay's pocket. I made one more circuit of our rooms and determined we could live without what we left behind if we had no choice.

We didn't bump into either teen as we exited the inn, and while Asa loaded the SUV, I called Clay to me.

"Hairs, please." I accepted the long strands he stole from Trinity and inspected them, discarding two of the five samples for being rootless. "Hold out your hands, pointer fingers extended."

"This sounds like the start of a fart joke or one kinky evening."

Gently, so as not to break it, I wound one strand around his left knuckle and then his right, leaving an inch gap between them.

"I'm going to recite a spell," I told him. "When I give you the signal, you break the hair in two."

Halfway through the process, I gave him a thumbs-up, and he jerked apart his hands.

"What did I just do?" He waited for me to finish, keeping hold of the ends. "Do you need these?"

"You can let them go." I stepped in front of Asa. "You're next."

I repeated the process with him and then with myself.

"What did we just do?" Asa repeated the question. "What did I miss?"

"Clay has no hair, but the wigs are his. They were made for him. Someone with enough power and enough intent could twist that link and use it against Clay." I rested my hand on Asa's shoulder. "I'm not sure Trinity was grabbing for your hair so much as she was grabbing for *a* hair."

"She'll soon have access to our rooms while we're out." Clay put it together. "She could harvest strands from both of you. I would have been the problem child. A good wig doesn't shed much or often."

Not when you had them spelled to preserve them, they didn't.

With that done, we piled into the SUV, and Asa angled toward me.

"Was it wise to do that in clear view of the house?"

"We couldn't risk it." I fastened my seat belt. "Hair is too dangerous to leave in enemy hands."

Few hotels were on offer, and none of them had much in the way of amenities. As in, no cooking for us. I could imagine Clay grumbling, but he didn't make a peep. This was about Colby, not him or his late-night cravings for cookies. Though, to be honest, I had to make a better showing of insomnia baking for him.

Lately, if I woke in the night...I mean...Asa was right there.

Warm, hard, and willing to distract me until I fell asleep again.

"Let's get you guys checked in." I opened my door. "I'll be back with the keys."

What I wanted was a moment alone to inspect the place before I left Colby there to get over her scare. I walked in to find an older woman manning the check-in desk, a tray of nachos in one hand and a slushy in the other. Her nametag read *Myrtle*, and it was smeared with cheese.

She set both down and wiped her hands when I approached her. "How may I help you?"

"Do you have a room available? Twin queens would be ideal."

"Sure thing." She paused what she was watching on TV. "Business is slow, now that..."

I waited for her to finish her thought, but she click-clacked on the keyboard instead.

"Now that what, if you don't mind me asking?"

"The murders," she confided as she reached for a chip. "A town this size? Feels like half the people are dead." She crunched down. "Sure you want that room?"

"I did hear something about a kidnapping. A fire too, I think."

"I heard two crazies snatched a kid right out of his seat, over at the Waffle Iron. They were yelling at him in tongues and calling him a demon spawn." She slurped her drink. "They set fire to the place on their way out. The kid hasn't been found, and neither has the arsonist. Neither have the owners." Another crunch to gauge my interest. "For that matter, no one remembers the last time they saw the Amhersts. It's got some folks wondering if it's an insurance fraud thing. Like maybe the restaurant was going belly up, so they offered the kid a cut of the profits if he helped make it look more legit. It's not like they don't have a fallback plan. They own that old Victorian. The Amherst Inn."

"But there are kids staying at the inn," I began, realizing my mistake. "I noticed them on the drive in."

"Oh." Her next gulp gave her a brain freeze. "Yes." She rubbed her forehead. "Them."

"Are they the Amhersts' kids, or are they guests?"

"Trinity and Markus Amherst. They dress up and go tramping through the woods at night." She crinkled a straw wrapper with vigor. "They scared the bejesus out of me two months ago. I was out walking, and I heard chanting. It was just getting dark, so I wasn't too worried, but it was damn strange."

Already, this had the hallmarks of a Very Bad Idea, in my humble opinion.

"This is Raymond, after all." Her evident pride shone through.

"Nothing bad ever happens here." She took pity on the wad of paper and discarded it. "Until recently." She carried on. "I stumbled across the Amherst teens pretending to cast spells." Another chip bit the dust. "What do they call it? Some kind of club. A fantasy, make-believe thing." She shook her empty drink. "Probably Harry Potter."

A lot of parents blamed Harry Potter for, well, everything. The list was long, and my time was short.

"LARPing, I believe."

"That's it." She awarded me a curt nod. "God only knows what that stands for."

I could spell it out, but I knew it didn't matter. She wanted someone to agree with her, not correct her.

"Did they see you?" I pressed. "Say anything to you?"

"No." She tossed her cup in the bin. "I saw them first and hid behind a tree, then I backed away slowly."

If what Colby saw was accurate, that bit of luck probably saved her life.

"Can you tell me where this occurred?"

"Just in the woods." Her expression cleared. "There was a stump, now that I think about it, but trees are trees." She caught my look. "Lynn Amherst is passionate about the preservation of the *picoides borealis*. Or she was." Her interest in her snack waned. "She found a mated pair nesting in those woods and policed them vigorously. Of course, she's dead now, and her son couldn't have cared less about the red-cockaded woodpecker. Those kids of his run wild through the woods without Lynn around to keep them in check. I doubt there's a pecker to be found on the property."

Oh, what Clay wouldn't give for an opening like that. "Does anyone else go into the woods?"

"Plenty of old-timers like me. We used to have a bird-watching club, but most of us have died off."

"Um." I struggled for a response. "I'm sorry to hear that."

"Why all the interest?" She dipped her finger in the cheese. "You looking to put down roots?"

"I'm FBI." I flashed her my badge. "My partner and I are investigating a string of arsons."

"Huh." She licked her finger clean. "I figured that was more of an ATF thing."

The Bureau of Alcohol, Tobacco, and Firearms was more likely, under the right circumstances, but I had a patch ready for the hole in my story.

"The missing persons case is our main interest."

Though we had already solved that portion, thanks, unfortunately, to Colby.

"That makes more sense." She turned to the printer. "Sign here, and I'll get your keys."

We finished the deal with the usual chitchat about where to eat and what to do in town.

The list for both was short, which made it easier to remember and narrowed our suspect pool.

Out at the SUV, I gave Clay the paperwork and keycard then fetched his and Colby's essentials.

"I got it." He took them from me. "You guys head out so you can get in place before full dark."

A prickle at the base of my neck warned me we were being watched, but I figured it was Myrtle.

"We need to see you in, actually." I led the way. "I have to use the bathroom."

The guys exchanged a weighted glance then followed me up and waited as I reclaimed the keycard and barged into the room. There wasn't much to recommend it, but it was clean and smelled nice.

"I had a chat with the lady who checked us in," I told them. "She was eyeballing us on our way up."

"Anything to worry about?" Asa tucked a few strands of hair behind my ear. "Or just curiosity?"

"Curiosity, I think." I recalled her nachos with longing. "She struck me as bored and happy to gossip."

On cases, those were my absolute favorite people to encounter.

"You want to cloak us," Asa guessed, lowering his hand. "What do you need me to do?"

"Just hold still."

Murmuring a concealment spell under my breath, I pictured Asa, his hair and eyes, his smile and laugh. I thought about how it felt to run my fingers over his body, how his skin smelled, how his naked body looked spread on the bed, waiting for me to join him.

A hot flash burned my nape, but I tried to play it cool.

The better you knew a person, the better you could hide them.

That was the excuse I allowed myself for picturing how he tasted when…

A low growl shocked me back into the moment.

Lips parted, Asa stood millimeters away from me, his breath ghosting over my mouth.

On his head, onyx and deadly, gleamed his horns.

"Oops," I whispered, our lips brushing. "I might have gotten carried away."

Fascination heightened his senses, making him hyperaware of when my thoughts took a downward turn. Which, for him, resulted in more of an—*ahem*—upward turn.

"I can't see you," Clay announced, "but I can hear you. Keep that in mind."

"You can't see either of us?" I spun toward him. "You're sure?"

"As far as I can tell, Colby and I are alone." He hesitated. "Except for the panting and breathy sighs."

Huh.

The visualization exercise had included things I wanted to do to Asa. That must have secured the spell on me as well. I would have to remember that going forward. It was a handy trick that cut down on magic expenditure.

"Clay—"

"Oh, Ace," he mimicked me. "You're so tall, dark, and horny."

A laugh slipped out of Asa, but I waited for what I knew would come next.

"Do me, Rue." Clay pitched his voice low. "Ride me like a pony."

This time, I burst into laughter, because he made it easy to picture using Asa's braids as reins.

Which I would never tell either of them.

Ever.

"Why are you like this?" I jabbed his cheek. "What's wrong with you?"

"I'm sexually frustrated, emotionally stunted, and also hilarious beyond all reason."

"I'm not the friend who tells you that you need to get laid." I poked him again. "Your taste in women is terrible."

"You're not wrong." He cocked a half smile. "Maybe Ace can set me up with a nice daemoness."

"*Nice* and *daemoness* don't often go together." Asa melted my bones with a look. "I got lucky with Rue."

Biting the inside of my cheek, I didn't correct him. I was trying to get better about taking compliments.

Even if they were one thousand percent wildly inaccurate.

"Shorty incoming," Clay warned as she peeked out of his pocket, breaching the spell that kept her in a bubble of quiet, the better for letting the grownups talk.

Instead of her usual chatter, we got silence as she took in her new surroundings.

"Do you want to play your game?" I cast about for her laptop. "I can set you up before I go."

Without a word, she ducked back into Clay's pocket, spooked by my disembodied voice.

"I'm not winning any contests here." I headed for the door. "Clay, we're out."

Twice the coverage meant twice the drain on my magic, so we needed to get going anyway.

"This isn't your fault," he protested. "You can't blame yourself."

"If I had a nickel for every time someone told me that, I could use Benjamins to wipe."

Frustrated I couldn't help Colby by waving a magic wand, I barreled out the door into the parking lot.

The thing about trauma? It lurked in the recesses of your brain, let you hope you had finally, *finally* won. Then it pounced, digging in its claws and reminding you of each and every scar you did your best to hide.

"Let's stop by the front desk," I told Asa in a huff. "I want to see what Myrtle is doing."

"All right."

We didn't go inside, as it would be hard to explain the door opening, but I did peer through the glass.

Elbows on the counter, she filed her nails while she watched the TV mounted in their tiny guest lounge.

"Good deal." I got my bearings. "The woods are about a twenty-minute walk that way."

"All right."

Checking both ways before stepping into nonexistent traffic, I prowled across the pockmarked road.

"Are you stuck?" I flicked him a glance on the other side. "Do you need me to feed you a quarter?"

"You stew. Often. Mostly about your responsibilities to your loved ones. I worried about pulling you out of those dark moods at first, but now I see it's part of your process." He noticed he had my attention. "I can't convince you what others do isn't your fault. I can't convince you you're not to blame when things go wrong. You require time and space to work through it until you convince yourself you did the best you could under the circumstances."

Unnerved by how well he read me, I cocked an eyebrow. "Who says I don't stew on guilt 24/7?"

"You're too busy," he reasoned. "Busier since we started sharing a bed."

A half-choked laugh forced through the knot in my chest. Smug looked good on him.

As we set off toward the woods, I gave what he had observed serious thought and decided he was right.

Weird.

When had I become a person capable of forgiving myself? Not shucking blame. Not immune to the consequences of my actions. But truly able to look at a situation, evaluate all factors, all participants, and determine I wasn't at fault?

Okay, so I wasn't *that* progressive.

Safer to say I was cutting myself slack when I never had before, not when it mattered, not when I cared.

In taking on Colby, I had duked it out with Atlas for the right to carry the weight of the world on my shoulders. I wanted to believe that meant I had made headway in becoming the person I wanted to be, but I wasn't sure if letting myself off the hook was progress or regression.

Aiming my gaze higher than my navel, I filled in Asa on my conversation with Myrtle.

"We have the Boo Brothers," he mulled it over, "who are an undefined variety of dead. We have an inn run by a white witch family. The parents are missing, and the kids are performing dark rites under the cover of LARPing. Their restaurant burned down. A familiar with it. And a teenage boy was kidnapped and killed behind their house."

"This feels like a side quest."

"How do you know about side quests?"

Fair question, given anything Mystic Realms leaked out of my ears. "Osmosis?"

Full dark had fallen by the time we reached the area, which made searching for clues harder but safer.

"They're onto us." Markus stomped into view dressed in the same jeans and tee as before. No wizard robes this time. "We have to be ready when they come back."

"You're paranoid." Trinity followed him wearing Clay's brunette wig, fiddling with it every few steps. "They're FBI. You saw the badge. Do you really think they let witches join the Bureau?"

Depending on the Bureau, they downright encouraged it. But that was beside the point.

"I found the witch in Mom and Dad's room, which means she magicked open the lock, because I sealed that door shut myself," Markus argued. "What do you think she was doing?"

"She probably got lost, like she said." Trinity removed the wig and flexed it on her hand. "How do you know she's a witch?" She jogged to catch up when she fell behind him. "They seemed normal to me."

They marched past our hiding place, and we hung back to give them a head start.

"They're not normal." Markus worked his jaw. "Come on." He set a brutal pace. "I'll prove it."

"We're not going *there* again, are we?" Trinity gave up on styling the wig. "Twice in one day?"

"They've been fed." He led us straight to the stump Myrtle mentioned. "They won't be any trouble."

A spasm twitched through Trinity's shoulders, but I couldn't tell if it was fear or anticipation.

Markus, on the other hand, was salivating for what came next.

The top of the stump, as near as I could tell, had been sanded to create a smooth surface. Moonlight hit the edge, and it shone, leading me to believe it had been coated in resin or polyurethane to preserve it.

From his pocket, Markus produced a switchblade and sliced across his palm. He flicked the blood onto the stump, which absorbed every drop, then he let Trinity layer on neon Band-Aids to cover the wound.

"Rise," he commanded, and the earth trembled beneath us. "Obey your master."

A blueish-gray haze seeped across the ground, a fog so thick and cold, I took a step back.

A standing apparition formed atop the stump, and another coalesced beside it.

The Boo Brothers.

Definitely dead then.

"What do you want?" Malcom, the older brother demanded. "Ain't you ever heard of *rest in peace?*"

"There is no peace here," Emmett said, his eyes black and bottomless. "Can we kill them yet?"

"Not yet." Malcom stepped down beside his brother. "One slip though, Marky, and you're lunch."

"You and your sister." Emmett stared a hole through Trinity. "I bet you scream real pretty."

Most things brought back after death came back wrong, and it sounded like the quasi-religious Boos had a different fixation now than in life. Or maybe death had cut away the excess to reveal their true selves.

"Enough with the theatrics." Markus stepped between them and his sister. "Can you sense witches?"

Hatred burned hot and fast in the Boos' eyes. "We smell you."

Confirmation the Amhersts had witch blood wasn't exactly a shock. Neither was the Boos' disgust.

"Other witches," Markus clarified through his gritted teeth. "Can you verify one was at the inn?"

"Maybe." Malcom clamped a hand on his brother's shoulder to still him. "What do we get in exchange?"

"To kill her when you find her." Markus offered me up without a blink. "Deal?"

"Deal," Emmett growled, his teeth bared. "Brother?"

"All right." He was slow to agree, sated from their earlier kill and not interested in glutting. "Let's go."

The four of them headed toward the inn while Asa and I watched their grim procession.

Just before they were out of sight, Malcom glanced over his shoulder...and winked at me.

"We need to go." Asa gripped my upper arm. "Now."

"You saw that, right?" I craned my neck after Malcom. "He knew we were there, but he let the Amhersts drag them to the inn to begin a search." I rushed after Asa. "What do you think's going on?"

"They're playing a game. With the Amhersts, and with us." He shepherded me away. "What are they?"

"The Amhersts or the Boos?"

"Either." He amended, "Both."

"The Amherst kids have white witch parents. If they went dark, none of us smelled black magic on them. If they haven't, they've done something equally stupid. I've never seen that level of sentience in a spirit. The Boos can bargain rather than accept orders. That's not revenant or poltergeist behavior."

Wary the Boos might change their minds and come hunting me, Asa and I jogged the whole way back to the hotel. Inside the room, I dropped our glamour to avoid spooking Colby again then got to work placing wards to keep out spirits.

Only once those protections were in place did we settle in to give Clay an update. "Any idea what we're dealing with?"

"Reminds me of lemures. Wandering and vengeful ghosts. Those aren't solid, though." He thought on it some more. "The consumption of entire meals, entire *people*, is a vrykolakas trait. They mainly eat livers and flesh. They're less corporeal but still able to interact with the world around them."

"How about we call them koalas and leave it at that?" I ignored the guys' synchronized eyerolls. "What's anchoring them here? What hold do the Amhersts have on them? And what are the Amhersts? Those are the big questions. We need to remove the Amhersts from the equation, and then take down the Boos. We can figure out the rest once the situation has been neutralized."

Clay lifted a finger for silence and brought his vibrating phone out of his pocket.

"Kerr." He listened for a minute. "I'm putting you on speaker."

"We have a report of Francis Franklin gutting a couple in

Natchez." Parish bit out the order almost as well as the director. "I want your team on it."

"We have a situation in Raymond." Asa sat on the desktop beside me. "We can't afford to leave yet."

"Francis is the greater threat." Parish brooked no argument. "I'll deploy a secondary team to Raymond."

The call ended with a click, and Clay stared at us in expectation, his whole body trembling.

"I can tell you're about to pop." I urged him on with a roll of my wrist. "Who is Francis Franklin?"

"Femme Fatale Frankie was a B-movie staple in slasher flicks. She was gorgeous, *and* a bean sidhe." He vibrated with excitement. "When her movies wrapped, her costars died. Every. Single. Time. Her fans loved it. Her costars, not so much. Eventually, no studio could afford to touch her."

"Did she do it?" I frowned. "Bean sidhes predict deaths. They're not the cause of them."

Among the fae, they were despised as a reminder that even the long-lived die eventually. They weren't popular among other factions either. People blamed them for being harbingers, but it wasn't like they were fulfilling the prophecy. They merely gave the warning they were genetically wired to impart.

"Police tried to make the charges stick, so did Black Hat, but there wasn't enough evidence."

"You met her," I realized. "Did you work the case?"

"Yes and yes." His gaze grew distant. "I might have asked her to marry me if she hadn't been killed by the wife of one of her former costars between police interviews. The wife was a literal goddess. She was convinced Frankie was having an affair with her husband. She believed Frankie killed her man when he refused to leave her. Frankie denied the allegations, but the guy was already dead. He couldn't say either way. Bean sidhe are tough, but a minor goddess is a major player."

Earth-walking goddesses, minor or not, were famous for their tempers. "How was she killed?"

"Arietta gutted her. Neck to navel." He turned solemn. "Waste of a beautiful woman."

"When you implied you two were in a relationship," Asa pried, "do you mean in your head or in reality?"

To hide my smile, I turned my head, but Clay knew me too well.

"This is your influence." Clay pointed a damning finger at me. "He used to be such a nice dae."

Swallowing my amusement, I prodded, "Answer the question."

"I never said we were in a relationship." He sniffed. "I said I might have asked her to marry me."

"So, the starlet was killed by a goddess, and now she's reenacting her death in Natchez."

"Does that mean the Boos are doing the same?" Asa frowned. "Acting out their deaths?"

"No one knows how they died," I admitted. "We'd have to solve that crime to know for sure."

The serpentine nature of their kills reminded me of a naga or another creature with snakelike qualities. They swallowed prey whole, then, after a period of time, bones were the end product. How was the flesh digested if the Boos weren't revenant-like? And if they weren't undead, did it mean that ghosts poop?

"I'll cross-reference what we know about their recent crimes against similar events occurring around the time of their disappearances." The tiny voice barely registered as Colby, but it grew stronger. "See if we can narrow the scope on a potential cause of death for them."

Are you sure? Are you okay? Are you ready for this?

Those were the things I longed to ask, but I didn't want to undermine her attempt to regain her footing.

"Clay?"

"You don't even have to ask." He sank onto the bed beside Colby. "Me and my best girl will wait here."

"Thank you." I jerked my chin at Asa then double-checked my kit. "We'll be back the second we can."

"Be safe," Colby whispered. "Promise me."

For so long, I had been her anchor. I hated to admit how good it felt when she said or did things that proved she might not have chosen me that dark night when she died, but she would choose me now.

"I promise." I leaned over the bed and kissed her soft forehead. "Don't let Clay get in trouble."

"Don't assign her impossible tasks," Clay chided. "Ace, take care of my second-best girl."

"I will." Asa followed in my footsteps and pressed his lips to Colby's cheek. "Be brave."

"I've got this," she told him. "I can do this."

"I know you can." He withdrew and took my hand. "We'll text as soon as we arrive."

Leaving Clay and Colby, Asa and I climbed into the SUV and set out for Natchez.

7

Ten minutes into our drive, Colby called me with a breathless note in her voice that left my palms slick.

"I was checking online for a match," she rushed out, "and I found another one."

"A match?" I recalled our last conversation. "You mean a killer with the Boos' MO?"

"A VacayNStay rental in Natchez with the same logo as the Amherst Inn hidden in the bottom left corner of their listing."

The vacation rental boom had turned many a home into a hotel in recent years. The more popular destinations got sliced and diced into B&B-style lodgings. You were on your own for meals, but you shared a house with a few other guests.

After Charleston, I was starting to view them as the bane of my existence. Apps made it too simple for paras to set traps to lure in prey. Mostly, they ensnared humans. But this was next level strange.

"Whatever the Amhersts are into," Clay added, "I bet the host is in it up to their necks too."

"Book us a suite for the next week," I said, covering our bases. "Do we know if the owners live on site?"

"Let me check." Colby grew more confident. "There's a note mentioning they stay on the premises."

"You are one brilliant moth, smarty fuzz butt." I grinned. "Do we know what the logo means yet?"

Silence on the end of the line warned me I had tread too close to a memory, and Colby shut down.

"The seal is part of the LARPer's logo on their website, but it's pinging in other searches too." Clay jumped in with her notes. "I'll let you know once we narrow it down."

"The Amherst kids said their club was the largest in the state." I was thinking out loud. "Do you think they meant LARPing? Or their online guild?"

"We're working on that now. A number that big? Probably online. Given how small Raymond is, they must have LARPer buddies flung across the nearby counties to amount to anything."

If whoever summoned Frankie was connected to the Amhersts, and their IRL members were that far-flung, then we had a summoning ring on our hands.

"If they recruited LARPers from their online guild," Asa added, "they'll be selective."

"Only those with magic, or the potential for magic," Clay agreed, "need apply."

"The logo must be how they identify one another." An *if you know, you know* thing. "Marking homes or businesses as safe havens, but safe for what? Meetings of their murder club?"

"The Kellies emailed an update." Colby sounded more determined than ever. "I have to go."

After she hung up, I sat there for a moment, allowing myself to breathe.

She was going to be okay. Already, she was climbing back to herself. This wouldn't break her.

"I'm going to read up on the LARPer site," I told Asa. "See what it can tell us."

Whoever designed the website knew what they were doing. It

wasn't the type of drag-and-drop or template site so many businesses used to cut costs. No, this had all the hallmarks of a passion project. I wasn't surprised to see the work credited to Markus Amherst at the bottom of the homepage.

"This says there are members from all over the state." I skimmed further. "They have weekly online meetings and monthly in-person gatherings. There's a painfully long set of interview questions if you'd like to be considered as a prospect, but anyone 'with magic in their hearts' is welcome to apply."

"That means this problem could be more widespread than we first thought."

"This says you gain access to the membership roster once your application has been approved." I mulled over that. "Probably so you can pair up in various MMRPGs."

There was no telling what contact information would be provided. Probably not names, addresses, or phone numbers. That was too old school. I was leaning toward social media and player handles with email addresses buried within a funnel of forwarding addresses.

"There's also a link to the sister's online wig store." I clicked it. "She's got some nice pieces."

I got the creeps imagining she might keep trophies of her commissions to forge links to her clients.

That was why I was so quick to make sure no hairs we left behind at the Amherst Inn could be used against us. Wigs with synthetic hair were a gray area, but wigs made from donated hair? That could get dangerous fast. Especially since a girl like Trinity, creating her own styles, could even reverse-engineer a spell if she hid a rooted strand of her hair where it was unlikely to be noticed by the buyer.

"What are you thinking?" Asa cut his eyes toward me. "You're quiet."

"Just recalling how very many ways we can get screwed if we leave behind a single strand of hair." I let my head fall back against the seat. "There's a spell I used to perform before leaving any room I had spent time in, back when I was paranoid other Black Hat agents were out to get me."

To be fair, I had given them plenty of reasons for retaliation. I still had a baggy of hairs in the safe that belonged to former coworkers who made their animosity clear. Like Marty. I really ought to burn those and rid myself of the temptation.

Back when I first ran from the Bureau, I expected those people to hunt me, and I wanted insurance. Now I had no reason to hold on to them, except out of habit. Or spite. Most of them were dead anyway. Black Hat agents don't live long, and those few were no exception.

Pages and pages of photos from previous gatherings proved the group was active, and the captions on each picture showed the website was updated frequently. That meant, within reason, the information was recent and accurate. It also gave Colby a jumping-off point to begin identifying the people in those photos to give us a list of suspects for the summoning ring.

A stinging pressure behind my eyes yanked me from my thoughts with a visceral tug.

Reality blurred around me, pitching my stomach until I tasted bile. Convinced the SUV had been hit, that we must be tumbling into a ditch, I startled when my vision cleared to show the same stretch of road.

A dozen blood-red roses that smelled of copper and sulfur filled my arms, their thorns ripping furrows in my skin. Reeling, I swung my head toward Asa, panic a heartbeat in my throat, but he gave no indication his world had tilted. That meant I was the only one whose brain got tossed in the washer on spin cycle.

"What happened?" I couldn't hear over the thundering of my pulse. "Where did these come from?"

The steering wheel groaned beneath Asa's fingers. "Father sent them."

"Goddess bless." I dumped them in the floorboard. "The thorns are an inch long."

"Clay would find it amusing my father has a crush on you."

"Yes, well, Clay finds it amusing to make his belly button talk too." I gestured to the bloodthirsty gift. "What do we do about this?" I kicked the bouquet for good measure. "Your dad needs to take a hint."

"We stop for the night."

"That was the plan," I said slowly. "In Natchez."

"The strain from the portal means our bodies are convinced they haven't slept in twenty-four hours." He kept stealing glances at the messy floorboard. "We might be walking into another Amherst Inn situation. We need to find a *safe* hotel, get some food and sleep, and come at this tomorrow."

"Parish will have a fit."

"We're no good to him dead on our feet."

"All right." I was easy to convince. "I'll update Colby."

>>I'll book you a room in Washington. It's about fifteen minutes outside Natchez. I'll adjust your reservation at March Manor online so your check-in is tomorrow.

>Many blessings upon your antennaed head.

>>You definitely need sleep. You're being weirder than usual.

>Thanks?

>>It wasn't a compliment.

>>I'm also ordering pad see ew and drunken noodles to be delivered from a local Thai restaurant.

>You're definitely my favorite moth.

>>Sleep. Eat. Brain tomorrow.

That might have been the most beautiful thing anyone had ever said to me.

Our lodgings for the night appeared on my right, and he cut into the parking lot with a squeal of tires.

"Asa?"

He got out, circled the SUV, and opened my door. He reached in, gathered the bouquet, and tossed it on the asphalt. I took the initiative, slid out, and stomped until every petal was bruised. I thought that would be it, that the purpose was catharsis, but Asa had other plans.

Crouching above the mess, he waved a hand over it, an incantation on his lips, and the debris swirled away to nothing.

"How…?" I gawked at him. "You never mentioned you could do magic."

"As I've said, Father is a big believer the word *no* doesn't exist. He spells his gifts to appear, and he gives the target of his affection the opportunity to return to sender. He considers it foreplay. Daemons enjoy the hunt." He warned me, "This isn't a solution. He'll push until he gets what he wants, or I kill him."

For Asa to reject a present on my behalf would only cause his father to double down until he heard direct from me. But then his suggestion registered, and my tongue turned to sand in my mouth.

"Kill him?" I forced my chapped lips to move. "Then you would be High King. That's not a solution either."

"No," he agreed. "It's not."

"We'll figure it out."

Fisting the front of his shirt, I led him inside to work up an appetite before dinner arrived.

8

Had Asa not set an alarm, I might not have woken at dusk. Or dawn. Or dusk the next day.

Used to paying the toll for travel between this world and the Hael pocket realm, Asa had a headache to my hangover. I inhaled the three breakfast burritos he ordered before we showered and wished he had bought ten more. Fluffy eggs, crisp smoked bacon, avocado, crunchy hashbrowns, cotija cheese, pickled jalapeños, and chipotle aioli. What wasn't to love?

We took our spicy Café de Olla to go, which gave me time to answer the backlog of texts and calls from Parish, and the Natchez team, demanding our ETA while Asa drove us to our next potential link in the summoner's ring.

The VacayNStay was a grand old colonial with a historically accurate blue-on-blue color palette. Fountain in the front, pulsing in time with a light show, and a garden in the back, hung with fairy lights. Perfect for a romantic stroll. The lawn was thick and lush. Impressive. And the circular driveway had been extended into more of a Q than an O, with guest parking in the tiny lot—more of a strip —off the side of the house.

Definitely not a place you rolled up to and thought, *This is it. This is where it all ends.*

The Amherst kids could take a lesson from the resident summoner on subtlety.

There were three other cars, two with out-of-state plates. Those must be guests, the same as us. That would make sneaking around that much harder, but it also gave us a layer of insulation among others.

Before we got tangled up in our next line of inquiry, I shot Clay a text.

>*We're here.*

>>*Keep us updated.*

"Do you think Markus warned his friends?" Asa left our things in the SUV. "It might cause problems."

"If he did, and they can identify us, this will all be over quickly." The Amhersts could have snapped pictures of us on their phones at any given time. They were likely more inclined to do so after we asked them not to. "We played it straight with the Amhersts." Mostly. They knew we were Bureau, just not which one. "What's our ploy here?"

"Honeymooners," he suggested. "That might earn us fewer interruptions."

"Hmm." I pretended to consider his idea. "It would also explain why we have no clothes."

Just what we had on our backs, both of us rumpled from yesterday's adventures.

"Oh?"

"I ripped them off you." I popped a button on his shirt. "They're in tatters down the interstate."

"And your clothes?" He leaned in closer. "What happened to them?"

"You," I said simply.

Leaning down, he brushed his mouth over mine and latched his arms around my waist.

"We're being watched." His breath coasted over my lips. "Is Operation Honeymoon a go?"

"We're already making out in the parking lot," I murmured. "I would hate to blow our cover."

With a flourish, Asa twirled me into a dance that tangled my feet with his in a way that made me want to kick his legs from under him and ride him down to the ground. Heat in his eyes, he dipped me until my hair brushed the gravel then dragged a fingertip from my chin to the valley between my breasts.

This would have looked so much more convincing if I were in a dress to flatter his black suit.

Oh well.

We work with what we're given.

Loud claps snapped me to attention, and I found a woman in her midsixties swooning on the porch.

"That was lovely." She continued her applause. "How romantic."

"Hi." I let Asa pull me upright and tuck me under his arm. "We have a reservation."

"Are you two having an affair? With that much passion, you can't be married."

The question caught me off guard, and I stood there, struck dumb.

"Yes," Asa confided with utter seriousness. "I hope that's all right." He gazed at me, full of mischief. "I'm going to marry this one, one day. As soon as the divorce goes through."

"I'm sorry your previous marriage didn't work out, but it's clearly for the best. You two are magic together." She held open the door. "Come on in, and I'll get your room key."

Face pressed into Asa's side, I whispered, "I'm sorry to hear about your previous marriage too."

"Yes, well, my wife had an affair with a fish farmer. I'm vegan, so the betrayal was twice as painful."

There was a familiar element about the story he was telling, but I couldn't put my finger on it.

Then it hit me.

That was the plot of the last improbable shifter novel I read, one about an octopus and a manatee.

I *knew* he had been reading over my shoulder, and he cast himself in the role of the wronged manatee.

"When you roe, you roe, I guess." I patted his hand. "What can you do?"

Before he could hit me with a zinger about fish eggs, the woman waved us into the home.

"I'm Lucy March," she introduced herself in the living room turned lobby. She hustled to a spindly chair set before an antique desk with a hutch full of keys that acted as the check-in area. "I live just down there." She pointed to a door at the end of the hall. "You're welcome to use the kitchen, but it's a shared space. There are rules posted on the fridge." She smiled as she passed over our key, an actual metal one plucked off its hook. "Enjoy yourselves."

"We will," Asa promised her, drawing me against him in a clench pose. "Thank you for your hospitality."

I didn't have to fake my blush when Ms. March mouthed, *Lucky girl.*

As it happened, our room was on the bottom floor, so we didn't have far to go to examine our lodgings. It also meant that Ms. March stared a hole in our backs until we shut the door behind us.

"I can't help but notice how close our room is to hers." I twitched my nose. "Voyeur, much?"

"The lot is full." Asa pinned me to the door with his hips. "It might be the last available room."

"I can't be the only one picturing her holding a glass to the wall to listen in on us."

"You were," Asa said on a sigh, "until you slotted that mental picture into my head."

Hands on his shoulders, creeping up to his neck, I stilled my fingers. "It's quiet."

"The lot is full," he repeated, cocking his head to listen. "Where are the other guests?"

"Feel up to taking a walk?"

"I'm definitely feeling up," he lamented, bracing his forehead against mine. "Give me a minute."

"Maybe I can help with that."

Sliding my back down the door, I traded my grip on his shoulders for one on his hips. I hit my knees, and Asa groaned, his fingers tangling in my hair. I unfastened his belt, opened the button on his slacks, and tugged down his zipper. He was hot and hard under my hands as I freed him from his boxers and took him into my mouth.

"Rue." Asa's hands spasmed as I drew him deeper. "Gods."

The taste of him was imprinted on my brain, and I savored it as a low growl slipped past his lips. His spine locked, his orgasm swift and brutal, and I grinned as his knees failed him. He hit the carpet before me, wobbly as an unset salted cajeta chocolate flan, his self-control unraveled in record time.

Yeah.

I was proud of myself.

"Your turn." He reached for my waistband. "It's only fair."

"You'll have to owe me." I shivered as he sank his hand down the front of my pants. "We should—"

"—be right here, right now, doing this." He dipped into my underwear. "I love you, Rue."

"I love you too," I panted as his fingers found me slick and eager. "Very much." I bucked against his hand as he entered me. "Very, *very* much." As his thumb stroked that tiny bundle of nerves, I quivered with need. "Very, very, *very* much."

Delicious tension coiled low in my gut, and I rode him faster, blushing as he watched me.

"You're so beautiful." He raked his fingers through my hair, cupped the back of my head, and brought me in for a kiss that ignited the burn between my thighs into an inferno. "And you're mine."

The last word held a promise, that he would protect me from his father.

And I would protect him.

The sweep of his tongue bumped his piercing into my teeth. He broke the kiss to nip his way across my jaw, and when he sank his teeth into my throat hard enough to bruise, I came apart in his hand.

"We have work to do." I couldn't catch my breath. "How am I supposed to brain now?"

All I wanted to do after that was, well, *him*. But we had a case, and possibly an eavesdropper.

Neither of which did anything to cool the heat swirling through me when I noticed Asa wasn't done yet.

A text from Clay foiled my evil plot to straddle Asa before he zipped his pants.

>>*You've got a live one.*

>>*Make that a dead one.*

>*Break that down for me.*

>>*A man was eviscerated outside the Shots Fired bar two hours ago. A secondary team has already secured the scene. They're waiting on you. Maybe actually go this time?*

>*To think I almost regretted not having you around to share my breakfast burritos with.*

>>*You ate breakfast burritos? Without me? How could you?*

>*Over the lips, past the gums, look out stomach, here it comes?*

After blanking the screen, I started to rise, only to realize Asa's hand was still down my pants.

"We can't investigate like this." I looked pointedly down. "We don't want people to get the wrong idea."

"That you literally lead me around by your—" he flexed his fingers, "—sparkling personality."

"Nice save." I shoved him back. "Especially since, judging by your wrist, I can tell your poor hand was trapped down there by my fat roll." I rubbed my stomach. "I've been eating too many cupcakes lately."

Even now that we spent all our time together, he still sent *I miss you* cupcakes as a delicious reminder of our early courtship. Just not in bulk.

"You can never eat too many cupcakes." He got our feet under us. "And I wasn't trapped." He steadied me. "I didn't want to leave."

Fresh heat spilled into my cheeks. "We should clean up and get going."

Before he could corner me in the bathroom, I ducked in and locked the door behind me. I pulled my hair into a messy bun, washed up, and attempted to appear professional in my day-old tee and jeans. The lump under my shirt confirmed the grimoire was safe in its cage around my neck, undetected so far.

I might not have been bold enough to use the mistletoe necklace Asa gave me every time I wanted a kiss from him, but I liked having the option. I missed it, what it stood for, and I couldn't wait to get home and swap the pendant for the charm's comforting weight.

"Your turn," I called while trading places with Asa. "We need to pick up fresh outfits in town."

Unlike me, Asa didn't shut the door. He had no problem attending business with an audience of one, which worked for me, because I had no problem watching him. I should have let the man have a shred of privacy, especially when I preferred the door shut, but sex had changed him.

Our bond deepened by the day, and the farther its hooks sank into me, the more it relaxed him.

Things that would have embarrassed him once, he didn't bat an eye at now. I wished my transformation was as impressive, but no. I was still awkward with words and better with my hands. Or mouth.

While I enjoyed the show, I cast a cleansing spell to remove hairs, blood, and other bodily fluids from the premises. It was a good habit to get back into since I was working full-time. Honestly, I should have been doing it all along.

Asa emerged with his hair tidied in neat braids and his clothes back in order.

Pity.

I liked him rumpled.

"Ready?" He dipped his head to kiss me. "We don't want to keep the agents waiting."

"Oh sure," I teased. "Now that your pants are zipped, you're a consummate professional."

His fingers dropped to the button on his pants, and I forced my eyes to shut, my heel to pivot.

"I have been a terrible influence on you." I yanked open the door before I changed my mind. "Oh."

Ms. March stood in the hall, not pretending she hadn't been listening in. "Leaving so soon?"

"We have dinner reservations in town," Asa lied smoothly. "Did you need anything before we go?"

"Me? No." She patted one of her rosy cheeks. "I'm right as rain. Thanks for asking."

We gave her a second to take the hint she had to budge before we could eke past her.

"I bet you a dollar," I told him in the yard, "she invites herself into our room while we're gone."

Cute little old lady she might be, but she struck me as the kind who would sniff her guests' pillows.

"I would lose that bet."

The ride to the crime scene didn't take long, and I was glad to see Marty wasn't the AIC, agent in charge. I was less thrilled when I recognized the trainee standing behind the vampire.

The vampire was a familiar face, but I was terrible with names. I hadn't cared to match one to the other back when we had a case or two in common. I hadn't cared about much of anything except chasing my next black magic high.

The last time I saw him was in Charleston, along with his black witch junior agent, who still appeared just as starstruck as he had then.

"I'm Fergal," the AIC introduced himself, reading my blank expression with ease. "This is Walters."

Time to pack away Rue and bring forth the black witch persona they anticipated, which made me tired.

"What have we got?" I didn't acknowledge his introduction beyond a nod. "Clay mentioned a body."

"The victim was human," Walters said, clearly bored. "He was eviscerated." He dragged his feet over to a tarp and peeled it down. "Probably the most exciting thing to ever happen to him."

Yeah, I was sure the victim's last thoughts walked that exact line.

Woo-hoo! Brutally murdered, what a way to go. This is the best. The absolute best. Oh, hey. I pooped myself.

Asa stepped up beside me, and Walters bristled at his proximity. "I'm sure he was thrilled."

The vampire startled to hear Asa speak, but Walters was new. He didn't know Asa to be afraid of him.

"He's just a human." Walters nudged the body with his toe. "What does it matter?"

That, Asa might have forgiven him, but the boy took it one step further and spit on the corpse.

Asa slammed the boy's head against the brick wall of the neighboring club before Walters could so much as squeak a protest. "All life matters."

Proving he was a total idiot, Walters reached for the wand hidden down his pant leg. "Back the fuck off."

Metal glinted, catching the streetlight, and it dawned on me he hadn't gone for his wand but a dagger. A cold ball of dread settled in my gut as I lunged to intercept the weapon. But in shoving Asa, I knocked Walters's aim off course, and his blade caught on Asa's braid rather than plunging into his chest.

Warm blood spattered my face, arced across Asa's jaw, and painted the wall above Walters.

Shrieking in horror, Walters scooped up his amputated hand and tried to stick it back on. It fell off with a thump, and Walters's eyes rolled up in his head. His knees buckled, and he hit the pavement in a heap.

Fergal latched his mouth around the stump, attempting to use his saliva to seal the wound, but it was a catastrophic injury.

"I ought to let him bleed out." I jerked Walters out of Fergal's hands. "But he's ruining the crime scene."

Drawing my wand, I tapped Walters's wrist bone, focusing my intent to cauterize the injury.

The agony shot his eyes wide open, and he lifted his barbequed arm with a tremble on his lips.

"My h-h-hand," he stuttered. "Where is my h-h-hand?"

"I have it." Fergal collected the gruesome trophy. "Perhaps Ms. Hollis knows someone who can reattach it."

"I'm sure I do." I pocketed my wand. "However, I don't, as a rule, help morons who attack my mate."

Mate.

The word had slipped out, and there was no calling it back. I think…maybe…I didn't want to?

"I'll take him to the medic." Fergal gripped his trainee by the upper arm. "I'll be back when I can."

"You guys are going to get us in so much trouble one of these days," I groused to the *y'nai*, and I swear I heard an answering rustle of laughter. "I'm willing to give you a pass this one time." I kept my face stern, though I had no idea where they were hiding. Probably behind me. Better to focus on the person I could see, the one chuckling at my slip. "He cut your hair."

"Better my hair than my heart." He cradled my cheek in his palm. "*Mate.*"

"Heard that, did you?" I could have kicked myself for saying it in front of other agents. "I was making a point."

"That you would have done the *y'nai*'s job for it if Walters had succeeded?"

"I want to believe I would have stopped there." I smoothed the poor, abused braid and gritted my teeth against the couple of flyaways Walters managed before the *y'nai* intervened. "I'm not sure I would have." I stared up at him. "I'm not exactly rational where you're concerned."

"I don't mind." His lips twitched. "Not at all."

"That only makes you just as twisted as me." I tugged his braid then let it go. "Come on. Time to work."

We took photos and video of the body for our personal records, but Fergal was thorough. There were no clues he hadn't already identified and flagged in his report. Parish had wasted resources ordering us here. Our time would have been better spent in Raymond, hunting the Boos, than horning in on Fergal's case.

"We've got a witness," a young man dressed in black told us. "Filmed the whole thing on her phone."

When he got close enough, I could tell he was aquatic fae by the faint scent that clung to him. The smell wasn't saltwater or fresh, but it was as if my brain made the identification without consulting my other senses. Must be a species I had come across and remembered, even if I couldn't access the name.

"Can I see?" I noticed the device in his hand. "Is that her cell?"

"Sure is." He pressed a few more buttons. "I got the video cued up for you."

I reached for the device, but he yanked his hand back, and I froze. "Problem?"

"Do I set this somewhere, or...?" His gaze flicked to the bloody puddle. "I like my hands where they are."

"As long as you don't go for his hair, you're fine." I snatched the phone before he could bolt. "Or mine."

"I like how you slid that in there." He laughed. "Slick." He glanced at Asa. "We haven't met, but I watched your recent challenges with my dad. Your combat skills are impressive." He dropped to one knee and placed his fist over his heart. "Jase Isiforos, Miserae."

Jerked from the action on screen, I pressed pause. "You inflict misery on people?"

A dismissive flick of Asa's fingers, and the daemon rose. "Pleasure to meet you, Jase."

"You don't end up a Black Hat by spreading joy and happiness." Jase grinned. "Nice to meet you, Rue."

He backed into the shadows then spun on his heel and returned to his team.

Since he appeared to be in possession of that rarest commodity—common sense—I committed Jase's name to memory in case we needed a solid agent later, then hit play. "Oh, boy."

Leaning over my shoulder, Asa watched the brutal murder with me. I kept having to dismiss notifications on posts the witness had made, leading me to believe she had shared her horror story on social media. A solid Black Hat presence meant the Kellies, not the cleaners, would be responsible for expunging that mess.

What was wrong with people that they filmed a murder rather than helped the victim?

"The spirit matches the photos in Frankie's file." Asa studied her. "Her form is comparable to the Boos."

"She's definitely tangible." I zoomed in on the snarl curling her lips. "Definitely pissed off too."

"Did you see that?" Asa paused the video, rewound it. "In the crowd?"

Nudging up the volume, I replayed the section he indicated and spotted a purple-robed wizard with staff in hand. She beamed from ear to ear, danced her way to a better vantage point, and generally acted like she had won a million dollars from a scratch card.

"Ms. March." I cranked my head toward Asa. "She's older than I expected for an accomplice."

After meeting the Amherst kids, I had formed the wrong impression. I expected to be hunting teens. The presumption was sloppy detective work on my part. I knew better than to make sweeping assumptions.

The robe and website logo were damning, but a peek at that

handy-dandy club roster would go a long way toward linking the Amhersts and Ms. March, if we could get our hands on it.

"Kids aren't the only ones who enjoy a temporary escape from reality."

"Hey, Isiforos," I called into the gloom. "Come here."

A minute or two later, he reemerged with raised eyebrows. "Questions?"

Curious about his take on things, I asked, "What do you think we're dealing with here?"

"Vengeful spirit." He clucked his tongue. "I don't know what that guy did to piss her off, but he did it good."

"Thanks, Isiforos." I caught his eye. "Here." I tossed him the witness's phone. "Send me a copy, please."

"*Please?*" He tilted his head. "Keep talking like that, and you'll ruin your bad reputation."

"Yeah." I scratched some dried blood off my cheek that had begun to itch. "I'm real worried about it."

Point in fact, I *was* worried. The stink was wearing off me. The pendant's aura was cloaking mine now. It wasn't too far off an idea I had early into bonding with Colby. I was starting to think this might work out. The pendant kept the grimoire safe, and their combined black magic funk kept my change of heart from showing every time one of these predators breathed in my direction.

Except, with the grimoire involved, I was always wary whenever I started thinking it was a good idea to keep it close versus flinging it into the nearest volcano.

"Need anything else?" Isiforos readjusted the tarp over the body. "We're about to move him, if you're done."

"We're done." I shot Clay a text to update him and tell him to watch out for the video. "So, clothes?"

After the run-in with Walters, we had to accept our outfits were destined for the trash bin.

"There's a supercenter two blocks away." Asa buttoned his jacket to better hide his shirt. "Will that do?"

"I'm good with whatever." I swept my gaze down him. "You're the fashion plate."

"I didn't choose the uniform." He smoothed his ruined shirt. "The uniform chose me."

A failed attempt at patricide got Asa recruited, so he wasn't wrong about not having a say.

"Not your fault you make it look good, huh?" I couldn't help my smile. "Let's see if your mojo works on off-the-rack clothes too."

And if he needed a second opinion that required sharing his dressing room, I would make that sacrifice.

9

The small problem of blood spatter we cured with brown paper towels in the bathrooms. They scoured a few layers of skin off in the process, but the exfoliation did enhance my youthful glow. We were heading back to the inn, where we could have showered before we changed, but a sharp-eyed security guard, his stealth skills zero, had followed our shopping spree with a tad too much interest.

Probably on account of the blood on our clothes, in our hair, and on our faces when we walked in.

We ended up returning to the bathrooms after a trip to the register to change into our new outfits. I was not a fan of this plan, but better to risk stains than get arrested on suspicion of murder and require a bail out from Clay. I finished changing well before Asa, but his discount store debut was worth the wait.

Clothes did not make the daemon. The daemon made the clothes.

Asa proved it when he strolled out wearing a magazine-spread-worthy suit cobbled together from their limited selection. Meanwhile, in my element, I had hit the sales rack only to discover several key pieces of my existing wardrobe marked as clearance. As if they had gone out of style.

Pfft.

Cheap never goes out of style.

I would have been insulted if I hadn't found dupes of all my favorite pieces to trundle back to Samford.

Dinner was burgers and fries in a moving vehicle, from a chain restaurant no less.

Had Clay been here, he would have cried over the soggy buns, the limp fries, and the flat drinks.

Aware of the trauma it would inflict, I texted him whatever was the opposite of food porn for a laugh.

For me.

>>*I hate you.*

>>*You deserve those fries for what you've done.*

>*I'll bring you back a combo.*

>>*Do it, and you're dead to me.*

The steady *tick, tick, tick* of the blinker drew my focus away from tormenting Clay long enough to orient myself. We were back at the colonial, which had gone dark due to the late hour, lending it a creepy vibe. Or maybe it was the memory of Ms. March cheering on Frankie like I had the daemon that spooked me.

"The cars haven't moved." I ducked my head to see the second floor. "No lights on upstairs."

"Lights are on downstairs." Asa checked with me. "Either Ms. March is in her room…or ours."

"Thanks for that." I shoved him. "Good thing I didn't want to sleep tonight."

We had proof she had been present when Frankie killed her second victim, but we needed more than that.

"You find this creepy, right?" I craned my neck as Asa parked next to one of the guest's cars, giving us an excuse to snoop. An old Mustang GT Fastback sat beside me in mint condition, minus the layer of pollen caking it bumper to bumper. Clay would kill for that car. Part of me wondered if Ms. March already had. "This one's been sitting for a while." I checked the other vehicles. "These too."

"That doesn't bode well for our fellow guests."

This time, our hostess didn't greet us at the door, but we heard lively voices in the vicinity of her room.

With our accommodations so close to hers, we didn't even have to come up with an excuse to do some eavesdropping of our own.

"Take out the mage," Ms. March hollered. "He's on your left. No, not that left. Your—"

A man yelled obscenities as an orc bellowed and explosions rang out down the hall.

As we neared our room, the door to our immediate right swung open to reveal Ms. March wearing an expensive-looking headset.

Behind her, spread on the bed, was the wizard's robe from the video, complete with a knobby staff I suspected might be constructed from EVA foam, like Trinity's armor, for her to swing it so easily. The design of her robe convinced me it had been sewn from the same pattern as Markus's. One of Trinity's custom orders? Paired with the staff, I placed the odds at better than good she was the supplier.

"I thought I heard footsteps." She shut the door behind her with a firm *click*. "How was dinner?"

The change in our clothes was noted, but she didn't ask, and we didn't tell.

"Delicious." Asa patted his flat stomach. "We ate too much."

"My cousin has a similar headset." I pointed to hers. "He's a gamer. Plays Mystic Realms, I think."

"One of my grandsons plays that." She slid the headset off and hid it down by her side. "My hearing isn't what it used to be, so I use the Bluetooth to do those Facechat calls with my kids and grandkids."

Had I not lived with the world's foremost expert on Mystic Realms, I might have believed her, but I did, so I didn't. Not to brag, but I was somewhat of an expert on orc death cries, screams, and bellows. What we walked in on reminded me of the orc horde Colby and her guild slaughtered to steal their emeralds. I was willing to bet Ms. March and her guild had been trying (and failing) to liberate precious gems too.

"Do you mind if I ask you about something we heard in town?" I rubbed my arms and hunched my shoulders. "Maybe I should wait until morning. It's getting late, and I don't want to upset your sleep."

"Nonsense." She reached for my hand and patted it. "You mean the murder."

As expected, she made the leap in logic and stuck the landing.

"Yes." I pretended relief that she put it into words for me. "Has that ever happened here before?"

"You're perfectly safe." She made a sandwich of my hand between hers. "You don't have to fret."

That wasn't an answer, and her too-warm, too-soft hands were making my palms sweat.

"Oh good." I broke from her and tucked myself under Asa's arm. "We'll let you get back to your game."

"My *call*," she corrected me, a flush in her cheeks as if she were embarrassed to have been called out for playing. "You two enjoy the rest of your night."

"We will." I faked a yawn. "Ready for bed, honey bunny?"

A twitch in Asa's cheek betrayed his amusement as he took my elbow and guided me into our room.

Once the door shut behind us, I set about warding the space and soundproofing our side. I had done the spell so many times at this point, it was as natural as breathing. I didn't register pulling on the bond with Colby, but it was too big of a spell for me to do alone. I chalked it up to practice and didn't sweat it.

To avoid losing the entire night, always a possibility with Asa, he and I took turns in the shower.

After we got clean, we climbed in bed with our laptops, and I dialed Clay, switching on speakerphone.

"That video was intense," Colby answered, proving we were on speaker too. "I might never sleep again."

"She beat me to the clip," Clay explained. "And she's smiling, so don't believe her."

Thanks to Camber and Arden, Colby had developed a taste for horror movies. *I* never let her watch them, but somehow she always knew the plots the next day. I suspected she crawled along the ceiling in her smallest form and camped out in the shadows so I wouldn't catch her.

"This is like *Game Over*." Her mood soared. "I can't believe I didn't see it before."

"That sounds like the title of a movie I would never agree to let you watch."

"It does," she agreed gleefully. "Let's rent it."

"Are you sure that's a good use of our time?" I regretted my skepticism was showing when she was finally perking up again. "Can't you give us a summation?"

"You need to see this," she urged. "We can use the group watch feature."

"Rented," Clay chimed in, not waiting for my answer. "Click the link I sent you, and you're in."

"Thaaanks." I did as I was told. Might as well. I was outvoted. "Do we synchronize watches or what?"

"It's automatic," Colby assured us, proving her vast experience with the app. "Just tell us when."

Asa adjusted so that his back rested against the headboard, and he pulled a small bag onto his lap that held knitting supplies. Sometimes I envied his ability to indulge in his hobby while doing something else. Put a book in my hands, and my brain left on a mini-vacation to another world and left this one behind. I loved that about reading, but it wasn't something you could multitask with movie watching or casework.

"When," I told them once Asa was click-clacking away, and I was leaning against him.

Thirty minutes later, I began to understand what Colby meant. The similarities were disturbing. The plot, if you were feeling generous, contained marked similarities to our case. No LARPers, but instead gamers who had had enough with bullying and decided to take revenge on their tormenters by summoning their favorite video game bosses to kill them.

Easy to see how the movie might have planted the seed, but it was far from a how-to manual.

Someone with real arcane knowledge taught the Amhersts how to summon and where to find the Boos.

"When was this movie released?" I figured Colby would know. "How widespread?"

"About a year ago," she told me. "It didn't make it into theaters."

"Do you think this could have been in the planning stages for that long?" Asa kept his eyes on the screen to ensure one of us was paying attention. "There are obvious nods to the movie in our case, but who taught the Amhersts to summon? How did they know where to find the Boos' remains? Why them? There's no game or LARP link there. The Boos died before Mystic Realms was released."

"Summoning fictional characters is, well, fiction." That meant they couldn't recreate the movie exactly. "Instead, the LARPers chose to summon paranormal pop culture icons with bloody histories. Maybe the choice is based on the summoners' proximity to the burial sites? Except that leaves us with the problem of how the LARPers are finding these guys in bulk. Someone must be feeding them that intel."

"You're going to miss the best part," Colby fussed. "Watch the last ten minutes. It's worth it."

The last ten minutes were a bloodbath where the gamers lost control of their boss, and the boss killed them. Their deaths were chalked up to yet another murder in a long string of them, and the bosses were yanked back to their reality, into their games. The crimes went down as unsolved mysteries.

"That was not a satisfying ending," I remarked. "You liked that?"

"The point," she said in her best *kids know better than everyone* voice, "is the creations turned on their creators."

"The Boos are already threatening the Amhersts." I recalled that wink from Malcom but still couldn't make sense of it. "As the first summoners on our radar, their clocks are ticking the loudest."

"I called a buddy in Savannah." Clay ended the shared movie. "A necromancer."

"That has bad idea written all over it," I muttered. "They get tetchy when anyone brings anything back to life without paying their consultation fee."

"She doesn't need the money, and she cares more about saving lives than crunching numbers."

"Another ex of yours?"

"Just an old friend who got a raw deal. She's not a fan of the Society. That's why I trust her. She's not swayed by politics. She's been the victim of them too often."

The Society for Post-Life Management was the necromancer ruling body, and they were based in Savannah, Georgia. Since his contact was also in Savannah, she had a finger on the pulse of the Society.

"What did she have to say?" I had trouble picturing a helpful necromancer, one who didn't charge by the hour. Or by the question. "Anything useful?"

"The summoners would have had to inter the remains of their boss of choice in graveyard dirt from their original grave but rebury them on property owned by the summoner who wanted to control them. She believes they're onryō, a rare type of vengeful spirit that preys on those who wronged them in life. They can interact with objects and people, the better to murder the people with aforementioned objects." He paused, as if checking his notes. "Since ours aren't naturally occurring, they're attacking their summoners' tormentors rather than their own."

Gold star for Colby.

The kid was right on the money with that gorefest we watched earlier.

"What level of magic is required for an undertaking of that size?"

"I like how you said *undertaking*." He chortled. "She claims most of the magic is in the bones, and in the death itself. The victims—in this case, our bosses—were targeted for the popularity of their lore. It gives them life after death the same way gods get a kickback from being worshipped. Factor in their violent ends, and you've got magic waiting to be tapped by anyone with a thimbleful of skill. *And* they were all paranormal creatures. She's certain of that. Which means the Boos, whatever they were, weren't plain vanilla human."

"Does she think this is an untrained necromancer?"

"Not a chance." He explained, "Their magic, ironically enough, brings the dead back to life. Unlife?"

Vampires weren't alive so much as they were reanimated, the same with pets, but his contact was likely protecting trade secrets with broad answers. Necromancers were a secretive bunch. Taciturn and cheap.

"Let me guess." I pinched the bridge of my nose. "This is the work of a black witch."

We had been laboring under that assumption, given our past work on rogue cases, but it sucked to hear it confirmed that incidents were on the rise.

"That means the Amhersts have embraced the dark arts," Asa pointed out. "That doesn't look good for their parents."

By far and away the most popular method for a white witch child to cement their black witch status was to kill their witch parent or parents and eat their hearts. The most brutal of dark offerings, it was almost a rite of passage. The Amhersts had, almost certainly, claimed their first victims before they dug up the Boo Brothers' remains. With their parents MIA, I expected to locate those bodies before the case ended.

"We need to find the bosses' bones." I checked with Asa. "Can the daemon help with that?"

He had the best sense of smell but buried remains might prove tricky. Even for him. We weren't talking flesh, which helped us out by rotting and making a stink, we were talking bones. *Old* bones. Most of their scent would have faded during their time underground.

A buzz from Asa's phone gave me permission to cop a feel as I pulled it out of his pocket.

"Get Colby off the line." I gave Clay a moment to comply then answered. "Hollis."

"Agent Montenegro is with you," Parish rasped, "I presume?"

"His hands are full." I gave Asa a cheeky grin. "I'll put you on speaker."

"We have another case," Parish informed us. "Old Man Fang was spotted in Tupelo."

"No way," Clay breathed. "Old Man Fang?"

Parish hadn't given us permission to leave Clay behind in Raymond, not that we had asked, but if Parish heard Clay and thought he was here, I wasn't going to disabuse him of the notion.

"I know this one." I shocked everyone into silence. "Old Man Fang was a warg who—"

"The team in Natchez will remain in place under Fergal's command." Parish wasn't interested in my summation. "You're expected in Tupelo."

"All right." I couldn't shake a budding sense of unease. "We'll pack up and head out."

After the call ended, I returned the phone to Asa. "What do you bet Ms. March is standing in the hall?"

"Trying to listen in?" He put away his current project. "Hoping for another free show?"

"Is it wrong to feel murder-y when I think about her hearing how you sound when you come?"

A bloodcurdling scream filled the room, and I almost fell off my side of the bed.

"Clay?" Pulse thumping, I groped for my phone, for the source. "Clay, are you okay?"

"I can't hear you," he sang. *"I can't hear you. I can't hear you."*

"Clayton Kerr, are you all right?" I waited a beat. "Answer me. Right now. Or else."

"Can't hear. Nope. I can't. Not gonna listen. Ever again."

"He's fine." Asa mashed the button to end the shrill singsong. "Just traumatized."

"He's such a baby." I threw my phone. "Though I do *slightly* regret him hearing me say that."

Dirty talk wasn't a strength of mine. I couldn't make words sexy the way Asa could, and even he didn't do it on purpose. That might have been the most direct line I had ever spoken to a man, and it figured Clay would overhear it.

"You're jealous." Asa let his supplies hit the floor. "You don't want to share me with Murder Granny."

As he climbed over me, I slid lower onto the mattress, allowing him to straddle me more comfortably.

"I don't want to share any part of you with anyone," I confessed. "I would stuff you in this pendant if I could." I slapped his shoulder when he laughed. "I don't want to hear it. You'd do the same to me in a heartbeat." I craned my neck to kiss him. "You're special. You know that, right?"

"To you." He pressed the words against my lips, a brand. "Only ever to you."

"Yeah, well, everyone else is an idiot." I slung my arms around his neck. "They missed out."

"We should go." He shifted until he settled between my thighs. "Tupelo is several hours away."

A knock on our door shattered the moment and proved Murder Granny had the same flawless timing as Clay where Asa and I and nakedness were concerned.

"We're about to reenact one of the most romantic moments in our relationship." I nudged him back, got to my feet, and loaded our new belongings. "We're going to sneak out this window." I gave it an experimental tug to ensure it wasn't painted closed. "Then we're going to run to the SUV like scalded cats and burn rubber."

"That's not how that night ended," he reminded me, his hips pressing into my butt, his lips on my ear.

Leaning against him, I fought the urge to groan as his hands explored over my clothes. "Have you ever necked in an SUV?"

"No." He bit mine to make a point. "I can't say that I have."

"Then our night isn't over yet."

Our night was *so* over.

I could tell the second I caught a glimpse of the carnage Old Man Fang left behind as his calling card. It was textbook, identical to the stories Meg had told me over the years. I wished Dad was here to see it. Old Man Fang's legends were the kinds of stories I could imagine a black witch dad telling his daughter over a campfire.

"Well, if it isn't the director's prize pony. This must be a special occasion for him to trot you out."

Dread in my gut, I whirled toward the voice, but not in time to fend off the attack.

"I haven't seen you in forever," Evette squealed, tackling me in a hug that smelled like lemon drops. She was cecaelian. Basically, a mermaid with tentacles. "Not since we drank Bourbon Street dry." She pulled back, but her hands were everywhere. Even the six I couldn't see, thanks to her natural ability to camouflage. She was lucky my hair was in a bun when she pounced. "Where have you been hiding?"

"I ran away from home." I pried her off me. "Asa, this is Evette."

"You brought me a present?" She clapped, her eyes flickering a luminescent green. "He's so pretty."

"He's mine." I gripped her upper arm and yanked her back. "Do. Not. Touch."

She wet her full lips with her greenish tongue and debated whether to listen to me. We hadn't been friends, but we had gotten into a lot of trouble together when I was younger. Usually after she wore that exact expression.

"He's a daemon prince." I kept a civil tone. "His person is sacred, particularly his hair."

"How big is your altar?" She fluttered her lashes at him. "Should I worship you on my knees?"

All of a sudden, I felt certain anyone with eight arms could stand to lose one. Or six.

"Touch me," Asa said, polite as you can be, "and Rue will slit your throat."

Shock burst across her face, and she glanced back at me to find my athame in hand. "He's not wrong."

"It would be a mercy," he continued, voice flat. "As I understand it, cecaelia can't survive without all eight of their arms. Lore says they can't swim without them and lose their way in the sea. They get lost and wander until they die of a broken heart from homesickness."

"That's barbaric." Evette flexed her hands, her eyes narrowing on me. "Forgot who I was talking to for a beat." She flipped her hair over her shoulder and strutted off, swaying her hips. "Finch, you handle this."

While Finch scuttled to us, we crouched over the body and began an examination. There was no mystery here. A large warg had gone wolf and ripped a guy open from chin to navel. Most of his organs were MIA, and blood spread like brushstrokes where the warg had lapped up the puddle with his tongue.

"They made a mistake with this one," I told Asa quietly. "Meg will know where to find his bones."

"She might have known where they were buried, but can she tell where they were moved?"

"I hear you go by Rue Hollis these days." Finch measured me with a glance. "Evette's right. You've been gone a long time. We all figured you were dead." He tilted his head. "You're not dead, are you?" He cracked a yellowed smile. "The things we've been seeing lately make it hard to tell."

"Asa, this is Finch. Finch, Asa." I answered the question in Asa's eyes. "The three of us took a few classes together. We worked a few cases together too."

"Until you got Roy killed." Finch chuckled, as if the death of my first TO amused him. Roy had sucked as a training officer, but he hadn't deserved to die like that. "That's when you got saddled with the golem."

That golem was the best friend I had ever had, but facts were facts. "Still am, actually."

"Guess the director likes you under his thumb."

"Guess so."

"What can you tell us about the victim?" Asa interrupted our awkward reminiscing, thank the goddess.

"He worked as a butcher in a grocery store in town. Human. He fell for the old *I hit a dog* ploy."

Man drives home late. Warg runs in front of car. Man hits warg. Warg plays dead. Man gets eaten.

"Who found him?" I picked up where Asa left off. "And when?"

"A human teen on her way home from work found him in the road, called the cops. We've been monitoring their frequencies heavily since this what-the-fuckery started. The Bureau dispatched a unit to contain the situation, and then Parish gave us a heads-up you were on your way."

"My team, you mean."

Finch delighted in correcting me. "I mean *you*."

Stinging prickles coasted down my spine, that sense of wrongness blossoming.

"You are the black magic specialist." Asa brushed his thumb along my cheek. "This case is in your wheelhouse."

"I wouldn't touch her if I was you." Finch chuckled. "Last guy who tried without her permission ended up missing his hand." His beady eyes twinkled at me. "Hell of a thing."

This was the ideal opening for Asa to bluster about how we were in fascination or claim we were already mates, which was a lie that got easier the more often we told it, but he remained quiet. I appreciated that he let me handle my own PR. I had been a myth within Black Hat, but I was very much flesh and blood now. I had an identity to either reinforce or discard, and he was letting me choose which way to go.

"Asa is my mate." I averted my face from his. "He's the only man who can touch me and keep his hands."

That was almost true. Hair was the trigger for *y'nai*, but Finch didn't need to know that.

"You have a mate?" Finch recoiled. *"You?"* His lip curled up on one side as he gave Asa a closer look. "You're a damn fool for tying your life to hers. I hope the sex is worth it. She's only going to break your heart." He lifted a shoulder. "And then eat it."

A crackle of flame teased the corner of my eye as the daemon burst from Asa's skin with a ripping noise that did *not* bode well for his new suit.

"Rue mine." He clamped his hand around Finch's throat. "Rue love me."

"Rue loves power," he rasped, then his lips fell slack. "You're that daemon prince." He laughed, bitter and sharp. "No wonder she chose you."

The daemon picked Finch off the ground and slung him across the road into the bushes. "Finch dumb."

"You got that right." I petted his hair to soothe him. "But I wasn't a nice person back when he knew me."

That version of me? He wasn't wrong about her. Even a little.

"Still dumb," he huffed. "Rue mine." He gathered me into a spine-popping hug. "Rue love me."

"I do love you. Both of you." I laughed under my breath. "But you need to put me down."

"I hold Rue." He nuzzled me. "Rue second-best friend."

"You're killing my tough guy rep." I caught up to what he was saying and gasped. *"Traitor."*

"Colby play with me *and* feed me oranges." He turned solemn. "Prevent scurvy."

"Goddess bless," I muttered. "She's brainwashed you."

The odds of him catching scurvy were about the same as me caving to that expansion pack.

"It okay to be jelly." He patted my head. "Asa still love you most."

The daemon was spending way too much time with Colby if he was picking up her lingo, but I was amused that he had a favorite person that wasn't me. More proof he and Asa were separate entities.

"While you're here—" I indicated the body, "—can you examine the scene for me?"

Given the opportunity, I texted Colby for a favor.

>*Can you have a few of Asa's good suits sent to the hotel?*
>>*Store bought not holding up?*
>*The daemon just shredded one like tissue paper.*
>>*I'll push the requisition through. You should have them by morning.*
>*I'll owe you a basket of oranges for this.*

The daemon, busy with his task, hadn't noticed I was multitasking and began his report.

"Warg." He didn't have to scent the air to tell. "Hungry warg."

"Looks that way." I didn't want to lead him into anything, but I had to ask, "Do you smell magic?"

The daemon crouched over the body, inhaling in long breaths. "Smell like dirt and thunder light."

"Lightning?" I waited for his nod. "The magic or the body?"

"Magic." He leaned down, nose almost brushing the victim's throat. "But not magic." He frowned. "Death." His scowl grew more pronounced. "Old death."

"The killer was a ghost," I told him, sounding like an absolute lunatic. "Can you track him?"

"Not sure," he admitted. "Smell like graveyard storm."

Based on what Clay's contact reported, I could see how that

might be the case. Ghosts didn't secrete oils or sweat or any number of things that gave a person their scent. It would be down to the magic animating it. Or a fresh kill.

"Thanks." I gave him one last pet. "Can I have Asa back?"

This time, there was no negotiation, for which I was thankful. I gave Asa a moment to collect himself then texted Colby with a job.

> The killer was definitely a warg. The daemon thinks he can track it, but we need a starting point.

>>I've already booked you into the Laurie Motel. It's got the same seal as the others incorporated into its logo. There's no check-in office or manager on site. You get your code via the app, punch it in, and let yourself into your room. Looks like there's a number for a maintenance guy if you have questions.

>>Markus Amherst is listed as the website designer.

>You're brilliant. You know that?"

>>Yep.

>And modest.

>>Also yep.

>And the daemon told me I'm his second-best friend now, so thanks for that.

>>I taught him the Mystic Mambo. He's forever in my debt.

Of course, she was responsible for his victory dance.

>>I'm emailing your Laurie Motel confirmation. For tomorrow. I booked you somewhere safe to crash tonight. Ordering food now. Looks like pizza is your only hope this late.

A beat later, my phone pinged.

>I love you.

>>I know.

Relieved to hear she was back on track, I updated Asa, who was in bad shape. His discount clothes might have looked good on, but they weren't of the stretchy variety. His outfit was ruined. There was no saving it. If not for his strategically placed hands, I might have had to murder gawkers.

"You'll be okay, right, Finch?" I leaned over him. "Want me to call Evette?"

"Gods, no." Grass rustled in the ditch. "I'll just rest here a minute."

After recording the scene and discovering nothing undocumented, Asa and I returned to the SUV.

"I imagine that was the equivalent to a high school reunion for you," Asa teased. "How did it go?"

"I remembered why I became friends with Evette. Eight hands made it easy for us to pick pockets and use other people's money to buy ourselves drinks. She was also popular with guys, for obvious reasons." I lost the fight against a nostalgic laugh. "Her catchphrase was *no holes barred*." Asa shifted on his seat, and I couldn't resist asking, "Did that make you pucker?"

"I don't know what you mean."

Oh, he did, but I wouldn't hold it against him. We all had our limits, and he was only now exploring his.

"Finch was always trailing after Evette." I switched subjects. "Looks like he still is. He's a crane shifter."

"A crane shifter named Finch."

"I can't remember his actual name." A common problem for me. "Evette started calling him that, and it stuck."

A burn in my chest I had learned to identify as shame spread through me at how we had treated him. How we had treated everyone. I didn't select victims the way she did. I tended to abuse everyone who got in my way equally, which wasn't any better. It might have even been worse.

"You outgrew them."

"We weren't friends." I had known that then, and I knew it now. "Evette sought me out because she wanted to climb high in the ranks as fast as possible. Everyone knew the director favored me, but not why. She figured if she stuck with me, we'd both make it to the top. Finch, as I said, was a third wheel. He doesn't have much in the way of ambition, aside from earning Evette's approval."

"I don't understand what makes a woman like that appealing. Why would he stay?"

"He's not a glutton for abuse, if that's what worries you. She kissed him the first time she saw him, because he was new and cute and covered in blood from the reason Black Hat recruited him in the first place. Her saliva is addictive. As long as she swaps spit with him every so often, she can string him along for the rest of his life. Or hers." I cut my eyes toward Asa. "Remind you of anyone?"

"I do recall being fixated on your saliva," he mused. "Are you sure *you* don't have cecaelian ancestors?"

With aquatic daemons in my pedigree, I wouldn't be surprised to learn I had distant octopedal relations.

"Hey, now, *I* wasn't the problem." I jabbed him for good measure. "*You* were the problem."

"I was an innocent dae, swept into a whirlwind romance with a gray witch—"

"A gray witch?" I twisted to face him as he pulled onto the road. "Why do you say that?"

"Your father mentioned blending his power with your mother's skill to produce a magic that isn't one or the other. You're using your training as a black witch to harness white magic, and Colby's magic." He searched my face to see if I was upset. "You're the closest thing to a gray witch I can imagine exists."

"It's funny you say that." I plugged in the directions to our hotel. "I've been thinking along the same lines. It feels more honest." I decided that was the right word. "I'm not out practicing black magic, but my white magic was peculiar before Colby." I considered his words. "Practicing one craft while pulling on knowledge and training from another gives me mixed results sometimes."

Back in Samford, when my days were filled with tinctures and salves, I hadn't used enough power to grasp the discrepancies. I was magic lite. These days, I was slinging spells left and right, and the end product wasn't like anything I had ever done or seen.

"How do you feel about it?"

"Ugh." I flopped my head to one side. "I hate that word."

Feel.

Blech.

A soft crease at the corners of his eyes told me my joke had landed without hurting him, which meant I was getting better at this relationship thing. But the lift of his eyebrows told me I wasn't off the hook.

"It feels more authentic," I decided. "What do you think about me downgrading my classification?"

"You're not upholding your old reputation. You're carving out a new one. I fully support that." His lips tipped up at one corner. "Based on tonight's events, I would say our coworkers are as afraid of you as ever. I don't think you have to worry on that score either."

Had the stink radiating off the pendant not tricked the noses of the people who ran in my circles early in my career, I would have been outed on the spot. They would have known I had changed, even if they couldn't tell how. That wiggle room was what got people in trouble. Was I weaker? Stronger? Deadlier?

Too often, they bowed to their predatory instincts. They chose to test me, and then they paid the price.

"You're so sweet." I kissed his cheek. "Every girl dreams of being the monster under the bed."

"I would prefer to be the monster *in* your bed."

"You're not a monster. You're too cuddly for that."

Which he proved after we gorged on fig and goat cheese pizza then passed out in a tangle of limbs.

10

Thanks to Clay's brief obsession with home renovation shows, I decided the Laurie was a no-tell motel in another life. The seedy side of town was blossoming, its businesses either rehabbed or on their way. The result was trendy stores, trendy colors, and trendy people walking cracked sidewalks without a fresh can of pepper spray tucked into their palms or tasers hidden in their oversized bougie purses.

The Laurie itself was one story, an L shape, with a sparkling pool out front to attract roadside customers.

Part of me appreciated that these days, businesses owned by individuals could provide no-contact check-ins. It was quicker, easier to hide when you showed up with blood spatter, and less invasive.

Plus, a locker system allowed guests to receive mail, which meant we now had Asa's new suits.

But, if the pattern held, whoever owned this place was likely responsible for summoning Old Man Fang. We needed to verify that. Quickly. Before Parish yanked us out of Tupelo as he had the previous towns.

This case was starting to feel more like a game of hot potato than an assignment.

"I'd like to touch base with Meg. See if she's got the inside scoop on Old Man Fang."

We found our room, let ourselves in, and I searched for anything that might hold water.

What I found was a petal-pink box with a chocolatier's name stamped on the top.

"That looks pricey for a welcome gift." I flipped the lid. "Do you think the previous guest forgot it?"

A grid of nine elegant compartments with handwritten labels informed me of the contents.

Champagne gummy bears, cold brew cordials, ganache hearts on top. Dark demitasse squares, raspberry crescents, praline stars filled the center. Chocolate lava cake, crème brûlée, and black forest cake truffles rounded out the bottom row.

Asa took one look, and his fingers curled into fists at his sides. "Another gift from Father."

"How can you tell?" I sniffed them. "They only smell chocolatey to me."

"The chocolatier is a desirae daemon. He can imbue his products with those emotions. Father sends the altered treats to his future conquests to make them more open to his suggestions."

"Let me make sure I understand this." I slammed the lid shut. "He sent me roofied candy?"

A muscle ticked in his jaw. "Yes."

"Teach me how to return to sender?" I drew my wand, tapped the box top, and reduced its vile contents to melty goo. "This time, I want him to know for certain who's rejecting him."

"All right." He forced his fingers open. "Flatten your palm above the object you wish to spurn." He demonstrated, and his hand quivered with his fury. "Then speak these words."

He enunciated them clearly in daemonish, and, being a witch, once was enough for me to commit them to memory. The power in my voice was also enough to activate the *return to sender* spell on the first try.

"That is super handy." I walked into his embrace and placed his arms around me. "Thank you."

"I won't let him hurt you." He fisted the back of my shirt. "Even if it requires a coronation to do it."

"I know." I kissed the spot over his heart. "Help me find a bowl?"

Asa cupped my face between his palms, lowered his mouth to mine, and accepted my reassurance his heart was the only one I craved.

Which, okay, a black witch—*former* black witch—admitting that would terrify rather than comfort most.

I let him break the kiss, breathe me in, and settle his nerves while I plotted his father's eventual demise.

No child should grow up believing they were unlovable, that parts of them ought to remain hidden. They shouldn't doubt their acceptance by their peers or conceal who they are to fit their parents'—or anyone else's—idea of who they ought to be.

When he withdrew, he had fewer lines biting the corners of his mouth and tightening his eyes. I couldn't tear down his *wrong* opinion of himself overnight, but I was willing to put in the work to renovate his confidence.

"Found the ice bucket." Asa lifted what resembled a desktop trash can with a liner. "Will this do?"

Meg would pitch a hissy if she figured out I was summoning her in plastic, but she would have to deal.

After prying it from his tense fingers, I filled it with water. "I'll make it work."

Cross-legged on the bed, I sat with the ice bucket cradled between my thighs. A prick of my finger with my athame produced the drop of blood required for a dial tone to call my mother's oldest friend.

"Megara, I summon thee." More blood, more intent. "Megara, I summon thee."

No surprise, she made me jump through flaming hoops before she deigned to answer. Business as usual.

"Thrice I bid thee." Even more blood, even more intent. "And thrice I tithe thee."

I ran a fingertip along the edge of the bucket, and the water rippled in dark eddies.

"Hear me," I called in a resonate voice. "Arise."

A face appeared wreathed in smoke, not from theatrics, but from the cigarette hanging from her bottom lip. Her makeup was smeared, and her lipstick was smudged across her chin. Her hair was tousled, and a feline grin told me she was downright proud of herself.

"Darling," she answered, taking a long draw. "How can I help you?"

"I'm working a case, and I was hoping to ask you a few questions. If you're not too busy."

"Just finished up, actually." Her smile grew sharp. "Ask away, but it will cost you."

Her consultation fee went toward providing for the pack she had left behind, so I didn't mind the bill.

"No problem," I assured her. "Transfer incoming."

"Then I'm at your disposal." She leaned forward, fingers steepled. "You need legal advice?"

"I need lore advice." I debated how to break it to her but decided she liked it straight. "Old Man Fang has been resurrected. Kind of? We're waffling on the lingo. He was summoned, and he made his first kill tonight. Can you tell us where he was buried? I'm hoping the daemon can track his scent from there, give us some idea who took his bones."

A temper I had only ever seen provoked by mention of my parents' deaths cut a snarl across her face.

"They. Did. What?"

"He's the latest in a string of old boogeymen that have risen and begun killing innocents."

"The only ones who knew where he was kept were pack. Even then, only his direct descendants were told." She took a calming breath. "Whoever did this has a familial warg contact, one who knew the exact location of his ancestors' burial grounds." A growl pumped through her chest. "I'll contact the head of the family. They'll be in touch after they've questioned their own people." Her eyes glowed. "And dearest? There's no charge for this. Thank you for bringing it to my attention."

"We appreciate any help you can give us," Asa assured her, "and we'll be paying that fee."

Her anger dropped a notch, and she nodded at Asa. "You found one of the good ones, Rue."

"I can tell you a different type of horror story," I offered, "if it will make you feel better."

I hated to upset Meg, hated more that she couldn't act on her fury, that she was dependent upon others to do what she would have done gladly. Maybe a side note might break the ice and let her temper cool.

"This must be good." She gestured at Asa. "His scowl says he's ready to murder over it."

"The High King of Hael has a crush on me." I kept my voice light. "He wants me to have his babies."

A loud crack jerked my head around to find Asa had broken one of the bedposts. Snapped it clean in two and left him with what resembled an ornate baseball bat. He frowned at his hand, at the wood, at me.

"Looks like your mate finds your anecdote as amusing as I do." She lit another cigarette. "If Stavros has his eye on you, you must be careful." She flicked Asa a glance. "Or you'll wake up with Asa's brother in your belly."

The snap of Asa breaking his bat in two startled me to the point I almost dumped out Meg.

"I was trying to lighten the mood." I wavered on who to comfort first. "Asa, it's all right."

Shaking splinters off his hand, he dipped his chin. "I'm going to walk around the building a few times."

He didn't wait for me to say goodbye, and that stung, but it was my fault for riling him.

"It's more than the comment, isn't it?"

"Yeah." I tore my gaze from the door and focused on Meg. "Stavros sent me flowers, and candy."

"That's not good." She took a long draw. "It's not funny either." She pointed the red ember at me. "Don't yank that daemon's tail. He believes anyone saying *no* is playing coy." She pointed to the hair bracelet on my wrist. "Ask your man. He can tell you. His father takes what he wants."

"When I tell Clay a bad joke, he calls it terrible then moves on with his life." I couldn't tear my gaze away from the door Asa had walked out. "Apparently, when I tell Asa a bad joke, he storms off to prevent himself from portaling to murder his father."

Never one to talk about Clay unless forced, Meg skirted the mention. "You're his mate."

"What does that have to do—?"

"You're his mate."

"But I—?"

"You're his mate."

"We're not actually mated," I rushed out before she could interrupt again. "We're just..."

"Having sex, bandying about the L word, and planning a future together."

"Um." I fumbled for a smart response. "Well..." I avoided her eyes. "Yes?"

"I'm a warg. I've seen every shade of mating there is, and yours has begun. You've moved past the denial stage into the *maybe it's just physical* stage, while Asa is ready to place his crown on your head."

"He didn't grow up with the best examples of love to follow, so how is he so good at this?"

"Children raised in split households often wonder *what if*. They daydream about what it would be like if their parents reconciled or to have one home they all shared."

"But he knew about his father," I reasoned. "What Stavros did to his mother."

"I doubt his mother told him until he came of age, or until his trips to Hael commenced. The truth of his conception might have shattered his hopes for his parents, but I guarantee he spent so many years wrapped up in the fantasy of it that he wants it for himself. He believes he can have it. With you."

"That's a lot of responsibility," I said lamely. "What if I don't live up to the hype?"

"You won't," she assured me. "You can't."

"That's comforting." I scowled at her. "Then what's the point in trying?"

"Don't conform," she advised me. "Smash through his preconceptions. Show him who you really are, what you really want, how life with you will really be. If he sticks around, and I have no doubt he will, then you'll have the best of both worlds. Someone who loves you for yourself and is willing to build the best possible version of the future for the both of you."

"I ought to go apologize." I rubbed the base of my neck. "I'll do better with the jokes."

Clearly, Asa had been stewing since the rose incident to be chill in the moment but blow a gasket now.

"You'll do fine," she assured me. "That boy's crazy about you."

"I'll go find him." I checked with her. "You'll be in touch?"

"One of my kinsmen will, yes." Her light mood darkened. "Old Man Fang is a legend for a reason."

The story claimed he went insane after eating a powerful black witch and began eating members of his pack until only his mate remained. It was said he even consumed their children before she shot him with a silver bullet through the heart. The lore also claimed she buried him in a silver casket to punish him into his afterlife.

"I'll be careful."

With a doubtful huff, she swirled into nothing, and I got up to dump and rinse the ice bucket. As eager as I was to rush after Asa, an open link to the other side was asking for trouble. The second Meg left, so did the water that had held her.

Done with tidying, I stepped outside to find Asa. I didn't have to go far before I heard voices. His, and a woman's. Their low conversation made me think it wasn't a casual meeting. Before I decided if I should interrupt, Asa must have caught my scent or heard me. He turned around, spotted me, and grimaced.

A slight woman with rose-gold hair pressed a hand to his chest and leaned around the corner to see what snagged his attention. Her lips glittered, glossy and full. Her nose was a pert little button. I pegged her age mid to late twenties, but that could have been a glamour.

Dull pain radiated through my chest when he wrapped his arms around her and hauled her back into their nook with an urgent warning.

He was hiding *her*.

From *me*.

The dull roar in my ears usually reserved itself for those who had trespassed against him, but I was deaf to Asa as he put himself between her and me.

He was protecting *her*.

From *me*.

An itch in the back of my throat had me swallowing hard to erase the phantom taste of her blood as I imagined biting into her heart like a ripe apple. Warm with copper juices and meat that would sustain my power. The pinch of hunger contracted my stomach, twisting it, cramping it, and that black magic voice from my past whispered I should devour her for the crime of touching my mate, clinging to him, clutching him. But he read my intent, and he approached me with his hands held in front of him.

He was ready to take *me* down.

For *her*.

An inhuman snarl revved up my throat, and my fingertips sharpened to daggers. I waited until he put a few feet between him and her, and I pulled on my bond with Colby for the strength to ram my shoulder into his with bruising force. I spun him aside, and he hit the wall. With the path clear, I sprinted for the woman.

"Wait." He found his balance. "Don't."

Fire erupted behind me as I lunged with my claws out, but my roar was crushed along with my ribs.

"Bad Rue." The daemon had grabbed me around the middle, deflating my lungs as he dangled me from my waist several feet above the sidewalk. "No hurt Callula."

"I won't hurt her." I kicked and clawed at him. "I'll *kill* her."

"Rue cute." The daemon squeezed me in a hug. "Don't be jelly."

"I'm not cute," I snarled. "I'm about to commit murder."

"I'm not sure Asa would appreciate that." The woman strode forward. "I'm Callula Alfre Montenegro."

"This Asa's mom," the daemon explained. "Lady Callula."

"Oh." I lost the furor pounding in my head and deflated in his hold. "Well, this is awkward."

"Rue be good?" The daemon cast me side-eye. "If I put down?"

"I'll behave," I tried to make it a promise. "I apologize for the whole attempted murder thing."

"Rue love me." The daemon thrust his hair at me. "Pet."

Happy that forgiveness was earned on one front, I returned my focus to Lady Callula, whose gaze stuck to the daemon as I ran my fingers through his hair.

"You're such a brat." I yanked the silky strands. "Why is Asa's mom here?"

"Asa's mother?" Callula squared her shoulders. "I'm *his* mother as well."

A frown knit the daemon's brow, and he folded his arms across his chest, saying nothing in return.

Had she ever come right out and claimed him? Or had he read more into her tone than I had?

"I apologize, again, for my misstep." I was making a great impression, I could tell. "He referred to you as 'Asa's mom,' and I did the same without thinking."

"You're friendly with that—?" She bit down on her next words. "You're close to that part of him?"

"I am." I heard the testiness in my voice. "And we are." I elbowed him. "I'm his second-best friend."

"Asa mentioned he met someone." Her gaze sharpened. "I didn't think he'd choose a witch."

"We get that a lot." I shrugged like the slight didn't matter. "Good thing love conquers all."

"You love him?" Her doubt stung me, but it was the daemon she fixated on. "All of him?"

"That's how love works." I might not be a pro, but I knew this to be true. "I'm all-in."

"Do you think, as a witch, you could bind him?"

Ba-bump.

A rush of anger so cold it scalded crashed over me, deafening me, sweeping away all my good intentions until her heart became the only sound in my world. "What do you mean?"

Ba-bump. Ba-bump.

"His daemon half," she explained, as if it were obvious. "Could you bind it to his fae half?"

Ba-bump. Ba-bump. Ba-bump.

Light strobed behind my eyes, and then I was holding my athame to her delicate throat. "Come again?"

"You can't mean to share your life with *both* of them?" Her horror was palpable. "That's unseemly."

"Lady, I'm a black witch. I've done the worst things you can imagine and then some. Usually, I was smiling while I did them. Laughing even. But to bind the daemon to the fae as one personality would be to strip away the facets of the man I fell in love with, and I would rather slice you in half than tear him down the middle."

Tears filled her eyes and tumbled down her cheeks, and her bottom lip trembled as she held in a sob.

She must not have experience with blades being pointed at her throat.

As my maybe future mother-in-law, she better get used to it if she had more of these bright ideas.

"I'm done here." I paused in front of the daemon. "Even if Asa and I don't work out, if she ever tries to cage you, come to me. I don't care where I am or what I'm doing. You come to me, and I'll fix it."

With a sour taste in the back of my throat, I returned to our room.

Alone.

This was not how I pictured meeting his mother would go. I hadn't meant to act like a jealous harpy, but with the restrictions placed on Asa's person, I was floored to see another woman fondling him. Though, I guess with it being his mom, it wasn't technically *fondling*, but still.

How had she gotten here? What did she want? Did I care?

I was still so mad at her gall in asking me to bind her son, I wanted to stab something.

I sank onto the bed and scrubbed my face with my palms. I didn't look up when Asa entered the room. I didn't peek when he knelt in front of me. I didn't blink when he pried away my hands. I stared at a stain on the carpet that reminded me of Saturn and waited for him to reprimand me for scaring his mother.

"Come here." Asa dragged me into his arms, and I pressed my face into his neck. "I'm not mad."

"I am," I mumbled against his skin. "She asked me to bind you."

"I know." He nuzzled me. "I heard."

A throat cleared behind him, and I found Callula, lovely as ever, standing in the open doorway.

"I would apologize again," I said, throat tight, "but we both know I wouldn't mean it."

"I would settle for your word you won't attack me again."

"Don't provoke me again," I countered, "and I won't."

"That's fair," she allowed and shut the door behind her. "I shouldn't have tested your loyalty, but Asa is my only child. I worried when he told me he was in fascination with a black witch." Her gaze penetrated me. "Though I do wonder at that. Your magic is...interesting...but not as dark as I expected it to be."

"My loyalty?" A dangerous adrenaline high shot up my pulse. "You asked me to *bind* Asa."

Her idea of vetting me was worse than when I jokingly suggested Stavros had been the one testing me.

"It was the worst thing I could think of," she admitted. "I hadn't expected to see you tonight, or I would have prepared a more suitable and less antagonistic approach."

Call it instinct, but I didn't believe her for a hot minute. "That would have been nice."

"My son has been greedy with you and kept you all to himself." She risked a step closer. "I understand why, now. He's had so little acceptance in his life. Then there was you."

"Then there was me," I repeated, keeping hold of Asa like she might snatch him back.

"I didn't want you to make the same mistakes with him I did." She twisted a ring on her finger. "I wanted to know you could love all of him, every part, before I gave my blessing. Mating is forever, you understand. I had to know he was as loved as he deserves to be."

"It wasn't your place," Asa growled softly. "You have no right to play your games with her."

"I'm your mother," she growled back. "I have every right."

"Why did you hide her from me?" I released him and sat back. "You're lucky I didn't gut her."

"She arrived unannounced." He rose and sat beside me. "I caught your scent, knew how it would look, and tried to protect her until I could introduce you."

"Fascination heightens emotions," his mother explained, as if I didn't know. "He was right to worry."

The effort of not punching her in the face made my fingers twitch, and her smarmy attitude didn't help.

"She's aware, Mother." Asa sounded tired, and the fight drained out of me. "I'm so sorry, Rue."

"We both could have handled this better, but make no mistake. This is not your fault." I left no doubt of who was to blame, in my humble opinion. "What was so important she made a surprise appearance?"

With tempers running high, it felt safer directing the question to him rather than her.

"High Priestess Naeema sent me to deliver this." She reached into her robes and pulled out a carved box she wisely passed to Asa to give to me. "It will protect Rue as long as she wears it."

"Wear it?" I cracked the lid and sucked in a gasp. "It's beautiful."

A delicate gold choker with an intricate pattern that reminded me of hand-knit lace rested on a bed of blue velvet, but there was no clasp on either end.

"Grandmother sent this?" Asa touched it with reverence. "It's a very generous gift."

"It will hide you from Stavros," she told me. "He won't be able to track you, or my son, when he's with you." Her gaze went unfocused on the bed behind me. "Even if your treacherous *y'nai* bring Stavros to your door, he won't sense you."

"This is Tinkkit, isn't it?" I swallowed when she nodded once. "That means it was made for me."

The ancient fae art required the crafter to imbue their individual projects with intent for the specific recipient, almost a wish for them, and the magic in the craft took over from there.

"Asa can remove it." She lifted it, and the fine links caught the light. "Anyone of our bloodline can." She let a flicker of insecurity show. "Mother keyed the transference of its power to me. I must fasten it around your neck, with your permission."

Instinct swung my gaze to Asa, who nodded, and the stare he

locked on his mother held a promise of violence if this was anything other than what she claimed it to be.

I won't lie.

It was kind of hot.

"All right." I fought against my breathlessness. "I'll allow it."

Given her height and slight build, I elected to kneel on the floor to give her the best access to me without my hair posing a risk to her. Since she was Asa's family, she might be immune when it came to me. But, given my violent reaction to her, and the questionable loyalty of the *y'nai*, she might not be.

"Hold still." Her fingers gripped my shoulders gently. "This will tingle, but it won't burn."

Cool metal touched my nape, flooding me with serenity, and the oppressive darkness I had struggled against since fashioning the grimoire into an accessory lifted until I could breathe easy again.

Busy soaking up the relief, I startled when Callula yelped and stumbled back.

"How…?" Her voice trembled. "What…?" She thumped against the door. "I don't understand."

"Asa?" I checked my neck, but I only felt the one chain. No choker. "What happened?"

Slowly, I faced her, uncertain if her fear was directed at me or the jewelry or both.

"Mother." Asa helped her to her feet then sat her in a wobbly task chair. "We need a moment alone."

Worry carved grooves across Asa's forehead as he led me out to the SUV where he locked us in.

"Can you ward this?" He didn't crank the engine or fasten his seat belt. "How long would it take?"

"Not long." I shut my eyes and drew on the well of magic within me to push out a temporary shield. "Got it." Out of breath, I slumped back against my seat. "How bad is it?"

"The choker vanished when it touched the pendant's chain."

"Of course it did." I pulled the pendant out from under my shirt. "Well, that answers that."

Golden threads wove through the original chain, bright against its ancient patina.

"The pendant, or the grimoire, absorbed the choker." Asa smoothed his thumb over the striking result. "I can still sense Grandmother's magic within it."

"I feel it." I stared down at the oddly beautiful combination. "Her magic, I mean. Her intent?" I wasn't sure of the proper term. "It's soothing, like a cold shower on a hot day. The grimoire isn't pressing down on me. I don't feel it, or the pendant. Their presence is just…gone."

"Perhaps the chain interpreted Grandmother's wishes in an unexpected way."

"Hmm." I mulled over that. "I wonder if calling the grimoire out would separate them."

"Would it hurt you to try?" Asa considered me. "Is it worth freeing the grimoire, even for a moment?"

"I'm not sure." I examined the pendant, which hadn't changed. "Nothing ventured, nothing gained."

Before he could talk me out of it, I murmured the incantation. The grimoire popped out, and I caught it on my lap. I swear it almost hummed as if it were pleased to be free of its constraints.

With the book in my hands, I tried again. This time, I focused on the chain. I could sense it on the edge of my awareness, pulsing with light, with warmth, with love infused by its creator. But it refused to budge. It was well and truly stuck.

"Well, it was worth a shot." I returned the grimoire, which fought me every step. "So, your mom."

"Your introduction didn't go how I imagined, but she takes extreme measures where my father is concerned." He took my hand. "She's entitled to that, but it was hard to hear her test you on your ability to love both halves of me. As if it was the worst obstacle we've faced."

"Her heart was in the right place." I made myself believe it. "She's aware of her faults, and she wants better for you than what she could give. I can respect that. She might not have gone about it the best way, but it shows she cares." I leaned into his touch. "For both of you."

Asa was all about seizing the moments given to us between cases, and I was ready to grab one now.

Sadly, not the one in his pants.

"There's something I've been meaning to talk to you about." I shrugged off my unease, given the nature of his mother's test, but I was asking for the right reasons. "Can you keep a secret from the daemon?"

"Yes," he said without reservation, and his trust sparked warmth in my chest.

A little afraid of his reaction, I asked, "How do you feel about skimming some baby name sites with me?"

11

Callula had regained her calm by the time we returned to our room, and she had dredged up smiles that could pass as authentic for both of us. Her ability to mask her emotions was impressive, since I was certain she hadn't magically become okay with what happened to her mother's choker.

As much as I wished Asa could reassure her, he couldn't explain the reason behind its disappearance without exposing the grimoire. And whatever abomination I created when the choker fused with the pendant concealing it.

"I've done what I came to do." She embraced Asa and kissed his cheek. "I should return home."

"Safe travels." I stiffened when she hugged me too. "It was nice to meet you."

"I'll be on my best behavior next time." She bussed my cheek. "I can't wait to see what beautiful children you two make." She hesitated at the door. "I hope the choker will lend you some protection, wherever it's gone."

"I hope so too." I touched the fused chain. "Thank your mother for me."

"She's eager to make your acquaintance." Callula exited the room. "Until next time, dears."

After the door shut behind her, I slumped into the vacant task chair. "What is it with your family?"

"You'll have to be more specific, I'm afraid."

"Babies." I stared up at him. "Can I meet someone who doesn't want to see me knocked up?"

Too late, I realized I was digging at the same wound that Meg had chided me for, but Asa was grinning.

"Clay has always wanted to be an uncle to a passel of nieces and nephews."

Ha. Ha.

No.

"Now you're just being mean." I hesitated. "How many is a passel anyway?"

A buzz in my pocket drew my attention to my phone, which flashed an unfamiliar number. "Hollis."

"Meg passed along your intel," a deep voice rumbled. "I'd like to offer you my services, free of charge."

"We appreciate that, Mr....?"

"You can call me Derry."

"Okay, Derry." I should have guessed he would be Meg's choice of champion. "When can we meet?"

"Now." He came off grim. "I was already on my way when Meg's intermediary touched base with me." A beeping noise filled his end of the line. "The local pack thought they had a rogue on their hands, but one of their elders recognized Old Man Fang and reached out to me."

With their pack in regular contact with Meg, who provided legal services to anyone who could afford her advice, I could see why other wargs might think Derry would know how to handle a vengeful spirit.

Not that I would ever tell Meg I had just mentally lumped her in with those.

Oops.

"Tell us where you are, and we'll meet you there in ten." He rattled off an address I memorized then ended the call. "Derry is the current alpha of Meg's pack." I thumped the phone against my thigh. "He's crossing state lines to help. That's a big deal."

Shifters, more than any other faction, carried the stigma of being mindless beasts when they turned and for being animalistic while in their human forms. For the most part, that wasn't true. Four-legged predators were far less likely to be frivolous killers than the two-legged varieties. But people did enjoy their classic monsters.

Word of a feral warg killing humans, even a dead one raised for that purpose, could be a PR nightmare.

As we left our room, I noticed a light on in the maintenance office. I hesitated a step but walked on to the SUV. No one in their right mind kept an alpha waiting when he was willing to extend a hand—or a nose—to aid in an ongoing investigation. Particularly since he stood a better chance in a fight with Old Man Fang than we did, if we found him.

The GPS led us to a cemetery on the outskirts of town where a fit man in his midforties leaned against a truck parked off the shoulder of the road. His eyes gleamed gold in the shine of the headlights, confirming this was our alpha warg. His hair was cut short, red-gold, and his scruffy beard was styled with care.

Alphas were all about appearance. They had to be. Otherwise, the pack they so lovingly tended would rise up, rip out their throat, and crown a stronger king, or queen, to rule them.

"Rue Hollis," he greeted me with a half-smile. "Our most frequent customer."

"Meg's worth it." I walked up to shake his hand. "She's a dear friend."

"She says the same about you." He flicked Asa a glance. "You, she just calls the Jawbreaker."

"The Jawbreaker?" I got a bad feeling about this, but I asked him anyway. "Why would she do that?"

"What do you do with hard candy?"

"You put it in your mouth."

"And?"

"You suck on it."

Derry allowed a small laugh to escape before he strode to Asa and shook his hand. "Good to meet you."

Right then, I decided I liked Derry. Anyone who treated Asa with respect earned the same from me.

"You as well." Asa dipped his chin. "We appreciate your help, and the heads-up on the nickname."

"Don't let Meg get to you. She had everyone calling me Dirty Santa for six years after an unfortunate Christmas incident involving a Santa suit, the stripper playlist for my mate's pole dancing classes, and a bottle of hot sauce."

A genuine smile broke across Asa's face, and I wanted to clutch my hands to my black heart.

Then I felt mildly creepy for the maternal *aww* moment at him making a potential friend.

"This is where Old Man Fang was buried?" I attempted to play it cool and not hover. "Any idea where?"

"Can you smell it?" Derry asked Asa. "It's giving me hives from here."

"Silver," he agreed. "I have the same reaction to the ironwork."

"I didn't realize smelling it bothered you." I pressed a hand into his chest. "It won't hurt you, will it?"

"Not unless he licks the rust off the ornaments." Derry snickered at my scowl then set off beside Asa. "My mate's the same way. She acts like I'm going to step out the front door on the way to work, trip, and fall on a piece of antique silverware that stabs me through the heart."

Asa strangled his chuckle when he caught me switching my glare to him, but I was secretly delighted.

"To be fair, Rue has picked iron bullets out of me." Asa kept pace with Derry. "She saved my life."

"I respect the ferocity of alpha females." Derry raised his hands. "Mine scented colloidal silver mixed in with my wine." He paused. "That I only drink with my mate so she doesn't have to drink alone." He cleared his throat. "She tried to become my official food and drink taster, as if I would consent to that."

Hanging back, I texted Clay while Asa and Derry bonded over their mates smothering them.

>*We're at a cemetery with backup, hunting Old Man Fang's burial site.*

>>*You're braver than me. I wouldn't step foot in one with the way things have been going.*

>*You got anything?*

>>*The motel owner is too cheap to pay for Wi-Fi for his guests, so it's a safe bet he's not our guy.*

>*Who does that leave?*

>>*There's one long-term renter Colby found through means she says you're better off not knowing.*

>*You've got his room number?*

>>*Do we look like amateurs to you?*

"Rue." Asa dragged me from my phone. "The glow."

>*I'll touch base when we finish up here.*

"Clay says he's got a lead for us when we can juggle it."

"Probably best we don't talk from this point in," Derry told me. "Just in case."

The advice was sound, so I put away my phone and tuned in our surroundings. I didn't expect to bump into trouble out here. Old Man Fang's remains had been removed in order to place him under the spellcaster's control, but I was happy to turn this operation over to Derry.

Ahead, a dark mound of earth beneath a blackened headstone marked our destination. No name graced the raw hunk of marble, and no mementoes had been left to honor the dead. Under the dirt, however, a brutal reminder of the grave's occupant rested within the shadowy depths.

A tarnished cage of pure silver, just as the story had claimed.

Derry crouched and drew air into his lungs, careful not to get too close. It made me wonder if silver residue leaching into the soil was a concern, which flipped into worry over potential rust particles.

"We're alone," he announced. "No ghosts, summoners, or anything else I can sense."

Asa held up a finger then let flames take him as he grew into the daemon.

"Damn," Derry breathed. "Meg was right. You are a big fella."

"Eat lots of cookies," the daemon told him solemnly. "Smell grave?"

"Knock yourself out." Derry shot to his feet when the daemon leapt into the grave. "Careful in there."

A twinge made me brace for him to imply the daemon was clumsy or careless, but Derry was in awe.

"I'd give you a hand up," he told the daemon, "but I can't get that close. There's silver dust mixed in with the dirt."

Well, that explained that. They really didn't want this guy to rise. Pity someone ignored those wishes.

"Can get out." The daemon climbed up without a hitch. "Got scent."

"You're a tracker too?" Derry's eyes brightened. "You ever consider hunting with a pack?"

The offer froze both the daemon and me in place, but he recovered first.

"Rue pack." He wiggled his fingers at me. "Hunt with her for bad people."

"Nah." Derry yanked off his shirt. "I mean a real hunt. For deer, mostly." He kicked off his shoes. "We get calls to put down problem animals too. Cougars and the like that have developed a taste for people. You should come." He shoved down his pants. "The way I hear it, Rue's mom used to run with our pack back in the day. I doubt anyone would care if you gave it a go."

"Rue come too?"

"That's up to her." He pivoted toward me. "You want to run with the wolves?"

Right now, I wanted to ignore the fact he was butt naked and giving me a full frontal.

"I'll take it under consideration." I kept my eyes averted. "I'm not much for hunting."

The blood, the death, the heart offered up to the one who made the killing bite...

"It's not the same as a pack run," he agreed. "Those are about family time and playing, building pack bonds." He stepped behind a bush. "I'll need about fifteen minutes."

For what almost popped out of my mouth before it hit me.

He was shifting.

Right there.

With us to overhear his grunts and pants as his body snapped and reformed into a new shape.

Mom had been considered pack. Meg had loved her like a sister. I understood that gave me leeway with their pack, but it was access I never cashed in on. I was content maintaining my ties to Meg and financially supporting her pack in exchange for her help in legal matters. I never stopped to consider the pack might view me as adopted kin, but Meg was their matriarch. It should have occurred to me before.

The daemon loped over to me, grinning wide. "Go on hunt with Derry?"

"I want *you* to go." I patted his arm. "He seems nice, and a hunt like that would be amazing."

I would miss Asa something fierce if they went too far for too long, but it would be the experience of a lifetime for the daemon.

"You pet." He thrust his hair into my hand. "I show Rue best hunting pose."

The pose was not a pose, but a variation on the Mystic Mambo. I really had to warn Derry what he had gotten himself into with the daemon. If he busted out moves like these while they were on a hunt, prey would hear them coming a hundred miles away.

A cold nose bumped the back of my hand, and I jerked when a lean gray wolf lolled his tongue at me.

"Ready?" The daemon walked up to Derry. "Race me?"

The wolf gave an eager yip, his tail wagging, and it made me wonder if Derry was behind the wheel or if he was more of a copilot in this form. Maybe four legs simply made him happier and more playful. The daemon was certainly both those things.

"You can race to the end of the cemetery road, but that's it." I set my hands on my hips. "Any farther, and you might be seen." Pack magic might blur the lines until folks saw a dog instead of a wolf, but a crimson-skinned daemon with ebony horns and muscles for days was hard to miss. "Are you sure...?"

They didn't let me get out the rest of my question before they took off like a shot.

"I'm glad we had this talk," I told a cloud of dust then muttered, "I hope they track as fast as they run."

Ten minutes later, I caught up to them and tried hard not to notice the daemon playing fetch with the wolf. An alpha wolf. With a stick as long as my forearm.

And if I happened to snap a few pictures, maybe a short video, then I was documenting the damage. Yeah. Property damage. That was it. Not creating a blackmail folder. Because that would be wrong.

"Oh crap." I jogged up to them. "That's not a stick."

The door to a nearby mausoleum hung at an odd angle, and the daemon looked way too innocent for his own good. Up close, I could tell the stick wasn't just as long as my forearm, it was an ulna.

"Go put that back where you found it." I ignored the daemon's sulk. "We have a case to solve."

The grumble in Derry's throat turned into a huff and a human-like head bob as he pitched in.

Once they set things to rights, I gestured for Derry to lead the way. This time, I walked behind him and left the daemon to follow me. Neither seemed happy about the arrangement, but I could schedule them a playdate later.

After we rounded up our summoning ring and banished all the vengeful spirits.

A transformation overcame Derry when he crossed the property line leaving the cemetery. Not as dramatic as the whole man-to-wolf thing he had going on, but it was impressive, nonetheless. Here was the predator I had anticipated, nose to the ground, ears perked for any sounds.

We walked three miles, according to my watch's fitness app, and I set a pin when the guys stalled out.

The daemon circled around me, picking up on whatever Derry had located, and the pair stared at one another in silent understanding. Then the daemon pivoted toward me, plucked me up like a feather, and hauled me into a nearby tree. As I found my voice to yell at him for overreacting, a blue onryō shot straight at Derry, slamming into him with a deafening crunch.

The wolf was twice his size and three times as vicious as they bit and clawed and snarled at one another.

"I'm useless up here." I climbed out of the daemon's arms onto a limb. "I need contact for my magic to work."

"Derry-wolf want test theory," the daemon explained. "Told him bad idea."

"We'll give them sixty seconds, and then we're going down there."

"Deal." The daemon grinned. "Rue have best ideas."

"I have terrible ideas that get us into trouble." I tapped him on the chin. "You just like trouble."

"Best..." he parted his hair, ready to pass me a section, "...ideas."

"Time," I called without having glanced at my watch. "We need to break this up before it goes too far."

The thing about ghosts was they were already dead. Theories were well and good, and I was all for testing them, but there were limits. Derry had a mate and a pack depending on him. I didn't doubt he was capable in a fight, but I put myself into his mate's shoes too easily. For her sake, I couldn't stand by.

"Hold on." The daemon scooped me into his arms and dropped from the tree. "Watch back."

"Thanks." I drew from Colby, readying a containment spell that ought to work on Fang. "Hey, you."

The wolves ignored me in favor of shredding themselves down to the bone.

Derry was winded, bleeding, and favoring one paw.

Despite his grievous injuries, Old Man Fang was not.

"Ugly," I yelled, illuminating the tip of my wand. "Come get some."

"That rude." The daemon cut me a scowl of disapproval. "Deadwolf can't help he not pretty."

"That's not—" I bit my tongue as the spectral wolf lunged for my throat. "Sorry, fella." I meant to tap him with my wand, but his fur was sticky, his skin gelatinous. He was solid, but my wand punched through him like paper. I flung the spell on the tip of my tongue and cringed as goo exploded. "Eww."

Blobs of glowing jelly rained down on us, and they began jiggling before they hit the ground.

"I saw that going differently in my mind." I dragged a hand down my face. "You've got to be kidding me."

As we looked on, the bits wiggled and rolled until they bumped into one another and began to form an arm that hauled itself toward another large blob that took on the shape of a leg. On and on, the process continued with disturbingly fascinating results.

"Derry hurt." The daemon didn't wait for permission. He lifted the wolf in his arms. "Take to motel?"

One look at the alpha assured me I had no time to waste on further attempts at containment or banishment. We had to get Derry medical care. Fast. And we had to be careful how we went about it.

Derry hadn't mentioned how many packmates had made the trip with him, but no alpha traveled solo in foreign pack territory. I wanted to believe we could trust those he had chosen, but I refused to chance it.

"Let's go back to where he shifted," I decided. "His phone must be in his pants."

From there, assuming I could unlock it, I could find his mate's number and call her for instructions.

"Hurry." The daemon snuggled the giant wolf against his chest. "It okay, Derry-wolf."

My sense of smell might not be on par with theirs, but I had a decent memory and ran ahead to the cemetery. I located Derry's clothes and pulled out his phone then breathed a sigh of relief when it wasn't password protected. He made it even easier with an ICE icon in the center of his home screen.

Clearly, this scenario played out often enough with wargs they disabled security during shifts and kept their emergency contact front and center on their home screen.

With no time to waste, I mashed the button and waited for someone to answer. "Um, hi?"

"What has he done now?" A woman with a throaty voice sighed at me. "How many bones are broken?"

"Not sure," I answered. "Can I ask who I'm speaking with?"

"Marita Mayhew, the long-suffering mate of the man whose phone you're holding."

Given it was his phone, and his emergency contact, that was good enough for me.

"Derry got in a fight with Old Man Fang, and he's lost a lot of blood. He's unconscious, but I wasn't sure what to do with him. I don't want him to face repercussions from the pack if he's seen in a compromised state."

"Rue Hollis," she said after a beat. "Of course you would know how to treat him. Give me ten minutes."

The call ended as the daemon arrived, and I gestured for him to lay Derry on the grass.

Warg healing is a miraculous thing to behold, which explained why I didn't sweat his recovery. Odds were good he would be awake and grumpy by the time his mate arrived. Or so I told myself. Until I saw the oozing green mucus weeping from his wounds and knew we had problems.

Wishing I could give her a heads-up but knowing I didn't have the time, I dropped to my knees beside Derry and yanked on Colby. Hard. I pulled her energy through me and channeled it into Derry with a touch of my wand. Her warm, healing light pulsed within him, and the goop leaked from his pores as the foul magic was purged from his system.

I did all I could and prayed it was enough as I sat back and waited for his mate to arrive.

She didn't keep me long.

"Derry Lamont Mayhew," that same voice from the phone snarled. "I'm going to wring your neck."

"Hi." I scrambled to my feet. "I'm Rue."

"Hey, Rue." Her expression was equal parts annoyance and exasperation. "Nice to finally meet you. I'm Marita, Numbskull's mate."

Hands on hips, she stared down at Derry and watched until he twitched before her shoulders lowered a fraction. She was good at hiding her concern, but it lived in her, the way the gnawing concern for Asa had been branded onto my bones.

"Old Man Fang did this?" She toed Derry in the side. "Impressive carnage."

"Yeah." I wiped slime off my fingers onto my pants. "Impressive."

"You must think I'm crazy." She laughed. "This damn fool man heard about the revenant or whatever it is and almost wet his pants. All the guys in the pack talk about how they could have ripped out Old Man Fang's throat if they had been alive at the time. Derry couldn't believe he was getting a chance to prove it." She crouched over him and jabbed him between the eyes. "He smells…" She lifted her head. "You spelled him?"

"Healed him," I corrected, feeling twitchy. "Old Man Fang's bite wasn't agreeing with him."

"I can imagine." She plopped down on the ground. "You don't have to babysit him. I'll stay until he can shift back. That will help accelerate the healing." She settled in beside him. "Thanks for saving him from himself."

"No problem." I scuffed my shoe in the dirt. "Do you have someone who can patch up a mausoleum?"

Laughter shook her shoulders, like she could already tell this story was going to be good. "Yes?"

In exchange for a photo of her husband playing fetch, she arranged for the damage to be repaired so the family wouldn't walk into a hot mess the next time they visited the cemetery.

"That's all our t's crossed." I checked with the daemon. "You ready?"

"Bye, Derry-wolf." The daemon pressed his hair into my hand. "Rue pet, I track."

"I can find my way back." I dropped his hair. "Thanks for the offer, though."

Hiding my smile, I set off and left him to keep up with me this time.

"Rue pet." He shoved his hair back into my hand. "I protect."

"I can take care of myself." I passed it back to him. "I exploded Fang, remember?"

"Found grave." His grin showed every tooth in his head. "Want to see?"

"That's why he attacked?" I hadn't been sure we tracked Fang that far before he struck. "Show me."

"You pet." He thrust more hair at me. "I show."

The tables turned on me so fast, I got whiplash.

"Fine." Fighting off a smile that only encouraged bad behavior, I tugged on him. "Let's go."

12

Without fail, the daemon returned us to the scene of the attack. Old Man Fang was gone, which I had expected, but I was hopeful this search might net us our first cache of bones. The area was overgrown with weeds and brambles, but I didn't notice any disturbed earth that screamed *fresh grave ahoy*.

Ahoy?

Really?

Now Colby had me talking like a pirate.

"Here." The daemon pointed to an animal den. "Bones hidden."

"Okay." I turned on my phone's flashlight. "Let's take a look."

Bright against the darkness of the hole, a piece of folded paper leaned against an exposed root.

"That not bones." The daemon shifted closer. "Bones gone?"

The same indescribable sense of foreboding that kept prodding me urged me to read the note.

"No one ever found your father's remains," I read aloud. "Your mother was much easier to locate."

A cold stone splashed in my gut, and I wanted to vomit at the implication someone had desecrated her grave, taken her remains, and planned to wield her as an instrument for their own ends.

"This is a lie." I fought off the clench of my fist, the urge to crumple it. "They don't have Mom."

Her remains had been identified, a death certificate issued, and then they disappeared without a trace. I searched for her. Everywhere. I concluded that, for whatever twisted reason, the director had secreted them away so that neither she nor I would know any peace. But, as I grew older, I began questioning whether eagerness to blame all my problems on the director had biased me against other options.

Until I learned Dad was alive.

Now I was certain, and it gutted me that even in death, the director's only use for Mom was as leverage.

"Rue." Asa had traded forms while I read. "We need to contact your father."

Unused to having Dad as a backup option, I blanked at the idea then leapt onboard. "You're right."

Without checking the time, I dialed Aiden, who answered slightly out of breath. "What's up?"

"I need you to write my dad." I clutched the paper in my hand. "Tell him to meet me in Tupelo. ASAP."

"Are you sure he'll go for that?"

"Tell him Mom's bones have been taken."

A beat of silence relayed his horror at the revelation. "Do you need me?"

"I want to say yes." I could use emotional support from another family member, which was downright bizarre to think. "But I don't want to bring you to Black Hat's attention, and you're doing a more important job by looking after the girls for me."

"I'll send the message now." His disappointment came through loud and clear. "Let me know if you change your mind."

"I will." I tried for chipper. "If you want field experience, we'll talk about it when I get home, okay?"

I couldn't afford for him to think that because I worked for Black Hat, it was an endorsement. The same went for Asa and Clay. We had been forced into service because we were dangerous, not because we wanted to make a difference and felt we could do that through them. We had been transparent in our dealings with Aedan, but if he wanted in on the action, we had to strip the meat down to the bone.

"Yeah. All right." He hesitated. "I'll touch base if he replies."

"Thanks."

I ended the call, feeling better for having that link to Samford. To *home*. I wished I could call the girls for a quick pick-me-up, but I was chicken. Rue Hollis, and her small-town life, were unraveling. The girls were pressing for answers I couldn't give, and it would drive a wedge between us if I didn't get in front of it.

"You heard?" I checked with Asa, who nodded. "We need to interrogate that guest."

"Are you okay?" He caught my arm. "What that note implies..."

That I might see Mom again. That she might kill someone. That I might have just ripped out Dad's heart.

As hard as it would be for me to see her, she was more of an idea to me than a person. To Dad? She was a razor-sharp memory that hadn't faded after all this time. He could barely speak her name without his voice going tight or agony leaking into his eyes.

"I can't think about it." I broke free of him. "It's too much." I gathered my nerve. "We're focusing on our best lead to solve the case as a whole, which is Old Man Fang."

The big problem with fascination was how high it cranked my emotions. I was getting better at figuring out what to do with my feelings, but I wasn't a pro. Far from it. The cocktail of feeling swishing around in my gut made me nauseous, and I couldn't afford to feed that gnawing anxiety.

"All right." Asa let it drop, and I heard the impact. "We'll focus on Old Man Fang."

We didn't speak on the ride to the motel, and I kept rubbing my thumb over the note until I quit before I worried a hole through it.

Focus.

Angling my body toward my window, I let the blurred scenery fill my vision and my head with streaks of color. It felt like blocking out Asa, which wasn't fair, but I couldn't control the instinct to withdraw. Still, I reached back for his hand, and he laced our fingers.

It was enough.

I couldn't offer him what he deserved by any metric, and I was grateful he accepted so little from me.

"I love you," I blurted then locked my jaw and glared at my reflection.

"I know."

That should have been it, but this time it wasn't enough. Fascination pecked and picked until I caved to its whims and regurgitated feelings all over us both. "I'm mad at the situation, not you."

"I know."

"Do black witches have nothing better to do with their time than target the fuck out of me?"

The harsh language caused his fingers to twitch in shock, but the old me had learned the art of swearing at Clay's knee. It could only get worse from here if I didn't rein in the habit before it broke free.

"Fuck," I exhaled, reeling in that breach. "I miss that word."

"You can whisper it in my ear whenever you feel the urge."

A surprised laugh spluttered out of me, and once again, it was enough. The tension in me broke open, and I could stand to meet my reflection without wanting to punch her in the face for the crime of allowing my black heart to bleed for a woman I barely remembered and the man who would break the world to have her returned to him.

"I've ruined you." I focused on his image in the glass. "You're almost as pervy as me."

"We have the rest of our lives for me to catch up," he said smoothly. "Assuming you let me hang around that long."

"I'll take it under consideration."

I scooted closer, leaned my head against his shoulder, and tried not to think too hard about how certain I already was that I couldn't live without him.

⸻

The lights were out at the motel, which should have been our first clue something was wrong. But I was tired, sticky, and willing to pretend we could interview our latest suspect and best hope of solving the case without it all going to Hael in a handbasket.

What?

I can be optimistic. It's allowed. It's impractical, and I usually regret it later, but I still indulge on occasion.

"Do you smell that?" Asa stepped up beside me. "Ozone."

"Burnt circuits." That was what it reminded me of. "What do you think happened?"

"Whoever is pulling Old Man Fang's strings knows you're onto them." He sniffed the air again. "The power is on down the street. Whatever happened, it's localized to the motel."

Finch's earlier assertion that Parish had sent *me*, and not my team, kept seeping into my thoughts.

Had Parish known about Mom? Did he know about Dad? Or was he simply acting in his capacity as the deputy director?

I was the black magic expert, as Asa had reminded me, and I got tapped for cases involving the dark arts.

A summoning ring of black witches crafting violent spirit manifestations was right up my alley.

"Let me touch base with Colby." I shot her a text. "I doubt we get lucky, but we might find something."

>Room number for our summoner?

>>Lucky thirteen.

>>Based on the security footage, you've got another black witch on your hands.

>You have a lot of fingers in a lot of pies for someone who doesn't eat pie.

>>*What can I say? I have a lot of fingers.*

Technically, she had none. But she made up in arms what she lacked in individual digits.

>>*Be safe.*

>*Always.*

After pocketing my cell, I drew my wand but kept it down by my thigh. "Let's go."

We cut a path to the room, the ozone smell intensifying, and I kicked the door open.

Yes, I could have knocked first, but violence against inanimate objects was cathartic.

The one area where I was on par with the guys' hearing was in the detection of heartbeats. But once the door swung open, I could tell by that clawing, hungry pit in my stomach that the summoner was gone.

"You take the left side, and I'll take the right." I checked under the bed before I stripped it, searching for any hidden nastiness that might hurt someone else later. I combed over the pillow for hairs, but the black witch knew enough not to leave those behind. "Nothing."

Except for an indigo wizard's robes with glittering silver moons embroidered on the hem.

These guys must use the same costumer, and I had been in her workspace.

Lucky me.

Asa shook his head, confirming he had come up empty too. "How is he controlling Old Man Fang?"

"The necromancer claimed the bones had to be buried on land belonging to the summoner," I recalled. "Grave dirt was required too." I searched the room. "Do you think the black witch lives in town? Maybe they buried the bones locally but hid out at the motel to throw us off their scent."

"That would make him smarter than the others, but it doesn't explain the logo on the motel's site."

"True." I wasn't sure how to account for that. "We'll add that to the list of things we don't know."

Assuming I could find the end of it. It must stretch for miles by now. At least as far back as Raymond.

"With the summoner on the run, we might earn a reprieve from Old Man Fang."

"We can hope." That would make my day. "Do you want to drop in on the maintenance guy?"

If that wasn't him before, he was here now. Complaints would have come piling in from guests when the power went out, especially after they noticed it was isolated to their rooms and not a city- or block-wide issue.

We gave the summoner's room one last chance to prove useful, but we turned up nothing new.

Halfway to the office, a harried man with an impressive beard shoved out the door on his cell.

"This is my livelihood. I need power restored *now*. Keep screwing with me, and I will forward all complaint calls to this extension." He ended the call with a growl, then he spotted us. "The power's out. I got it. I can see it for myself." He stomped off toward the parking lot.

"Thanks."

"We're not here about the power." Asa prowled up behind him. "We're here about a long-term guest."

"Shit fire and hold the mayo." The man spun, found Asa in his personal space, and puffed out his chest. "I don't know who you think you are, but—"

"Agent Montenegro, with the FBI." Asa held his badge an inch from the man's nose. "We need to ask you a few questions."

"Yeah." He ruffled his hair. "I knew this would bite me on the ass." He gestured us back the way he had come. "Let's do this in the office." He let us in and sank into a chair behind a small desk. "Hang on. I've got flashlights in here somewhere." He produced four, turned them on, and set them at the corners of his desk. Their shine bouncing off the ceiling did a decent job of lighting the room. "Okay, shoot."

"What do you know about—" Asa consulted his phone, "—Johnathan Smithfield?"

"He works in IT," the man said. "He travels a lot for work. My boss has strict policies about long-term renters. He's against it. Doesn't want any squatter problems down the line, you know? But this guy, Smithfield, he paid me in cash for the month." He drummed his fingers on the desk. "Plus a little extra."

"Your boss doesn't know about him, I take it." I watched him. "Or the kickbacks you're taking."

"Kickback," he insisted. "I've never broken the rules, not until now."

"What made this offer special?"

"I don't know." He scratched his chin through his beard. "I told him no, that a week was as good as I could do, but then..." He frowned. "He came back, made the same offer, and I took him up on it."

A light persuasion spell or charm was nothing compared to the complexity of the magic the summoner was already using. There was a chance this guy had stuck to his guns but that our black witch swayed him with magic.

"Did you see or talk to him otherwise?" Asa asked. "Did you interact with him after that?"

"No." He jiggled his leg. "He had food delivered, but that was it. He never left his room that I saw, but I keep weird hours, mostly catching up on maintenance crap. This place is falling down around my ears, but the boss don't want to hear that."

After he finished venting, we encouraged him back on topic, but he didn't have much to add.

Most of their bookings were handled online, through the same app as the others. Smithfield had shown up in person. He also paid in cash, so there was no ID or credit card on file. Effectively, he was a dead end.

Once that lead was exhausted, I made our goodbyes, and we climbed into the SUV where I called Clay.

"Tell me something good."

"The crunchy outer edge of a brownie." He made a dreamy sigh. "Makes me crave your brownie brittle."

"I'll bake some when we get home," I promised, "but that's not what I meant."

"Old Man Fang's handler is more powerful than the others." He quit joking. "He used a spell to come and go without being seen at the hotel, but Colby found the one time he couldn't disappear himself."

"At check-in?"

"Yep." Clay's glee was tangible. "The hotel was at two-thirds capacity with lots of pool activity. He had to play it safe and let himself be seen. He made multiple trips to his car to bring in his luggage, a seriously nice desktop computer setup, bags of junk food, and boxes of energy drinks."

"The maintenance guy says the owner has a limit on how long he allows guests to stay at the motel, but he awarded Smithfield an open-ended stay anyway. His confusion, paired with what we know so far, leads me to believe Smithfield used persuasion on him." Smithfield had to appear in person for that to work, which was dicey, but it kept his identification off the books. "That lends weight to your theory that he's more powerful than the others."

"Ladies and gents," Clay announced in a booming voice, "we might have found our ringleader."

As tidy as that would be, I had my doubts. "Unless the sequence of summonings is meant to escalate."

"I prefer my idea," he grumbled, sinking into the certainty things would get worse before they got better.

"Can your necromancer buddy explain how Smithfield is controlling Old Man Fang without burying his remains on property he owns?"

"Who says he didn't?" Clay crunched on a snack in the background. "Shorty has a theory."

"For starters, Johnathan Smithfield isn't his real name." She snorted. "Who uses John Smith as an alias?"

Silence was the only answer, given I hadn't put it together.

"It's Bernard Lacky," she chattered on without noticing my pause. "He's a black witch."

As usual, I found myself asking my little moth girl, "How do you know these things?"

"She hacked the Kellies and used their proprietary facial recognition software to identify him." Clay steadily munched. "Using the screengrabs from the surveillance footage, she found a match."

"I located a deed to a property in his name." Colby continued to amaze. "It's three miles from your location. It's family land. Inherited. He's never lived there, and there are no structures on the property, but it's near a cemetery."

"That sounds about on par with where Derry took us." I checked with Asa. "Where we found the note."

"Note?" Clay quit snacking. "What note?"

I slid my hand into my pocket, fingers caressing the crumpled edge, but I couldn't make my voice work.

"Lacky claims to have access to Vonda Winterbourne's bones." Asa rested his hand on my thigh. "Rue has already had Aedan contact—"

"Saint," I croaked. "We shouldn't use his name."

Ears were everywhere. Eyes too. Dad was safer if we got in the habit of using a nickname for him, and Mom had given him the perfect one.

"We haven't received word from Saint or Aedan," Asa continued, "but if Saint believes the threat is credible, then I can't imagine he won't come."

"And if he does," I predicted numbly, "there will be a bloodbath."

"Aww, hell, yes." Clay whooped in the background, eager to see action. "Colby and I are packing up and heading your way."

Colby sucked in a sharp breath at his swearing, but I could hear the thrill in it.

Given my earlier lapse, I let his go without fussing, earning me a raised eyebrow from Asa that I repaid with a shrug.

"Are you sure that's wise?" Asa's brow pinched. "Having Colby so close to...?"

"...a black witch," I finished for him. "Dad won't hurt her." I made myself believe it. "But I don't want to wave her under his nose either."

"Shorty will be fine." Clay made it a promise. "We're bored sitting here with nothing to do."

"I have dragons to raise," she said loftily, "but Clay is driving me crazy with his pacing."

"Rude." He sucked in a sharp breath. "I thought we were besties."

"We are," she said, "but I can't cook, or eat what you cook, and those are your top two hobbies."

"We do have a surplus of croquembouche." He sounded sheepish. "I made a fort."

Uncertain I heard him right but afraid I had, I asked anyway, "You made a croquembouche...fort?"

"Choux pastry puffs make surprisingly good building blocks, and caramel is the best glue."

"Okay." Torn between fear of Clay being unsupervised in a kitchen and dread burning me up from the inside whenever I thought about Mom, I caved to his request. "I could use the moral support."

"I must have leftover caramel in my ears." Clay whistled. "That almost sounded like a plea for help."

"If that's what you heard, then you do have caramel in your ears."

"We can be there in a few hours." Clay clapped his hands. "Don't have any fun without us."

Leaning across me, Asa ended the call then kissed my neck. "Do we wait for them?"

And hope Dad caught up to us? Or not? I couldn't decide which would be worse. "I don't know."

"Then I vote we get a room in a hotel without a resident black witch and nap." Asa smoothed his fingertips under my eyes. "You need rest to face this."

Sleep wouldn't help. Nothing would. Except if the note were a cruel prank.

A text from an unfamiliar number lit up my screen, and I braced for the news.

>>*Did your daemon leave anything behind in the mausoleum?*

The mausoleum? *Oh*. This must be Marita's number.

>*No?*

>>*The coffin the guys raided for their throw toy was a concrete box in the center of the structure.*

>>*It was also chockful of random religious paraphernalia that smells like roadkill.*

>>*One piece has been smashed to bits, but the base is intact. A vase, I think. Not sure if the guys did that or if it was already that way.*

Hope we had discovered the Boos' cache made me grateful I had asked Marita for the favor.

>*That's evidence in our case. Can you lock it up, maybe put some guards on it?*

>>*Sure thing.*

>*Thanks. I'll pick it up soon.*

Soon might be a slight exaggeration. I didn't trust anyone else to secure the items, the worst of which would end up in my care, but I couldn't circle back yet.

Impact rattled us in our seats, and we flinched at the massive dent in the roof above our heads.

Wand in hand, I leapt out the door and pivoted to see what manner of monster had found us. *"Dad?"*

He vibrated with rage that should have burned hot but turned him stone-cold. For a beat, there was nothing in his eyes when he looked at me. I don't think he knew me or registered anything except a threat to the mate that was beyond needing him to defend her.

The black wings I saw him with last fanned out to either side of him, hidden from human sight, but not from me. He stepped off the roof and landed on the asphalt before me, his eyes dark and fathomless. A muscle twitched in his neck, and his gaze flipped down to where the pendant hid beneath my shirt.

For a heartbeat, two, I forgot how to breathe in the face of his all-consuming fury.

"Where?"

That was all he got out before his locked jaw caged any further conversation.

"We don't know." I hated admitting that to him. "A suspect we have reason to believe is already in control of one onryō left me this note."

Dad snatched the paper out of my hand and skimmed it, cruel darkness billowing around him.

"My *wife*." He crumpled the threat in his hand. "They would dare?"

The ball erupted into black flames that smelled of old blood and dirt, and Dad blew the ashes off his palm. Rather than disperse, they glittered with a spark of that same ember and caught a ride on a nonexistent wind toward the street.

"This will lead us to the person who wrote the note."

He didn't spare us another thought before prowling across the road in pursuit of the trail.

Asa and I exchanged a look then trotted after him. I let Asa guide me as I texted Clay a warning. If we were still out with Dad when he arrived, I didn't want him to get Colby anywhere near us. Not until I was certain I could trust Dad. With the pendant heating against my skin, I had more than a few doubts.

Dark artifacts want to be used for their intended purpose, they crave it, and Saint was all potential. If the grimoire was to be believed, Saint contributed to its pages. Above any other, it would long for its original masters. Any one of them would do, but it falling into Dad's hands would mean the book hit the jackpot.

As much as I wanted to believe Dad possessed a daughter-seeking radar, I couldn't discount the possibility it was the grimoire's power signature he traced to me. The choker, assuming the pendant/grimoire hadn't destroyed its intent, protected me from Stavros. Not him.

With punishing strides, Dad devoured the ground between the motel and where we found the note. He located the animal den and stuck his hand in without hesitation. Tension strung him tight when he withdrew, and he showed us a delicate finger bone on his palm. A distal phalange, if I wasn't mistaken.

"My love," he breathed across the fragment, closing his fist, "they will pay for this in blood."

Agony streaked his features as he pocketed the bone, but I couldn't shake its miraculous appearance.

"That wasn't here earlier." I turned to Asa. "You would have scented it."

"A distraction." He cut his eyes toward Dad. "Lacky wants to slow Rue down."

Again, I heard Finch in my head, and again I couldn't shake the sensation of a target on my back.

"Parish gave us a heads-up you were on your way."

"My team, you mean."

Finch delighted in correcting me. "I mean you.*"*

Why had Parish specified me?

Had he known about Mom? Had he hoped Dad would intervene? Was I working a case or acting as bait?

"We lost the spell," I realized as the area grew darker. "Can we get it back?"

"No," Saint rasped, "but I can catch it."

Faster than I could ask how, he vanished into shadow, leaping from dark pool to dark pool in pursuit.

"I have it," a cold voice whirled around me. "Follow the spark."

A sizzling pop ignited in front of me, and the spastic glitter of a floating orb shot off in the direction Dad had gone. The whole thing reminded me of tales from those who followed will-o'-the-wisps into midnight forests and were led to their doom, but I had brought Dad here. He was my responsibility.

Asa and I rushed again, almost losing sight of the spark, but its explosion as it returned to Dad lit the way to him. The burnt-black magic from earlier fluttered onward, and he tracked it with purpose. Its edges glowed red, as if igniting, and then extinguished in a huff of smoke.

"We're here." Dad reached for his wand. "Be on your guard."

As usual, Colby's reports were correct. This was a barren tract of land that might have once been a homestead, but all reminders of it had been reclaimed by tangled vines and thorny bushes. There were plenty of places to hide, if you didn't mind getting poison oak or ivy, but I doubted our summoner was hiding under one of the wild blackberry bushes, where his hands would be limited in their motions.

Entering the woods from this direction, I couldn't decide if this was where Old Man Fang attacked Derry. Then again, it didn't have to be. I could have checked the pin I set earlier, but his bones had been relocated. The summoner couldn't have moved them far, but he owned several acres. Needle in a haystack, anyone? Thank the goddess for Dad's quick spell.

A frantic buzz in my pocket left me certain things had somehow managed to get worse.

Asa touched my arm to reassure me he would watch my back while I checked my cell.

>>*Answer your phone.*

The number was unfamiliar, but there were teams in every city with three to five agents in each.

>*In the field.*

>>*Fine.*

>>*Check your email.*

A beat later, I had my answer as to the identity of the mystery texter.

Parish.

We had another case.

13

"We've got another onryō." I reread the email. "Parish wants us in Plantersville ASAP."

"That's just down the road." Asa checked the address given for the incident. "Southeast of our location."

The space around my father exploded into darkness as his wings unfurled, and he jettisoned into the sky.

"Losing sight of him can't be good." I did my best to steady my nerves. "We have to go after him."

"Any word on who was summoned this time?"

A hard lump formed in my throat. "She has yet to be identified."

"That doesn't mean it's your mother." Asa rubbed my back. "It could be anyone."

Without warning, the daemon burst into crackling existence, ripping Asa from me.

"What's wrong?" I grabbed for his arm, but he shook me off. "What is it?"

He circled the area, sniffing the air, then swung his head toward me with a deep and abiding sadness.

"Rue come."

Following his hunch, we crashed through the underbrush until he located a dilapidated chimney that was little more than a crumbling stump of handmade brick.

"Rue mom dead."

"Yeah." I fought the tightness in my voice. "For years now."

"No." He came to me, took my hands gently in his, and tugged me forward. "Rue mom dead *here*."

Across the way, sitting on the damp earth with her back to a tree, was my mother. I recognized her in the foggy way you recalled a photo you had seen too often to be sure if you truly remembered or if you had only fabricated a recollection based on that captured moment.

Sixty seconds.

That was how long it took the daemon to locate her.

That was how long it took for my world to jerk to a grinding halt.

"You should run." She kept her head down, gaze locked on her feet. "I mean it, baby."

"Mom?" I searched for her summoner. "Where did you come from?"

Based on the pattern of our assignments, I expected the next onryō to be in Plantersville with its summoner.

"He brought me back." She glanced up, and her eyes were soulless pits. "For you."

"Mom?" I rocked forward onto the balls of my feet. "You can understand me?"

"*Run.*" A sob broke free of her chest. "I can't hold back much longer."

Desperation blazed a path through me, and I saw a way clear of this standoff.

Whispering the enchantment under my breath, I began summoning the grimoire. Not far enough to let it out. Just far enough I hoped its fluctuating magic would catch Dad's attention.

Had he been tracking me via the book, he would pick up on its signature in a heartbeat.

"Lacky?" I inched closer. "Is that who you mean?"

"Rue." The daemon gripped my upper arm. "Look."

Mom had meant what she said literally, her hands clenching the roots to hold herself still. The strain in her body became evident the longer I stood there, and then her fingers lost their purchase.

Her magic slammed into my knee. The joint wrenched, popped, and I hit the ground on all fours.

A trembling wand hung from Mom's fingers, the tip glowing bright, and tears wet her face.

"I can't control myself." She blasted me again. *"Run."*

The daemon saved me from myself, yanking me up and tucking me under his arm. He ran as fast as he could, weaving through trees, putting as much space between Mom and me as possible. Distance helped. The farther we got from her, the less the compulsion laid on her compelled her to act.

Without her bones, we had no way to stop her. I could blast her apart, as I had Old Man Fang, but this was my *mom*.

I wasn't sure I was strong enough to end her, not after a lifetime of the director telling me I had been the one who killed her. I didn't want to make his lies my truth. Even though she was already dead, I didn't want to be the reason she winked out of existence for good.

A distant worry sprouted in my mind, a tickle in my brain as a certainty took root.

Whoever possessed her bones had kept them close. For decades. That explained why I couldn't contact Mom, why Meg couldn't find her either. She hadn't been on the other side of the veil. She had been trapped here, and I could only imagine one person who would have treated her so cruelly. The man I had suspected from the start.

The director.

But if he had her bones, and she had been summoned, that must mean...

...he was here.

The only person who knew his whereabouts was Parish, and

Parish wouldn't tell me even if I ripped out his heart and ate it in front of him. It was the principle of the thing. He hadn't survived being the director's right hand this long by giving away his boss's secrets.

A branch raked through my hair as the daemon hiked me higher on his shoulder, but the whoosh of debris flying past kept me from checking behind us. The pain radiating through my back told me I had taken a projectile to the left of my spine, but I had to suck it up and deal.

A mournful howl pierced the night, others raising up that voice, and hope surged through me.

The sound distracted Mom too, who searched for the source and forgot to attempt to murder me.

A massive wolf I recognized as Derry dashed out of the darkness and fell in step with the daemon. Four other wolves emerged, flanking us, herding us toward some distant point. Their yips and barks told me they were having a blast, which made me wonder if they thought Old Man Fang was on their heels and not Mom. Either way, I was grateful for the assist.

"Derry-wolf says this way," the daemon cut into my thoughts. "Old cemetery."

A crumbling stone marked the corner of a family cemetery that hadn't seen visitors in decades, based on the overgrowth. A long slab proclaimed it the Lacky family cemetery, not Old Man Fang's original resting place.

The daemon skidded past the markers, almost dropping me in the process. Using his momentum against him, I broke his hold and flipped over his arm. I landed on my feet, my knee screaming from impact, and freed up my hands for casting.

I didn't want to attack my mother, but I would if there was no other choice.

You can't value the dead above the living.

Twisting to glance over my shoulder, I groped for the edges of a wound I couldn't see. "Can you help?"

The daemon grumbled about scurvy, proving Colby failed to define it for him, then fell silent.

"Nothing there." He lifted my shirt and sniffed, which tickled. "Old scar. Smells weird. That it."

"That can't be good." I had plenty of scars, but none that had ever tickled his nose. I reassessed my knee while I was at it, and it took my weight without buckling. I was healing. Fast. But how? "Do you think the choker…?"

The daemon parted his lips to answer, but the wolves broke into warning snarls that deafened me.

On legs that fought against bending, Mom approached me, her battle with the compulsion evident.

"You need to end this," Mom murmured, her voice a thousand whispers. "I don't want to hurt you."

She didn't step a toe over the invisible line onto sanctified ground, for which I was grateful.

Of all the things I could have asked, that I wanted to say, I had to know. "Who did this to you?"

A pinprick of red marked her pupils and grew until her eyes had been devoured by crimson.

"He wants your father." Strain thinned her voice. "Don't let him win. Not again. Not this time."

"The director," I pressed for confirmation, but her focus blurred as she fought against herself.

No blame passed her lips, proving whoever summoned her had made sure she couldn't out them.

"Please, baby, end this." She hugged herself, trapping her wand under her arm. "My bones…"

"How?" I stepped forward, lulled by her moment of lucidity. "How do I give you peace?"

"Burn my bones and salt the earth where you find them."

"I…" I shored up my courage. "I will." But I had to locate them first. "Do you know where they are?"

"He buried pieces of me everywhere," she confessed. "I can't find myself, only my target."

Me.

"Why would the director do this?" I couldn't imagine his endgame. "Why the charade?"

"The director?" A deep line carved across her brow. "He—"

A shadow passed over the moon, and the wargs packed in close around me, all of them gazing skyward. I didn't have to look. I could feel in my bones who had come, and I began to fear he might struggle harder choosing the living over the dead than I did if his heartbroken awe was any indication.

"Howl." He landed before her, his wings quivering as if he couldn't believe it. "You're here."

"I was sent for our baby." She flung herself against his chest. "Please, help me."

"Come with me." He scooped her in his arms. "You always did love to fly."

A watery laugh escaped her that turned into an anguished cry of pain.

"I can't fight it much longer." She cupped his cheek in her palm. "End this."

"I would sooner the sun burn out than give you up again," he said, and I could tell we both believed him.

"I can't live like this." She bit her bottom lip. "*Exist* like this." She pleaded with him. "I'm not real."

"You're real enough for me." He held her tighter, like he would never let go. "I'll fix this, Howl, I swear it."

"My Saint." She tipped her chin for a kiss that forced me to turn my head. "You can't fix everything."

"I can try."

Without a backward glance, he launched into the sky, taking the immediate threat with him.

If it hurt, that they had been so lost in each other neither of their gazes had found me, I couldn't show it.

And it worried me, that flaring the grimoire alerted Dad in record time.

"This won't end well." I watched them until they were a speck on the horizon. "Not well at all."

"Your father has one of her finger bones." Asa must have shifted while I was busy tucking away my pain. "Perhaps he can bury it in land they owned and award her some control over her actions."

"She's been in limbo all this time." I basked in my shame at leaving her there. "He needs to let her go."

As always, Asa heard more than I said, and he drew me against his side. "This doesn't make you weak."

"I barely remember her. I'm not sure I *do* remember her. I shouldn't have locked up like that."

"She's your mother." Asa rested his chin on my head. "No one blames you for not wanting to hurt her."

"She's dead." I forced myself to say it. "I can't hurt her." I swallowed again. "She asked me to end it."

Whatever afterlife she believed awaited her, she had hoped I would help her reach it. An act of mercy. An act of love. Instead, I performed an act of cowardice. I allowed her to be taken by a man who would rather die than live without her.

"Let's circle back to the den." I wiped my face dry with my tee. "Maybe we missed something."

"Your father has a piece of her now," Asa reminded me. "He'll find the rest."

That was what I was afraid of.

"None of this makes sense." I balled my hands into fists. "Why involve her?"

Why involve *me*?

Selfish? Yes. Whiny? Also yes. But come on. Did karma really have no one else to pick on?

"She fought a compulsion to kill you, specifically." He sounded thoughtful. "That confirms Colby's *Game Over* theory. The murders weren't random."

"We need to take a closer look at our victims, dig up their connections to their specific summoner."

The best cyber sleuth in the business was on her way to us, but I figured I could give her a head start.

"Hey." I didn't waste time on pleasantries when I dialed Colby. "We need to be looking for a link between the summoners and their victims. They weren't random. They were targeted."

"I know."

"Oh." I should have known better than to think I was ahead of her, but I did have one confession left she couldn't know. "Well, we didn't figure out they were assassins until the last victim got away."

"Got away?" Colby click-clacked in the background. "No one has gotten away."

"I did."

"What do you mean *you* did?" Clay bellowed in my ear. "Who came after you?"

A child's first word is often a variation on *mother*.

Funny how I couldn't get out a single one of them.

"They sent her mother," Asa told Clay for me. "Saint collected her before anyone was hurt."

A fountain of profanity spewed from Clay's mouth, and I swore I could feel his spittle rain down on me.

"Mom couldn't name him, but the director is behind this. He must be." I yanked myself back from the edge. "I don't know if she meant the entire thing or just her part of it."

"We know he's out of the office." Asa lent his weight to my worry. "If he carried those bones with him, they would have offered him a bargaining chip if he ran into your father before he was ready to face him."

I'll trade my life for the bones of your wife, that I murdered and hid from you while I imprisoned you and raised your only child to be a psychopath.

The sad thing was, I could see the director believing that was insurance enough to save his hide.

He really had no idea who his son was or what Dad was capable of if he thought he would survive this.

"About that." Clay hemmed and hawed. "Colby and I have been working that angle since you guys left."

"You've been hunting the director." Asa pounced on the lead. "Have you found him?"

"He's still at the compound," Colby told us. "Rogue agents attacked him on the grounds."

"Parish was with him," Clay continued. "He scooped up the director and ran with him inside. The compound was locked down for twenty-four hours, and all traces of the attack were erased." He hesitated. "It must be bad, if they don't want anyone to know how bad it is."

The director might be my grandfather, but I couldn't find an ounce of pity for him in me.

"Travel provides him with a safer cover," Asa agreed, "one that might keep him in power a little longer."

"Wait." I heard my theory hissing like a popped balloon. "Then who…?"

"Did I mention we haven't sat on our hands the past few days?" Clay sounded proud enough to burst. "Colby is a verified member of the Mystic Realms Live Guild."

"I tracked down our suspects' emails, handles, and social media links." Her enthusiasm was contagious. "I can link the Amhersts to Ms. March and Lacky. There are six others we suspect are waiting on their turn to go active. Each more powerful than the last. I'm still cracking those identities."

"That's amazing." I pressed a hand against my chest. "*You're* amazing, smarty fuzz butt."

Six was so much better than the sixty members on the Amherst's original roster.

"It gets better," Clay rushed out. "Tell them the rest."

"The ringleader's handle is Advent."

"Any idea who he or she is?"

"Yeah." She drew out the word, giving me time to dread the reveal. "I chatted with him earlier."

"I'm sorry." I attempted to find my Zen, but it was MIA. "You *chatted* with him?"

"In the game. In a side chat." She huffed at me. "Relax."

Secret Agent Moth could fuss all she wanted. I would never *relax* over direct contact with a suspect.

"Anyway, he vetted me some, and I let him. I was even super helpful and sent him a link to my website."

"You have a website?"

A smile warmed her voice. "I do now."

"This is taking too long," Clay added his two cents, "and Rue won't understand half of it anyway."

"Thanks." I would have smacked him if I could reach him. "Your support and encouragement are truly limitless."

"The link to my website was malware," she explained patiently. "Malware is malicious software."

"Okay."

"When he clicked the infected link, he gave the malware permission to download onto his laptop."

"Okay."

"The malware was actually spyware, and it gave me access to his computer."

"Okay."

"He has multiple email accounts, which, most people do, you know?"

"I totally knew that."

"He had an account for gaming, under Advent Infinity. I made copies of correspondence that links him to the Amhersts, Ms. March, and Lacky." Her pause held an unexpected gravity. "His primary email, however, was for work. It took me longer to crack its encryption, but I've got it now." She blew out a slow exhale. "Advent? He's Jai Parish."

"The dragon?" I slotted those pieces into what we already knew, or tried to, but most didn't fit. "He's already the director's right hand. What does he have to gain? Control of the entire Bureau?"

"You say that like it's as disgusting as bathing in a tub full of slugs," Clay intoned, "but we're talking about the *Black Hat Bureau*."

"I know that." I dug my nails into my palms. "I don't need a refresher course on family history."

As the founder's granddaughter, and a victim of his constant scheming, I wore no blinders. I never had. I hadn't been afforded the luxury.

"That's the problem. You view it as the family business, but it's not. It's an organization that has taken on a life of its own. Your grandfather awarded himself the power to punish any member of any faction at his discretion. He chooses who lives, who dies, who serves."

The bitterness in those last two words speared me through the heart. "I'm aware."

"I don't think you are," he insisted. "People outside the organization don't care who runs it as long as it runs smoothly. They're willing to turn a blind eye to us creeping in the shadows, cleaning up their messes, making their worst villains go away. Dollface, I think you fall in that category. I think you're happy to be there. To pretend the director is the worst fate to befall us, but he's not. Trust me. The Bureau is a powerful tool, and in the wrong hands, it will become a weapon against anyone the new director decides to punish."

"The whole premise behind the Black Hats are we enforce justice."

"Whose justice?" he demanded of me. "Whose orders do we follow to the letter or else?"

"We stop dangerous predators. We protect the paranormal community from discovery. We might not be doing the job out of the goodness of our hearts, but we put in the work."

"I love you for your idealism," Asa entered the conversation, "but Clay is right that it matters who runs the bureau. As bad as it is, it can get worse. Things can *always* get worse."

"Parish isn't walking away from this. Even if I trusted the director to slap him on the wrist, and I don't, Dad won't give him the chance. He'll kill Parish for the insult to my mother." I focused on Clay. "We need to anticipate what comes next. *Who* comes next. After Parish. Do you have anyone on the inside who's in a position to snag the promotion?"

"No one in my pocket is that high in the organization, no."

As persona non grata in the Bureau, I had no strings to pull that wouldn't garrote me in the process.

Asa, who wasn't in the habit of making friends or forging alliances, didn't have anything to add either.

"One step at a time." Asa massaged between my shoulders. "The director will recover. He always does. He'll name a second. Things will go on as they have."

"If you believe that, then why push back? Why agree with Clay?"

"He thinks you can do a better job than Parish. Or the director." Clay made it sound obvious. "That's why."

"A dead bird in a cat's belly could do better," I argued. "That's not saying much."

"You care." Asa made it sound obvious. "That alone qualifies you."

"You want me chained behind a desk for the rest of my life?" I recoiled from the idea. "I'm not going to be the director, or the director's pet. I don't want that much power. I can't handle it. It would corrupt me, and people would die." Their endorsement terrified me. "I don't want it."

This much, Asa and I had in common. Ambitious families. Powerful fathers. And the weight of expectation that came along with it. As if either of us wanted to step into the roles we had rebelled against all our lives. As if either of us wanted to become the next director or the next high king. As if either of us owed our blood lines for anything, let alone for being born and forced into the role of heir.

Goddess bless, what a mess.

The world was safer with the Bureau in it, I believed that, but could I stand in Dad's path to preserve it?

Dad, who had spirited away my mother rather than work with me to release her.

Dad, who had stared a hole in my chest as if he could sense the nearness of the grimoire.

Dad, who was eager to fulfill his bargains and be done with a life he no longer wanted to live.

And Parish, that bastard, had handed Dad the perfect distraction to keep him off the director's back.

A black witch, such as my father, had no afterlife ahead of him. Mom, on the other hand, as a white witch, would join Meg. Unless the fuzzy area of gray magic they practiced together blurred those edges too much one way or another for them both.

How far would Dad go to spend one more day, week, month, year with Mom?

And how would I convince him to ever let her go?

14

"I've got him."

The tense conversation ground to a halt, and shame hit me that I had forgotten Colby was listening in.

"I've got him," she repeated, her voice squeaking as it rose. "I've triangulated his cell phone signal."

How we leapt from tracking Parish's computer to his cell flew over my head, but Colby was in her element.

"Where is he?" Clay whooped with glee. "Let's nail that bast—" he cleared his throat, "—bad man."

"I have his coordinates." Colby gave us all a second to pull up map apps. "Ready?"

We all grunted agreement, eager to punch in the numbers and find where the case took us next.

Before we finished, I could tell Asa and I weren't going to like the answer.

"He's here." I pinpointed our location on the map. "In Tupelo."

"About a quarter mile away." Clay narrowed it down. "He's moving in the opposite direction from you."

"He sicced Mom on me." I pivoted toward the signal. "Then he watched to see what would happen."

Either she killed me, I banished her, or...I delivered the director's own personal boogeyman to him.

"He was gambling on you being in contact with Saint." Asa worried one of his earrings. "You were the bait, and your mother was the trap. Saint won't rest until he's collected all her bones, and there's no telling where they're hidden."

"That narrows the scope," Clay agreed. "Parish now has a grid where your father will eventually strike."

"He must have taken Mom's bones from wherever the director was hiding them." I kept an eye on the directions Colby sent to lead me straight to Parish. "I wouldn't be surprised if the director locked them in a box under his bed."

To learn my parents, *both* my parents, might have been beneath my feet for all those years made the dark yearnings within me stir with a hunger for vengeance against my grandfather and the atrocities he had committed in the name of building his legacy.

A legacy that had ultimately rejected him, time and time again.

"We need a plan." Asa strode beside me. "We don't know if Parish is working alone."

"That might be why he liberally sprinkled so many teams in the surrounding area rather than let us do our thing. There are dozens of agents within a two-hour radius of you." Clay grunted. "That means he's got all the backup he needs."

"We find where he's holed up," I gritted out, "who he brought with him, and we wait for backup."

Our lives were tied, Colby's and mine, and I couldn't throw hers away because I didn't want perspective.

"You're going to wait for little ol' me?" Clay tittered in a falsetto. "Why, I'm positively flattered."

"We'll be there in ten." Colby updated us. "We'll meet you beside Bistro Americana."

"Mmm." Clay made a happy noise. "I wonder if they serve steak frites with béarnaise butter? Or mussels with caramelized fennel and leeks? Maybe an elegant smoked whitefish tartar with herb oil?"

"You're getting close." Colby spoke over Clay's ramblings. "I'll switch to texting for stealth."

The call ended, and I forced myself to breathe in and out.

We had directions. We had backup en route. We had our ringleader.

"It's all right to be angry," Asa said from beside me. "At Parish, the director." He hesitated. "At Saint."

"He didn't even look at me." I mashed my lips together, but the words kept coming, pried out by the fascination roiling through me. "Once he saw her, that was it. I ceased to exit. He only cared about her."

"I can't imagine what he must have felt, seeing her again. Or you, meeting her in that state."

"This isn't the first time he's chosen her over me." I hadn't realized that Dad's reappearance had sliced me that deeply, or that the wound had been festering since the night I first saw him. "He made a vow that would end his life after he avenged my mother. He decided there and then to make me an orphan. He didn't care that he was leaving a child behind. He only cared his wife was dead."

"Rue..."

"I wanted him to be my dad." I swallowed past a tight throat. "I wanted him to stay." I shook my head. "He doesn't care about me, Asa. He doesn't love me. Maybe one love is all a black witch can manage."

There was an argument to be made that Dad was half crazed from his time beneath the compound. That he wasn't of sound mind or body. But I reverted to the small child I had been when I last saw him, and I wanted him to pick me.

Me.

Twice now, he had chosen Mom instead, and that cut deep.

Enough to draw tears that threatened to blur my view of what lay ahead.

"Is there a point where we have so much sex that fascination stops making me a weepy mess?" I checked with Asa, who choked on air beside me. "Is there a magic number? Should we have been keeping count?"

"That's not how fascination works," he said, his voice strained. "I wish I could make this better for you."

"You've been making everything better for me since the day I met you."

"I thought you wanted to kill me then?"

"I wanted to punch your face in. Lucky for you, your good looks distracted me." I allowed myself a moment of levity. "Almost as much as your butt in those slacks is distracting me right now."

"It's the spandex," he confided. "It really sculps and lifts."

A snort blasted out of me, startling a nearby bird from its perch. "I can't believe you went there."

"Clay said that once, after the drycleaners mixed up our pants. He was able to pull mine on, but it was a stretch." Asa's lips hooked up to one side. "He went as far as to order a pair in his size, but he wore them to a food truck show one weekend and caught the reflection of his food baby and vowed to never wear them again."

"As many food babies as he's carried, I'm amazed he's not the father of hundreds of thousands."

We reached the meeting point but lingered outside rather than venturing into the restaurant.

"You're not your father," Asa said after a while of me staring down the road.

The impact of those words coming from Asa, who feared that most of all, forced me to face him.

"I love you enough to become something more terrible than I have ever been if I lose you."

"And you love Colby enough not to put her in the middle of what's between us."

"That doesn't mean I don't want to." I pressed my face into his chest and looped my arms around his waist. "I love her, so much, but you..." I tipped my head back. "I can understand why Dad did what he did in the moment. He didn't want to live in a world without Mom. There *was* no world without her."

"You won't make that choice." He breathed me in. "You would never take that decision from Colby."

"I want to believe you're right." I turned when gravel crunched behind us. "But it gets harder every time I see your slacks lift and sculp your butt to ever imagine my life without that view."

Laughter crinkled the corners of his eyes, and he captured my mouth in a kiss that tapped his newest piercing against my teeth. "I never should have told you that."

"Ugh." Clay pretended to talk into his phone to enable him to speak freely with Colby. "If we leave them alone too long, they're like ice cream left out in the sun. They turn into gooey puddles of pure sugar."

"I like gooey puddles of pure sugar," Colby said from within his pocket. "But yeah. They're gross."

"Totally." Clay wrinkled his nose as he walked up and stole a hug from me. "So gross."

Again those stupid tears threatened to prick my eyes, and I found myself holding on to Clay for too long.

"It's all right, Dollface." He kissed the top of my head. "You can cry all you want. It's good for you."

"I hate crying." I shoved away from him. "I hate feelings."

"Feelings hate you too." He ruffled my hair like a big brother. "That's why they've ganged up on you."

"I want to punch them all in their touchy-feely faces."

"I know you do." He tweaked my chin. "You know what will make you feel better?"

Like a lady, I sniffed and wiped tears and snot on my shirt. "Punching someone else in the face?"

"That's my girl." A throat cleared in the vicinity of his pocket. "My second-best girl, that is."

This again? Really? I was starting to develop a complex. "Et tu, Clay?"

First the daemon demoted me, then my dad—or first my dad?—ditched me, and now Clay dumped me.

"You've been neglecting me lately." He lifted a shoulder. "Colby was there for me in my time of need."

"I held his hand," she confirmed, "when they announced the winner of *The Great British Bake Off*."

A rustle of fabric drew my attention to Clay's pocket where Colby's antennae stuck up on high alert.

"He's on the move." Colby peeked out to point the way. "We can catch him at the intersection."

"I don't suppose you can tell if he's got backup with him?"

"No." Her frustration was evident. "There are no cameras in the area, so my vision is limited."

Of course, my little hacker moth would have tried before it occurred to me to ask. "That's okay."

"We'll do it the old-fashioned way," Clay agreed. "You guys go down two blocks then cut north. Colby and I will head northeast. Eyes and ears open, people."

They peeled off and began their recon from a safer distance while Asa and I waded into the thick of it by trailing Parish directly. We could have tracked him by the thick cloud of smoke curling over his shoulder as he pinched a cigarette between his lips. The scent that followed him wasn't chemically treated tobacco but brimstone and death.

We didn't have much to hide behind, but that worked for us as much as against us. We kept a clear line of sight on Parish, who was on his phone, distracted and alone, puffing away, while he strolled through a town where he had just kicked a hornet's nest then stomped it flat.

"He's baiting us." I hung back. "There's no way he's this oblivious."

Parish had a reputation, but that wouldn't protect him if he kept his head down while enemies were circling him. And if he had been in that clearing, then he knew we were enemies. There was nothing else we could be after what he did to my mother.

A quick text to Clay told them to hang back while we watched for his next move.

"I can smell you," Parish said, putting away his phone and his pretense. "You might as well come out."

That sounded like a terrible idea, so we held our ground, waiting to see if he was bluffing.

"Show some spine." He removed his jacket, let it hit the road, then began rolling up his sleeves. "Do you really want to die cowering?"

Only Asa's grip on my upper arm kept me from launching myself at Parish and clawing off his face.

"I'm old," Clay called, shrugging out of his suit jacket. "Insults won't make me move any faster."

His jacket, and the moth within, he draped over a branch, giving Colby cover to escape. As Parish had, he rolled his sleeves up over his forearms.

"You're eternal," Parish countered. "Age means even less to you than it does to my kind."

"I bet you miss the old days when you could set fire to any old village you wanted, steal the maidens, and eat the humans."

"You have no idea." Parish thrust his hands into his pockets, the picture of calm. "Life was simpler then."

"Food tastes better than ever, plus you can pay people to cook for you, so you'll have to forgive me if I disagree."

A faint tingle in the back of my mind confirmed my familiar was nearby, and she was working magic.

"Where are the others?" Parish glanced up and down the street. "You're never alone."

"We're all alone, in the end."

As the lament settled into the space between them, Clay broke into a run, pumping his arms, aiming for Parish.

Their bone-jarring impact made my heart squeeze. Before Parish landed his counterstrike, light exploded from the trees. A hair-thin bubble of iridescence expanded to encapsulate them within a shimmery ward that would protect the innocent from their brawl.

Good call, smarty fuzz butt.

Drawing in a full breath, as if readying himself to spew fire, Parish instead burst into his dragon.

Brilliant red and gold scales glittered across his massive body, and his wings arched high overhead. Horns ringed the crown of his skull, and spikes lined his tail. He watched Clay through narrowed yellow eyes, almost luminescent in the streetlights, and his voice rolled like thunder across the pavement.

"You would dare?" Another gulp of air, and Parish spat fire at Clay. "Burn, golem."

Had Asa not wrapped me in a bear hug from behind, locking me in place, I would have run straight to Clay. As it was, I gave serious thought to stomping Asa's foot or jolting him with magic to break free.

"Fire won't harm him," Asa reminded me. "He can survive anything as long as his *shem* remains intact."

Survive it? Yeah. But it would *hurt*.

The torrent of flames lasted only so long as Parish had breath, and then he was left panting for air.

Meanwhile, Clay was…

"If you wanted to see me naked—" Clay dusted ash off his chest, "—all you had to do was ask." He touched his scalp. "Damn it, I liked that wig." He folded his arms across his chest. "It made me look taller."

"He's buying us time." I squirmed in Asa's grip. I couldn't help it. "We have to help him."

"That's not what he's doing." Asa released me and yanked me to my feet as he stood. "Look."

The sky above us roiled with churning clouds and streaks of lightning. Wind picked up, buffeting Parish's wings until he snapped them shut to avoid being blown backward. His roar was deafening as he reared onto his hind legs, swiping at the barrier until his claws left visible marks.

Enormous wings that stank of rot and copper exploded into view as Colby's freshman attempt at solo warding failed, and the creature at their center folded them in tight then dove straight for the dragon's open maw.

"That's my dad." I ran toward them. "Good goddess, what is he doing?"

Forget Clay and the daemon's roughhousing back home. This was a true clash of titans.

And no magic protected the citizens caught out in town from having front row seats.

The black magic spell Dad used to conjure his wings expanded until his size rivaled the dragon beneath him. As a piercing shriek rent the night, I conceded he resembled a giant bird of prey more than a man.

Wicked talons spread wide, he dove and sank them into Parish, ripping open his side.

An indrawn breath tore my focus from the battle as I sought the source behind us.

"Look, Momma, look." A small boy pointed at the brawl. "Are they filming a movie?"

"I don't..." Her voice trailed off as she got an eyeful of the scene unfolding. "Come on, Wren."

"Don't let them leave." I shoved Asa toward them. "Round up anyone else who saw and contain them."

Refusing to budge from his spot by my side, he speared me with his penetrating gaze. "What are you going to do?"

"First, I'm going to help Colby raise her ward again. Then I'm going to cast an illusion over the block to prevent any more witnesses. After that I...have no idea."

"Solid plan." He kissed me quickly. "Be safe."

"You too."

The familiar connection thrummed between Colby and me, warm and bright, and I set out at a jog around the perimeter, anchoring the spell to buildings, to lampposts, to curbs. I drew on the threads binding us to weave a powerful ward shrouded with a complex illusion that would have pushed me even at my black witch best.

"Rue."

Heart clenching, I paused to scan for the owner of that tiny voice. "What are you doing?"

"Helping you." Colby smacked into my shoulder and wrapped her arms around my neck. "We're stronger together." She buried her face against me. "I might also be a tiny bit scared. I didn't realize dragons were *that* big. The eggs in Mystic Realms can't be to scale. Do you think your dad will be okay?"

Shoving worries for Dad aside, I focused on her. "You need to hide. Dad can't know about you."

A pang shot through me, and I flinched away from confirmation I didn't trust him, no matter how much I might want to, not with her.

Colby, it seemed, was the ultimate test of faith with me, and he didn't make the cut.

"Hairbow mode activate." She shrank to her smallest self. "Hair or bra?"

"Bra," I decided. "Hold on to the strap, like old times."

Fewer and fewer of my bras had tiny Velcro patches sewn onto the upper straps these days. A wardrobe staple there in the beginning, I had phased them out over time. The idea had been whenever Colby was overwhelmed, she could climb in my shirt and hold on to the loop side with the delicate claws on her feet. Nowadays, I was busier spelling the various shirt and jacket pockets in Clay's wardrobe to suit her.

"Avoid the chain and the pendant if you can," I warned her. "Retreat into the cup if necessary."

"Eww." She wriggled against me. "I'll take my chances with the strap."

Once she was secure, I resumed my careful prowl around the outskirts, keeping a wary eye on the combatants.

The smell of blood got my adrenaline pumping, and my heart was a drum within my chest. I could all but taste how that dragon heart would flavor my tongue with iron and salt. And power. So much power.

"Rue?" Colby rested her head against my chest. "Are you okay?"

"No." I tried very hard not to lie to her. "But I will be."

"Will Clay be all right?"

"Not much can hurt Clay." I kept going, kept weaving my spell. "Maybe avert your eyes, though. The dragon burnt off his clothes."

"Oh no." A faint vibration from a laugh she tried to swallow hit me. "His poor wig."

"This case has been brutal on his hairdrobe for sure."

With us combining our focus, we managed to finish setting anchors without ending up charbroiled from the effort. Then came the fun part, summoning enough power between us to raise the barrier without falling to old habits. I could have taken a bite out of a heart and done it without breaking a sweat, but I would rather let the humans watch the monster brawl than cave in now.

There comes a point where you must stop looking back on the person you were and judging the person you are by their standards. You can't be two people at once. You're either New You or Old You. There is no in between.

Me? I had a crick in my neck from looking over my shoulder.

Finally, I was ready to...maybe not forgive...but cut my younger self a break for doing whatever it took to survive.

"This is going to be rough." I found us a sheltered position where I could keep an eye on Dad and Parish. "We've never pulled this much magic."

"We can do it." Her wings twitched with determination. "We got this."

Heart in my throat, I began the spell under my breath and let everything else slide out of focus until the churning of power within me spilled from my fingertips and burned bright on the tip of my tongue. The words grew sharper, gruffer, and the illusion snapped into position with an audible click that caused Dad and Parish to pause and reassess.

Dad understood first, but he didn't seem to care one whit.

Parish, on the other hand, went ballistic. Biting, snapping, clawing. He attacked the ward, desperate to escape my father, but there was nowhere for him to run.

When Parish turned his back on Dad, Dad shot a bolt of blue-black lightning into his spine. Parish jolted from the shock, twitching and flailing, hitting the ground with an impact that rumbled the streets. I expected Dad to finish him, but he only hovered and watched as Clay grabbed the dragon by the tail and yanked him away from the barrier. As if they had coordinated it, Dad touched down beside Clay, who kept his grip on Parish, and he dismissed his whirling shadows.

Darkness pulsed in the air around Dad as he prowled toward Parish's great head and fisted one of his horns.

"You will tell me where to find the rest of her bones, or I will tear off your scales, one by one. I will cauterize the wounds to prevent regrowth, and you will be left defenseless against the attacks of your kind. I will shred your wings to ribbons so that you can't outfly your challengers. I will sand your horns and spikes smooth and dull. And then I will lock you in a silver cage and ship you to your aunt and uncle, and let them decide the punishment for your crimes against your ilk."

For that threat to carry any weight, Parish must have been turned over to Black Hat by his relatives.

And here Dad was, offering to return him to their tender embrace gift-wrapped for their pleasure.

"I would rather an ice lizard castrate me than help you."

"If you're interested in castration," Clay drawled. "I have a pamphlet around here somewhere."

Before Parish got a word in edgewise, Dad struck him with a spear of black magic.

"The great Hiram Nádasdy, brought to his knees over a white witch yet again." Parish laughed, a wet and hacking noise. "You were the greatest of us all, and you have sunk the lowest." He whipped his tail, but Clay caught and subdued it. "When I heard you had escaped, I knew the right bait to lure you out. All I had to do was get the director out of his own way long enough for me to do what needed to be done."

"You expect us to believe you're loyal to the director?" Clay took the words right out of my mouth. "You're admitting that you're responsible, directly or indirectly, for the attack that sent him to his own infirmary."

"He admires strength and cunning."

"You know what he doesn't admire?" Clay chuckled, low and cold. "Independent thinkers." He jerked his head toward my dad. "Ask him." He scanned the night. "Or his daughter."

"They are traitors to the Bureau and to the Nádasdy legacy. It's no coincidence rogue black witches have banded together after the director's granddaughter resurfaced. Or that her father escaped after decades of confinement in secrecy. Elspeth intends to claim her birthright. She wants to bring the director to his knees and destroy the Black Hat Bureau and all it stands for."

Vertigo swept through me at hearing them discuss me as the Nádasdy heir so baldly.

No one knew that. *No one.* Yet the director had told Parish. Or had Parish figured it out for himself?

Either way, he had me confused with someone else. Say, my father. Those were his goals, not mine.

And Parish, tired of living under the Sword of Damocles since Dad escaped the compound, had gambled that recapturing Dad would redeem him in the director's eyes. He didn't want to be the next Mikkelsen, a victim to my grandfather's rage, but he didn't hide himself within his web of misdirection well enough. The gamers were all cannon fodder meant to take the fall if his plan failed to bear fruit, but he miscalculated the greater danger. His preemptive strike missed the target. By a mile. Or fifty.

And now, fresh grief tracking down his cheeks, Dad would kill him for it.

"You have no idea what my daughter's ambitions are, or what she's capable of," Dad growled the threat. "She's better than us, better than the Bureau. She doesn't want your seat at the table. She doesn't want any of this. She craves the same things I once did. A life. A family. Her freedom." He blasted Parish again. "People like you don't understand." *Again.* "We were forced to live another man's dreams." *Again.* "And when we dared to dream our own, he destroyed them."

"He can't take much more," Clay warned him. "Lay off unless you want barbeque for dinner."

"He would rather die than help me." Dad sounded past caring. "And I won't let him live."

The next bolt of magic struck, and it didn't stop until Parish's twitching body hit the pavement and the stink of charred flesh clogged my nose. A moment later, Parish quit moving, and the street fell silent.

Following protocol to the letter, Dad touched the dragon with the tip of his wand, and its hulking corpse disintegrated into ash the wind scattered across the pavement. Done with that, he rested his palm against the barrier, and it collapsed around him as if it were nothing.

"I have to go."

Dad cast his voice to where I hunkered down with Colby, and I stepped from my hiding place.

He pressed a piece of paper into Clay's hand, met my eyes, and rolled his shoulders.

Magic burst from either side of his spine, exploded into those same giant wings, and he flew away.

When Clay didn't join us, I figured he was avoiding how he was on Team Dad in the fight while the rest of us were relegated to onlookers. That, or he was in mourning for his wig. Either way, I went to check on him. I wanted my team secure before I attended the humans Asa had gathered to contain the incident.

On the way, I scooped up the jacket Parish had discarded and pocketed his phone as evidence.

"Oh no." I located Clay frozen near the spot where he left his jacket. "Hold on, Clay, I've got you."

Circling around, I expected damage to his *shem*, but the design remained whole and untouched on his forehead. As I stood there, studying him, he broke out in shivers, and then he began to cough.

"Hey." His voice came out graveled and low. "What are you doing here?"

"The fight's over," I told him slowly, giving him a second to catch his breath. "I came to check on you."

"What fight?"

"Are you okay?" I ducked down to search his face. "I checked your *shem*, but…"

A light breeze swirled hair into my eyes and ash into my lungs.

From the horror spreading across Clay's face, it must have tickled him too.

"Where are my clothes?" He cupped the space between his thighs then crossed his legs. "What the hell?"

That about summed it up from my point of view too.

15

"What's the last thing you remember?" I helped Clay knot his suit jacket like an apron to cover his front. His anatomy was his business. No one else's. Sadly, his backside was a view we all had to endure. "Let's start there."

The note Dad had pressed into his hand resided in my pocket, but I hadn't worked up the nerve to read it. Clay didn't know who it was meant for, and if it wasn't intended for me, I wasn't sure I could deal with Dad passing me over again.

"We were on our way here..." He scratched his scalp and earned ashy fingertips. "Where's my hair?"

"The dragon got your wig too." I took his hand and led him to an out-of-the-way space. I helped him sit on a carpet of pine needles beneath the trees and lean against a trunk. "It was Parish."

"Why was Parish here?" He shifted to get comfortable. "Fucking pine needles."

"You're having a short-term memory problem." I touched his shoulder. "Just stay put, okay?"

"I'm not going out there naked. The world isn't ready for that."

"I'll stay with him," Colby volunteered. "I don't want him to forget again and wander off."

"Good call." I helped her out of my shirt then set her on his shoulder. "I'll be back soon."

Without a handy pocket to hide in, Colby was exposed. But, I rationalized, she could fly up into the trees if she required cover. Plus, naked Clay would prove a distraction if he was discovered before I got back to him. That would give her time to escape.

"Do me a favor." I handed her the note. "Does this have any bearing on our present circumstances?"

Chicken I might be, but idiot I was not. I couldn't afford to ignore what might prove to be a lifesaving tip, even if I wanted to believe ignorance was bliss for a while longer.

"No," she said softly and passed it back. "You can read it later."

"It's for me?" I bit my tongue, but it was too late. She was already nodding. "Okay." I forced a smile. "Later then."

After a quick sweep of the area, both to ensure Clay and Colby were secure and to escape her pity, I went in search of Asa.

Cleanup on this scale required professionals, but I couldn't help spinning out possible scenarios.

Earthquakes got a bad rap in monster-infested cities, but it wasn't a popular excuse in Mississippi. Hurricane would have worked better, but those didn't appear out of thin air. Tornado?

With the options available to me, that sounded the most believable.

An EF5 was nicknamed the Finger of God for a reason. Damage from those storms was catastrophic.

"Rue." Asa flagged me down. "Over here."

After jogging across the street, I smacked into his chest, breathless. It was the exercise. Not the urge to sob on his shoulder about my daddy issues. He gathered me against him and kissed my forehead as if he sensed the wild spin of my thoughts. Too soon, he released me, and we were forced back to the task at hand.

He had corralled nineteen people in a sub shop and offered to pay for their food if they waited out some vague emergency important enough for the FBI to be on scene. That had done the trick, but now I had a lot of memories to wipe and not much time to do it.

Small events gave you a larger window to act. Big events dug in and seized hold of the mind, rooting the memory. If I screwed this up, these people were at risk of being tornado victims on the nightly news.

"I can erase this event," I confided in Asa, "and I can suggest an excuse, but I can't create a true memory."

Better that they lost an hour of time than their lives. The showdown outside had disastrous potential if even one person filmed Dad or Parish in their other forms and uploaded it to their social media sites. I didn't have any mind-altering tea for them to drink, which meant I had to reach into their brains and jiggle the wires myself.

"I called the cleaners after I rounded up everyone," he assured me. "They'll handle the fine-tuning."

"Good." I wanted to shut my eyes and sleep for a week. "That's the best news I've heard all night."

As I approached the first table, I noticed a kid eating dino nuggets and inspiration struck.

"Can I have everyone's attention, please?"

Thankfully, they were eager for an update. Especially after noticing the blood and dust on me.

Once I held their entire focus, down to the last child, I yanked hard on Colby and summoned a light mist from my wand that spread through the restaurant. As the patrons inhaled, the spell latched on, and *click* went their brains. They switched off, leaving me front and center before a roomful of zombielike stares.

"A monster movie was being filmed downtown tonight. What you saw were animatronic creatures doing battle for the final showdown. The buildings will be repaired by the production company in a timely manner." I smiled, and, as one, they smiled back. "Everything is okay. Every*one* is okay. We need your cooperation for a bit longer, and then we'll let you all go home."

The room nodded in sync then fell into staring at me again, their empty eyes following my every move as I met Asa at the door.

"Clay helped Dad fight off Parish," I told him quietly, "but he doesn't remember any of it."

"That's not like Clay." Asa scanned the street behind me. "His mind is like a vault."

"Exactly." I hated to think it, let alone say it. "But there's a key."

The director.

He gave Clay orders, and Clay always followed them to the letter. He had no choice.

But, as much as I would love to pin this on him, he wasn't here. So where did that leave us?

Tires squealing drew us out on the sidewalk as three vans skidded into the parking spaces in front of the restaurant. Men and women dressed in biohazard suits spilled onto the street, broke into teams, and set about earning the title of *cleaner*. Each one carried a kit resembling a tacklebox, and one of them hefted a case of the supernatural equivalent of bear spray with a yellow sticker reading EXPERIMENTAL.

Kudos to them for trusting an R&D project to save them from a rampaging dragon.

"Thank the goddess. I really didn't want to be responsible for scrambling this many people's brains."

These folks stood a much better chance of making a full recovery with pros on the job.

"I hoped the cleaners would arrive in time for me to join you, but I didn't trust the humans to stay put."

Put more than two people together, mix in an ounce of excitement, and you became an instant cat herder.

"You were right to keep watch over them. It's not their fault Parish earned a smackdown, or that Dad was too enraged to see straight. This is an incident with a capital *I*. They exposed themselves to humans in a populated area with no attempt to deescalate the situation."

As far as I could tell, Dad didn't care who got hurt so long as he got answers from Parish. I had to hand it to him. One sure-fire way to dethrone the director and abolish Black Hat was revealing the existence of the supernatural community. And if the cleaners missed one speck of evidence tonight during their wipe down, that was exactly what he had done.

"Let's greet them." He rested his hand at the small of my back and guided me. "Then we can go."

"I need to make a statement." And yet, I allowed myself to be led. "This is going to get…sticky."

"The cleaners will have their hands busy with the humans," he reasoned. "They can find you later."

"After I've had time to think up a good story?"

"Precisely."

With the director wounded, and his second-in-command dead, the Bureau was rudderless.

We had to do one of two things: Get the director back on his feet or elect our own interim director.

The latter was laughable, really. Who could we trust? No one.

Anyone who snatched leadership out of the jaws of this turmoil wasn't looking to save the Bureau, or its agents. More than likely, they would run Black Hat into the ground faster than you can say *chupacabra*. I doubted anyone left would make that power grab except as an escape route.

With the title came the power to abolish the Bureau, to release the agents from their service, to free the prisoners in the belly of the compound.

Agents, pardoned from their duties, would fall into old habits and wreak havoc.

Prisoners, half-starved and brutalized, would devour entire towns to sate their hungers.

The world would descend into bloody chaos, and humans would never trust the night again.

Asa handled the cleaners when I failed to rise above my churning thoughts, but I came alert in time to show him where I parked Clay and Colby.

"Ready to go?" I offered Clay a hand. "We'll bring the SUV around so you don't have to flash anyone."

"They should be so lucky." He let me help him up with a grunt. "This butt is a work of art."

His creator had been a master sculptor, so there was no arguing the point, but I didn't let that stop me.

"I'm prime beef," he continued, sounding more like himself. "Grade A."

Leaning around him, I took in the crosshatch pattern in his skin from sitting on the pine needles for so long. "You've got the grill marks for sure."

We chose another hotel, unrelated to our cases, and booked a double queen to share. It was the best option they had, and none of us minded the closeness after the insanity of a night that somehow felt longer than the day of the challenge. Clay still had no memory past leaving his hotel, and Colby was disturbed by how normal he seemed during their trip.

When acting on orders, Clay was himself before, during, and after. That was the most unsettling part of his curse of servitude. He had no choice in what he did, or sometimes said, and memory of those events were at the discretion of his master.

All that meant I had seen this before, and it shook me to see it again with fresh eyes.

Blame the tiny shoot of conscience blossoming in my mind, or the rush of *feelings* Asa had inspired, but I had forgotten how misery, shame, and fear swirled across his face in a smear of uncertainty when he woke with no recollection of his actions.

On the balcony, forearms braced on the railing, I stared out at the scenic recycling center parking lot across the street and turned my options over and over and over in my head.

The director would be out for blood after what Parish did to him. He would want to make an example out of him. But Parish was off the table.

So...did I let Dad take the fall?

Or did I accept the blame?

We had cost the director a prime opportunity to string up one of his top people to quell the rising rebellion, and he would expect one of us to pay for it out of our hides.

Already, the urge to run from my problems—*again*—twitched in my calves.

The choice was easy last time. Now? Not so much.

There was more than Colby to consider. I had Asa, Clay, and my whole life in Samford.

Selfish as it made me, I didn't want to give up any of that. I had gotten greedy, and I wanted it all.

Hours.

I had hours to find a solution.

Hours until my grasp on Samford slipped as I tumbled into free fall.

"Mind if I join you?" Clay didn't wait for permission before shoving in next to me. "I know how he did it."

"How who did what?" I had so much spinning in my head, I was out of room for more. "Parish?"

"Your dad." He let me come to terms with that. "I was given orders long ago to obey Hiram."

"The director never rescinded them because Dad was, as far as anyone knew, dead."

Either the director never intended for Dad to step foot out of his cell again, or he couldn't retract it.

And Dad must have known it, if he singled Clay out sometime prior to his run-in with Parish to ensure he had backup he could trust with his secret.

"That's what I'm thinking."

A flutter behind my breastbone tempted me with hope. "Does that mean...?"

"No." He leaned more heavily into me. "He can't release me from service."

"This was more like the director adding users to his Netflix account than handing out his password," Colby explained as she joined us.

"That actually made sense." I shot Colby a grin. "I'm getting better at tech speak."

Head down, she got real quiet, real fast.

"You pre dumbed it down for me, didn't you?"

"Maybe." She sandwiched two fuzzy hands together. "A tiny bit."

The flare of amusement I felt for her shenanigans grew cold in the face of reality. "What should I do?"

Clay knew me well enough to know what I was asking him.

"You should visit the director at the compound, give your report in person, and assess his condition." Clay's jaw bulged as he ground his teeth. "That might earn you, and Samford, leniency."

Admit Dad killed Parish or confess I did. Neither were great options.

With cleaners swarming the place, I wasn't sure I could take the blame even if I wanted to when their findings might thwart any attempt I made to shield Dad from exposure to the masses.

"He's not sentimental." I considered his proposal. "He'll want a detailed rundown of events."

"He won't kill you," Asa said quietly, joining our huddle. "As long as your father is alive, the director needs leverage to bring him to heel, and your mother's bones are lost." He stared out at the night. "He could cage you, Rue. Bait to lure Hiram right where he wants him. If you walk into the compound, you might not walk out again."

"Samford is safer with me in a cage," I confessed, throat tight. "The girls would be too."

"There's another option," Colby said softly. "I don't know if you'll go for it."

"I'm open to suggestions." I leaned back. "What's on your mind?"

"What if we join your dad's resistance?" She twitched her antennae. "He said no before, but now…"

"The director can't afford not to punish someone." Asa knew it as well as I did. "He won't out your father except as a last resort."

To admit his son, who had challenged his authority before, was not only alive but an active participant in this latest resistance would torpedo his reputation. Add to that my disappearance for ten years then my triumphant return, minus the public spectacle, and agents would decide he was growing weak.

And that was before news of his attack leaked, which it would, and Parish's death hit the grapevine.

"If I run again, he goes after Samford." I shut my eyes. "I can't have that on my conscience."

"What if we put protections in place?" Clay rubbed his naked scalp. "We could hire mercenaries."

"I'm sorry, but what?" I whipped my head toward him. *"Mercenaries?"*

"You can't trust mercenaries," Colby informed us. "They'll always work for the highest bidder."

"I agree." That it was game-based logic didn't change it was real-world applicable. "No mercenaries."

"I have an alternative." Asa's head fell back. "Father gifted me a centuria for my thirteenth birthday."

"Command of a centuria?" Clay watched him. "Or slaves?"

"Slaves." Asa let me see what the admission cost him in front of Clay. "Families seeking his favor tithed him their firstborn child on the day I was born. Those children were trained as legionaries from my birth to be loyal to me. They were meant to be the core of my royal guards when I ascended to the throne of the high king."

"It sounds rather past tense." That was the only way I could frame it. "What happened to them?"

"I tried to free them, but they refused to leave my service."

"Brainwashed." The metal railing crumpled in Clay's fist. "And there's no saving them. Not when they were molded as children. Not for that kind of life. I doubt they realize they're not soldiers, they're servants."

I too had been forged young, but Clay had taken me in hand and taught me to think for myself. The least we could do was put the same tools in theirs and offer them a chance at carving their own futures.

"Where are they now?" I did my best to absorb this latest turn. "What do they do?"

"They provide security for my estate in Hael." His chin dipped toward his chest. "It keeps them safe and gives them a purpose." His voice went soft. "It's a waste of their lives, their talents, but I can't make them see it no matter how hard I try to convince them otherwise. They were trained for this, raised for this. They don't know anything else, and they refuse to learn another way."

Elite fighters left to babysit an empty estate. I bet they were bored out of their skulls.

"Can we trust them?" I wasn't in a position to turn down help. "How loyal is loyal?"

"They're blood sworn to me." His lips twisted in a grimace. "They obey only me."

"How certain are you of that?" Clay rubbed a hand down his face. "We have to tread carefully here."

"Father ordered three officers to slit their own throats." He swallowed. "They did it without hesitation."

"That means they answer to him too," I pointed out. "That makes them too dangerous to use."

"That was before the transference ceremony," he explained. "He wanted a spectacle, so he created one. He issued the same command after the centuria was bound to me, and they didn't so much as twitch."

"How sure are you that wasn't more theater?" Clay wondered. "He could have staged it ahead of time."

Y'nai might be Stavros's preferred spies when it came to Asa, but a centuria his son believed to be within his control was even better for reporting his activities back to his father.

"Grandmother visited me that night. She brought a shawl her mother knitted for her, one that forces the wearer to speak truth." A faint smile made a brief appearance. "She interrogated them, and after she was satisfied they were earnest, she cast her own binding over them. Any who harm me will die by their own hand." He cut me a glance from under his lashes. "We can trust them. She made sure of that."

"Your grandmother sounds amazing."

"The shawl disintegrated after that." His grief over its loss twisted his features. "Her one heirloom from her mother, and she spent its magic protecting me."

"I'll say it again." I took his hand. "Your grandmother sounds amazing."

"She is." He allowed himself a smile. "She's going to love you."

For my sake, I hoped so. I didn't want to get on her bad side. That much was certain.

"Thank you." I squeezed his fingers. "I can imagine how much you hate leaning on that connection."

Maybe life in Samford would agree with the centuria, as it had with me and Aedan, and they would flourish.

"For you," he said, his jaw tight, "I'm willing to renew those old ties."

A persistent buzz from Clay's phone sucked the air from my lungs, aware any moment I might lose my choice and be forced in one direction or another.

"Kerr." He leaned against the railing. "That sounds like a *you* problem, Marty."

The name alone had me rolling my eyes, despite the grim circumstances.

"He needs orders," Asa told me, eavesdropping on their conversation. "No one can get in touch with Parish."

"Orders for what?"

"There's still a case to solve, as far as they know."

"Right." I massaged an ache in the center of my forehead. "I knew that."

The ringleader was down, but there were still others waiting on their turn for otherworldly revenge.

"You have bigger things on your mind." He kissed the spot I was quickly rubbing raw. "But the summoning ring must be stopped, with or without us."

"Give me the phone." I reached for it then girded my loins. "Marty, you're in Natchez, right?"

"Who the fuck put you on the phone? Pass me back to Kerr."

"Apprehend Lucy March. She's a summoner. Likely a black witch. Contain her, and you contain Frankie. Lean on her to get the location of Frankie's bones. Burn them, mix the ashes with her grave dirt, and salt the earth. Got it?" I recalled our eerie accommodations. "Find out what happened to her guests while you're at it."

They hadn't been on Parish's list, but *something* happened to them. A trial run for Frankie, maybe?

"You're out of your godsdamned mind if you think I'm taking orders from you."

"Bernard Lacky is on the run. Find him. He's responsible for Old Man Fang."

"Are you deaf?" Marty laughed, a bright choking noise. "I ain't listening to you, witch bitch."

"Parish is dead." I wasn't sure I made the decision to tell him so much as it fell out of my mouth. "The director will be looking to promote. You caught his attention with the last case, right? The one in Charleston? You rounding up this summoning ring will make you look good. Maybe good enough to step into Parish's shoes."

For once, Marty kept his mouth shut. I imagined the gerbil in the wheel of his brain waking from a long nap.

"Okay." He thought about it. "Give me the others, and I'll take this case off your hands."

"Thanks." I forced my jaw to unlock and fed him Colby's research. "That's all I've got."

The call ended, and the mental picture of Marty dancing a jig popped into my head.

"You lied." Clay clucked his tongue. "The director probably doesn't even remember his name."

"Marty horning in on all the other individual investigations will give us a breather." I even threw him the waitlist of summoners who hadn't gone active yet. "He won't tell a soul Parish is dead, but he will tell everyone that he's acting on Parish's behalf and that if they take issue with it, they can contact Parish. Except they can't, because Parish is dead. That sticks Marty in an endless loop of authority."

"You didn't give up the Amhersts." Clay pried his fingers off the railing. "You going to recruit them?"

Hearing him put my plans into words, I couldn't control my flinch.

"They're killers, but they're also kids." I forced myself to shrug. "And we left our stuff there."

"You're such a softie." Clay shook his head. "We left you under that hot Alabama sun for too long."

"Yeah, yeah, yeah."

As much as I wanted to ask Clay to swing by the mausoleum to pick up the Boos' collection while I slept, I couldn't trust him. Not while Dad, who collected dark artifacts too, could command him to steal them. With more battles ahead, Dad would use any and all resources at his disposal. Including my friend.

Already, I was deciding how to use the hoard to finally identify the Boo Brothers' mysterious benefactor. I fully expected the trail to lead straight to Black Hat. To a black witch, most likely. One of our rogues.

Thank the goddess Parish hadn't won, or else the director would have a fresh armory instead of me.

For now, all I could do was text Marita, beg for an extension, and promise to pick up the goods at dusk.

That done, I shoved past the guys, picked the closest bed, and flopped down face-first.

16

Morning came early. The only reason I didn't threaten to throat punch the sun was the warm dae curled around me. I was under the cover, and he was on top of them. That confused me until I heard the flutter of sleeping moth wings and recalled that we were all sharing a room.

"Stop wiggling," Asa growled behind me, his voice heavy with sleep...and desire.

"Make me," I whispered back, grinding against him playfully.

A pillow smacked me in the face, and I spluttered, swatting it aside as another struck me.

"Look who's awake." Clay rested on his mattress, propped up on one elbow. "Perv One and Perv Two."

"And you thought violence was the answer?"

"With you two?" He pretended to consider it. "Yes."

"Any word on Marty's progress?"

"Ms. March has been detained for questioning. She doesn't have much magic, but she's stubborn as a mule. They're going to truth spell her if she doesn't cooperate soon, and that won't end well for her."

A truth spell was a last resort with suspects who had no value beyond the information they carried. The process wasn't a spell, per se, but it did involve a specific type of fae magic that ripped chunks of information out of a person's head then rendered them comatose.

Pointless, really, given the nature of the case. Seize the electronics, and you tied the case up with a bow.

Not my circus, not my monkeys.

"The truth spell was Marty's idea," I decided. "I never should have told him about Parish."

"He would have found out eventually. This way, he handles cleanup, and you get to save two young lives." He flopped back against his pillow. "It's not perfect, but it's not a bad deal either."

"Unless those young lives attack us, and we have to save ourselves."

"Always a possibility," Clay admitted. "That's the job."

"The Amhersts are seventeen and eighteen. Old enough to know right from wrong. They decided to embrace the dark arts." Asa made it sound simple when it was anything but. "They chose to murder innocents to get their next black magic high."

"You're right." I rolled onto my back. "That doesn't make it suck any less."

"No," he agreed, resting his chin on my shoulder. "It doesn't."

"Come on." Clay threw back his covers and swung his legs over the edge of the bed. "Time to go."

The comforter hit Colby and jarred her awake, her wide eyes blurry in the bright room.

"*Kill him,*" she blurted then seemed to realize where she was and who was with her. "Oh, uh, sorry?"

"If you tell me you even dream about murdering orcs, we're going to have a serious talk, young lady."

"Then I won't tell you." She stretched out her wings and yawned. "But it involved a pirate ship…"

"Goddess bless," I muttered. "It's too early for this."

"You expressed concerns about my dreams." She woke up fast. "I was only easing your fears."

"I expressed concern." Those poor orcs would be shark bait soon. "You expressed an infomercial."

Folding her arms—all of them—across her chest, she pouted at having been called out.

"Let's go." I rolled out of bed, but Clay shoved me back down and sprinted to the bathroom. *"Jerk."*

"Dibs," he called as he slammed the door. "I call dibs."

"That's not how dibs works," I yelled after him then pointed at Colby. "Don't encourage him."

Colby, who had been giggling, pasted on a solemn expression I wouldn't buy on sale at the dollar store.

While we waited for the diva, who had somehow managed to travel with all his remaining wigs in their protective cases, the rest of us pulled on what clothes we had available and ordered room service for breakfast. This was going to be a long day, and a full stomach would go a long way toward improving it.

The Amherst Inn hadn't changed since our last visit. From the outside, it appeared to be sinking in, and it made me curious how long this charade of rot had been in the making for people in town to accept it as a natural progression of neglect.

The glamour alone would have sent most prospective guests around the loop in the driveway on their way somewhere better, yet there were signs, such as our modern suites, that Mr. and Mrs. Amherst had been overhauling their inheritance prior to their disappearances.

Rather than give Trinity and Markus a heads-up we were coming for them, we left the SUV in the parking lot of the hotel where Clay and Colby had been staying. The short walk across the street to the woods gave me time to quash worries about my future to focus on the Amhersts' fate.

"I knew you'd be back." Malcom Holmstrom stepped into my path. "Didn't I say, Emmett?"

A beat later, his younger brother emerged. "Sure did."

Barely past noon, and these jokers were walking about as if the sun wasn't a deterrent for them.

"Those punk kids told us to hunt you down," Malcom explained, "but why waste the energy?"

"I thought you hated all things paranormal?" I kept them talking to get an idea if they were running on autopilot or if their summoners were nearby. "Yet you're killing on command? For witches."

"Don't have much choice." Malcom gestured down at himself. "Damn kids have our nuts in a vise."

"Then why the saucy wink that night in the woods? You seemed plenty in control of yourself then."

"Ours is a sacred mission, and those kids have no right to dictate our kills. The Lord does that."

"We only kill the damned," Emmett added. "Not innocent humans."

"You understand that *innocent* and *human* aren't synonymous, yes?"

And, based on our intel, their streak of murdering humans they pegged as paranormals was still going strong. If they hadn't figured that out yet, there was no point in educating them. They would be dead soon enough.

Dead again?

Dead for good?

Whatever.

"Don't try to get in our heads." Malcom clicked his tongue at me. "We're smarter than that."

"That wasn't an attempt at reverse psychology so much as it was an observation, but sure."

"You're pretty." Emmett studied me. "I can feel how evil you are, witch. Evil shouldn't be pretty."

"I thought about cosmetic surgery. A mole here, a chin hair there, but it was out of my price range."

"She thinks she's funny." Emmett prowled closer. "You're not funny, little witch." He lunged, his jaw unhinging, stretching until he could have fit my whole head in his mouth. "You're dead."

Yanking magic from Colby, I blasted Emmett, who exploded into ectoplasmic lumps that jiggled and wiggled as they began merging into a cohesive whole again.

"You're gonna die for that." Malcom ran at me, his lips parting. "No one hurts my brother."

"Sorry, but I'm too busy to die right now." I repeated the effort, blasting Malcom to bits before he showed me his fillings. "Have your people call my people, and we'll set something up for later."

"Let's go." Clay nudged me toward the house. "They won't stay jelly for long."

We reached the house without issue, but raised voices warned us the siblings weren't happy. We crept to the azalea bushes planted beneath the kitchen window overlooking the backyard and hunkered down to listen in. The curtains had been drawn, so there was little chance of us being seen, and their voices were loud enough I doubted we would be overheard either.

"The Boos should have returned by now," Markus snapped. "Something is wrong."

"You're paranoid," Trinity countered. "They're dragging their feet, as usual."

"What if those agents circled back? They're not just going to forget about us. What if they found the bones?"

"We would know if our onryōs had been vanquished, wouldn't we?"

"I don't know." His footsteps retreated as he began pacing. "Any word from Aspect?"

"He hasn't been online."

"What about Bowser or Dreadnaught?"

"Nothing since yesterday."

"Aspect said he would be in touch. It's been three days. He never goes that long between check-ins."

"Maybe they caught him." I could almost hear her shrug. "He's the one passing out arcane information. Maybe he gave the spell to the wrong person, and they turned on him. Or maybe one of the others summoned a badass they couldn't control, and it killed them."

The silence told me Markus was considering this as a possibility.

"We need to find the Boos." His heavier footsteps grew closer. "Let's go yank on their chains."

"Good grief." Trinity huffed. "I have three orders to fill. I can't keep running off to play with your toys."

"You helped me summon them, so it's your responsibility to help me control them."

"I wouldn't be stuck traipsing around in the woods if you hadn't been determined to have the Boo Brothers."

"They weren't my pick, and you know it." His annoyance rang clear. "Aspect chose the Boos for us." He didn't sound happy about it either. "Two of us, two of them."

"Just think." She sighed. "You could have summoned the Baymont Butcher, Trixie Vein, or Gigi Savage."

"Either way, you owe me," he clipped out. "For Dad."

Another quiet descended that was somehow louder than the first.

"I'm sorry." Markus exhaled. "I shouldn't have gone there. What he did to you..."

"He deserved to die," she said without an ounce of remorse.

"No argument here."

The rustle of clothing and shuffle of feet made me think they might have hugged, but it was brief.

"Let's go." She forced a brighter tone. "I have to be ready for the big tournament next Saturday."

"Forget the tournament." He joked with her. "I'm still waiting for an upgrade on my beard."

The siblings' banter made them easy to track as they exited the house and entered the yard, all smiles and chatter. They had committed atrocious acts, and they didn't care. They had gone dark side too long ago to save if their cavalier attitudes were any indication.

We eased around the side of the house and intercepted them before they reached the tree line.

"Markus and Trinity," I began, and that was all the warning they required to bolt.

The brother appeared to be the instigator, so I wanted more people on him.

"Clay, you and Asa go after Markus." I jerked my chin at the girl. "I'll go after Trinity."

The guys weren't happy with their assignments, but oh well.

"This only ends one way," I shouted to her. "Surrender, and you can save your brother."

"You're a black witch," she panted. "You just want my heart."

The oddities of my heritage and powers urged me to embrace my new truth. "I'm a gray witch."

"You must really think I'm dumb. There's no such thing." Her voice rose to a fever pitch, a spell falling from her lips that trailed to me. "Malcom, I summon thee."

"Crap." I put on a fresh burst of speed, determined to seize her before he caught me. "Trinity, *stop*."

Two thirds of the eldest Holmstrom brother materialized before me, and I smacked right into him.

"Oh, hello." He shoved me back while I was off balance, then swiped my leg out from under me. "I was hoping we'd meet again."

"You're starting to sound like a broken record."

"Well," he said, chuckling, his hand going to the absent portion of his head, "I am missing half my brain."

"I can't tell much difference, to be honest."

Back on my feet, I kicked his hip, spun him, then thrust my wand up toward his chin. He leapt aside, dodging the strike, then rolled under my defenses to pop up in my face. His eyes were wild with exhilaration, and his chest pumped despite the fact his heart had long ceased its beating.

"This is going to be fun." He punched up, catching me in the gut. "Never killed a *gray* witch before."

A sharp hurt radiated through me from the point of impact, and that was when I understood.

"You *stabbed* me. That's so…" I pulled the ectoplasmic blade from my gut, and it turned to goop in my hand, "…disgusting." I brought my knee up between his legs, and he doubled over panting. "If I get ghost cooties from this, I'm going to carve your bones into beads and pass them out to witch covens as souvenirs."

"You bitch." He squinted up at me. "That fucking *hurt*."

"Use your brain." *Awkward.* "The half you have left." I barreled on. "You're dead. Your heart doesn't have to beat. Your lungs don't have to fill. You don't have to experience pain. You're *dead*, capiche?"

His reactions were based on responses he would have had while he was alive, not stimuli he felt now.

"Hey." He straightened to his full height. "You're right." He laughed. "Mind over matter."

When his fist plowed into my face—once, twice, three times without flinching—I realized the enormity of my mistake. Now that he knew he didn't *have* to feel pain, he was choosing not to, and Trinity was getting away.

"I probably deserved that," I admitted, ducking his next strike. "But, as much fun as this has been, I've got a summoner to catch."

Before he could get in close again, I stabbed him through with my wand and lit him up until he exploded. A permanent solution it was not, but I was running low on options. And the bigger problem was sprinting away at breakneck speed.

Once he was scattered, I ran in the direction I last saw Trinity. About the time I started to fear I had chosen wrong, I found her clutching her side and panting through a cramp. She spotted me and forced herself to run, but it was clear she wasn't used to the exercise.

Foam armor doesn't make you work for it like wearing the real thing.

"Last chance." I was closing in fast. "I don't want to hurt you."

"Then don't." She began to limp. "Leave us alone."

"I can't do that." I extended my arm and brushed her shoulder with the tip of my wand. Magic turned her muscles soft, and she collapsed in a heap I almost tripped over. "Sorry, kid, but you've got hard choices ahead of you." I wanted her to decide *before* she saw her brother. "You need to answer some questions for me, and then we're going to talk about your options."

Exhaustion paired with the spell left her too weak to do more than mumble an affirmative.

"You and Markus summoned the Boo Brothers." I started off easy. "How did you do it?"

"Advent." Her breath hitched. "New guy in the guild. Played with us for months. Got tight with Markus. Even streamed a few movies together."

"Movies like *Game Over*?"

A flicker of surprise lightened her eyes, and she stammered, "Y-yeah."

"And then?"

"Markus bragged we were witches, said he bet he could summon an avatar like in the movie. Advent asked if we ever cast any spells." Tears slid down her cheeks. "Markus said no, and Advent hooked him up with a few easy ones to see if they would work."

And just like that, the Amhersts handed Parish the perfect vehicle for their revenge.

"I'm guessing they did."

"No." Her voice went softer. "They didn't."

"Did Advent have a cure for that?"

"H-he told us if we wanted magic, real magic, we should kill our parents. That we would become more powerful if we..." she wet her lips, "...ate their hearts."

Already knowing the answer, I still asked her. "And did you?"

"Our dad knocked us around a lot, and our mom let him." Her jaw flexed. "One night, he hit me so hard, I was unconscious for twenty minutes. Markus was terrified. He thought Dad had finally killed me." Her cheeks flushed. "Markus killed him instead." Her eyes dilated. "I couldn't believe it."

"What happened next?"

"He told me we were in this together, that I had to do my part." The tremble in her voice might have been remorse...or it might have been excitement. "I had to kill Mom to make us even."

"Did you?"

"I didn't think I could eat her heart. It was this bloody, messy glob of raw meat."

The description alone was enough to have me tasting copper and craving salt.

"Markus went first. He took a bite out of Dad's heart, and he...changed. The spells that didn't work before worked then." She swallowed hard. "We knew our parents were witches, but they didn't practice. They didn't have enough magic. I think...maybe...that was why Dad hated us so much. Markus and I weren't powerful, but we had something. I think Dad...that he...wanted it, and since he couldn't have it, he decided to beat it out of us too."

The grandmother had power, which Mr. Amherst must have grown up envying. But for his kids to have a spark where he had none? I could see how that would turn him bitter, but it was no excuse. There was none for harming children.

"How many people did you kill?"

"Me?" Her eyes rounded. "None."

A glint of humor slipped her careful mask, and I discovered which side of the line she fell on.

"Malcom?" Trinity tried to recover the remorseful act, but I had seen through it. "He must have killed four, no five, people."

"Did Malcom choose the victims, or did you?"

"Let's see." Her forehead scrunched. "There was the cop who came to the inn after customers reported shouting, saw me bleeding in a corner, and left. There was a teacher who suggested therapy would help me cope with the abuse. She could have reported my parents, she could have saved us, but she didn't. Then there was the preacher who told us to pray for our parents. There was a boy from school who told me he loved me, used it to get in my pants, then posted it online for all his friends to enjoy." She counted them off on her fingers. "I feel like I'm leaving someone out, but that's four."

"Do you feel any remorse?"

"Do you think they lost any sleep over me?"

"You understand there are consequences for your actions."

"Worth it," she told me. "No regrets."

Had the defiant glint in her eyes not reminded me so much of myself, I might have joined the long line of people who had turned their backs on this girl and decided she was someone else's problem. But I thought about Clay, and how the hand of friendship he extended had pulled my head above the waterline when I was drowning in the same black magic addiction thrumming through Trinity.

Finally, I brought her around to a topic that had been preying on me. "Why Mystic Realms?"

"Mystic Realms is iconic. It's the most popular MMORPG *ever*. Nothing else comes close. There were like twelve million subscribers last I checked, and over one hundred million accounts." Her enthusiasm leaked through. "If you were going to recruit gamers for, well, anything, that's the place to do it."

Niggling fears that Parish had chosen Mystic Realms for Colby-related reasons subsided, mostly.

"Fair enough." I could see the logic. "Why LARPers?"

"Markus and I had a club, so it was easier to explain meeting up with the others as role-playing."

That tracked, which put me further at ease, allowing me to hope Colby remained a secret a while longer.

"Tell me where you buried the bones, and I'll cut you a deal."

"You're not going to let me go." She scoffed. "Not after that speech."

"You're too dangerous to be released unmonitored," I agreed, "but that doesn't mean you're hopeless."

"Feeling maternal?" Her voice dripped with acid. "You and your boyfriend looking to adopt?"

"I work for the Black Hat Bureau." I watched for her reaction but saw none. "Do you know what that is?"

"Do you really think, based on what I've said, that our family sat around the dining table and had discussions on magic?" She cocked her head as the name sank in. "I thought you said you were FBI."

"Black Hat is like the FBI, but for people like us. The agents are just like you. Killers who are given a choice. Join or die." I drew in a sharp breath. "The choice is yours."

"You're a killer?" She swept her gaze over me. "You seem too…do-goody."

"Join up, and you'll find out just how do-goody I am. I have a reputation I've earned, and I'm not proud of it."

"What about Markus?" Interest spiked her tone. "Will he be given the same choice?"

"We ask separately to ensure you don't influence one another. It's a lifetime commitment. You must be dedicated to the role, or you won't last long. You won't be partnered with your brother, either, since he's part of the reason we're having this chat, but you'll be able to visit him during your off time. If you survive training. You won't be kept apart unless you give the Bureau reason to put those measures in place."

"I'll have to be an agent the rest of my life?"

"That's the deal."

Eternal servitude or immediate demise.

"Not much of a choice, is it?"

"You already made the big decisions. These are the consequences."

"Can I still…?" Her gaze dipped to her hands. "It probably sounds lame to you, but can I still LARP?"

"Depends," I said wryly. "Can you LARP without murdering anyone?"

"I'm in it for the wigs, and the costumes."

A game.

It was all a game to her.

The summoning. The evil spirits. The deaths.

"As long as it doesn't hurt anyone else, you'll be free to do your own thing in your downtime."

"Okay." She rose to her feet. "I'll show you where I buried the bones."

We walked together, side by side, and I kept a close eye out for her onryō. I used the time to check the wound in my side. It wasn't deep, but it leaked goop. It also tingled while the raw edges knit themselves together. Black, white, or gray, spontaneous healing wasn't in the witch repertoire. I hadn't done it, which meant it had been done to me. But how? Or worse, by whom?

Was the grimoire responsible? The choker? The pendant, at least, wasn't capable of magic.

Or it hadn't been. Until I fed it a grimoire. And it ate a blessed choker.

As the kids say…FML.

"Do you like being an agent?"

The question caught me off guard, but I wouldn't lie to her. "It has its moments."

"Will I have to kill anyone?"

She didn't sound excited by the prospect of a license to kill, merely curious.

"Yeah." I didn't want to sugarcoat that either. "In the field, it's kill or be killed on most cases."

The conversation orbited the history of Black Hat and the duties of the agents. I answered all her questions to the best of my ability without allowing my relationship with the director to taint the facts. Mostly. Impossible to wipe the slate clean between him and me, even for her benefit.

"There." She indicated a point between two trees. "Under the poison oak."

"I've got your first assignment." I jerked my chin toward the spot. "Start digging."

"Can't you magic the dirt out of the way?"

"I'm not a magical excavator, no." That would be a handy talent, though. "But I can heal you after, so don't worry about a rash."

"You're a black witch." She stared a hole through me. "How can you heal?"

"I'm a gray witch," I reminded her. "I *was* a black witch, but I embraced light magic. Except it doesn't quite work like that after you've been tainted. Now I'm stuck in the middle."

"You can do that?"

"It's the hardest thing I've ever done, but it's worth it."

Unlike me, she didn't have Colby lighting a path back to white magic. But maybe, if she showed signs of a genuine desire to change, I could help guide her onto steadier ground. Right now, she was dizzy with the information I had given her. Probably terrified of what it all meant. She might think she wanted to be good, in light of getting caught. But only time would tell. I could ask Colby to keep tabs on her, but that was the best I could do until Trinity had fully assimilated into Black Hat and proven what type of agent she would become.

Wrinkling her nose, Trinity knelt among the weeds and began scooping the soft dirt with her hands. A few inches into her hole, she produced the first bone, and I inwardly sighed with relief that she had been honest about this much anyway. As the pile grew higher, I rolled my shoulders to dispel a prickling down my spine.

A smudge of blue teased the corner of my eye, and I whirled in time to duck the punch Malcom threw at me. Even less of him was present than the last time, which made me think the more you exploded them, the harder it was for them to come back together.

Good to know.

"You're not rolling over for her," he barked at Trinity. "Put those bones back where you got them."

"I control you." She dug faster, her breaths coming quicker. "Not the other way around."

Malcom lunged for her, and she screamed, but he pulled up short, unable to harm his summoner.

"You think she's going to let you go after what you've done?" He growled. "You're going to burn, witch."

While he was distracted, I rushed him, jabbing my wand into his wiggly mass. "No, she's not."

Magic burst forth, and he melted into a puddle at my feet.

"That's new." I put Trinity back to work. "Maybe there's a limit on how many times they can reform."

More good news, but my observations wouldn't help Asa or Clay. They had Markus and Emmett on their hands, and no magic to detonate the onryō. We had to hurry this along, before the guys got hurt. If I could get my hands on both skeletons, I could end this.

"That's it." Trinity tossed a skull onto the pile. "The tiny bits are in the plastic container."

When I realized what I was seeing, I wanted to bang my head against the tree. "This is only Malcom."

"Advent told us we each had to do it alone and keep the location to ourselves."

"Okay." I gestured her aside. "Stand back."

Drawing on Colby, I spoke the words to reduce the bones to ash then grappled with my kit to locate a small vial. I knelt beside the hole, swept the ashes into it, dumped in the salt, and gave it a stir.

A foul odor wafted up to curl around me, and Trinity's knees buckled with a violent jerk.

The bond between onryō and summoner had been broken.

Thank the goddess.

Quickly, I filled in the hole, tamped it down hard, and set a simple ward around the area that would dissolve over time with exposure to the elements. Overkill? Maybe. I didn't have time to dwell on it.

Pushing to my feet, I went to Trinity and checked her pulse. Steady. I patted her down to ensure no nasty surprises waited for me, but all she had on her was a pottery shard turned keychain that throbbed with magic. One I was willing to bet matched the smashed vase from the mausoleum.

Heaving her upright, I propped her back against a tree and used a binding spell to pin her arms behind her. One less thing to worry about.

With her secure, I went in search of the guys. I didn't have to go far before I heard the daemon bellow. I homed in on his rage and let it guide me. Soon, Clay's shouts entered the mix, and I knew I was on the right track. As I burst through a clump of wild blueberry bushes, I spotted them.

Clay held Markus in check while the daemon fought Emmett with varying degrees of success.

The daemon was coated in green slime, and it slicked his feet, making him slide when he moved too fast. His fury only grew as the onryō bobbed and weaved out of his grasp, immune to the goo. One wrong step, and the daemon went down on his side.

I took advantage of the opening and rushed Emmett from behind. I clutched his arm, lighting him up with a thought, and he splattered us and the surrounding area. Markus, stunned by the apparent defeat of his champion, quit struggling to glare at me with so much hate, I felt it like a slap in the face.

"Where's my sister?" He scanned over my shoulder. "What have you done with her?"

Ignoring his demands, I asked Clay, "Have you searched him?"

"Not yet." He began patting him down. "Looking for anything in particular?"

"A pottery shard." I held up Trinity's. "Like this one."

The sight of her keychain sent Markus into a fit. "What have you done with Trini?"

"She's safe," I assured him. "We'll fetch her when we're done here."

"Got it." Clay held up another keychain. "What is it?"

Since Marita texted, I had my theories, but why not go to the source? "Answer the question."

"A bunch of weird crap was buried with the Boo Brothers," Markus clipped out. "It looked like thrift store rejects to me, but Advent claimed they were powerful relics that would help us with our quest."

Our *quest*.

Further evidence these kids had too much black magic swirling through them to care they were killers.

"What was special about the vase?"

"He told us to smash it and send everyone in the ring a piece." His lips pulled back over his teeth. "It conceals the smell of black magic."

Well, that was one mystery solved. I bet there was another shard in the inn itself to keep out the stink even while the Amhersts weren't home. Same for the other locations.

"You can't leave Trini alone." He jerked against Clay. "Emmett isn't under her control."

"Emmett is sludge, so let's have a chat before he pulls himself back together."

"I have nothing to say to you until you let me see my sister."

"Then we're at an impasse. Guess we'll just stand here and wait on Emmett to regenerate. Do you think he can sense his brother's dead? Again? What do you bet he hunts down your sister first thing to confirm it?" I hated playing hardball, but this kid needed a wake-up call. "That would suck, huh? She's tied up at the moment. I wonder what Emmett—?"

"What do you want?" He connected the dots. "The bones?"

"Got it in one." I hooked my hands on my hips. "Will you lead us to them?"

Gaze swinging between the globs of ectoplasm and the direction I came from, he stalled. "I..."

"Looks like he's made his choice." I jerked my chin at Clay. "I'll bind him, and we'll bring him in."

"No." He fought against Clay's immoveable hold. "I'll show you." He grew frantic. "Please. Just help her."

"Bones first." I didn't want to give him a chance to flake on us. "We handle that, and she's safe."

Fury and guilt and maybe a tinge of relief twisted his features until I couldn't be sure how he felt. Maybe, after everything, he didn't know either.

"This way." He yanked on Clay. "Emmett is buried near the house."

"Really?" That edged us closer to his sister, and I wasn't buying it. "You sure about that?"

Frustration twitched the skin beneath his eye, but he held firm to his story. "The bones are in a stump."

"The stump where you fed them that teen?"

An epiphany struck, and I finally had my answer for the Boos' uncanny ability to manifest in daylight. The land was the key. Their bones were buried there, yes, but they had been fed there as well. That was how they drew strength to rival the sun. That same tether explained why they didn't chase me out of town or hunt me down after I left. They couldn't. They were leashed. Trapped. They could only go so far or *poof*.

"You saw that?" He pulled up short. "How...?"

"Doesn't matter." I knew the stump's whereabouts, so I led us there, careful to cut a wide swath around Trinity's location. "I know you're a killer. Your sister filled in the blanks for me. She confessed to the murders." Malcom's kills, at least. "Do you have anything to add?"

"If Trini told you, then you already know."

A diplomatic answer, which meant any deaths in Raymond she hadn't confessed to would be added to his and Emmett's tab.

Only after we reached the stump, and Markus illustrated how to swing open the top, did we discover the bones nestled in a plastic bag filled with grave dirt. There were spells too, fresh off the printer. Supplies for those spells. And a notebook with a kill list that was refined over several pages where he and Trinity had passed it back and forth while arguing the merits of who deserved to die for what they allowed to be done to them. The reasons were sound, from their point of view, and it ended with the name of the boy who had filmed Trinity.

"Samuel Todd," I read the name. "He was the teen you killed after we checked in."

Ballsy of them to commit a murder within screaming distance of people who identified as FBI.

"I told Trini we had to act fast." His scowl cut deeper. "That something was off about you two."

"I'm going to give you the same choice I gave her." I slapped the book shut. "But I need to handle your buddy first." I passed the book and other materials to Clay then dumped the bones into the hidey-hole. "This won't take but a minute."

This time, when I reached for Colby's energy, I sensed the blip that was her exhaustion.

"Last one," I told her. "Can you handle it?"

From high above us, her tiny voice drifted down to me. "Do you really need to ask?"

"She makes a good point, Rue." Clay chuckled. "She's just like you. She would rather die in the process than admit she's too tired."

"Who said that?" Markus tensed. "Who else is out there?"

"Another member of our team." I ignored his mulish glower. "One you won't be meeting."

A high-pitched scream rent the night, and Markus twisted so hard, he broke free of Clay and ran.

"Go," I ordered Clay and the daemon. "I can handle this."

I made the mistake of watching them go before I refocused on my task, and impact from behind knocked me to one knee. I twisted, expecting to find Emmett, and I was half right. The bottom half. From his belt down, if you want to get technical.

No clue how he saw me or sensed me, but he had brought me down to his level. I wheeled back, but it was too late. His boot made contact with my jaw, and I saw stars.

Rising onto my elbows, I let him get a leg's length away before I kicked him in the junk hard enough to rattle his teeth. Not that he had any. Just as his brother had clung to habits of the living, so did Emmett. He hit his knees then fell forward, his crotch mashed into the grass while his feet kicked the dirt in agony.

Stretching my arm as far as it would go, I ignited the sack of bones. The haunted legs fell still and then reduced to a puddle. I flipped onto my stomach and rose to my knees over the stump. I stirred salt into the mix of ash and grave dirt then swung the top shut. A quick spell that didn't require Colby's assistance let me seal it closed so that Emmett wouldn't be disturbed again.

About the time I wobbled onto my feet, I heard the daemon crashing through the underbrush.

"Rue okay?" He wasted no time scooping me up and squishing me against him. "Ghost dead?"

"Ghost dead." I slumped against his shoulder, exhausted from the magic. "Why did Trinity scream?"

"Spider crawl on nose." He swung me into a bridal carry. "Not even big spider." He scoffed. "Tiny one."

With her hands tied, she had been forced to let it do its thing. I could sympathize. After my run-in with the giant spiders guarding my grandmother, I had developed a mild case of arachnophobia myself.

"I called Marty and explained our situation." Clay looked me over with concern. "His team is coming to scoop up the Amhersts."

"Tell him to collect the parents' remains while he's at it. The kids can tell him where to dig."

"Will do." He glanced over his shoulder. "I gave Markus *The Talk*, and he agreed to join. That nets us two new recruits." He hesitated. "You've never recruited. Anyone. Ever." He touched my arm. "You sure you're okay with this?"

Comfortable in the daemon's arms, a mumbled affirmation was all I could manage.

"Rue sleep." The daemon petted me. "I carry."

That sounded good to me, and as soon as Colby lit on my chest, it was lights out.

17

"To what do I owe this unexpected visit?"

Dressed in his Black Hat best, the director lounged in a wingback chair in his office. He appeared healthy, but he was a master of illusion. Had I not called ahead to request a private meeting, a courtesy from one predator to another, this conversation might have occurred in his room, with him in bed as he recovered from the grievous wounds I could smell on him from here.

The idea had been to arrive sporting bruises from the Boo Brothers' last stand as proof I had been in a fight for my life, but the swelling and discoloration had vanished before I could put them to good use.

"I came to deliver the news about Parish in person." I stood at parade rest behind the visitor's chair across from him. "He's dead." A slight tilt of the director's head was the only reaction he gave to this announcement, though he must know by now. "You and I don't see eye to eye on much, but we—"

"You recruited two young black witches. Siblings, I believe."

"I did." I knew it would convince him as few things would, that I was ready. "I thought it was time."

That snagged his interest, and he leaned forward, wincing before he could smooth his features. "Oh?"

"I want Parish's job." I did my best to appear earnest. "I want to fix what's wrong with the Bureau."

"You want to dismantle my legacy." He leaned back to ease the strain on what I suspected were abdominal wounds. "No." He flicked a dismissive hand. "I have another candidate in mind."

"Your candidate didn't kill Parish."

Silence flooded the room until our hearts, mine steady, his labored, were the only sounds.

"That's not possible." He looked me up and down. "I know who killed him."

"Oh?" I strove for innocence. "Who?"

Even now, when he knew Dad was responsible, he didn't risk speaking him into existence.

"Witnesses report a great black bird who smelled of carrion attacked the dragon."

"And?"

"Only one man has ever summoned such wings, and he died long ago without sharing his secrets."

For a second, I thought an understanding pulsed between us. The old *he knew that I knew that he knew that I knew* Dad was alive deal. But he wasn't willing to step up to that line, and I wasn't willing to cross it either.

"Or perhaps—" I tasted bile admitting this much, "—he wrote it all down."

"A grimoire?" The director's attention swung back to me. "*His* grimoire?"

Again, I waited for him to use his son's name or allude to my father, but he didn't.

"Do you want your proof, or don't you?" I acted bored. "Appoint me deputy director, and I'll show you my new trick."

"Done." His eagerness made me squirm. "The job is yours, *if* you can produce those wings."

The words I spent the hour beforehand practicing spilled from my lips as I raised my arms to either side. I smelled the magic before I saw it, ripping through my spine and anchoring itself in my flesh. I flexed the new appendages, blowing the director's hair back from the might of the gale they produced in such close quarters. Black tendrils curled over my shoulders, but soon the color leached to a silvery gray.

As fast as I had summoned them, I cut off the spell, hoping the director hadn't noticed the odd color.

"Marvelous."

That one word was the only bit of praise he had ever given me, and I could tell by the war of hatred and love across his face that he meant the word for his son, who had created this spell. Not for me, who had merely executed it.

Either Dad had known, after he fought with Parish, that I would end up here, or he sought to fulfill his promise to share the secret of flight if I wrote to him. Before he disappeared. With Mom. For good?

This, at least, gave me the grounds to prove I had killed Parish. Had I not known the director better, I might have suspected he made his bargain in haste to cling to the only person of his blood left. The truth was more likely that he needed me as his shield until Dad was in a grave. For real this time.

"Your magic," he began as I folded my hands behind my back again. "It's in flux."

So much for him not noticing. I should have known better than to think it would slip past him.

"Not in flux." I felt the truth in that. "Evolving."

"Careful the book doesn't evolve you beyond recognition," he said slyly. "What a pity that would be."

This was the hard part, the road I didn't want to go down, but I had to sell myself.

"I've mastered my addiction." I pasted on a cocky smile. "The grimoire won't best me."

Nestled in the valley between my breasts, the pendant pulsed. Just once. Before the choker quelled it.

"You're an addict, and you always will be." He seemed pleased by that. "If you're already using the book, then you'll be back to your old self in no time." He laced his fingers across his lap. "I'm glad you stopped by, Deputy Director. It's been a pleasure."

The lies had done their job, convincing him I was following in my father's footsteps and well on my way to eating my next heart. He must have assumed that Asa would fall by the wayside too. He was right about that. If my hungers controlled me, I wouldn't have room in my life for anything but sating them.

Almost out the door, the director called, "I expect a handwritten copy of that spell on my desk Monday."

Molars grinding, I crossed the threshold and strode out the front door of the compound with purpose.

This was not the life I wanted. This was not a job I ought to have. This was…our best chance at survival.

Asa waited for me in the SUV at the gate, and I'm not sure I had ever been so happy to see him.

"I would ask how it went," he said, "but I've already gotten the group text."

"Group text?" I strapped in. "What did it say?"

"I'm pleased to announce our new deputy director," he read, "my granddaughter, Elspeth Bathory."

"His…*granddaughter*?" I snatched his phone. "He outed me? To the entire bureau?"

"You're falling in line, as far as he knows." Asa plucked his phone from my fingers when it looked like I might cock my arm and throw it out the window. "He's letting everyone know to be on their guard around you."

"No." I slumped in my seat. "He's painting a target on my back and passing out free arrows."

As much as I wanted to stay curled up in a ball in my own bed, in my own house, we had preparations to make. I had secured the stolen artifacts in my safe last night, after we got home from Mississippi, but we had a meeting scheduled for the butt crack of dawn, and we couldn't afford to be late.

I'm not proud of the cereal bar I crammed in my mouth on the way out the door, but it had to be done. I offered to share, but Clay informed me he would rather die than eat breakfast out of a box claiming its contents were inspired by real fruitlike flavors.

On an overgrown tract of land outside Samford, the three of us walked into a barn full of daemons.

They were...terrifying.

It gave me hope they were up to the task.

"My lord," they boomed through the space as they hit their knees and slammed fists over their hearts.

A slight female with red skin and black leather dragonfly wings flitted over to us.

"Primipilus Moran," Asa greeted her. "It's good to see you."

"It's our pleasure to serve." She bobbed her head at me. "You must be Princess Rue."

A strangled noise caught in my throat, but I managed not to choke on my own spit. "That's me."

However, I did elbow Asa for not warning me about the use of the title.

I was *not* a princess.

"Forgive me, sire, but your orders confuse me." She linked her hands at her spine. "The missive led me to believe you wish for us to protect this town." She waited a beat. "Full of humans."

"Those are your orders, yes." He gave her a moment to digest that. "However, if you're unable to fulfill that simple task, then I'm more than happy to appoint a new centurion." He gestured to a male behind her with orange spikes jutting down his sides. "Tiago would serve in your place with honor."

"Yes, sire." Tiago jogged over. "It would be my pleasure."

Moran whipped a blade from her belt, pivoted toward Tiago, and sank it in his gut then kicked him over to groan and bleed on the moldering hay.

"That won't be necessary, sire." A line furrowed her brow. "I merely wished to ensure our first mission for you is a successful one. If you desire these humans be protected, then we will guard them with our lives to our last man."

Sympathy for Moran's plight won out over caution. Here she was, called into service for the first time, and rather than a battleground, she found herself assigned to a quiet town full of mortals. I could see why she would be confused, maybe a little offended too.

"I assume we have your discretion." I waited for her nod. "Then I will tell you this. I'm planning a coup against my grandfather." Her blank expression told me word hadn't reached them, but it would soon. "The director of the Black Hat Bureau."

The slight widening of her eyes was all the surprise she betrayed, but an eager glint quickly replaced it.

"You have chosen your mate well," she congratulated Asa. "She is a fiercer creature than I had heard."

"Yes, well, this town is my home. These people—these humans—are my family. I'm giving you the most important task I will ever assign." I read her doubt and was quick to allay her worries. "Enemies have already attacked my chosen family, and that was before I picked a side. The director, and all his enemies and allies, will target this place. It's your job to ensure I don't lose the war by coming home to fight every battle for myself."

"Yes, my lady." She bowed lower than before. "It is our honor to serve and protect."

"My cousin will be our liaison." I couldn't think of a better go-between than Aedan. He had a personal stake in the outcome of any fight. And, as much as I hated to admit it, her name was Arden. "He's Aquatae. I assume that won't be an issue for you?"

"We have several in our number," she assured me. "Our legion is comprised of many different species."

"Good." I shook her hand. "It was a pleasure to meet you."

Leaving Asa to finalize our plans, I stepped out for some air to find Clay wearing an odd little smile.

"You made a boo-boo." He tweaked my nose. "You told her your cousin would play liaison."

"And?" It hit me a minute later. "I admitted my cousin is a daemon."

If she dug into my family history, she might realize I was Haelian Sea royalty, and that would not do.

"Don't beat yourself up over it." He shrugged. "Now that you're mated to a daemon, people will feel validated for suspecting your dad wasn't pure black witch." He watched me sag on my bones. "Moran is sworn into Asa's service. Hand down an order not to spread the gossip, if that's a yowling cat you want to wrap in a straitjacket and then shove back into the bag before you toss it in a river."

"I'm glad you caught it." I turned to go back but bumped into Asa halfway. "I need a word with Moran."

"She won't tell anyone about Aedan's relationship to you. Neither will the others."

"Did everyone catch that but me?" I slumped where I stood. "I'm slipping."

"You're exhausted, and you're stressed about your father. And your mother. And your grandfather."

"I'm the deputy director." I heard myself say it, but it didn't sound real. *"Me."* The person who, a year ago, would have cheered Dad on while he burned down the establishment. "I can't brain right now."

"That's why you have me." Asa gripped my shoulders, steadied me. "And Colby. And Clay. And Aedan."

The way he broke it up made it easier for me to balance the scales in my mind. I had a lot on my plate, but I had even more going for me. I could do this. I could make this work until I decided which team to ultimately choose. Either way, Dad wouldn't survive, and that gutted me.

Almost as much as him ditching me for the ghost of my mother.

"I couldn't do this without you." I pressed my face into his shirt. "Even if you did let them call me *princess*."

"I could have gone with Future Queen of my Heart."

"Hardy har har." I tweaked his nipple and savored his yelp. "Let's go home."

"About that." Asa pointed up to where Moran hovered above us, her outline shimmering with daemonic glamour. "She's escorting us."

"You know what's most annoying about that?"

"That you requested them, issued their orders, and therefore can't complain if they fulfill them?"

"Yes," I grumbled without heat. "That."

"Careful what you wish for," he began, his lips tipping up at one corner.

"A dae prince might just give it to you?"

"Yes," he agreed with a different kind of heat seeping into his gaze. "That."

18

Few things set my soul at ease as much as coming home. It didn't matter if I had been gone for a week, a day, or an hour. I experienced the same rush of *ohthankgoddessI'mbackwhereIbelong* every single time I pulled up the driveway and saw my little house, on my little plot of land, in my little town.

Knowing Colby was safe inside? Within our wards? Comfy at her rig?

Priceless.

As Asa threw the SUV into park, Moran and two other females rushed to open the doors for us. I wanted to wave them off, to tell them we could do it ourselves, but I had to take it slow with them. A lifetime of conditioning wasn't going to wash out in a day. So, I smiled, thanked them, and tamped down my guilt.

About to offer them refreshments, I threw out a hand for balance as the world tilted under my feet in a vertigo spin that reminded me of…the rose delivery. The way reality twisted around me and only me.

No. No. No.

I was not dealing with this today.

An explosion of heat fanned my spine, and I whirled to find the last thing I wanted to deal with.

Orion Pollux Stavros, High King of Hael, future FIL, and royal pain in my butt smiled at me.

In his hands, he held out a tray of cupcakes from the fancy bakery Asa used to send me treats.

Up to this point, I had been annoyed with his sense of entitlement. Now the violation as he stole a thing that belonged to Asa and me alone tempted me to immolate him.

"You've returned my gifts." He ignored his son, convincing me ash was a good look for him. "I'm hurt."

Too tired to play, I strode toward him with my hands empty and down at my sides where he could see them. I didn't want him to tense before I got close enough to slap yet another Band-Aid on yet another problem in our ever-growing stack.

Among them the fact Stavros might not be able to track me while I wore the choker/pendant/grimoire, but he knew where I lived, and the *y'nai* were quick to tattle my arrival. Their loyalty to Stavros was the only excuse I could fathom for his immaculate timing.

"I don't have time for this." I accepted part of the weight of the tray. "I don't have time for you."

Maybe he thought I was flirting. Maybe the words didn't fit my actions. Maybe he was just an idiot.

Grip firm on the corner, I spoke the words Asa taught me to get rid of unwanted gifts.

The cupcakes, and the daemon king holding them, vanished.

Gasps rose behind me, and I turned to find Moran and the others watching with slack jaws.

"Don't you ever get tired of him being all *I'm a sexy king, come have my babies*?"

Crickets sang in the distance. A frog or two joined in. The warriors before me? Not a peep.

"Really?" I stared at them. "No one?"

"They aren't in a position to ignore the high king," Asa reminded me. "They may not be magically bound to obey him, but they have no choice if he commands them, as his subjects, to his bed. Whether or not they agree with you, they will never refuse him."

"Good point." I rubbed the back of my neck. "I'm happy to tell Stavros he's an asshat enough for all of us." I dropped my arm. "Blink once for yes. Keep staring for no."

They kept staring, which was disheartening, until I noticed tears gathering in the corners of their eyes. I had the privilege to tell Stavros where to stick it. (Hint: Not in me.) I also had the power to back up any threats I made to him. These females, they didn't have that option.

"I need to grab a shower." I dipped my chin. "Aedan will be in touch."

Cheeks warm, I made it halfway to the wards before a light tap on my shoulder brought me up short.

"Moran?" I blanked on her title, but I remembered her name. Progress! "Can I help you?"

"I…" Her eyes glistened. "Thank you." She set her jaw, and they cleared. "I will remember the look on his face until the end of my days." She took my hand and bent over it, pressing it to her forehead. "I am yours to command, Princess. Ask it, and it will be done."

"Thanks." I patted her shoulder awkwardly. "I appreciate that."

With a tight smile, she leapt into the sky. The others followed suit, allowing the wind to dry their tears.

"Princess Rue." Clay toyed with the ends of my hair. "I should start braiding your hair into a crown."

"I'm not a princess," I grumped. "I'm not wearing a crown made out of hair."

"I bet you would if your spit muffin donated for it."

"This again?" I rubbed the bracelet on my wrist that was so much a part of me these days. "I wouldn't wear a crown made out of his hair either." I squinted at him, noticed his grin, and decided, "However, I would love to see you braid *his* hair into a crown. He's the prince, after all."

"That's not happening," Asa assured us.

"You have to sleep sometime," Clay said cheerfully. "When you do, I'll be there."

"No, you won't."

"Rue will be there," he amended. "She's Team Hair Crown."

A laugh I desperately needed loosened the tightness in my throat.

Though Valentine's was still days away, I could no longer see that far into our uncertain futures.

That ambiguousness convinced me we should celebrate even the Hallmark holidays before the next disaster struck. Plus, it gave me an excuse to give a long overdue gift to someone who truly deserved it.

"Come on." I hit the front steps. "We have a holiday to further commercialize."

"Rue got me present?" The daemon sat on the couch. Bounced, really. "Give me."

"Here you go." I handed him the pink and red box. "Go on." I nudged him. "Open it."

Paper ripped, the ribbon snapped, and the box tore as he dug in. He pulled out a simple sterling bracelet with a name etched into the front and a message stamped on the inside of the band. It opened and closed with magic, and it was designed for shifters who lived in cities and wanted to wear a collar with identifying information when they changed forms. But that was getting ahead of things.

"Blayton Skinflayer Montenegro," he read, his forehead creasing. "Who Blayton?"

"You are," I told him. "If you want to be."

"That my name?" He rubbed his thumb across the engraving. "What inside?"

"You'll have to look." I turned it in his hand. "It's a message from Asa, since he couldn't be here."

"You will always be my brother," he read in a stilted voice. "Asa say that?"

"He chose the bracelet, the quote, all of it."

And Aedan made it happen while we were out of town.

"Except the name," Colby piped up. "We all pitched in to choose one."

"Blayton is a family name on your mother's side, and Skinflayer was Colby's pick."

"Blayton Skinflayer Montenegro," he said again. "I have name." He checked with me. "Mine?"

"All yours," I agreed. "Unless you don't like it."

"I like." His smile lit up the room. "I go by Skinflayer?"

"It's your name." I patted his knee. "You can be Blay or Blayton or, yeah, Skinflayer."

"Skinny," Clay volunteered. "Works for me."

"You don't have to pick one or the other," I reminded him. "Everyone calls me Rue, but Clay calls me Dollface. We could introduce you as Blayton and call you Skinflayer or Skinny in private."

"Hmm." He passed me his hair. "You pet." He turned the bracelet in his hands. "I think."

"How did I know?" I raked my fingers through the silky length. "You don't have to decide tonight, big guy."

"Rue call me Blay." He held out his gift. "Put on?"

"Sure thing." I let his hair go, which earned me a pout, then opened the lock. "Want to know a secret?"

"Yes," he rushed out. "Tell me."

"Asa can't wear it. It will only appear when you do." I snapped it shut then spelled it closed. "Very nice."

"It mine?" He shook his wrist to watch it glint. "All mine?"

"All yours."

Flames engulfed him, leaving Asa sitting where the daemon —*Blay*—had been. Just as fast, Asa was ripped away as...Blay... reclaimed their body and leapt to his feet. He scooped up Colby, and they danced in the living room, both of them so happy it made my chest hurt.

Clay dropped onto the couch beside me and draped his arm across my shoulders. "You okay with not spending Valentine's Day with your guy?"

Oh. We would be celebrating. Later. After everyone else had gone to bed. But I wouldn't tell Clay that.

Call it my Valentine's gift to him.

"More than okay." I excused myself, went to my room, then returned and plunked down beside him. "You and me? We're going to eat full-price chocolate until we get sick. Then we're going to drink wine until we think learning the Mystic Mambo is the best idea *ever*."

Already reaching for a throw on the back of the couch, he lifted one corner for me to slide under beside him. "Can we watch *The Princess Bride*?"

Snuggling in next to him, Blay and Colby murdering orcs in the next room, I sighed happily. "As you wish."

ABOUT THE AUTHOR

USA Today best-selling author Hailey Edwards writes about questionable applications of otherwise perfectly good magic, the transformative power of love, the family you choose for yourself, and blowing stuff up. Not necessarily all at once. That could get messy.

www.HaileyEdwards.net

ALSO BY HAILEY EDWARDS

Black Hat Bureau

Black Hat, White Witch #1

Black Arts, White Craft #2

Black Truth, White Lies #3

Black Soul, White Heart #3.5

Black Wings, Gray Skies #4

Gray Witch #5

The Foundling

Bayou Born #1

Bone Driven #2

Death Knell #3

Rise Against #4

End Game #5

The Beginner's Guide to Necromancy

How to Save an Undead Life #1

How to Claim an Undead Soul #2

How to Break an Undead Heart #3

How to Dance an Undead Waltz #4

How to Live an Undead Lie #5

How to Wake an Undead City #6

How to Kiss an Undead Bride #7

How to Survive an Undead Honeymoon #8

How to Rattle an Undead Couple #9

The Potentate of Atlanta

Shadow of Doubt #1

Pack of Lies #2

Change of Heart #3

Proof of Life #4

Moment of Truth #5

Badge of Honor #6

Black Dog Series

Dog with a Bone #1

Dog Days of Summer #1.5

Heir of the Dog #2

Lie Down with Dogs #3

Old Dog, New Tricks #4

Black Dog Series Novellas

Stone-Cold Fox

Gemini Series

Dead in the Water #1

Head Above Water #2

Hell or High Water #3

Gemini Series Novellas

Fish Out of Water

Lorimar Pack Series

Promise the Moon #1

Wolf at the Door #2

Over the Moon #3

Araneae Nation

A Heart of Ice #.5

A Hint of Frost #1

A Feast of Souls #2

A Cast of Shadows #2.5

A Time of Dying #3

A Kiss of Venom #3.5

A Breath of Winter #4

A Veil of Secrets #5

Daughters of Askara

Everlong #1

Evermine #2

Eversworn #3

Wicked Kin

Soul Weaver #1

Printed in Great Britain
by Amazon

Made in Milan
A novel by
Stephen J. Alexander

Stephen J. Alexander comes from Shrewsbury, England. He now lives in the French Alps with his wife and two children.

Titles by this author:

Peter and the Dwarf Planets (Olympia Publishers, 2018)

Made in Milan (Third Edition KDP; 2021)

Falling Strong
(The Sequel to Made in Milan Coming Soon on KDP)

Please follow me at:

https://olympiapublishers.com/authors/stephen-j-alexander/

https://www.amazon.co.uk/Stephen-J-Alexander

https://www.goodreads.com/author/show/19074010.Stephen_J_Alexander

Twitter: @dwarfplanets5

Instagram: stephen_alexander_author

Facebook: www.facebook.com/dwarfplanets5

To Florence

PART ONE – THE MEETING

Him

I can see her looking over at me from her table. I always clock everything in a crowded space; something I picked up from my dad. He never sat with his back to a room and claimed it was an Italian thing.

For the record, I'm alone, drinking an aperitif in an old bar on a side street just off the fashionable *Alzaia Naviglio Grande* in Milan. I found the place in a copy of *Lonely Planet* from 2016. It's survived *The Lockdown* as well as Italy's sometimes violent bailout battles with the E.U. in the early 2020s and more. So, I'm guessing it must be an ok place. I've only been out in this city once before as part of a group back in '26. We were working and most of the crew were so annoyingly American after a beer or two, I'd kept myself to myself all evening and slipped back to bed at the hotel the first chance I got.

Me being back in Italy now and my dad's seating phobias *are* purely coincidental. Dad, or papa as I called him, was not a Sicilian gangster and I simply like sitting, especially in a new place, where I've got a clear view of where I'm at.

I guess we were kind of similar like that, preferring our own company over a party, and secretly people watching for inspiration. Dad taught me to read stories in individuals' gestures and postures and he loved observing and contemplating the many ways different people interact. Above all though, my father liked to surreptitiously feast his eyes on beautiful women. He loved the idea that if he stared for long enough, he'd somehow be able to draw a reactionary glance back from them, though at that point, he always looked away in haste. Or, at least that's what he'd told me in his old age. If he ever did go any further with his anthropological pursuits, I certainly never knew anything about it.

Anyway, back in the here and now: Her hair is long, straight and dark. Her eyes are a piercing blue adding a certain intensity to her face that I find very alluring. She's got olive skin, typical of a local girl, and as our eyes briefly meet across the room, I feel a sudden chill forcing me to lower my gaze towards the *Spritz* that I'd been sipping. My fingers, nervously detached, rotate the little glass slowly round and round on its spot before I find the courage to look up again.

There's a man sitting opposite her. He looks bored. They haven't spoken in what seems like an age when without much ado, he suddenly just gets up and excuses himself with a polite little bow of the head. On his way out he lightly brushes my table. "*Scusi*" he mutters softly, as he shuffles by.

I turn my head to watch him, trying to find a story to explain his quick getaway. He looks about thirty, a similar age to me, and handsome in a swarthy kind of way. I watch him all the way to the door and in that briefest of moments, the girl has got up, stalked over, drawn up a chair and sat herself down opposite *me*.

"Hello," she says. She speaks English. "You. You don't look Italian. But you *do* look like you might be interesting, and I really need interesting right now. May I sit?"

Her

Paolo and I have been finished for some time. It's just so hard to let go completely. We meet for coffee from time to time, usually in the morning. I talk to him about my work and my travels. Paolo talks about his paintings. He's a penniless artist who dreams of getting a big exhibition someday. I really envy his freedom. I like how he lives on the fringes, untroubled by alarm clocks, the metro and all the other trappings of what he calls 'wage slavery.' But, it's just not something I can do with him anymore. It was great when we were younger. But now, I can't explain it.

I've been working for the same company for over eight years since I graduated from the university here in Milan. I have a really good position and unlike most Italians in this decade, I do still get to travel abroad because of my job and I love that. So, you could say I'm comfortable and happy with my life as it is. Only, I'm getting bored. Yes. I *am* bored. I'm no more interested in Corporate Financial Risk Management which is how I earn my living, than I am in following an ageing dreamer with no salary at all.

This evening, Paolo invited me out to eat with him. But it's Friday night. I've just escaped the office and I'm in the mood for some fun, and not really the kind of depressed artist conversation he wanted to have as we take an *aperitivo*. I know he still has strong feelings for me, and I do love him very much, just not in the way he wants. I've moved on and I can't help it. If I tell him about some of the interesting people I've met lately both here and on my travels, he'll only get jealous and defensive. The silence is palpable. He looks down at his beer. I nervously nudge my wine glass and begin to scan the room around us.

This is a popular place on *Via Corsico,* especially just before dinnertime, and the room's full of happy faces, young and old. Yet, in amongst the gallery, I find myself drawn. I'm looking straight at a young man sitting alone. His eyes flit around and I watch him, hoping he's not scanning for the arrival of someone else. But, I'm fairly sure he's not. He looks interesting; quite possibly a foreigner as I so often am for work. I think I know my own type.

I'm pondering whether he'd be offended if I went over to him when suddenly, our eyes meet. I'd been studying him perhaps too closely. Damn it! He's looked right back at me. We've crossed paths. It was so brief. I smile awkwardly to hide my embarrassment, but he's looked away and probably won't look up again.

As I turn back to Paolo who's been mumbling something at me I didn't hear, I smile at him ruefully and he instantly gets it. We know each other far too well and he gets offended easily if he doesn't have my undivided attention. I can tell when Paolo's upset. He isn't a huffy puffy man. He just glazes over all forlorn and then gets up and excuses himself. He's sorry. He really should get back to his work he says, and in the blink of an eye, he's up and gone, and I find myself pulled as if by some supernatural force, out of my seat and over to an empty chair opposite the interesting stranger.

I've never done anything like this before and if I'd stopped for one moment to think, I'd probably never do anything like this again. But it's done now. Too late.

"Hello," I say in my best English accent. "You. You don't look Italian. But you *do* look like you might be interesting, and I really need interesting right now. May I sit?"

Him

"Y-Yes," I stutter, completely taken aback.

I mean, what woman ever fronts up to a man like this in a bar? Deadbeat B-movies I've channel hopped onto after midnight back in the States often have 1980s neon lit bar settings with hot lone nymphos coming onto young single guys in flecked grey business suits with their sleeves rolled up to the elbows. Those seedy looking yuppies always get their impossible fantasies realised with the backdrop of some vilely synthesised electronic Euro pop.

But here in Europe, post *Male Enlightenment* in the summer of '24, neither men nor women really ever make moves on each other in bars anymore, like, ever! Sure, it is fine to look, but making a move, especially for a man is frowned upon to say the least; seen as very old-school at best. Human courtship is conducted 100% through dating apps on hologram home entertainment systems (H.H.E.S.) and dates are *'pre-programmed'* to use the modern parlance.

"Thank you," she coos ever so politely as she reaches up a hand and beckons over a passing waiter. "Do you like red wine?" She flashes me a quick glance before assertively addressing the young man dressed in black and white in her native Italian.

Just as with the man she'd been sitting with, I turn to watch the waiter scurry away. I have a reservation for one at the nearby *Il Brellin* in ten minutes and I'm starting to feel quite hungry. I'm sure that if we turned up there together, they'd be more than happy to accommodate her at my little table. But before I can ask, she beats me to the punch.

"I've ordered a bottle of red wine, two glasses and some snacks for you. We can go get a meal later if you're really as interesting as you look," she says. "Me. I'm in the mood for drinks and fun tonight. What about you?"

Watching her lips, still mildly shocked at my good fortune, the words seem to spill from her mouth and I register them individually but struggle with the narrative. She's beautiful, and as I wonder whether or not she realises that herself or whether she's mistaken me for someone else, she sits forward and notices me.

"Cat *has* got your tongue?" she asks. It's the first tiny flaw in her English, and seems to break me out of my trance.
"I'm sorry," I say shaking my head from side to side, weirdly but deliberately. "You're Italian, I guess? But your English is really, *really* good! And I see you even know one of our expressions?"

She blushes. A vulnerability to flattery might suggest she doesn't realise how attractive I find her.

"What's your name?" I blurt out.

We're interrupted by the arrival of several *Stuzzichini*, some tomato bread and the wine she ordered. She's speaking really quickly to the waiter as he uncorks the bottle and seems to want *me* to do the traditional taste and nod test.

This isn't at all what I'd had in mind for dinner and the reservation I've just missed was hard to get. I feel my phone vibrating in my pocket, and I'm sure it's them. But I don't pick up. I'm a millennial with much older tastes. 7 and 8G phones are more of a burden to me than the freedom they're meant to bring.

The waiter strides away again and immediately she grips the bottle, filling both her glass and mine up to the rim. I make a shocked face. It's not very continental and more than a bit ironic. "What?" she says aghast before jumping straight into a shouted "*Salute!*" extending her glass towards me. "By the way, I'm Alice. And, no-one flies abroad without the 'R.P.' anymore. What are you doing in Milan on your own on a weekend?"

"Cheers," I reply, raising my glass and suddenly feeling quite cagey.

If this is going to turn into a crazy night with she who it appears is called Alice, it's going to be best for me if I deflect the personal questions back onto her for the time being. And, that is exactly what I do, rather deftly, if I may say so myself.

It turns out that Alice is a banker by profession. She regularly travels on business to and from London, Paris and other mainly European capitals by *E-Train* where possible, but she says she always flies to England. It's apparently much quicker for European business people to get past security in a British airport than at railway stations. I nod in agreement. That makes a lot of sense to me. With tourists having been restricted to *E-Trains* and driving across Europe in at least a hybrid vehicle since France came up with their *Papier de Raison* known globally as an *R.P.* in 2023, the rail and sea border between there and England does tend to clog.

As she talks I figure she must be well trusted by her company. She must also be well qualified, and probably well off. There are so many alternatives to meeting face to face post pandemic that large companies only ever send out their best people. She speaks English and French, apparently a passable Spanish, fair German and Dutch on top of her native Italian and as I watch her talk, she's definitely in a celebratory mood tonight. I think she's amazing and I try to take in everything she says about her bank, though I've never been that fond of them myself. I have my money in one or possibly two of them. But it's my agent's job to take care of all that.

I'm soon completely losing myself in her world. The unexpected wine on an empty stomach, her Friday night enthusiasm and the rollercoaster tone of her voice all combine. Also, without warning she's ordered a second bottle from a passing waitress and continues to speak more and more animatedly after she gets me to admit to being English and starts to describe just how much she loves the place. She works a lot in London.

I watch her casually drink two, maybe three glasses more, topping us both up as she goes, before she starts on about how she once spent three weeks in Cardiff.

She's not at all what I imagined a banker to be like as she raves on about how great Milan's music scene is and how she'd love to show me. I pick at my cold cuts, cheeses, and olives every time my belly rumbles and I drink her wine as she pours. Alice touches none of the food but she seems happy enough as she is.

She comes from a village on Lake Como, not too far away from Milan. She says she would like to take me there one day to meet her family, but swiftly changes the subject when I look startled by the suggestion.

I eventually rest my chin on my upturned palm, starting to feel the dull effect of far too much red wine, and I watch her rattle on contentedly in front of me. I take my time to memorise this moment. Low hanging bauble lights of varying sizes cast cool contours across the room, and the background din of the bar feels far away from us here on centre stage.

Alice's bright blue eyes dazzle through the shadow cast around our table in wonderful juxtaposition with her long ebony hair. I like everything about her up to this point. She has on a simple black polo-neck sweater and jeans, not showy. Just sweet. She comes across as a very down-to-earth girl. From downplaying the importance of her important job, giggling at me when I say she's got a lovely smile and her straightforward chic dress sense, I worry for how this might end, before anything's even begun.

When Alice gets up to go to the bathroom, I notice her *Converse* trainers and tell her I've got a pair of those too. Hanging over the back of her chair is a small but stylish black leather handbag. She also wears a delicate, thin black band in her hair that's barely noticeable in our low-lit surrounds but does enough to subtly evoke a sweet style.

When she returns to the table, I pick up on the only signs of what I assume must be her wealth and status - a pair of small round white pearl earrings, visible as she runs a nervous hand through her hair and looks at me, clearly thinking about something. She also wears a rather large, masculine looking *TAG Heuer* watch. The whole *look* suits her perfectly.

Nonetheless, and rather oddly you may think, singularly the most interesting thing to have struck me about Alice this evening is something far more profound than a pair of earrings or trainers.

Today is Friday 24th October, 2031. As a species, we have somehow or other survived well into the fourth decade of the 21st Century. Yet no one, but no one, lives without being digitally connected all of the time. Now, Alice and I are both born of *that same* techno-age! In fact, I have learned from her during the course of the evening that we *are* the same age! And, people in general, all over the planet have been device-addicted for well over twenty years now, getting more and more woefully hooked with every new advance. Yet, Alice has not once reached for a mobile device since I first set eyes on her. Admittedly, she did go to the bathroom once, but she wasn't there long enough to have scrolled through her social media apps... And, really, I can't even begin to express how happy this makes me feel now that I'm thinking about it.

Suddenly she just blurts out of nowhere, "I'm going home. Are you going to come with me?"

She has already waved the waiter back over with his card reader and taken out a purse full of what looks like several gold visa cards.

"I can pay," I offer.

But, she shakes her head at me looking stern all of a sudden. I take the hint and thank her. Alice pays for everything without saying another word. Then, she's on her feet, swaying ever so slightly, and heading towards the door. I watch her from our table trying to work out what I'm going to do next. And, holding onto the door, she turns around, smiles and beckons me over to her.

"Are you happy to take me home then?"

"Yes, of course," I reply.

Alice

Looking back at him, I could walk away now and forget this evening ever happened. But I don't.

Above the usual clamour of a busy bar, I'm not sure whether I caught him tell me his name or not. I think he might be called Peter Scott, or Scott or just Pete, I don't know. But it really wouldn't be a good move now, holding the door, to ask for his name again after I've just asked him to take me home.

I watch him gather himself together back at the table. He's so scruffy, like looking good is not one of his priorities. He's wearing a dull mauve pullover at least one size too big for him and his hair seems to just sit, like a wet brown mop.

When he stands, I watch him stride towards me through a crowd and notice straight away how tall he is. His long legs reach up to what I'm sure will be a beautifully shaped bum, yet, his cheap taste in jeans is obvious. At least the *Doctor Marten's* he appears to have on his feet show some style. But he has such a lovely face, I feel like something fits; like we're destined to be together tonight.

All evening I've glanced at him as I talked; gazed as he did. He's so handsome from the sincere interest in his curiously dark brown eyes to the way he speaks, both gently and awkwardly radiating a sweetness. I love the way he asks me so many questions and gets completely lost in my replies. Then, at last it's his accent. He could talk to me all night long in that soft English tone. I've been blushing all evening whenever his voice quickened with enthusiasm for one of my silly ideas and I'm sure he's noticed.

"Are you happy to take me home then?" I ask again at the door.

"Yes, of course," he says. So, I take him by the hand, deliberately intertwining our fingers, denying him the chance to change his mind.

Him

Outside in the autumnal night air, I stop Alice in her tracks as she tries to drag me away. Holding up the hand that she's taken from me, I jokily examine the form of our entangled fingers. She, all the while, glares back at me like a rabbit caught in the headlights, looking like she wants to ask a question but apprehensive of where it'll lead. What's certain before the moment completely passes, is that someone needs to make a move or forever rue a missed opportunity. And, that someone appears to be me. Her look is demanding me to act.

Hesitantly, I pull her towards me and she rises onto her tip-toes in my embrace. I stop. Our noses are almost touching. I look into her eyes for a sign. Anything. I can feel her breath, warm and gentle against my cheek. It's beautiful.

My heart beats faster and faster as my lips brush delicately over hers like butterfly wings, sweet, soft and fragranced with red wine and strawberry chap stick.

We're still holding hands when her other moves up behind my back and eases me closer. I move my head back to look her in the eyes only for her to use them to draw me back to her. I'm breathing deeply, completely caught up in a sensation I have not felt in a long, long time. I am waking from an emotional coma, like a child learning lessons in love for the first time, and it's my first proper kiss since before the *Sunset* incident stripped me of all desire. She reaches forward and kisses me back, slowly at first, tenderly fingering the nape of my neck and feeling her way between my opening lips with her tongue.

She trembles a little in my arms as our tongues connect for the first time and I feel electricity surge through my body. A reckless passion is awakened in me. I run my fingers through her ebony hair and then hold her closer still as she again presses my open mouth to hers, the intensity building to a delicious crescendo – the goosebumps moment when I open my eyes to find her still there, staring back at me, still breathing heavily. Playfully, Alice leans in again and gently bites my lower lip. She then breaks away smiling and says, "I think we're blocking the doorway." I grin back at her like a naughty teenager out with a new accomplice. Then I cradle her head against my shoulder as we walk. Every five or six steps though, we seem to stop, turn and exchange playful glances. I've no idea where we are but I'm gliding, happily giddy with Alice.

We turn a corner, Alice is guiding me onto the pathway running down beside *Il Naviglio Grande* where all the lights and sounds coming from the restaurants and bars on either side of the canal give the whole place a fuzzy, warm, romantic feeling. Seeing such beauty, I'm transported out of my body into a whole new world. Here, I am not a lonely thirty-two-year-old man with the weight of the world on his shoulders. Nor in this world am I being treated for recurring nightmares in which I owe something to someone that has no price nor can ever be repaid.

"It's so pretty here, don't you think?" she asks.

"Yes, it is. Do you live far?"

Straight away, I wish I hadn't just said that. I am still thinking about our kiss. I don't want her to think…

"No. Not far," she replies quickly. "But can I show you somewhere on the way? I mean, unless you need to wake up really early tomorrow?"

"No. It's Saturday. I'm fine," I say. "I want to go wherever you want me to go."

Alice pauses to ponder. Then, she twirls around quite suddenly and takes me by both hands before beginning to apologise really unnecessarily for something she thinks she's done wrong.

"I'm sorry," she says. "I never once asked how you find yourself alone in Milan on a Friday night. Where are you staying? Do you live here or are you just travelling through?" She grins nervously.

"I'm working here," I reply quickly enough. "I have a valid *R.P.* and a meeting on Monday at midday, but I flew in early. I thought I'd give myself the weekend. A bit of sightseeing."

"Oh. Okay," she nods. She seems reassured. "Come on then."

We walk again. Then a few paces further along, she turns me around. "So, what work do you do? I'm sorry. I should have asked earlier. I... May I ask that or...?"

"You may ask me, yes."

"But?" she counters.

"But nothing," I say smiling. "It's just that I'd rather not talk about what I do while we're standing in the street. Can we talk someplace else? Is that okay?"

"Are you a spy?" she asks in a hushed voice. "What did you say your name was again? Peter? Scott? Or...? Are you James Bond?" She laughs at her own joke, but I can see she believes I'm hiding a secret and she's desperate to know what it is. Girls do seem to love a bit of mystery with men, I find.

"I'll tell all when we get back to your place. I'm expecting the Spanish inquisition," I say.

"Italian, Please! And, I knew it! You're a spy aren't you! British intelligence?"

"Shhh, keep your voice down."

"Oh my God!" she says. "It's true. You *are* a spy."

There's a brief pause. Drunken thinking is going on here before she finishes off with, "you're not going to murder me if I let you in my apartment, are you?"

I laugh. "Only if you don't have the plans that I'm looking for."

"I don't know what you mean," she says stifling a giggle, and she turns me around another corner to where a lot of young people have spilled out onto the street in front of a jazz bar.

"Come to *Blues Canal* with me," she pleads tugging me through the crowd towards the sound of live jazz music bursting through the door. "Just one drink? I love this place. I love the music."

We sit at Table 52, as close to the stage as Alice can get us, and table service is as quick as the rhythm being thumped out by the three guys on stage. "What would you like?" she calls out over the music. "More wine?"

"I fancy a whisky in a place like this! Neat. No ice."

I love jazz music. I tend to listen to it at home though on my headphones and I do like a little glass of scotch on the side. It's been a long time since I was out in such a lively place. It could be so easy to aggravate my condition in here. But the company does help and I'm absorbed in the busy, upbeat vibe.

"Good," she says and places our order.

I take a moment to scan the room and it doesn't disappoint. It's wild and cool, and nothing at all like I'm used to on a Friday night back in England or L.A.. In fact, the only thing missing from the whole classic jazz scene in here is the cigarette smoke that fills the air in films from the twentieth century.

When two whiskies arrive, I resist the urge to ask. I also call the waiter back and slip him a fifty before Alice can pull out her card collection again.

"I don't really drink whisky," she smiles.

I kiss her again, just lightly. Just checking this isn't a dream. She purses her lips and briefly closes her eyes to my touch. "I know," I say.

We sit close. We're facing a stage some twelve feet away where a really young-looking pianist is thrashing out the embers of a track that an older drummer and guitarist are supporting him on. It's frenetic and I don't know it, but the pianist looks crazy cool and completely lost in it.

"They're a local trio," shouts Alice. "They play here a lot."

Then, after the applause, the room falls eerily quiet.

The guitarist comes to his mike to address the audience. He's a really laidback guy, probably in his mid-forties, and he speaks in Italian with the kind of rhythmical voice I'd expect to find in a place like this.

"He says they're going to play a number that is not jazz. The leader says he wants to pay his respects to a great English group," translates Alice into my ear.

He's still talking, and Alice waits like an interpreter, to continue her explanation. "The song will convey the writer's dismay..." She's so fluent and quick she could work for the U.N.

"The song's from 1968, but we're living difficult times still now; since '*2020*' was followed by the *Depression*, the endless refugee crises, and with Africa, Central America and Australasia's soaring mortality rates where it's becoming impossible for humanity to exist anywhere but close to the coast. The song's about our inability to realise our potential to love."

Without warning, she abruptly stops translating and turns away to watch the stage. I wonder if there's something wrong, and I reach out to hold her hand, squeezing it reassuringly and getting the same back. I wonder if she's just guessed what they're about to play and she appears moved. If that's by the song, the world and local events or all three, I don't know. But I do immediately recognise the opening. In these special surrounds and accompanying such an amazing girl as Alice, I can't help but spare another quick thought for my dad. He loved *The Beatles* and is the reason why I do too.

On the small stage, an acoustic intro is performed perfectly, leading into a moving rendition of the song. A solitary tear runs down Alice's cheek and I can't help but feel moved by the reverence with which the whole club treats such a hauntingly beautiful piece of music.

I move the back of my hand gently over to wipe away her sadness and I whisper the words in her ear in time to the music, "*... while my guitar gently weeps...*"

For this, she turns her face back towards mine, takes my hand in hers again and kisses me full on, open-mouthed right there at the table. And I love it. I love the fireworks tingling up my back and I love the way our bodies melt so perfectly together. When we pull apart this time and open our eyes, we stare at each other for longer. The guitarist is allowing his guitar to weep some more in an extension of the original and I see wonder and love in her eyes. Alice is studying me passionately. She bites her lip and looks away. "I live near here," she says. "Shall we go?"

Polite applause is followed by another song as we wind our way hand in hand back outside and I'm completely blown away with only Alice on my mind.

We cross a footbridge onto the opposite side of the canal and walk until the lights and the noise from the bars disappear behind us and we're standing outside a modern looking apartment building. It's flanked on one side by several much older looking buildings and by a small park on the other. Alice announces that we've arrived and then quips, "You won't hurt me will you Mr. Bond?" as she reaches into her bag for the front door key. I think she's trying to look coy, teasing me. And it's working.

I smile to myself in the dark. And, as we enter the building and walk past several mailboxes in the foyer, Alice moves ahead to feel for the light switch as the front door clicks shut behind us.

"It's too late for regret now," I say, immediately conscious of sounding a bit stupid. But she doesn't seem to notice.

We kiss again in the lift all the way up to the top floor. I'm normally scared stiff in elevators but not right now. Alice leans against the side and presses the button behind her back. She pulls me towards her and grasps onto my pullover in the middle, taking control, as, on tiptoes again she reaches her lips up to brush mine, teasing me, demanding more.
"You live in the penthouse?" I ask when the door opens onto a short corridor with just one door leading off it.

"Please," she says, as we approach her apartment.

"And you live here alone?"
"I...I want to share it. Would you like to share it with me? Tonight?"

Alice stutters, notably before the last word. I hope I haven't touched a raw nerve. She's nervously fumbling in her bag for a key and I watch her, forcing my hands into my tight pockets for no good reason other than I suddenly feel awkward in the corridor light and don't have anywhere else to put them.

The wide-open space her front door opens onto accounts for about ninety percent of Alice's apartment and I look all about me in awe. There's ambient lighting all around a clean modern kitchen area and central breakfast bar flowing onto a vast sitting area with a huge inviting, low white leather sofa. In one corner close to the front of the room is a grand old black concert piano. And, glass patio doors surround the front and far side of the whole place. The bright lights of the *Navigli* quarter and down as far as *Porta di Genova* stare back at us through the night sky. It's a truly magnificent flat and view.

"Go sit on the sofa, and I'll bring food and drink," she hollers, probably from her bedroom.

I'm standing alone in the shadows in a one of Milan's finest and best located penthouses. I'm consciously happy for the first time in ages, and the girl who invited me in is incredible. I'm always ready if something goes wrong as it so often has done in the past. But I might just as easily be falling in love. I've known Alice for one solitary evening but worryingly, I think I like her. Damn it. It can surely only end badly. It is a relationship doomed by distance anyway. And, then there's my job. *The Carpet*'s surely not for her, though she'd look beautiful on it with me. Should I tell her how I'm feeling? No. 'I love you' on a first date can only end with me standing alone back at the entrance below and in no time at all. And she'd definitely not want to hold my hand again in the lift.

I sit down on the sofa like she wanted me to, and wait.

Alice

I don't know why I do a lot of the things I do, but I've never been known for my spontaneity. Tonight though, it seems all that just changed. And, I'm having a good time.

He pauses outside the door and for the briefest of moments I'm really nervous. It's like he's weighing up whether or not he actually wants to be here. Well, it's now or never, I'm thinking. Maybe if I try to kiss him he'll make up his mind and then we can walk before we freeze to death.

Suddenly, his eyes widen. I attempt a shy smile, and I think we both know what's coming next. He pulls me slowly towards him and I feel safe again next to the warmth of his torso through that worn pullover. I'm wishing he'd just hurry up. I can feel my eyes misting over. My heart is beating out of my chest he's so handsome, and I am melting into those chocolate brown eyes of his. I so don't want him to notice I might cry. Why doesn't he just…?

…Not before time, he leans forward and our lips meet for the first time. He is so soft, so gentle yet his lips against mine feel like they belong there and always have. I want more, and I show him, pulling him closer still and passionately opening him up.

I've drunk a lot more wine than I usually do. As we walk, him cradling my head on his shoulder, my excited nervousness is momentarily tempered by fear. Am I about to take a strange man right into my home where…? No, surely not. I feel safe on his arm. His kiss is as delicate as a gentle breeze in summer and there's a tender sadness in those doe eyes that insights a passion and curiosity in me that I really need right now. An escape.

We turn onto Via Casale, just a little detour, and I plead with him to come for drink in *Blues Canal*. I tell myself as I pull him along after me that if he likes it here, I'll love him forever.

This is my favourite bar in all the world. Some of the hippest people in town have been coming here for over seventy years. And, it's just around the corner from where I live. Over the years, I've made lots of friends here. It's the kind of place that's always welcoming, and where I've spent many an evening unwinding after arriving back in Milan.

It's turning into a magical night. The bar is heaving, yet a table for two right by the stage is free and calling out to us. A waiter is immediately on hand and quickly back with our drinks. Then, we've only been there for one song when the leader of the local trio on stage starts talking intelligent politics to introduce why he wants to pay homage to my favourite musicians of all time.

In the last few years, this bar has been a den for the *still politicised few*; the lefties, the greens, the old schoolers who're not burned out on 8G hologram-chatting to the detriment of their ability to think for themselves anymore. As the guitarist at his mike brings people's attention to some of his latest humanitarian causes and starts to play *The Beatles'* track he says brings into question our capacity as a species to really and truly *'love'* one another, I look away into space for a moment. I know I'm going to cry if not for the issues some people less fortunate must face, then for the chills that spill up my back every time I hear George Harrison's guitar gently weep.

I know I can love. I know I want to love. I know I will love. And, the man sitting next to me tonight could be my one true love, as he whispers the lyrics of the song back to me and caresses away my tears. But, it's so true that many people around the world can't or won't love, and this for me is so sad, it moves me.

I kiss him again. I want him to feel all my loving intentions, to flood his senses with how much he means to me right now in this moment. We leave as the rest of the audience applaud and the band start to play a regular favourite of theirs, "*Innamorati a Milano.*" As we push through crowds towards the door, I smile to myself at how apt this song might turn out to be.

I lead him quickly back to my apartment. I don't think about the impression it might leave on him when he realises I live in the penthouse. I've never brought a man here before. Maybe he should be honoured I've invited him. Then again, maybe I should just stop overthinking what presumptions he might have and open the door. I live in a big loft in central Milan. So what? I work for a bank.

I look at him. He looks ill at ease with his hands unnaturally squeezed into his pockets. I'm so happy we've made it here though. And, I want this to continue to be a special night. I so want him to want it to be special too. I'm thirty-two years old and it's probably high time I shared my home with more than just my music collection and a fancy mood lighting app.

I turn my key in the door, and suddenly feel his awkwardness. It's as if I've said something wrong. I think he thinks so.

I blush pure crimson as we go inside and don't want him to see me. I close the door behind him, head bowed, and rush to my bedroom, I say, to change my clothes.

I call out to him to sit. I say I'll prepare food and something to drink. Then I quickly remove my accessories and put my hair up. I inform *Echo Spot 12* that I'd like something classic, sassy and moody to play on low volume throughout the apartment. I completely trust *ES* to do that. I've only had him a month but he always seems to pick exactly what I want.

Finally, like an actor in the wings, I take a deep breath and go back to him as *Caetano* sings *Paloma*. A beautiful choice for finding new love.

Him

Alice heats up some pizza and brings over another bottle of wine with two large glasses. "They never give tall glasses for wine in Italian bars," she says. "If you want to drink for drinking's sake, you buy your own and do it at home."

After placing everything on a low set glass coffee table in the middle of her enormous lounge, she uncorks the bottle as deftly as the waiter did it before, and pours.

I'm too comfortable to move and so stay, sitting upright, crossed legged like a school child and in easy reach of the table. Alice cradles her glass on the sofa next to me. She kisses me delicately on the mouth before sitting back against the seat to give herself space to look. She stares down at me half hidden behind her drink, and eventually asks again what I was reluctant to answer in the street. She's blunt and so sudden, I have to stifle a fit of the giggles.

"C'mon," she demands. "I told you my life story in the bar." "*Okay,*" I say between cramming pizza into my mouth and washing it down with a gulp of what I embarrassingly then realise tastes like quality red wine. "Tell me where you got the *Steinway* in the corner and I'll tell you anything you want to know."

"It's not a *Steinway*," she snaps. "It's *Fazioli*, so better."

"You're kidding me, right?"

"What are you asking me?" she says suddenly. She sets her drink down and rises back to her feet, waving her arms around. I guess I've hit a raw nerve and immediately start to back track. She's really passionate about her piano but as she rages away, I can't help but find this *look* really sexy.

"If it's about 'can an Italian piano maker be better than a *Steinway*', then *yes* it can! My piano is better than any *Steinway I've* ever played. Then again, if it is an assumption that *Steinway* means *quality*, then this is just the typical reaction of a non-musician. Did you perhaps see someone on TV playing a *Steinway?*"

"Perhaps," I stutter.

"So, you admit it. You don't know what you're talking about when it comes to pianos?"

"And, I thought you were a banker?" I laugh, still trying to diffuse her. I get the sense she's having none of it though.

"You can think whatever you want," she says sitting back down and taking her glass again. "But I can't have you talk about my piano. Not yet anyway. I still don't know what or who you even *are* yet, and you're a guest in my home."

I pause. Is it that time already? Alice widens her beautiful blue eyes imploringly, and I know.

"So?" she asks finally. She looks so attractive and curious and agitated all at the same time. I know I'm going to have to start talking about myself. And, that's when I deviate completely off grid!

"Have you heard of Peter Allan-Ferris?"

After a brief quizzical pause for thought Alice replies. "Urm… yes. Wasn't he that American actor?"

"Yes."

"Didn't he die of an overdose or something a few years ago?"

"Yes and no," I say. "He died on February 1st, '27 and he was only twenty-seven years old. He'd have been just a year younger than me now. And it was no overdose by the way. I reckon he was poisoned. Someone, and we don't know who, messed with his MDMA that night. But…"

She doesn't say anything. Alice simply looks confused, like as if to say 'what the hell are you on about? Is this even relevant to us tonight?' I know that's what she's thinking. If roles were reversed, I'd be thinking the exact same thing. Anyway, when she shrugs, I go on.

"…Of course, it helps popular myth and the fake news media narrative that it's chalked up as just another O.D. in L.A.. Like, oh, there's another member of the twenty-seven club and, it's what they do isn't it? Those," I take a sip of Dutch courage before finishing my line, "…*film stars*?"

"Okay," says Alice. "Where are you going with all of this?" She's still lost and I don't blame her. But, I've opened a can of worms and I'm kind of obliged to be clearer now, right? Right. The painful truth I've deliberately avoided for the last four years except with my shrink, Juan Pablo, is about to come out.

"Alice. I was with him that night. I was *with* him," I persist. "Peter Allan-Ferris was my best friend. We were best friends, you know?"

"No. I'm not sure I follow," she answers. She looks calmer than I feel though, and it makes me go all apologetic on her.

"Look. I'm sorry Alice," I say. "I said in the street that I didn't want to talk about my job because it's… Look, I'm not a spy! And, I'm not a murderer either." I force a lame smile. "But, I'm not just going to tell someone I meet in a bar what my name is."

'*Shit. That probably came out all wrong, and it's too late to take it back.*'

"So, you're not called Peter Scott?" she asks innocently. "I don't understand you at all."

"No," I say. "I'm not Peter Scott because there is no Peter Scott… Okay?" Then, "there are probably seven or eight thousand Peter Scotts on *Facebook*. I'm just not one of them."

Alice falls silent and I look at her pleadingly.

It's not my fault I'm the way I am. I've never wanted to open up or be opened up by anyone. I'm happy on my own aren't I? Then, this girl might be different. I stare at her and see only a beautiful innocence I just want to lose myself in right now.

Only, she's now glaring back at me. Still silent. I have to tell her. I just don't know how or where to begin...
It's just one big bad movie script. The media storm that's become my life in the last seven or eight years. In and out of Hollywood, no real attachment to anywhere. Then, after Pete crashed and burned, I've self-medicated sleep, blurring the lines between reality and fake with no one but an expensive old Argentine to turn to whenever I lose my shit completely. And, I've been living out of a suitcase for way too long as well, and I don't like what I see when I look in all those different hotel mirrors.

"Continue," she says suddenly. She must really be into me. I'd have thrown me out by now, or at least shouted something like, "what's your bloody name you weirdo?"

"Look, I travel under the name 'Peter Scott'. Allan-Ferris, was my best friend. It's kind of a homage thing. That and I like going incognito."

She shrugs again. She's waiting. Her happy face has gone but she's still too curious to show how impatient I must be making her.

"Do you know any of his best films before he died?" I ask her.

Another shrug. She makes a facial gesture like she doesn't really care and my heart leaps for joy. She probably doesn't have time for stupid American films, and I can just say my name and she'll never have heard of me anyway and, then she goes and speaks again, and I melt into a pool of water and come crashing down onto her sofa.

"I saw him once, in a *silly* comedy called '*If I could make it there...*'"

"It's called 'If I *can* make it there...'"

"I'm sorry. It's a foreign film. I don't know the exact name. My brother showed me it."

"And I'm sorry too. It *is definitely* a very silly film. You're right." I sigh with relief, and beam from ear to ear, buoyed by her opinion. She surely thinks I'm nuts.

"Look. Pete also starred in a psychodrama called *The Dream* back in '24, a year after the *silly comedy,* and, he was in the middle of shooting a film called *The Truth and the Light* when he died."

"Ok," replies Alice. "But you're not his ghost. Why are you going on about *him* when it's *you* I want to get to know?"

"Alice," I say. "*The Truth and the Light*" has been resurrected. It's just about to come out of post-production. It just needs a signature. Then, it's getting released for Christmas in Pete's memory and in time for next year's Oscars. I am in Italy this week to promote the film. That's what my meeting on Monday is all about. You know the *Gallia Excelsior*, right?"

"Of course, I do" she replies. "Everyone in Milan knows this hotel. Are you...?"

I interrupt her and hold up my hands apologetically.
"None of my films have ever been nominated before. If this one is well timed enough it will be my first nomination, and if we win and Peter is acknowledged... wow!" I pause for breath.

Just as Alice cried earlier on, I now wipe away a small tear with my sleeve. She stands up and crosses to her kitchen without uttering another word.

I just turn my head and watch her. She presses something on the *ES12* and poses a question into the usual beam of white light pointing up at the ceiling. "Echo, chi ha diretto il film, *La verità e la luce*, che uscirà questo Natale?" She asks in Italian but I more or less understand. I know what she's doing, and I don't interrupt her a second time. A large three-dimensional hologram of me wearing a tuxedo and walking arm in arm with a French actress that I know all too well appears on Alice's kitchen worktop. It's a much-used *3D meme* from the Cannes red carpet where in naïve, happier times, we premiered *The Dream* in the spring of 2025.

Alice stands the other side of the hologram and I see her silhouette through my image staring up in complete bewilderment as *Wikitalk2025* starts to explain what I can only assume is my life story in Italian. I stand up wanting to go to her, but she notices me and clicks the image off just as quickly as it came on.

"I'm sorry Alice," I say. "I always travel under his name. I do it to protect myself."

She's already walking back towards me as I talk. Not another word is spoken before she reaches out a hand again, and again I take it. We kiss and everything else in the room falls away around us. Her soft warmth comforts and reassures me far more than words ever could.
We break off and I feel her breath shaky and shallow against my cheek. I open my eyes to see her looking right back at me. "Thank you," I say.

"Why?" she replies, bewilderment suddenly mixed with passion.

"For understanding."

Alice leans back out of our embrace and silently leads me by the hand over towards her *Fazioli* where she sits and beckons that I sit close, next to her.

"Do you want to hear an Italian Steinway?" she giggles, her voice still shaking a little.

"What are you going to play?"

"I don't know" she replies. "A medley for *The* Nathaniel Scott, in *my* apartment perhaps?"

"Please. Call me Nathan," I say. "Close friends don't call me Nathaniel."

"But I'm not a close friend," she quips in a flash. "I'm someone who…" She stops there. There's no need for more words. She gazes into my eyes briefly. Then she turns away and starts to play the haunting opening to The Beatles' *"You never give me your money."*

In that instant, I learn all that I need to know about Alice. She plays with passion and as I listen, I look out past her and the piano. Against the backdrop of the calm Milan skyline at night, and with the most beautiful soundtrack, Alice and I have found each other. Two lost souls from a bygone era in love in 2031.

Alice

It's been a while since I last entertained anyone in my apartment. I'm so nervous about getting this right. I give him some nice pizza that I baked yesterday evening. My brother grew the tomatoes and basil on his balcony. The cheese is organic. I hope he likes it. I open one of my best bottles of red, *Sassiaia 2015*. It's a super smooth wine and I'm going to try to relax with a glass as he tells me who he is. I trust my instincts. He isn't dangerous, at least not criminally so. But, there's something mysterious about him. Could he really be a British spy? In northern Italy?

I watch him hungrily devour my pizza and suddenly feel really guilty that I'd kept him from his dinner earlier on. My guilt evaporates after he gulps from his glass of rouge as if it were fruit juice and makes some bizarre observations about my *Fazioli*.

I completely overreact in defence of my instrument but when we're speaking about my one and only prize possession he will have to learn this about me. My piano is my beating heart. It is everything to me. The *Fazioli* in my apartment was a thirteenth birthday gift from my parents, constructed for me personally in 2012. I performed at international events heralding the abilities of so called, "*Prodigies*" throughout my childhood and it was on this very instrument that I practised and perfected many of my concerts.

I really was supposed to have become a great composer or something like that. I even shared the stage once in London with the acclaimed English composer, pianist and on that occasion violinist Alma Deutscher. She was only eight years old at the time, back in 2013, compared to my still innocent fourteen. Yet she showed me my place! Alma was just a little kid. She was not at all horrible to me. But I knew after sharing the stage with her... Sadly, it was after that performance when I realized that a career in music was not for me. It was like the moment when Antonio Salieri must have realised that Amadeus could not be beaten. All point was taken away. I'm not competitive. I knew I was competent. Applause does that to a person. And, as a child, when you're told you're special all the time, you tend to believe it, especially as it is the trusted adults who are telling you this. But I am no fool either. Unlike the adults who stood and watched and clapped and cheered the little children as they made music like Mozart, Alma and I knew what we were doing. And I knew in an instant that I could never be as good, naturally, as she was.

Still, my beautiful *Fazioli*, at great pains and cost to my parents and I, has followed me from my family home on Lake Como to this apartment. I would be lost without it though I don't compose or play classical pieces on it anymore. *The Beatles'* entire back catalogue is my biggest musical passion. *The Beatles* and jazz piano. This is my life away from work.

As we sit there and he talks in circles, I'm kind of tuning in and out of what he's saying. Drinking a lot of red wine on an empty stomach is never a good idea I'm beginning to realise, no matter how good the company. I nibble some of my pizza and try to focus. He seems to want to tell me something really complicated and I'm confused as to why. I only want to know what his name is and what he's doing in Milan.

"So, you're not called Peter Scott?" I ask eventually. And, this brings up a further question from me. Did he lie about his name to begin with? Did I just bring a complete stranger into my house? Oh God! Red wine will be the death of me!

Saying that, he actually looks like he's going to cry at the moment and I wonder whether I should be getting up and offering him a Kleenex. I don't know. It's kind of obvious really that he's got something to do with the media or films, or both. But seriously, I don't know why he's so afraid to talk about it. He's not an actor I've ever seen before and all that celebrity stuff is of no more interest to me than the subtle differences between a *Fazioli* and a *Steinway* are to him. I'm more curious about the man behind the mask. And, his being so handsome on the outside helps enormously too.

So, okay. A dead film star called Peter Allan-Ferris who I barely recognise from a couple of old films released just after the first pandemic, was his friend. He was there when the guy died. He suspects foul play and hates himself for not being able to do anything to stop it… Or at least I think that's what he's been raving on about all this time. And yet, I still don't know the name of the man on my sofa eating my pizza and drinking my wine!

He looks at me, really serious all of a sudden. I am beginning to wonder if I should be scared.

He launches into another speech about an abandoned film called *The Truth and the Light.* It was supposed to have brought Allan-Ferris his first major awards as a film actor. Upon the announcement of his death, production had stopped. But now it turns out that the film has actually been completed and will soon be released in honour of the actor this Christmas.

He looks like he's about to sob again when he mentions the 2032 Oscars. Then, just like that, he stops talking altogether and sips on his drink, spent of energy.

I'm still not sure I follow what's going on but if he's not going to say, I'll have to find out for myself. And, if this *Truth and Light* is *his* movie, then this is a really ironic situation we find ourselves in.

I turn on my *Spot12* and ask it who directed *The Truth and the Light*. I can see him watching me through the *3D Wiki-grams* of himself.

I don't care about his fame or his red carpets. I don't care anymore than he probably does about the world of international banking. Right now, I just want to connect with this beautiful man who's standing in my living room looking lost and scared. I want to connect with the real person behind the name, Nathaniel Scott, Hollywood Film Director.

He's quite probably a lot of different things to a lot of different people. And, seeing the difficulty he seems to have living with the whole fame thing, and the way he puts down his own films, I can see he's not happy with whatever pressures he places on himself. But, none of it matters and there are no words in any language that I can say to make him better. There's only love.

We hold each other again and I am there, lost in his arms, looking into his eyes and thinking, 'this is the real thing. This is the real thing.' Our lips touch and I feel fire race right through my body. I could so easily get addicted to kissing this man. We part and I struggle to stop my breath from shaking. Then, he says, "thank you," and though I ask him why, I know.

"Call me Nathan," he says. "Close friends don't call me Nathaniel."

"But I'm not a close friend," I say. "I'm someone who…" I stop myself from asking '…*you met in a bar?*' I'll save that line for if he ever hurts me. I feel so good and yet so vulnerable right now. Control of my heart is now completely out of my hands and I hope he feels the same way too.

Tonight, we'll be ok though. Tonight, we'll stay together. Tonight.

Nathan

We stay at her piano until we finish the wine bottle. She smiles as she plays and I sing her favourite ballads back to her. Her pearly white teeth are as perfect as the ivories she's tapping with such beautiful energetic ease. Her fingers are slender and her nails, well-kept and polished clear. I briefly look at my own chewed efforts and wonder what she could possibly find attractive about me. My lower front teeth are bent as well and I'm reminded of a conversation I once had at *Warner* with a Foley guy who said I should get my teeth done then sell him whatever they remove for his prop box.

She tells me she's crazy about *The Beatles*. She doesn't know why. She puts it down to how some of the songs, mainly ballads send a chill up her back whenever she hears them. Having studied music as a child she's had her mind opened to so many different influences most of which come from a time long before our own.

I tell her about my dad and how he'd passed away. But how he'd been a huge fan himself and had passed that love on down to me. Then, I'm rattling on about a night I spent in Girona, Catalonia with *The Beatles'* first drummer.

"Pete? Oh no, another Pete!"

"Yes," I say. "It's no big deal though. It was just a really strange night out. Pete Best just kept saying the same thing over and over... He was like, 'who is this guy? He keeps going on about *Cliff Bennett and The Rebel Rousers.*'"

"Who are they?"

"Not anywhere near as big as *The Beatles*," I reply. "They're an English group that toured with the Fab Five as they would've been then, in Germany in the early days. My granddad's cousin was their bassist."

"And why was Pete Best so bothered by that? Should he not have bowed down himself to the great Nathaniel Scott?"

"No way! I was just a student back then, in 2018. Pete Best was old, but he was still cool."

"Wow," she says. "I saw Paul once. In concert. It was years ago. I was sixteen at the time. And, do you know what? He forgot the words to the song we started off with before."

"What did he do?"

"Oh, he just made up some new ones on the spot. It was so cool!"

"You're so lucky," I groan. "I've never seen Paul or Ringo for real and I guess it's too late now."

I scan the room for a clock of some sort. Neither of us has looked at a mobile device, and my Smart watch is in the hotel tonight getting its once per week charge. I'm scared to ask her what time it is as I don't really want our private party to end, and even worse, I don't want Alice to think I'm getting bored.

Anyway, she has no clock. There's probably one attached to the oven, but I'm too myopic to see that from the lounge. The only obvious sign indicating how long we've been sitting together is the dawn that's starting to break through the two walls of glass surrounding us.

I'm beginning to think that if we don't go to bed soon, I'm going to ask her if she wants to take a stroll with me in the early morning light to find fresh coffee and warm pastries. Or we could just go out and watch as the cleaning carts beep their way along the canal side and the shutters start to roll up on another working day. I've always found early mornings a beautiful time to be awake, especially when you know you've no work pressure lying ahead of you. Just observing the world as it wakes up, hearing birdsong and smelling fresh warm bread is such a delicious thought.

"You studied in Spain?" she asks, interrupting my daydream.

"No. Catalonia," I assert automatically. I'm really well versed in Iberian politics and have been an occasional supporter of the Catalan Republic. I say 'occasional' because it's not really my problem, and currently a guy I used to know very well seems to be spearheading the region into civil war. Whenever I've been in a place like Girona or Figueres where nobody speaks Spanish unless under duress though, I have appreciated there is an argument for self-determination and I'll even admit to having flag waved for the cause on more than one occasion in my youth.

"Oh. So, you speak Catalan?" she asks with interest.

"*Per suposat*" I say. "*Of course,* that means Of course."

"And Spanish too?"
"Por supuesto" I smile.
"And you say your mum's French, no?"
"Bien sûr" I say, laughing.

"Why are you laughing again? You mock me!"

"No," I grin cheekily.

"Arrogant man," she scoffs. "And I thought you were just a typical English…"

"Typical English what?" I ask. "Hollywood film director?"

"Arrogant!" she quips. "Just arrogant. Now, as you speak all these languages you'll have no problem learning Italian next, I hope?" And, she does genuinely sound hopeful that I will.

"Ok, but not now though, I'm too tired. Though I do have one, more, vital, question for you."

"Yes?"

"Internazionale or A.C.?" I ask tentatively. I love football. I won't deny it. And this is Milan after all.

"Calcio!!!?" she replies. "You ask me about soccer at dawn?"

"What?" I say, though not really as surprised as I make out, truth be told.

Alice turns back to her ivories and strikes out the intro to "*Here comes the Sun*" once through. I fall straight into her trap. I'm readying myself to launch into song when she stops abruptly and carefully closes the lid on our night's entertainment.

"I have had an amazing night out and in with you Nathaniel Scott," says Alice getting to her feet. "If this is just a dream, it's a really good one so thank you God. If this is really happening though, maybe you would like to stay with me and hold me in my bed? I would like that very much. I would be…"
I interrupt her. She looks really embarrassed all of a sudden and she has no reason to be. No reason at all. I quickly put two fingers towards her lips and ask that she stop.

"Are you coming or going?" she asks finally.

"I'm *staying*."

Alice reaches up and kisses me gently. Then, she pulls away ever so slightly and looks me up and down teasingly. I smile. Again, she eases herself up on her tiptoes, softly biting first her own lower lip, before in an instant, mine. I pull away gently and kiss her back, just a peck. I hold her stare. She bites her lip again, her head bowed but her eyes still trained on mine. She's so cute, I want her more than anything right now. She provokes me, again rubbing her pixie nose against mine and then my cheek. She's playing and I love it. I draw back this time. I'm studying her tired blue eyes, still sparkling ahead of the impending dawn. She takes me by the hand, lacing her fingers gracefully with mine. Finally, she comes down off her toes and pulls me slowly back across the room towards somewhere we both want to go…

Standing at the foot of her bed, we find ourselves still as statues, suddenly as nervous as a pair of teenagers experiencing love for the very first time. For a moment, I don't know what to do. She bites her lower lip again and tilts her head to one side. Alice is still playing shy as I start, then we both undress each other. She is a drug to me. All it took was that first kiss and addiction was instant.

I sit on the edge of the bed and pull her towards me. She is breathing shakily and shallow again and I feel her heart beat quicken against my body. Is *that* what love feels like? Passing my fingers gently through her hair I let it fall loose over her shoulders. She kisses me again soft and warm and as I open my mouth to her she moans with pleasure. The kissing intensifies and we move like two totally synchronised dance partners, our bodies fitting together like they were designed for only that.

When eventually our eyes meet again, she suddenly asks me in a hushed tone if I am ok. I could not be more okay right now, anywhere or with anyone else in the whole of this world. I'm just too shy to say so. "Yes," I say breathing erratically and nodding my head.

"Good," she replies. "Because, I need you to know something very important. I don't do this sort of thing often…"

"I know," I say.

"No, you don't know. We're going to get very intimate in a minute and you need to know that when we do, I'll very likely fall in love with you. So, for self-preservation…"

I try to speak, but she stops me.

"…For my sake, I need to know that this is really something you want too and…"

This time she does let me stop her. I don't speak. My eyes give me away. In this precise moment, I could not be more in love than I am with Alice.

Her hand glides across my face, just checking, and moves down over my arm to where I catch her hand in mine. We begin to move together as one, loving each other with our eyes as much as with our bodies, connected telepathically as we steady ourselves every so often, smiling breathlessly at one another, trying to extend the moment.
When it all comes to an end, we find ourselves still as statues once again, only this time, not afraid. Our bodies and souls mingle under a warm duvet, holding one another close, gazing into one another's eyes until sleep eventually steals us both away and into another day.

Alice

I absolutely adore playing music at any time of the day or night. As I sit next to Nathan at my piano, happy to finally know who my guest is, I suddenly can't control how excited I'm feeling. It's not that I seem to have just trapped a famous film maker in my apartment either. I'm not interested at all in the cult of celebrity. I could have been one myself had I wanted it more than I did at the time. And besides, he's not someone I'd consider a celebrity anyway. He works on the wrong side of the camera for a start.

I'm excited because he's gorgeous. He's tall; at least one metre-eighty-five, and then he's lean and muscular in all the right places. I felt his arms in the street. He works out for sure. And, his full head of brown hair that just seems to hang at odd angles like a mop has a kind of charm all of its own. He looks like a throwback to the 1990s, and though I haven't asked him yet, I suspect that's probably his intention. His nose is cute, his eyes, deep and brown like chocolate drops, and his lips... He kisses *by the book.* Yes, he kisses *by the book said Juliet of her Romeo.*

He can be so awkward and shy yet also mysterious and gentle and charming. But, he does, like all men seem to have his complications too. And, I know now that it wouldn't be possible for me to find a man who isn't complicated without finding that boring.

He seems unaware or unconcerned that what he does entertains so many people around the world. I have a feeling that my brother likes Nathan's comedy film a lot. But, I wouldn't tell either of them this. I don't really understand. If he hates his own film that's fine, but I wouldn't want him to say so to Marco.

I imagine they pay him well to make films. And, if those films make some people happy, he's a success. Anything else is irrelevant.

Also, and this is a very big thing! I've not seen him use a mobile telephone this whole night, not once. I left him to use the bathroom in the bar and he's maybe used the toilets once or twice himself. But he was never away from me for long enough to have checked his social media.

I never look at my phones unless I am working. I hate them, and my mama and papa always connect to me via the *Echo Spot Dial System for 3D Holochat* if they need me. They're both old-school. They were born in the 1960s and generally like to see who they are talking to. Marco, my brother, is the only dial tone for whom the volume is switched on with my personal mobile phone. He's nuts for tech. We're not similar at all, though I love him to absolute pieces all the same!

Living here in Milan, I likewise don't have any need for an *e-car*. I could walk to my office or run in less than an hour. But, more often than not I still choose the metro. Since the mid-2020s after the E.U. eventually decided we were better off in than out of their still unreformed union of bureaucratic thieves, more than three quarters of the entire system has become electric through external investment, and as such, environmentally friendly. I am very much an advocate of all things green.

Sadly, many of the trains running out to here in the canal district still need converting. It's a shame. Italy is more than playing its part in changing the world and I respect that. It could move quicker but it's not as bad as some places. That said, the metro is also a horrid place in the morning. Commuters fill the long chasms of the modern underground trains. The new metros are just long snakes of neon lit plastic and fibre glass casing housing thousands of worker ants all connected to mobile devices screening television shows missed from the night before down to social media platforms designed for life. All are masked, a hangover from the first pandemic, and all cover their ears with headphones and their eyes with shades. They are controlled; controlled, yet well connected even several hundred metres below the ground. I said to myself back in 2019, twenty years old and still at university here, that I would never become like that.

During the 2020s, Paolo and I joined a movement aimed at getting people to look away from the device. It was for a while at least well documented that social media was alienating people more than it brought us together. I often made my point in discussion that on the train journey from Milan back to the lake to visit my parents, I found much more of an inner peace looking out of the window at the lush green countryside as it rolled by, than by anything I could possibly view on an LCD screen. I've often found people agree with me and nod as I speak, yet, they and many, many others like them continue to distance themselves from one another in this way every single day. It's one thing saying something in conversation. But being and doing is something else entirely. From what I have seen tonight, Nathaniel Scott appears to be like me, a member of the anti-tech rebellion in a lost age, and I really hope so.

I have a really good feeling as we sit close together at my *Fazioli*. I just pray that the stars that aligned for us this evening, turn out to have really brought me my one and only – my soul mate.

I feel lucky. I don't have to go to work tomorrow. I usually don't stop. This week, I don't work again until Monday afternoon and that's only in my office here in *Porta Nuova*. I won't travel again until possibly Tuesday or Wednesday. I've heard noises around the office about someone needing to go to Prague next week and if that someone is me, then fine. It's a lovely, friendly city and I shouldn't need to fly to get there. There's an *e-bullet* from *Centrale* once per day only stopping twice, in Munich and Bratislava *en route*. But for now, I'm free and I'm home… with a *man* – Nathaniel who prefers to be called Nathan. And, he's drop dead gorgeous!

He's very serious when I play for him. He says he loves the way my fingers just glide over the keys so elegantly. And he; *he* sings like a songbird, connecting with my *Beatles'* ballads like no one I've ever met before – at least no one our age who can actually sing as well. When he does *The Long and Winding Road, Why don't you give me your money?* and *Blackbird,* I look up and catch him close his eyes, really feeling the passion in the lyrics, and my heart skips at least one beat. He can't even see with eyes shut just how much his connection is turning me on, yet he doesn't sing for praise either. He just loves the songs and wants to give voice to them for me.

Between tracks, Nathan tells me his funny stories. I don't know how much of it all is true, but as he grows in confidence around me and I with him, I just love listening to him more and more and tell him so.

He tells me he's fluent in four languages. I love this about him too. He's surely the first Englishman I've ever met who knows other languages besides his own. I love that we can vary our conversation from English into French. And, I tell him he'll need to learn Italian with me. I'm only kidding of course, but if, just if we became a couple, and he didn't speak Italian, my mum would not forgive me. My dad would not forgive him.

As dawn breaks over Milan, I nervously attempt some comedy of my own, playing the opening to '*Here comes the Sun*' then closing the piano just as he is about to sing the first line. I don't say so, but I am sorry. He looks so sad. But it is time for bed now. It's time, and I just want to hold him and love him and fall asleep with him in my arms.

I ask him if he is coming or going, but he doesn't really have an option. My heart is pounding against my chest as I stand before him on my toes and kiss him seductively. He looks so calm. So beautiful. His mop of hair falls forwards and I want to push it back; I want to push it back and back and…we kiss again. It's just a small one. I pray my instincts about him are right. I'm so fired up I'm losing control. I need to take something back. He looks at me. I bite my lip. I do it instinctively, but I know how he'll see a shy girl's innocence in the gesture. I watch, reading him like an open book before coming down off my toes and pulling him after me to my bedroom, turning a new page…

… And, he comes. We undress each other and I shiver. It's never cold in my apartment but I'm scared. I've only loved one man before today and now suddenly I'm falling again. In the blink of an eye, I've been sassy, brave and forward and now I'm exposed, helpless and in need of nothing but his devotion and caress. My insecurity rises, and I guess I'm being really dumb, but want to I ask him about Audrey Novel. I recognised her from the *3Dmeme on Wiki*. He was holding hands on a red carpet with one of the most beautiful women in the world, yet now he's on my bed and I can't believe what's happening to me.

I have to tell him. I do tell him. If he makes love to me I will fall in love with him and I won't be able to let him go. He has to love me back before we can be intimate in my bed. I don't do this kind of thing I tell him. I need him to understand I am a one-man woman and I am completely his for the taking if he feels that way too.

He reaches out and takes my hand firmly in his. My body is on fire. I stare into his eyes, and he back at me. I feel our souls connect, soon followed by our bodies. My back arches as I accept his love and that special bond of intimacy that we're now sharing sends my imagination wild with dreams of future togetherness and hope.

We finish and curl our bodies around each other. I look deeply into Nathan's chocolate drop eyes, and as sleep takes over, I feel joy. For now, at least, only joy.

Nathan

It's Saturday. I wake up in Alice's bedroom and notice straight away that I'm alone. The space where she lay beside me has gone cold. There are no windows in her room, which strikes me as a bit odd, so there's no natural light from what I assume must be at least early afternoon.

I sit up and as I do so, the whole room is illuminated automatically. The source of the light is not some hanging bulb but it appears to emanate from within the ceiling itself, and is only visible when on. Looking straight ahead at a long blank wall I suddenly blink as the *Samsung View* also alerts itself to the fact that someone has sat up in bed. The wall immediately becomes a giant options screen, all in Italian, backed by an enormous high-definition photograph of what I presume is Lake Como with some very attractive residences along its bank on one side of the image. I know from my own rented pad in L.A. and what the actor who owns it told me at length when I moved in, that the *S-View* is voice activated and that the first four generations of it only let recognised voices use it. My rented *SV* unit is third generation but the landlord set it up to hear my voice. It's in a kind of sunken lounge area that's cylindrical with a sofa wrapped around all of it bar the wall where the screen is and some faux industrial looking steps that lead down into this huge round pit from the kitchen up above. In all honesty, I rarely use it. It looks like a sink hole with a metal railing around it when the lamp down below is turned off and that's not cool. I don't watch much TV at all and I play music from an extravagant yet more conventional source: my original 1950s *Wurlitzer* Juke Box. Some relative of Tobey Maguire sold it to me a few years back for a cool $5000. I've also got a CD player for my albums. I've always liked to be able to hold the product in my hands, and being in my line of work, I often get the chance to have signed copies of everything I keep on my shelves too. Still, that is there, this is here and right now I need music to wake me up a bit. Hoping it's the *SV-5* I tentatively say, "music?" Then I go a little louder, "Music!" And finally, I shout "MUSIC!" But nothing happens.

I give up and head off still stark naked to use the toilet where it's often been that while weeing I've had some of my most creative ideas. It's always so annoying when this happens at home, because you can never write anything down when standing over the bowl. Here, I only need one word in Italian…

"*Musica?*" I shout up at the *SV* after practically running back from the bathroom. Surely, the Italian word for music can't be all that dissimilar to Spanish or Catalan. With fingers crossed I'm thinking 'maybe…'

… and I jump into the air with fright when a sudden buzzing sound booms quite loudly from an equally well-hidden sound system and the music options screen springs into life on the wall. "Wow! She's got a 5!" I say to myself. "*She's got a 5!*"

I feel as if I've just won on the lottery or something. That was weird! And still excitedly, I say, "*Mozart*, Go on! *Mozart*, per favore!"

Whenever I have a sore head in the morning, self-inflicted or not, it just has to be opera to drown it out! A good soprano or tenor on full blast with strong black coffee and painkillers if I can find any. But where's Alice?

Just then, the full list of *Mozart's* work scrolls digitally before me and I instantly call out, "*The Marriage of Figaro!*" My favourite. I listen to this one in the car on the L.A. freeway every day to help pass the time in those endless jams.

The only trouble is that like before, the machine's not reacting… She's got it totally configured in Italian. And, sitting back down on the edge of her bed, I have to admit, I don't know why I'd even be surprised that was the case.

"Sod it!" I reach for my jeans on the floor. I'm going to need that bloody mobile phone to translate the title for me, aren't I. Only, as I go for the pocket I discern that grabbing the Android is only going to piss me off in a million other ways, not least having to see the unwelcome damage staying out all night without looking at it has probably done to my inbox.

Lighting up on my outstretched palm, thankfully pre-set to silent, literally hundreds of missed texts and calls from the last two or three of days flash before my eyes. Most *are* business related and can be deleted or will have to wait until Monday. But of course, Audrey's been texting again too. It's only the usual, 'where are you?', 'why do you never pick up?' and something about her arrival in Milan being delayed to Monday morning. And… Delete.

Back to business, and the "*Hey Google*" app on *GooglePal10*. "Dude," I say. "What's '*The Marriage of Figaro* in Italian?'"

"Oh, hello Nathan." My sudden use of *GP* has overridden the muted volume. "Why are you calling me *Dude*? Why don't I even get a *good afternoon* or a *please* sir?"

He's got such a sterile British *Hal* voice. And, sarcasm really doesn't suit him. In fact, I'm sure I've tried to set him up to sound like a typical Venice surfer idiot before, but I'm no techie and it only ever crosses my mind to do anything about his default settings when he's in a bad mood, or I am with him.

"Ok *pal*. I forgot again. Sorry. *Pleeease*."

For about thirty seconds, nothing. The little spinning circle pans round and round on screen as if he's thinking. He won't need that long to connect. 8G is everywhere. He won't need that long to translate. And, I'm just starting to wonder if this *A.I.* has actually decided he hates his master when it speaks.

"I've consulted my Italian counterpart, and the following statement would seem to be the one that you are looking for: **Le Nozze di Figaro**."

I scroll the cursor over the words on screen that he's just said. Then I copy and paste them onto the memory card.

"Ok, thank you so much with a cherry on top my *G-Pal*. Have a nice day!" I reply with only a touch of facetiousness, as I slide the phone back into my pocket.

"What's left of it," says *G-Pal* as he's tucked away.

Back on my feet, after pulling on my underwear and jeans, yet still as semi-naked as a semi-naked man needing music in a windowless Italian girl's bedroom, I hold both of my arms out wide imploring to the heavens and, in my best-worst Italian accent I cry out, "**Le Nozze di Figaro!**"

Flopping backwards on the bed, I'm so proud of myself if only for a minute or two. "Oh Wolfgang! Wolfgang! So much better than Ibuprofen!" And, the volume setting is either sufficiently high already, or else the tone of my voice did for the front row seat at the opera that I now appear to have got.

Putting my t-shirt, socks and jumper back on, I glance down at the bottom of the *S-View* screen showing that it is nearly 2pm. And, a little shocked but still, happier for the noise, I wander back into the light of the rest of the apartment to see Alice. Only, she's still not there.

I eat some toothpaste from her tube and rub it across my teeth and gums with my finger. It can't hurt. I know I've not got the best set of '*gnashers*' in Hollywood anyway. But I'm only thirty-two. So, I'm not as worried as my dental insurer wants me to be, yet.

I sit on the loo and call the *Excelsior* to make sure no one has been desperately trying to get hold of me. They haven't. I flush, and at the same moment the front door clicks open and I hear her shout, "*Figaro*! Fantastico!"

I pause. Washing my hands in her bathroom sink and looking back at myself in her neon lit mirror for the briefest of moments, I wonder what next for Nathan Scott in this unexpected situation... Where do we go from here? Surely this is all too good to be true...
As I approach the kitchen, Alice rushes over and throws her arms around my neck. Our eyes meet for the first time in the light of day and I see right into her soul. Her loving nature is not easily hidden on that pretty, innocent face and as we're so close again it uses every ounce of inner strength that I can muster not to simply purse my lips to hers and kiss for what's left of the afternoon. Something's troubling me though. I don't know what exactly but I feel myself panicking. My breath tightens and I feel anxiety build in my chest.

"We are a mess today huh?" she asks as she pulls me excitedly back by the hand towards her breakfast bar. Two stools close together face away from the windows and their view on a now cloudy wet Milan day. There are two filter coffees steaming in their paper cups, fresh O.J. also in paper cups and a range of pastries.

"I have to eat better today," she says. "I mustn't let myself waste away." She smiles as she picks up one of the cups of orange. "I need Vitamin C too. I must have downed half a vineyard last night...Had to jog it off along the canal as soon as I got up...And, thank you so much for this beautiful morning music, Nathan." She leans over and kisses me softly.

"I see you have worked out the *S-View*. Your Italian must be better than you let on. Come on. Drink coffee. Shall we plan our day?"

"What's left of it," I reply.

We eat breakfast. I enjoy the coffee, Italian, long and black, just the way I like it. "I will have to get back to my hotel," I say. "I need to get cleaned up and get a change of clothes."

"Shall we go together?" asks Alice. It's a perfectly reasonable question. I know it is. But it doesn't stop my follow up. I predicted this would happen when I looked at myself in the bathroom mirror, and I so hate déjà vu situations.

"No, Alice. Trust me. That's not a good idea."

She looks crestfallen. From the way she furrows her beautiful brow over those sweet blue eyes, to the way her excited lips now droop at the edges, I know there's little I can say to make her understand. I drain my coffee cup and try to offer some words to the wise. But, as I speak it all just comes out completely wrong.

"There's no one at the *Excelsior* who will harm you directly if you come with me." I say.

"You're working at the *Gallia Excelsior* I know. But, you're staying there too? Wow!"

I ignore her and continue to dig myself a dishonourable exit. "Isn't *paparazzi* an Italian word? You surely know how these people operate, Alice? You know how they make money don't you?"

She looks down at her knees. It's as if she senses she's being palmed off; that everything we did last night wasn't at all what I'd allowed it to seem.

"They will be there. Somewhere at a distance, looking through their dirty phone camera lenses, pretending to be doing something else, hoping for a film director they know from their shitty sources has come to stay early in advance of a meeting in Milan on Monday. You can understand that can't you?"

"Not really?" she says looking up innocently and bearing in mind how she bit on her lower lip last night, probably quite deliberately this time too.

"Okay so," I continue. I'm suddenly animated, definitely hungover, and seemingly hellbent on destroying the only really beautiful thing that's happened to me in several years. I take her hand in mine and reluctantly, she lets me. I look down and start to cradle and massage her fingers. Her hand is limp to the touch. She thinks I'm dumping her. I'm distracted. Her fingers are so smooth and slender. I so don't need to be here right now. I want her to know that I am protecting her, but she's just not going to take it that way, whatever I say. I'm not going to be able to rescue this right now. I need air. I need to think.

"Okay fine," she says. "I get you. It's okay. I understand."

"No," I start up. "It's not like you think. We can go to my hotel. And, we can go to my room. You can wait. I will change. Then we can leave and go for dinner, drinks, dancing. Whatever you want. And then…"

She stops me. "Then, nothing," she says. "We can go to your room, but only if Nathaniel Scott wants to of course. And, we can't get a change of things. Instead, we could go *get* his things and I can give him this."

She passes me a set of apartment keys across the bar.

"Then, Nathaniel Scott could come and go as he pleases from my home here for this weekend, and of course whenever he's in Milan again in the future, he has a discreet, private, warm place to stay."

"And then?" I reply. I really, really want her logical solution. I want to hold her again. I want to explore body and soul with Alice all weekend. I don't want to go anywhere. But, I always muck things up. I always lose from a position of victory. And, I know this is going to be just the same before I even open my mouth to answer my own question.

"Please let me finish this time."

Alice bows her head again. She's completely resigned as I press on. I'm being paranoid. I'm being unreasonable. But, I'm afraid. Am I not allowed to be afraid?

"Two weeks from now," I say. "The world's tabloid press with their telescopic camera lenses will have someone camped outside your block waiting for you to come home from Paris or London or where ever! When you are alone in your flat some drone will film you playing your piano through the glass! Our faces will be all over *La Republica* and every celebrity journal from here to Hollywood! And, you. You won't be able to call the *polizia* because guess what?"

Alice doesn't answer. So, I do. "Because the paparazzi are above the law. They're just doing their jobs! That's why."

"So, what are you saying?" she demands. "You've had your fun? You pleased an Italian girl for one night only? Is that it?"

I glare back at her, shocked, and let go of her hand. I have no idea how to reply. I guess this must really look quite bad. I can't blame her for being upset. She looks steadfastly back at me and all at once I feel both painfully uncomfortable and emotional in a way I've never felt before around a woman.

For someone's own good, though I'm not quite sure whose, I will have to get up and walk away right now. But as I'm staring into the eyes of a young woman trying to look angry but not being able to hide her pain and sadness, I also know that I've fallen hopelessly in love with her. I know that when I walk out of this apartment alone, because I will, the profound sadness of something special being lost will be felt just as strongly on both sides of that shut door.

Of course, in an ideal world and not the one I think I inhabit I would just take her back in my arms now and tell her I love her then never, ever let her go again.

But, that's not my reality! My reality sucks. And, I've seen before with Pete and with Audrey in America just how much. I don't want all that for her.

"I've nothing left to say," I tell her as I head towards the door. "I just want to protect you."

"Yes," she says. Then, she's holding the apartment door open and waiting silently for me to leave.

I stand there forcing my hands into my pockets again and getting a sense of déjà vu. As Alice is doing her best to not make eye contact, I take a good long look across the open plan of her home, one more time. I guess I just wanted a memory to hang onto. When my eyes glide past the breakfast bar though, I suddenly get this urge. I'm an impulsive person. It's gotten me into all sorts of mischief over the years. Yet I don't seem to be able to stop myself whenever the compulsion hits.

I chance a final look at Alice's forlorn bent figure, clutching the doorframe like she's ready to slam it shut as soon as I pass. Then, I stride confidently back to the breakfast bar where I take a bite from the remains of a Danish pastry, simultaneously gathering up Alice's apartment keys and silently pocketing them.

"What are you doing back over there?" she asks.

"Eating," I reply. "And, picking up my phone."

"Oh, I didn't see you had one out."

"Yeh, I did. May I have your mobile telephone please Alice?"

She doesn't reply.

"You *do have* a mobile telephone?" I ask.

She is clearly still thinking in black. Of course, she is.

"Y-yes." She stutters and moves away from the open door to get it from a drawer in her kitchen worktop.

I take it from her shaky hand but then need to ask her to unlock. Getting it back again, I key in my personal number. I call myself so that I have her number too, then I hand her back the phone and retreat towards the door.
"Is that okay?" I ask. "Can I call you sometime?"

"I suppose so," says Alice.

"And, thank you. It was lovely to meet you."

"You too, but…"

"Yes?"

She stops herself. "It's okay. See you."
She kisses my cheek and ushers me out of the door. *Figaro* is still getting married in the background.

Alice

As I wake up to Saturday, midday has long since passed, but he still sleeps soundly, his arm across me, caressing. I slowly move out of bed keeping low to the ground. My *S-Vision* is set to put on the main room light and interactive screen as soon as someone sits up in bed. I forgot to disactivate it for him, and I don't want to wake him. He looks so peaceful.

Crawling out of the room on all fours, I grab my same clothes from last night. It is 12.35pm. The time at least is not so bad as I first thought. But the weather outside is. It's grey and looks like we've had some rain earlier on. I tie my hair in a ponytail and slip out of the apartment. I want to take a light jog along the canal bank then back around and through the park. Nothing too strenuous or I'd dress for it.

My priority is to get breakfast for Nathan. And, I need to eat too. My stomach rumbles at me as I get in the elevator and I snack on *M&Ms* from my wet weather coat pocket on the way down.

I jog. Just a little. I walk mainly. But I do complete my circuit. I arrive back at my block little more than a half hour later, and I'm feeling a lot happier about my wine consumption last night for a bit of light exercise.

Just beneath my apartment is a really small café. There's barely room to fit four customers in there at any one time and there's no seating indoors. But they do keep a beautiful range of cakes and small sandwiches on a weekend and they've got a quaint little coffee machine too. While I wait for a box of freshly baked pastries, I drink a macchiato and check my phone messages. I have two phones. I have taken the *social* mobile out with me. I don't dare to look at the *work* one still on charge in the apartment. No one is going to get away with sending me to Berlin at short notice while I have my handsome Englishman here in Milan with me.

Anyway, there's nothing in the social phone, except Paolo wishing me a wonderful evening without him, and my big brother Marco. As I pay the Saturday girl, I text Marco back. He is at a loose end this evening. His usually full social calendar has a free Saturday night on it, and when it does, he often calls his baby sister so that he and his husband can invite me around for dinner and grill me, not literally, about why I don't have a man yet to replace the mopey painter Paolo, when I'm apparently so incredibly gorgeous, says he...

Marco is an architect. He's 37 years old but soon 38 and he doesn't like to be reminded of it. He is married to Noah. Noah is Danish and 28 years old. He speaks good English and is an interior designer who owns his own company.

They met two years ago while contracted to the same job. They were married within six months and have never been out of each other's sight since. It's a strange relationship in some ways. I think Noah gives more than he takes and Marco gives out a lot more instructions than he takes back, but they live well with the dynamic and anyway, I'm the one they call, the "Sexy Spinster," in English oddly enough. So, I'm hardly qualified to pass comment on *their* relationship when I haven't had one of my own for more than a year now.

As I order two orange juices and two Americanos to go and as the girl turns to prepare them, I briefly consider inviting Marco and Noah over this evening to meet with Nathan. But, it's too soon... Yes. Way too soon.

Nathan is out of bed and in the bathroom when I get home. As I see him, I immediately run to wrap my arms around him. I take him by the hand and show him the breakfast I found for him. The fresh coffee aroma fills my senses and I just want to sit with him again, to hold his hand, plan our day, plan the rest of my life…

But something's wrong. Almost straight away I sense it. He wants to go back to his hotel to change his clothes and wash, and I want to go too. I had everything figured out down in the bakery and on my walk. We could collect his things from where ever he's staying and then we could come back here and he'd stay with me for the rest of his time in Milan and … I clearly got too carried away. I'm such an idiot. I told a man I would fall in love with him if we became intimate. I opened myself right up on a first date, and how stupid I was. We were already in bed naked before I told him my feelings. As if either of us was going to stop the inevitable from happening at that moment.

He won't let me come with him back to his hotel.

I plough on. For some reason, I think I will be able to convince him to change his mind. But the lecture about *paparazzi* and how he only wants to protect my innocence just isn't convincing me. I search in his eyes. They're still beautiful, but they're not giving anything away. I think he's had second thoughts about *us*. I feel humiliated.

I laid my heart bare to him. I've never been very good at hiding my feelings. I don't want to play games with anyone. I know what I like and I know what I don't. If he's now in the process of letting me down, I don't need it to be gentle. I don't want a lecture and I don't need Nathaniel Scott to protect *me* from anyone.

I bow my head in resignation twice as he fires on and on. Why is he patronising me? I am not a little girl. I can look after myself. And, no, I'm not from Hollywood. But that doesn't mean I haven't seen cameras and lights before. When I was a child, those cameras were turned on *me*! I was famous in my own right when *he* was probably just an ordinary school kid! And, now he's behaving like one. These paranoias he has about his privacy are crazy. They're crazy because *he* can choose how much or how little fame he wants. He's not a star in front of the camera like his friends. He holds the damned thing!!! He can choose!

Right now, I need him to leave my home, though I want him to stay forever. I want him to stay so that I can protect *him*! But, he doesn't seem to want that; not now anyway. And, on such a rainy day; perfect weather to put out last night's beautiful flame.

Still, something stops him from just getting up and leaving immediately. And, that same something stops me from just ejecting him from my apartment too. I look back into his eyes hoping for a sign that will lead me back into his loving soul.

He glares back at me though. I think he's trying to make me angry to give him justification for his own madness. He won't get it though. And, I see hope in this. I only want to love him. If he sees that… If he can only see that I won't fight him like he expects, I can let him walk out of that door and leave me now. But that won't be the end of the story.

He leaves for the *Excelsior* at *Centrale* and *Le Nozze di Figaro* continues to fill the apartment with life. I lean back on my front door and just stare straight ahead at nothing in particular. I've done all I can for now…

Nathan

I walk back to the hotel. It's about five kilometres and though wet and windy it's not cold for the time of year. I'm so lost in thought, a taxi ride with a chatty Italian would be too bizarre to cope with right now, and I don't understand the ticket machines in the metro. Even when you press the button marked *English*, it still makes no sense at all. An hour's fresh air will do me good and as I'm told by a woman in the street I ask directions from, I'll get to see *Il Duomo*, the iconic cathedral, if I've got my bearings right.

Back in the hotel lobby I want to talk to the receptionists about my plans for the next few days, but I can see they're all busy checking in two sheikhs in full Arabian costume ahead of an army of young men with travel bags on wheels. There's at least twenty of them and they're all wearing matching maroon and yellow tracksuits marked with a large badge that reads "*Roma*" under a picture of some kind of dog. I'm half tempted to stand in front of them all and wobble my knees around like Bruce Grobbelaar. I don't. It was my granddad who showed me the video from

1984, and these young lads wouldn't know what I was doing.

Hands in pockets, her keys seem to jump into my hand as I'm probing around in there for my electronic room card. I skulk towards the elevator unnoticed. I'll phone down after a wash.

The whirring noise that the lift makes as it ascends unnerves me as these things always do. But soon enough, I'm safely back inside my top floor room, sighing relief with my back against the closed white door. I scoop up my *S-Gear 12* off the charger where it has been all night and check the time. 4pm. "Good. There is still something left of the day," I say to myself.

I do love this watch, and as I do up the strap, I feel suddenly as if it's back where it belongs. I missed not wearing it last night. My arm felt kind of naked, and never more so than after meeting Alice with her *Tag Heuer*. It's another odd thing about me. I really don't like mobile phones much at all. They're a kind of necessary evil that I use and tolerate as everyone else swears by them. But I have always been a bit of a slave to time. I think being from Britain does that to a person.

Seated on the edge of the bed, I call down to room service and order a burger, fries, salad and a big bottle of *Coke*. I'm absolutely starving after my epic walk and I will tip them well if they're quick and don't undercook the meat like they do France.

I lie back and muse over the last twenty-four hours some more. I simply can't shake Alice off my mind. I look at my phone to see if she's messaged but there's nothing. Should I text her? No. I need to think this thing through rationally and alone.

I want nothing more than for her to be there next to me now. I'm not thinking about sex either. I just imagine lying right here, right now with Alice next to me. We're holding hands and looking up at the ceiling, breathing each other's scent, feeling each other's warmth. Content. Connected. In her company, I felt loved. It felt right like we belonged.

But, my train of thought keeps coming back round to the negative. I couldn't stop it on the hike over here and I can't still now. I mean, we can't... We can't do this whole weekend thing, whatever *it* is. If I go back to her, it's only going to be ten times worse and more difficult to say our 'goodbyes' again tomorrow. And, if we were to string this out 'till Monday it'd be more awful again! As if staring down all the flashing cameras and doing press interviews wasn't bad enough, Jim and Audrey will be there and I can't deal with all of them with a broken heart as well. No. I simply can't go back to her apartment. It's just not realistic.

Yes. On Tuesday afternoon after a brief detour to Heathrow, I'll fly back to L.A. to attend a vital studio meeting where I am expected to dutifully sign off on my latest and apparently "greatest" film. That's where my focus lies. So, why am I lying here trying to convince myself I need to do what I already know I'm going to do?

I take her keys out of my pocket and dangle them in the air in front of me. I should probably ask room service to get someone to take them back to her. Then again, no, I can't do that. I can't have them couriered. That would be implicating a third and possibly even a fourth party in my private affairs and…

There's a knock at the door. "Room Service!"

"I'm coming," I call back. Food for more thought.

Alice

Did I make an awful mistake getting up and approaching the handsome stranger in the bar last night? I'm starting to think I probably did. He's gone and though I know he's still in Milan, I'm not sure he'd want to see me even if I did try to contact him. I don't think he's a bad man for leaving me like he did. He must be carrying so much baggage from his life that he just can't allow himself to… I don't know… This has every probability of turning into a *real* Italian tragedy for me doesn't it! I just can't stop wanting him. I look to the sofa. I see him. I look to my piano. I see him. I don't want to go back into my bedroom right now.

I must be a complete fool. I felt, the moment I looked across and saw him, 'this one's dangerous.' There was something about him last night in the bar that shouted 'mysterious and edgy!' right at me. But I either ignored or tried to embrace the feeling.

Maybe last night, that was what I craved. Danger. Someone to rescue me from the mediocrity of my life and from falling back with Paolo for the lack of anything else. Last night, Nathaniel Scott had to come back to my apartment. I set out to seduce him. But when it worked and I did seduce him, maybe I just made it far too easy for him in the end.

So, why am I now here at my door still, heart beating like a teenager in love for the first time? Why am I staring towards the heavens too scared to look at my own home, fit to burst into tears at any moment? I was fine last night. I was strong before I walked over to him. I was in control. What's happened so drastically in that short space of time that's changed everything? Nothing's what.

This is ridiculous. I'm a strong, independent, intelligent woman. I've never been one to let my emotions go like this over a man.

...But then came Nathan. Nathan who loves *The Beatles, Mozart* and jazz! Nathan who is sensitive and sweet and tall and handsome. Nathan who sings like an angel, and appreciates good wine. Nathan who understands other cultures and speaks other languages. And, Nathan the film maker, independent, bold and free. Nathan could've been so perfect for me.

It's such a shame he won't be. He's running scared from so many imaginary foes. He's hiding from what he thinks he'll find lurking under his own shadow. He needs to trust when he doesn't even trust himself. He needs to let go of the past and stop fearing the future. But, I can only help him if he's prepared to allow me in. And sadly, I don't think he's capable.

I finally move away from the door. I've leant against it for more than half an hour. I may even have kissed it when he left.

I wallow over to clear away our breakfast, and spy a glimmer of hope amongst the paper debris. My keys are gone. He must have them...

I am now sitting; reclining into my deep soft sofa looking blankly out of the window. It can only be mid-afternoon but the sky is very grey today and I can make out lights already appearing in some of the taller buildings across the skyline.

I start thinking about his whole celebrity argument. What's that all about? Would he have wanted me and not be so desperate to protect me against his world if I were Audrey

Novel? Or, if I were famous too? I don't care if he's Nathaniel Scott of Hollywood. I wouldn't have even known what films he'd made if he hadn't told me himself!

"Che cosa c'è in un nome? Ciò che noi chiamiamo con il nome di rosa, anche se lo chiamassimo con un altro nome, serberebbe pur sempre lo stesso dolce profumo!" I shout Shakespeare right across my apartment aiming towards the windows and the rest of the city beyond. I know no one can hear me. But I am driving myself mad in here and I needed to let it out.

I start to whisper the word 'no' over and over. Hopefully, I'll fall asleep and wake up on another day somewhere else, maybe in the summertime down on the lake. Suddenly, my mobile phone rings and I leap up like up like I've been stung.

"Nathan?!" I pant as I reach it in the nick of time.

"Non, Nathan!" says another softly spoken male voice, followed by, "Chi è Nathan? È tuo caro fratello, Marco." It's my brother.

"Oh, ciao caro fratello. Nathan è un collega. Andiamo a Praga martedì." And it works. Telling him that Nathan is the name of a co-worker on my next business trip to Prague this week makes him back off with the questions, for now. Marco is well aware that my phone only ever rings at all when he calls, and that it's set up to play a really old song called *"Dancing Queen"* that he is totally in love with as his special ringtone.

Marco has called because I sent him a scatty text message earlier. He wants to know if I am okay. He's such a sweet man.

He and Noah have no plans this weekend and want to invite me over to eat with them in their apartment. And, as I talk to him trying not to sound too down, I pick up my watch. 5pm.

Outside, the overcast sky isn't helping. 'Nathan is not coming back,' I think to myself. 'The key is probably downstairs in the mailbox where he's dumped it when he left', so I *am* at a loose end and have no excuse to turn Marco down.

Marco is also very sensitive and alert to people's feelings, even over the telephone. He always had a keen antenna for people in need, and now, he can sense that I should not be alone tonight anyway. So, when he asks me so sweetly for a third time in as many minutes, I find it impossible to say anything other than, "yes, okay then. Tell Noah I will be there by eight."

"Sola?" he asks me.

"Sì. Tutta sola. Now go. Ciao Bello! I am working!"

"Stop it, and put-on make-up. Drink wine!" he says in English but with his awful Italian accent, before ringing off abruptly.

Nathan

It's gone six o'clock and I am showered, clean-shaven and fed, standing with a towel around my waist and drip drying at the window. I carelessly watch the car lights down below at the end of a dirty grey day in Milan, and ponder what to wear for the evening ahead.

The concierge has clearly taken great care to empty my entire suitcase into a variety of small compartments and onto several velvet lined hangers in the wardrobe. I'm looking for something a bit more *Milano* to wear tonight and I'm thinking of more live jazz to lose myself in and take my mind off Alice.

She hasn't been far from my thoughts all day. But, at every point when I start daydreaming about her, my working brain kicks in to end the paragraph. And, it always concludes that although the attraction is strong, I'm gonna have to let her go. It's just better that way.

Besides, Audrey's flying in on Monday morning. She's in Europe and is apparently looking forward to seeing me. Our work timetables haven't managed to give us any time together in nearly a year and as I text her back I know she'll be annoyed that I didn't check in with her earlier. Since she last left L.A. with no promise to return back in January, I just got used to not seeing her anymore. Now, her texts just wind up with most of the others.

I've been staying indoors on my own eating expensive take-out meals pretty much since Audrey left Los Angeles. In the last few years, Pete left us way too soon and then there was my dad too. If the Alice experience has taught me anything that I *can* continue with, it's getting back on my feet and heading back out into the world. I go for the black-tie look like Frank Sinatra. I want to eat well, see good music performed well and wake up early tomorrow morning back in this room, not hungover.

Yes. That's the plan. "That and these black shiny lace ups," I say to myself as I bend down and pick up one of three pairs of shoes I appear to have travelled here with.

Alice

It's just after six o'clock in the evening and I've just had a luxuriously warm, soapy shower. I felt his scent on my skin all afternoon, so now I know he's not coming back, I reached a point where I could take it no more. I've checked my phone for texts, as often as a school girl with a crush, every ten minutes since he left and…

He's had all day to call me or just to leave a little message to say he's thinking of me. But…

I begin to dress for Marco's and I'm going to take my time. I'll put on some make-up, drink a glass of wine and…

…Probably keep thinking of Nathan.

Just in case, on the off chance of him dropping by (and I know how stupid I'm being), I'm going to leave it to the very last minute before I summon a taxi. And at the same time, I do just have to accept that today, this is how things are. Tomorrow will be different though. Marco and Noah will see to that.

I dress in complete silence; slowly and taking care about my appearance in a way that I did not before I left to meet Paolo last night. As I feel sad, I wear black. I have a habit of colour coding my feelings right down to nail polish and underwear. I bet that would seem weird if I told people that's what I do. But, the good thing about black is it's also classy. So, tonight, I will be wearing 'black with panache', mental checklist at the ready:

Black lace underwear, on. Check. Gothic black nail polish, on. Check. *TAG Heuer,* on. Check. My pearl earrings that *nonna* gave me when I played for her on her eightieth birthday. Check! Black tights. Check. Tight fitting black cocktail dress, above the knee. Check. And mamma's black chiffon scarf to hug my shoulders against the chill night air in the absence of a man's caress. Check.

And, that leaves only my hair to take care of. Last night, it was carefree and down save for a little band that Paolo used to say made me look *'pretty.'* No matter how well dressed I am, I never feel pretty at work. So, I think it's good to feel that way sometimes even if Paolo didn't notice my smallest of efforts.

Right now, I'm standing here looking in the mirror and I'm actually distracted for a moment or two by how good I look when I make a real effort. Ok, so I certainly don't feel too great inside – I am that stupid girl who's looked at her phone for a non-incoming message from Nathan at 6pm, 6.10pm, 6.20pm, 6.30pm, 6.40pm, 6.50pm and at 7 o'clock after having done the same thing every ten minutes since half an hour after he left me all day long. But, I do scrub up well when I try, particularly it would seem, in black.

As it approaches 7.10pm and my internal clock is pulling me to look down at that blasted phone again, I quickly try to bundle my hair up and pin it out of the way in a messy chignon. It looks awful. I let it fall loose, and start again. And in so doing, I miss my 7.10pm vigil. I should be happy about that but... instead I glance again in vain at 7.16pm and then back on track again at 7.20pm.

It's almost time to telephone for a cab when I dig deep in my wardrobe and find some black heels. I haven't worn them out for quite some time. I don't like heels at all. They're so unnatural, yet in business, in some countries they apparently give me an edge.

Anyway, I look at myself one last time in the full-length mirror by my front door, and think…

…*Sei bellissima!* And heels huh? Hell's own heels for my brother's house? Like Cinderella, all dressed up and nowhere to go…

Nathan

It's almost seven o'clock and *Blues Canal* isn't nearby. I'll hail a cab from *Centrale* or ask for one at reception. No problem.

As I go to leave the room, I casually place both my hands into my pockets and realise I don't have my phone, my wallet or the room card. "Dumbass. You nearly locked yourself out," I say, talking to myself again.
I walk back over to the bed where I left my jeans and start to search the pockets eventually pulling out everything that I've done over the last twenty-four hours. There's loads of stuff. Sweet wrappers, sticky to the touch, tickets for a metro that robbed me and that I never ended up using anyway, some rubber earplugs my mum gave me for the plane, now covered in bits of pocket paper and fluff, and… Alice's keys. They jingle-jangle together as they land on the white of the hotel duvet and mysteriously appear to separate themselves from the rest of the items strewn all around.

I grab them up absentmindedly, but then end up holding them out in the palm of my hand. It's as if they're talking to me. I surely hope not! I drank a lot more wine yesterday than I've been accustomed to since I detoxed all summer. But I've been no stranger to hallucinations in the past.

I look at my phone to see if she's messaged me. She hasn't. Then, looking back at the keys, that fear's there again. It feels uncomfortable so I pocket them. Out of sight, out of mind. Then, this time I do leave the room and I do head back towards the elevator; my sole intention, to enjoy a Saturday night out in Milan.

Alice

It's approaching 7.30pm. I look again for Nathan's message but of course, it's not there. My frustration that there's no text, not even a simple 'hi', or 'I hope you're ok', is reaching its peak. My distaste for our ever worsening *'glued to mobile phone culture'*, has gone out of the window today. Today, I became a massive hypocrite. And, Nathan has done this to me. Nathan and *Samsung*. Thanks Nathan and *Samsung*. Welcome to the century you were designed for Alice…

Right now, I feel like a child unable to understand my own emotions. I can't control myself in loss, and let's face it, that's what this is. Yet, I still won't put the damn thing down. If I got just one message from him, just one *ding* to show that he loved last night, but that he's really sorry and my keys are down below in the mail box, that'd be enough. My heart would beat just that little bit slower again, so I could gather myself. And then, I'd feel I have the right to reply, and I'd tell him straight, with the confidence of the faceless texter, "Come back my love… Let's spend this night together… and…"

Instead, I send a text to Marco. "Do you need wine? I'm calling a taxi now."

"No to wine. Yes to 'Get in a taxi!' now!" is his instant response. My brother is one of those people who lives with his phone right there. He has no shame.

I reluctantly make that call. The controller tells me I can come down to the door below at 7.45pm. "Ok, grazie," I say. But really, this is no good. It means, in my crazy-woman head, that I will still be in at 7.40pm, and will be compelled to look again one last time for a text from him.

I sit at my breakfast bar staring down at the time on the dark screen of my telephone as each minute ticks by slower and slower to get to 7.40pm. And then, it does. And then, it passes. And, at 7.41pm, I can take no more. I open my door to leave the apartment. I'm going to try to enjoy my night and forget about…

…Nathan

"Damn! Damn! Damn! Sod it!" I say to myself. I am in the lift going back up again.

I check my watch. It's about twenty to eight.

Anyway, I am headed upwards too slowly for my liking. I'm alone and I'm silently praying I won't get stuck, just like I always think while travelling in these things, when finally, it makes its reassuring little pinging noise and the doors are flung open.

Next, just as I always do, I step out trying to look casual, trying to look for all the world to see that I am not some odd ball who's afraid of lifts, though feeling anything but, under my collar. I walk the short distance back along the brightly lit hallway and my thoughts quickly change to 'what in the hell are you doing Nathan?'

I am probably too late, but I just have to see…

...Alice

"Nathan?" It's been so long since I wore these shoes that I almost fall over when I see him standing there.

"Oh my..." He's looking at me with amazement, shock and fear etched right across his beautiful face! And, I'm completely stopped in my tracks. A deer in the headlights, weak at the knees, dithering on the spot. I well up then, and somewhere between Nathan starting to say, "you look absolutely amazing!" and the tears rolling down both my cheeks, I've kicked off my heels and leapt towards him.

The sun I want to orbit has come back into my system and I won't let him leave again. He catches me and lifts me up off the floor. I wrap my legs around his middle, I hold his cheeks between both hands, and feel the warmth of that tender kiss like gravity pulling me back to where we both belong.

We stay there, me floating, both silent and feeling each other's presence for quite some time. I play with his hair and he holds me tightly, clinging on to the moment.

When we eventually break away and my stockinged feet touch the ground again, I continue to look up at him and chuckle a little through my tears.

"Were you on your way out somewhere?" he asks.

"Y-yes, as a matter of fact I was... I mean I am."

"Oh. Okay. I'm sorry. Do you want me to come back at a more convenient time perhaps?"

He holds me close and I don't want him to ever let me go. "You see, I've been thinking," he says.

In his arms, looking up at him as I know I'll always want to do, I get a burst of the confidence that brought us together in the first place. "No. There's no other convenient time. I'm sorry about that," I say.

"Oh, Okay," he replies. "I should have called you I know. But, ..." I feel him try to move out of our embrace, but I don't let him. He's taken the bait.

"You see," I reply. "I have a taxi waiting for me and two very handsome men have invited me to dinner at their place."

"Oh, okay," he says again. His brow furrows and I keep gazing up at him. Every expression on Nathan's face draws me in further. I want to get up on my toes and kiss away this new forlorn look. I think better of it this time, though I keep looking.

"Cat's got your tongue?" I say finally. I'm trying to keep a straight face but he surely sees through me. Doesn't he?

"W-what would you like me to say now?" he asks softly.

And I reply slowly, deliberately. "Tonight, I'm invited to eat at the home of my big brother. He's called Marco. His *husband*, just so you know, is Danish. He's called Noah. I would love nothing more than to stay like this in your arms all night, Nathan. But I will be honest and tell you that it is far too late for me to cancel on them. I love them both too much to cry off on a promise like that."

"Okay,..." he says, equally slowly as if mimicking me. "Would you be allowed to have a '*plus one*' at your dinner party tonight at your brother and his *husband's* home? You see, like you, I'm all dressed up. But, seemingly unlike you, I have absolutely nowhere to go if I have to go there without you."

"Nathan," I begin. I think I can drop the *'slowly act'* now though. With every passing second in his company, I feel more and more relaxed again. "I've had the most shit afternoon I have ever had in my entire life I think, and…"
He interrupts. "Please. I would love to meet Marco and Noah. Please may I come with you to eat with your family?"

He says this so sweetly I couldn't refuse, not that I would have anyway. Besides which, when I send another text to Marco to tell him the taxi outside has left without me and I've had to order another one, and I then ask him if he would set up another place at the table, he's too thrilled to be upset at me.

"È Nathan?" he asks me.

"Si. È Nathan!" I message him back.

"Ok. Ciao Bella," he says. I know Marco. He loves to entertain new people and tonight he'll get Nathan to talk more about himself than I've managed so far. Of that, I am absolutely certain…

Nathan

Stepping into Marco and Noah's more modest sized yet also much more stylishly decorated apartment in what Alice tells me is the *Lambrate* area of Milan, I meet the slightly balding and portly architect straight away as he's over to lavish hugs and kisses on his sister in the doorway. His far younger looking, blonde, blue-eyed boy, Noah is right behind but isn't immediately visible until Marco moves aside. I'm nervous and clutch at Alice's hand, deliberately edging along after her so that she can best initiate the introductions.

Their hallway, if you could call it that, is short and narrow so there's not the space for four fully grown adults to stand talking, though they do anyway. I'm half French and have known all my life that practically everyone on mainland Europe has far more time for simply standing around making chit chat than the English, so it's not an issue. She squeezes my hand, reassuring me that we're on the move, and I do what I always do in new places and situations; hang back, try to keep calm and scope out my surroundings.

Next to the door, an antique wooden hat and coat stand sits majestically right next to a large ornate walnut book case. Three shelves of very neatly placed classic European literature and some travel guides, mainly for the far east and Asia are topped off with an enormous overhanging plant that almost touches the ceiling as well as the highest placed books. In front of the door is a big, framed photograph, professionally done, depicting *Nyhavn Harbour* in Copenhagen just before nightfall. I recognise it straight away. I met with some Catalans representing their exiled president, Carles Puigdemont there maybe ten or eleven years ago while freelancing with a Belgian film crew. The wood frame of the photo matches the style of the only other two pieces of furniture in the entrance, leaving me to imagine that it must've been Noah, the man responsible for this well-matched interior design.

We pass into the light of a much larger living space, less grand than Alice's, but immediately giving off much more of a lived in, loved and cared for feel. Looking beyond the kitchen-diner's modern chic towards a more retro sitting area, I again get a clear sense that Noah, the designer by trade, has lovingly placed his tasteful hallmark not just in the entrance, but all over their flat. The only thing they appear to be missing is the cherry on the top; a sedate Siamese cat sprawled on the sofa.

Both men radiate *une joie de vivre* and a warmth towards one another that I find instantly infectious. I don't think I have ever felt so at home in a new place as right here, right now. Marco is definitely a bit tipsy already and that's reassuring for a start. I've always drunk far too much in social situations, especially new ones, having been shy and awkward like that since I was a little kid. I don't know why I'm like this. I guess I'm just naturally more introverted than my little sister who has always been a kind of social magnet for everyone and everything she comes into contact with.

Noah is in control of the kitchen and doesn't appear to be drinking at the moment. Nonetheless, as we enter his dining area, he's already poured and is handing Alice and I either two huge goblets of *Chianti* or else two rouge-watered fish bowls, before ushering us both to take root somewhere.

I look about for somewhere to stand or sit, and Noah asks me how I'm feeling. His English is perfect and he speaks softly, with an American accent. I offer to help him finish up with making the dinner and Alice looks at me and smiles as she's quickly guided away on the arm of her brother and led towards his sitting area. I lean against a cupboard trying not to get in Noah's way and Alice winks back over her shoulder at me, encouraging me to relax.

"Let them go talk," says Noah. "She's away so much with her work and he misses her. Let me top you up."

"Thank you," I reply as he pours yet more wine into my already extremely full bowl. And, "Wow!" I say holding up the glass towards the light. "Either all of you in this family learned your English in England or you just like your wine big!"

"Oh no, I learned all *my* English just watching television back in Copenhagen. Then, much later, I studied Design at *Parsons* on 5th. Have you heard of it?"

"Oh no, I haven't. You mean Manhattan? I'm guessing *Parsons* is a college, right?"

"Yep," he goes. "And TV back home is perfect for learning English too. Danish kids are watching British *and* American shows from really young you know. We practically grow up bilingual! There's none of that awful dubbing that Italians have, and we get *Dr. Who*!"

"Oh, I know, I've lived all over Europe. They dub everywhere still now! Can you believe that?"

"I guess," he replies. "Probably more so because they're still all angry at England for Brexit!"

"That figures," I say.

"Then, I think Marco learned his English in Ireland," he cuts in. "He makes a lot of mistakes. It might be their funny accent, but I don't think he ever tried very hard to be honest. Probably just never fancied anyone over there!"

From the sofas a short distance away we hear Marco call out, "Nat-an, he is talking about my Engleesh? I'm a-sorry. Don't a-listen to heem. Iss not so bad? You get use to eet!"

Noah laughs to himself. "Yes dear," he hollers back. "It looks like we have an English night tonight though, so I suppose we *will* have to get used to it!"

I chuckle at his sarcasm, until Noah cuts in again.

"Alice, though. She is a star turn huh? She speaks most languages well. I think she learned yours in Cardiff, England."

"Ooh. I think you'll find that Cardiff is in Wales, sir. And you don't want to go offending a Welsh man."

"I'm so sorry. Are *you* Welsh?"

"Oh no, don't worry about it. I'm Scouse," I say. "From Liverpool."

"Ooh. Well, it's no wonder Alice fancies you then." And he shouts through to the lounge, "Alice D'Alessandro, you didn't tell us your new friend comes from Liverpool like your beloved *Beatles*!"

"I didn't know that," she calls back.

I'm finding Noah really easy to talk to and I'm happy about that. In recent years, I've become more of a fly on the wall than a real human being. I don't find interaction with new or old people easy, and Juan Pablo, my Argentine shrink was focusing all his attention on this problem just before I flew back into England last week.

But, this guy, Noah. He could be a chat show host if he wanted. He's made me feel well at ease from the minute I stepped into his kitchen, and though he doesn't know it, that's no mean feat. Right now, I'm so relaxed I could even handle an energetic dose of James Corden; a nice guy when you get to know him, but...

"Are you sure I can't help in anyway, Noah?"

"Oh no, thank you," he replies. "The table is set for four, you have a glass of wine and I've made pasta with Köttbullar. It's almost done."

"Is Köttbullar Danish?"

"Unfortunately, no. It's just Swedish for meatballs. I learned the recipe in New York from an old boyfriend." He ends his sentence in a hushed tone. "But at least it's Scandinavian! The pasta and the wine are from here and you are a *Beatle*," he laughs, before adding, "Marco says you work with Alice in the bank?"

"Oh no, I don't work for the bank."

"No. I didn't think so," he laughs. "All dressed up like Frank Sinatra for dinner? And you don't *move* like a banker either."

I chuckle at this. "How does a banker move, Noah?"

"Not like you," he says. "And I mean that..." he raises his hand across his mouth and whispers again, "...as a compliment."

"Thank you," I say as I sip my wine. "This flat looks great. Did you design it all?"

"Pfaff," he waves me away playfully before turning around and taking a pan full of meatballs off the hob and dropping it on the dining table with a big wood spoon sticking out of it. "You can bring the pasta if you want, Nathan. Drain it first. The sieve is by the sink."

I'm careful to take off my dinner jacket and roll up my shirt sleeves first, but Noah's watching me closely from behind.

"When you eat Nathan, you are going to get sauce all over that white shirt," he says. "Take it off and I'll get you and Alice a pair of polos from our spares. She always comes overdressed. It's no problem."

I thank him again and am just returning to my job at the sink when Noah suddenly and with no forewarning comes straight out and says, "You know Nathan, I'm sure I've seen you before. I don't know where right now, but I know it will come back to me. You've been to New York, haven't you?"

I don't know what to tell him. New York's a huge city. I always went out and met loads of different people whenever I've been working over there, but I don't remember meeting Noah. And, he's a really nice guy whose white-blonde Viking hair really stands out. I would definitely have remembered meeting him. Still, I say I've worked there on and off but not for a number of years...

And, weirdly enough, going back to my earlier train of thought, though I don't tell Noah this, my last trip to New York was when I first met James Corden and found him quite a tricky customer.

"Oh, okay, that must be it then," he says. "I can't place you but I'm sure we'll get there in the end. The evening is still young! Come on, let's plate up and get some wine down us! I sent Marco out drinks shopping this afternoon. That was my big mistake. There's surely more wine in this apartment now than there's water in the faucets! Trust me."

"I do," I reply.

Alice

I am really nervous yet hopeful about Nathan getting along with *"the guys!"* The surprise of seeing him there at my door just now has made me feel renewed, like anything's possible again. He holds my hand sweetly in the back of the taxi, but near squashes it going up in Marco's rickety old lift. His tender kiss outside their door, I think is his way of apologising to me. And, I accept. I accept. I accept, my brain completely on fire and goosebumps popping up in places I'd never felt them before.

In Italy it is customary to bring a gift of some sort to a meal. I say sorry to Marco but he is not bothered. He never is. He tells me I *did* bring something as he reaches out a hand to shake Nathan's and then eventually drags him into a bear hug when we move out of their poky little hallway and I let go of the hand that'd been clinging on to mine like a little boy lost since we left my place. Noah is standing right behind Marco, and when my brother moves aside, two large glasses of 'Chianti' he says, are passed straight to both of us.

I leave Nathan in the kitchen with Noah. He should be fine with the enormous glass of wine he's got to hold onto now. And me? I happily wink at him as I let Marco lead me and my drink away to himself in the sitting room. Parting, as Shakespeare once said, is such sweet sorrow and I find it difficult to tear my eyes away from his. Yet, I'm sure Noah will soon tell Nathan that it is customary whenever I arrive at their pad for my brother to want me all to himself, if only just for a short while.

Marco is on good form tonight and as I linger to gaze back at Nathan, he pulls me along after him insisting that Noah and he will be a hit even if my friend is a shy and boring banker like me. He guarantees that by the time we return to the kitchen, Noah will have dressed him appropriately to eat slop and the two will be toasting one another's good health.

My brother of course wants to know all about how courtship happens in banking. He often laughs at the kind of people he thinks I might mix with at work, and is desperate for me to talk him through Nathan and his job. He says that Nathan looks too handsome to be in banking and I just slap him on the arm playfully and tell him to stop. Then, finally I have to be firm and insist that if Marco wants to know all about Nathan, he will need to ask Nathan.

"Oooh…Misterioso!" he declares, staring down his nose at me and promising, if not to me then, most definitely to himself, to spend the whole evening grilling poor Nathan for what will be a second night in succession.

Changing the subject to Marco's current projects, he gets all serious for a moment and stops prying. I know that this is just the calm before the storm though. He'll get his fun later. It's either that, or he's heard Noah joking about his English from the kitchen. He shouts back in *Engleesh* and ignoring Noah's response he's quickly gesturing to me that the chiffon and the heels have no place in their apartment and will have to be removed before we can go anywhere near their dinner table.

Most surprisingly, it's Nathan who eventually calls us to eat. He shouts in French and I imagine his mum calling him to the table this way when he was a little boy. Only, Nathan's voice is so loud that Marco automatically puts his hand to his chest. *"Dio mio!"*

"Il est français?" asks Marco, hesitantly.
"Non. Sa maman," I reply.

"Alors, il est français. Tu viens de ta mère ma chérie. Tu viens de ta mère!"

"Oui," I say, "And, you know brother, if they laugh at your English, just talk to him in French. Noah doesn't know any does he?"

As we walk back to the table, Marco stops me and puts his finger to his lips. "Look," he says grinning. Noah and Nathan, now wearing an old Italian-blue polo shirt, are already sitting opposite one another toasting each other's health. "I told you didn't I?" exclaims a proud and ever so slightly inebriated Marco.

"Your favourite polo is hanging on the back there," says Noah. "Don't spoil your dress or he probably won't want to take you out dancing later."

I sit down and feel great. I glance at Nathan next to me and he beams back. Then Marco, opposite me, with a full glass and a burst of laughter proposes a questioning toast *"to four wonderful people for one night only, or for eternity?"*

Nathan

The serving up of dinner from the middle of the table begins well, with each of us invited to help ourselves. The chaos starts when I apparently don't take enough and Marco decides to play mum. As he stands up, definitely drunk, and begins to shovel heaps onto everyone's plate bar his own, more sauce and pasta ends up on the tablecloth than on any of the plates. "It is always like feeding time at the zoo when he gets started," says Noah cheerily.

"It's a Saturday!" shouts Marco. "Noah, Put some music on, we will listen while we eat then sing and dance later!"

He casts me a swift sideways glance, cheeky and playful. "I am normally on a vegan diet Nat-an. Noah always makes meatballs when Alice comes here! Perhaps he tries to say something with his food, I don't know!" He slings back another mouthful of wine and sways on his seat smiling to himself.

"That's not true," replies Noah. "I have made meatballs how many times for you Alice?"

"Twice at most?" she says politely. "And anyway Marco. You know, it's no big deal. Don't make a scene big brother! We're all five-day vegetarians here! We only go meaty when we've got guests! It's easier! You know that."

"Is it?" I ask, trying to sound innocent.

In Los Angeles recently, I've not eaten much at all except as fuel before the gym and at the end of the working day. I've been exercising a lot more often since my summer detox but I'd always thought lean meat was good protein and I quite often pig out on organic take-outs or my favourite, Chili burgers. Whenever I'm back in Europe, I see that most people these days live pretty much meat free. And, I've got no problem with that. Most of Hollywood has some kind of food hang up so I've seen it all before. But, I'm hungry and I've no problem at all with Swedish meatballs.

"Marco!" retorts Noah suddenly. "You know my meatballs are special. It's Köttbullar, dearest. Stop showing off! I'm more of an Eco Warrior than you've ever been!"

Turning to me, Noah continues, "I hope it's alright for you. The meat is from a Swedish Elk. It has travelled, I'm sorry.

But it's authentic and I bought it from a Swedish supplier I know here in Milan."

Then, back at Marco, "it's not some frozen cow's asshole that I bought last week from *Aldi*."

"Hey, Noah. Don't mind me," I say. "I'm happy. Your Elk tastes good."

And Marco nods. "Okay Noah," he says breathing heavily. "We are all happy. Good."

So, it appears to be 'Game Over'. The only trouble with that is that it'll surely soon be time for a new target, and as he'll never go for his *seester*...

"Nat-an, I'm sorry," says Marco. I haven't eaten the meat in a-maybe two or three weeks, and I was a-feeling happy about it. It's like… I don't know how to say it…"

"You were on a roll," I intervene. "You thought you were going good without and then…?"

"Yes, ees dat," replies Marco swaying forward again before suddenly squinting his eyes, piercing blue like his sister's, and trying desperately to look serious. "Now, what are you doing at the bank with my little seester?"

"He doesn't work at the bank," says Noah who's gotten up to put on some euro pop in the background.

"No," chips in Alice. "We met in a bar on Via Casale."

"Ooh, not UGO by any chance was eet? That is the best one on the street for me."

I try to keep my head down, happily tucking into a second dinner today and making a right royal mess with the sauce. Alice appears to have jumped in to save my blushes and I don't mind them all discussing me between themselves so long as it doesn't come down to what I *do actually do* that's not for the bank.

"When was this a-meeting?" asks Marco.

"Oh, not long ago," Alice replies. She wants me to help her out so reaches over and squeezes my hand gently. They talk some more, trying to tease information out of her about our friendship when finally, Noah turns to me again. "You don't live in Milan, do you Nathan?"

I go to answer him, but Alice jumps in first. "No," she says. "He lives in England but he does some work in America as well."

A brief pause in the conversation must be for thought. Then, Marco asks me, "what are you doing here?"

I'm still trying my best to look enthusiastic and busy with my Köttbullar and pretend like I've missed something he said. But, Marco's not one to let something go. That much is clear.

"Actually, I live in Los Angeles at the moment, but I was visiting my mum in England last week, and now I'm here on business this weekend."

"Oh?" says Alice quite suddenly, unexpectedly loudly and seemingly quite surprised herself. This prompts both our hosts to divert their attentions onto her.

"And when are you going back to Los Angeles, Nathan?" she asks, suddenly whirling fully round in her seat to face me.

I turn back to her, still chewing Elk, and both Marco and Noah's eyes follow us as if they're watching live theatre from their own dining room.

"Why Tuesday my dearest," I say playing to the crowd.

"So soon?" asks Noah, seemingly quite invested in the story.

"Yes? So soon?" repeats Alice. "You only arrived yesterday."

"But aren't you going to Praga on Tu-es-day?" Marco asks his sister, garnering him a glaring response, before finally, Noah's penny drops.

"Marco, look at them. They're in love. This is only their second date," he says all hushed, but deliberately audible.

I'm lagging behind a bit on the conversation, still hoping they're not going to bring up my job and only really having paid attention to what Alice last said to me. "Indeed, I did," I blurt out, and immediately wonder why Noah and Marco are staring at me open-mouthed.

"What? Did love her?" says Noah.

"Noooo," says Alice. "He only got here yesterday."

"Yes, I flew in from Manchester in the afternoon. I was visiting my mum in Liverpool last week. My dad passed away a while back, not long after I lost a very dear friend in America, and I became a bit shut off. It felt like I... like I hadn't seen my family enough. So, when I got the call to come here, I took a break and went there first."

"I understand you," says Noah. "I don't go to Copenhagen often enough either."

"Then go amore! Ciao bello! Ciao!" shouts Marco laughing as he goes. "I will stay here in the warmth and wait for you to return!" Then they wheel round to face each other and embrace affectionately. This would seem to be a running joke between them.

When they've finished, I don't really know what comes over me. Good food, too much wine *again,* and of course beautiful company.

"I work at the Gallia Excelsior on Monday, and then I have to fly back to L.A. on Tuesday. Wednesday is a big day for me over there."

"Wow Alice!" says a very animated Marco again. "A whirlwind romance! No more Paolo for you, I think! And, he's in the Excelsior! How do you earn your millions Natan? Are you a bank robber? Is my seester kidnapp-ed by you right now?"

He laughs again at his own brilliance and I watch Alice squirm uncomfortably, before reaching for her hand under the table. Marco raises his glass wanting me to make merry with him and I oblige, but only after looking for consensual eye contact from Alice whose hand is now squashing mine, I think, in revenge for the elevator.

"You look a beautiful couple anyway," says Marco. "A match, *Made in Milano!*"

"But Los Angeles is a long way from here," says Noah.

"Yes, indeed. Yes, it is," I say, my eyes still locked on Alice, and hers still locked on mine.

"What are you doing at *The Excelsior* on Monday?" asks Marco finally.

Alice and I are still gazing dreamily at one another when the question flies in. "Do you want to tell him cherie, or shall I?"

"Oh, baby. Please. I'd love to hear your story again myself. It was so interesting the first time. You tell him." She sounds so sarcastic I can't help but smile.

"Ooh. Intriguing!" says Noah.

Then, "yes Nat-an you are being Mr. Misterioso with us," says Drunk Marco, swaying even more on his chair than he was five minutes ago.

Alice is all the while gesturing with her hands and eyes that I have an audience and need to go on and tell my story. I think falling in love with Alice was easy. That was yesterday. I've struggled through the day to admit to myself that I could actually do this. But, every look, every glance, every touch of her hand right now makes me believe with more and more certainty. I feel so safe next to her, she's giving me a confidence I haven't had for years.

"I'm no mystery man!" I blurt out. "I'm sorry." I take a deep breath. "Look. Please don't shoot me down in flames," I say. "I'm a film director. I make really, *really* bad movies!"

There's a pause. They're all still looking at me like they're waiting for something else.

"Okay. Okay," I resume. "I'm a…I work in the… I mean I have a film coming to the cinema all over the world in two or three months. I have to go back to L.A. on Tuesday to sign it off as complete. It's a formality really, I should've done it before I came to Europe…"

There's another pause. I'm not quite sure what's happening and look at Alice again for reassurance. When I was a kid I used to wonder what was going on in people's heads when they seemed to completely zone out in thought. I would imagine one of those old toy monkeys that beat two sides of a drum with a little ball of wood on the end of a red string.

Right now, I can see the little monkey tap-tapping away in Marco's wine frazzled brain. But, not in Noah's. He looks quite different. For starters, I don't think he's had a whole lot to drink and he, rather more dangerously, I feel, seems to be thinking quite deeply about something else. So, it eventually gives me a little start when Marco at last seems to regain control of his senses first, and asks tentatively if I'm a *famous* film director…

"I don't know about famous," I say. "I have made some pretty terrible films over the years though."

"Like what?" asks Marco.

Alice rests her chin on one hand and looks at me as if urging me to go on.

"Like erm…" I start, trying to think of what he might have heard of. Noah at this point has gone surprisingly quiet and seems to be staring at me like he's had a Eureka moment and just worked out some really complicated sums.

"*If I can make it there…?*" I offer squeamishly.

Marco looks over at Noah and then at Alice. He is looking for a translation of the title and there appears to be a brief pause before Alice slowly recites the title to one of Marco's favourite dubbed comedies of the last ten years back to him in Italian. She's now gripping my hand tightly again under the table with her blackened nails digging into my skin, and I guess she's hoping all hell is not about to break loose when she finishes speaking. But, at least initially,…

…Marco's response is surprisingly calm. "Mio Dio," he says staring blankly ahead with his mouth wide open. Then he looks back at me without another word.

"I wrote it as well," I say. "I'm sorry if you don't like it. It was meant to be commercial. It…" Alice stops me by squeezing my hand hard and abruptly. I look at her and she shakes her head gently.

I don't understand. Is she protecting me from the wrath of her Hollywood hating brother? I gesture 'thank you' for stopping me with my eyes. But clearly, I've missed the point again entirely.

Then,… the bombshell!

"I knew it!" cries Noah rising to his feet. "I knew I had seen you before. Nathan is short for…You're Nathaniel Scott!!!"

"I'm sorry?" I ask.

"No! No, don't be sorry," says Noah. "It was *The Late Late Show*. It was a one-off filmed in New York. I was in the live audience. You were so shy that night. It was six or seven years ago. I remember the host guy. He was an old English man too."

"Yes, James Corden," I say.

"I don't know. He commented that you were young and successful and *too quiet* about it!" he said. "For me, this set you apart from all of the other guests on the show. And I went there to see good old Lady Gaga. That's it, yes! She had been unwell with *'the virus'* or some such, and had been advised not to fly. So, this Corden guy had brought the show to her in New York City instead!"

"Stefani's a lovely person," I say. "And James Corden's not as bad as all that. He gets paid by the Americans to be loud and brash. He's actually a really good guy. But, thank you Noah. Thank you for your kind words."

I want to change the subject. I get the gist suddenly that in their home my films might be quite welcomed. Also, by appearing humble on American TV, I seem to have left a good lasting impression on Noah.

Alice has slouched back in her chair brandishing her wine glass proudly in front of her. She turns, glassy eyed, round to me and playfully bites her lip. I smile knowingly back at her then kiss the back of her hand.

"May I have some more Chianti please Noah," I say as I finish my glass and hold it up to him. "I'm in the mood for a party if you are!"

"Of course, you may good sir. I feel honoured," he says as he goes to pour. Marco who had disappeared into the sitting room again on his own returns with an old DVD case that he wants me to sign for him.

"Oh please, I didn't know they still made DVDs. This will be an honour for me, Marco. It's like asking a musician to sign a vinyl," I say. "It's a real honour for me to have made such cool new friends here in Milan!"

Marco and Noah dart off into the lounge to put on some music that we can all sing and dance to together. Alice and I are alone at the table for just a few moments before we go hand in hand to join them.

"I love that you're enjoying yourself," she says.

"And, I love you," I reply.

Alice

My brother and Noah are a colourful double act. I think they'd make a great circus pair. Marco is the clown slopping Noah, the serious one's dinner efforts all over the place while barking out orders for the younger of the two who takes it all in his stride, assured in the knowledge that it's he who's really in control. I worry that Nathan, as a newcomer to their world will see a one-sidedness in their relationship that really isn't there. Noah usually does as he's told here when I'm about, but he seems to like it that way and there is always a lot of affection and some playful prodding too that makes the whole thing both comical to watch and very definitely only a game.

Marco loves playing around and as expected, it doesn't take him too long to start questioning Nathan about himself at table.

They quickly establish that he doesn't work for the bank with me, which goes down well. But then they both turn on me searching for gossip on where I found him and Nathan just keeps his head down and stuffs his face with meatballs.

It's nothing new for me to get this third degree at their dinner table. After Paolo, it has been nearly two long years of these two dropping constant hints about me needing a man in my life. I always survive though, and if honest, the only times I've ever thought about having a relationship with anything or anyone beyond my work or my piano are when I am being grilled about men by Marco and Noah.

It is all they normally talk about with me except when Marco suggested last Christmas that I should get a cat just for company in my huge, sparse living space. "All good spinsters need a cat," he'd said. "Or are you a secret witch?" asked Noah, before adding, "I don't mean that in a bad way. You could be a white witch or like that pretty girl out of Harry Potter? Witches do tend to live alone with a cat though don't they?"

At some point, I had to remind them both that this witch business was *their* fantasy, and I couldn't possibly be a witch as I didn't have and nor did I want to own a cat.

I speak superficially about my chance meeting with Nathan. I don't say who pounced first. That'd just be embarrassing. But even as I witter on, I think Noah's radar has quickly picked up that his newest dinner guest and I have only known each other for about twenty-four hours.

When he turns a question about why Nathan's even in Milan this weekend back on Nathan, I take the opportunity for a breather and sip some wine quietly glancing a smile over at my brother. But I'm worried that Marco will think I am crazy and impulsive, or worse, that he will notice that I might have fallen in love at first sight and shout it out in his flamboyant drunk style. I'm also panicking that Nathan will contradict me and show me up for having no real knowledge of my new boyfriend. And, that will make Marco think I've rented out my *'plus one'* from an escort agency to avoid having to take any more questions about my sorry love life.

Eventually though, my thought train goes completely off the rails and on to some *really* mad tangent that leads to panic. What if Nathan, who is looking and feeling to the touch far more relaxed this evening than he was yesterday, suddenly blurts out something about a girlfriend back in England? Or worse still…a wife and kids? In every scenario I imagine, the one and only similarity is that I end up looking like a complete and utter fool!

Then, as I could easily have predicted if I'd stopped to think, I go and dig my own grave. I've just confidently informed the table that my English man lives in England when poor Nathan who is fielding so many questions that he is still one behind the rest of us, announces that he actually lives in Los Angeles at the moment.

I don't really have an excuse for why I behave so shocked after that. I guess it never came up amongst all of the beautiful silences and the physical stuff of last night. I suppose that if his job is making commercial American movies, he is highly likely to need at least one home in the home of film.

But I do what I'm sure everyone would do to save face after being found out for something and, I just keep on digging. I dig and I dig until I find myself taking centre stage and a lead role in Marco and Noah's favourite type of human-interest drama. They fall silent in complete synchronization and watch across the table as a young woman, seemingly falling helplessly in love with a guy she's probably only just met finds out some quite important stuff about him with no forewarning and completely in public… And *cut!*

I'm very briefly upset, and I almost wish Nathan did have a wife back in England. I could more easily live with being in love with an unhappily married man in Europe than a handsome stranger who in two days' time will be so far away he's unlikely ever to come back and see me again.

It is thanks in the end, to my brother and Noah with their drunken interruptions and constant attempts at wit; that, and the fact that Nathan continues to hold my hand below the table and looks at me so lovingly, that I feel somehow reassured. I am so nervous this evening. I just need Nathan and no one else; I need his reassurance that the way I'm feeling is fine and that this weekend is not one huge, sorry mistake.

After a not too lengthy pause, Marco is swiftly on to him again about his work at the Excelsior. Nathan turns equally as quickly back to me as if now imploring the same moral support that I needed from him just moments before. We're clearly as hopeless as each other... A perfect match?

As I return his gaze this time though, I suddenly get a feeling hit me right in the gut that Nathan will be absolutely fine to tell these guys why he's in Milan. I'm in no mood to speak again for fear of further *faux pas*. Like last night, I'm starting to enjoy my wine again and Nathan's warmth radiates and washes over and right through me just by the touch of his hand. I gesture to Nathan, widening my eyes as far as I can, inviting him to talk on.

And talk he does... As Nathan opens up to my family and I watch him closely, both proud of him and steeling myself in case he starts denigrating his achievements in front of two guys who already love him, I see a very successful, very talented young guy squirm for no reason. Surely most people in his position would love the chance to show off what they've achieved. But Nathan's different. And, I read that in him. Nathan isn't the indifferent man he seems to want to project to everyone else. In only twenty-four hours, I've unmasked him. Nathan would just as soon put down his commercial successes and have everyone believe that he doesn't care. But, the trouble with him is that he cares too much. He takes it all very seriously, and though his modesty is all so sweet, I don't believe that making Hollywood movies is really what he wants to do. I don't know. Maybe he could stay here and make films closer to me, and I could be a muse to him?

When Nathan finishes telling his story, everyone's happy and Nathan tells the guys he's in the mood to party. That's when I know this is going to be another late night. Marco and Noah have never needed much of an excuse, and now it looks like I've helped set up a rather good one!

At a volume to punish the neighbours, three men and a karaoke machine go berserk to *Queen* and later, all sorts of different pop music from across the decades. I just sit and laugh with a glass, enjoying the spectacle.

"Nathan, if you want them to stop making you sing all the English stuff just tell them," I say. But he's enjoying it all as much as his two new play mates. And, I'm quite impressed. His vocal repertoire stretches way beyond *The Beatles*.

When the time eventually comes for us to go home and let their neighbours rest at least from Nathan's voice, we hand back the polo shirts, and Nathan gets back his white shirt and black jacket. But he's not quite finished. A quick word to Noah, and *"New York, New York!"* blares out of the Karaoke machine, the last song, they all promise me.

Marco fumbles around with his *iPhone*. I sit on the sofa with my chiffon over my shoulders and recline into Noah's arms. Nathan stands before us and basically, already having lost all inhibition, becomes Frank Sinatra. Marco is filming him and Nathan appears, in a good way, not to care about that either.

I shiver a little when he belts out the line, "*if I can make it there...*" and Noah who thinks I'm cold, cuddles me just a little bit tighter. But, I'm fine, again just gazing up at Nathan, lost in thought about lucky I am to have met him.

Nathan

There was a point, at about 7.30pm this evening when I stood alone in a dark hallway outside a row of letterboxes. I stood and stared at Alice D'Alessandro's name tag and flat number for a full ten minutes. I almost returned her keys. I was all set to leave her to go back to her normal life, much better off without me and my shit in it. But I couldn't. I had to see her just one more time.

Working in cinema, I come across a lot of attractive women. But, there's attractive and then there's something else. I'd spent all afternoon ruminating about this, and I couldn't and still can't now think of any other time when I've ever felt so drawn to one person as I am to Alice right now. In all the years I've been associated with show business, I've been on dates; I've even gotten close with Audrey before. But, nothing like this. I'd never felt sparks fly and my body melt at a simple kiss. Not until I met Alice.

And, there's her piano. The elegance with which she strikes melody from the keys; her graceful motion, eyes closed, feeling everything. She soothes me, pains me and warms my soul all at once; a puppet master in control with those amazing, long, slender fingers.

In short, Alice is one of a kind, and in spite of myself, I love everything about her and I want her now all the more for having walked away before.

After an amazing evening in with Marco and his loveable Viking, I'm now back at Alice's apartment, standing beside her enormous glass wall and looking down dreamily on the canal below. It's lit up like Christmas and fills me with that same glow that snowy winter nights spent with French relatives always did when I was a boy. I sip from a glass of water and reminisce on less complicated times past.

Alice is using the bathroom and says she'll be a while. She wants to put on something more comfortable, remove her makeup etc. Her *S-View,* or possibly the *ES12* in her kitchen is playing something jazzy and mellow on low volume, and she's uncorked yet another wine in anticipation of drawing out the party for as long as she can while we're here together.

Enveloped in almost total darkness, save for some cabinet lights in her kitchen and the orange glow cast by the streetlamps, it's so nice just being here, able to breathe for a moment. And, all really is going fine, I'm feeling, when suddenly, CRUNCH!

Reality bites back at my brain quickly. It starts as just a passing thought about Monday's press call. But it grows and finally decides to take root, sprouting up all of my *Audrey problems* and all the inevitable pangs of guilt that come with them. *"Stop!"* I say to myself. It was meant to be just in my head, but as the word unexpectedly jumps from my lips, so I find that Alice has silently returned and is pouring herself a glass right behind me.

"Are you ok?" she asks.

Alice

We've survived the Marco test!!! *Correction.* We've triumphed at the Marco test!!! *No. Try again.* Nathan has triumphed at the Marco test!!! I was just my usual clumsy self; drinking too much in company and saying things that I know little about at the wrong times. I honestly don't know what comes over me. For such a sharp, confident business woman by day, I certainly know how to land back to Earth with a bump every time my brother invites me over for dinner...

Still, this time was different. This time, both Marco and Noah pulled me aside for separate hugs and even whispered 'congratulations' at the door on our way out; not the usual, "ciao bella, don't get lost in stilettoes will you."

Apparently, I've hit the "*jackpot!*" with Nathan, whatever that's supposed to mean. And, that's the word that plays on my mind all the way home in the back of a taxi as Nathan plays delicately with my fingers, humming *New York, New York* to himself.

At the apartment, Nathan asks for a glass of water and I leave him with some music and a panoramic vision of night-time in Milan. Meanwhile, I stand beside my bathroom mirror and gently weep.

I'm happy for Marco and Noah. They'll probably party on 'till dawn now, or at least until a neighbour hits their ceiling with a broom handle. The unexpected houseguest experience they've just had will live in their memories for a long time regardless of what happens to Nathan and I. But, I'm sad about the *jackpot* comment, meant innocently enough of course... It's just that if that's what they really feel, then all that garbage about the paparazzi that Nathan complained about and that made him leave me earlier on, isn't garbage at all. He wasn't just having cold feet. He was actually trying to protect me from himself and from prying eyes who will, no matter how in love we are, only see our relationship as *me,* not him, having hit the *jackpot*!

...I dry my eyes and wipe away mascara that's run half way down my cheek. I stare at myself and focus. I have to go back to him and show him that he's the lucky one. Hollywood aside, he's just a guy (admittedly a really handsome, sexy one) who's met a girl he wants to be with. She's invited him home and he's waiting patiently for her to come out of the bathroom. She can be really pretty and sometimes sexy too when she wants to be. And, she does want to be, with him. So, who's the lucky one? I think maybe it's Nathan who's the real jackpot winner.

I sniff away the last of my little confidence blip, blow my nose and change into a pair of leggings and a t-shirt. I tie my hair up out of the way and slip into my cosy pink house slippers.

When I go back out there, I'm going to make him understand exactly where we both stand. He'll have no choice but to accept whatever I say. I have it all planned out in my head.

I'm going to take a last glass of wine from the kitchen. We're going to curl up together on the sofa to talk and relax. Later on, we'll make love, and he'll know exactly where he belongs after the cameras stop and the lights fade...

Nathan & Alice

Nathan spins around on his heel. "I'm sorry. I didn't see you there," he says.

"Who were you telling to stop?" asks Alice, showing concern.

"Oh, it's nothing. Honestly. I'm tired and I was just worrying about Monday, is all."

The last jazz track on Alice's playlist fades out and the moody introduction to *Glory Box* fills the room from the kitchen. Alice seems happy with Nathan's assurances that he's ok, and she glides over to be with him by the window.

He beams at her as she rises on her toes again, bites her lower lip, a tease she knows he likes, and then kisses him softly on the lips. They lock eyes as lips touch, and can both see, mingling with the sweet floral taste of *Chianti*, the promise of passion to follow.

"Are *you* ok?" he asks.

"I think so," says Alice. "I'm a bit tired but…"

"We could go to bed," replies Nathan. "When does Miss Alice want to go to bed tonight? It's just gone two."

"I'm in no hurry," she says, putting her glass down and placing a delicate, teasing kiss on his neck.

Nathan slips his hand smoothly over the nape of *her* neck, under the ponytail, massaging her lightly, his eyes trained steadily on hers. They kiss and Alice manoeuvres Nathan onto her sofa where she pulls him ever closer towards her, pressing her open lips against his and deepening the kiss. Then, when Alice hears Nathan groan with pleasure for the second time, she very deliberately breaks completely off, sits up straight and smiles wickedly at him.

"What's the matter?" he says, finding it difficult to hide his sudden frustration.

"We need to talk," she replies.

If Nathan had really been thinking about Alice's feelings earlier on and not just his own, he'd have realised they needed to talk as soon as she came out of the bathroom. And, if Alice didn't realise how cruel she'd just been when she pulled away so abruptly from Nathan's passionate kiss, she certainly came to her senses when she sat up to see the disappointment all over his face.

Right at that moment, both Alice and Nathan's basest instincts are screaming at them to just resume that kiss.

But Alice, definitely the stronger willed of the pair at this time, knows that she has already invested far too heavily in loving this guy, to allow for any repeat of the last twenty-four hours after dawn breaks on Sunday. She also believes that Nathan, though struggling with his ego, would like to reciprocate her feelings and more.

So, she needs to get this off her chest now before they can be intimate again.

Nathan is having the best time he's had in many years, and he's having it with a beautiful, intelligent, talented girl who to his surprise, appears to have taken a serious interest in him. She's not a film star and compared to him, her life seems uncomplicated. This is both really scary and very attractive to Nathan.

So, he needs to listen to Alice. His choice is simple: Allow her to fight for her man or stop her and leave before causing any more hurt.

PART TWO – THE CHALLENGE

Alice

He's staring at me, not saying anything. The moment lingers, and I tilt my head, attempting to smile at him. I'm so nervous again, anxious about what he's thinking. Suddenly, in one swift movement he hauls himself forward on the seat, rests his elbows on his knees and cups his head between his hands.

"Ok, let's talk," he says softly. "You start."

I gently ease myself back up close to him. All at once, I'm lost for words…

"W-what time's your flight on Tuesday?" I ask tentatively.

He stands, and paces back over to the window where he gazes straight ahead into the night sky.

"I love the view from here," he remarks. "And, it's 3 o'clock in the afternoon out of Malpensa, 7.30pm connection from Heathrow. Why?"

"I have a plan," I exclaim without hesitation. My heart skips and I find myself back on my feet too.

Nathan turns slowly around to face me. "Go on," he says. I pick up my wine for courage and stalk slowly over towards him, studying his eyes, talking as I move. It's like hunting. He's checking the bait, holding my eye, interested. I just need to stick to the scheme, and take extra special care with how I explain it to him. He may not be comfortable with everything I want, but it has to be non-negotiable.

"It's just after 2am," I say. "If you fly to London at 3pm on Tuesday, you'll need to be at the airport here checking in no later than 2.30pm. So, that, I think, gives us roughly 60 hours. That gives *us* 60 hours *together* here in Milan."

"But…"

"But nothing, I haven't finished yet," I snap. I am by this point right back within a metre of him, and I don't know why? Nerves, I guess. But, my next step is designed to make an impact. Slowly, I shuffle another pace nearer to him, smiling mischievously before rising up on my toes and grabbing hold of his lapels. "I'm going to finish saying what *we* are going to do in close up," I whisper.

Nathan simply stands his ground, still looking blankly at me.

"We," I resume, "…We, are going to spend the next 60 hours together, and we're going to treat them as if the world is about to end and there's nothing either of us can do about it. You only have me, and I only have you."

"First, *we* move you into here when we wake up. Then, I am going to take some annual leave from work this week. I've not taken anything in nearly two years so it's long overdue."

He wants and tries to speak but I am too quick for him, pressing just one finger lightly up to his lips and breathing, "shhh." All I know is that I want this man, and at least here for the next sixty hours, it has to be on my terms. It has to be this way so he learns to trust I can handle myself in his world. Then, I'll have him for keeps.

"I will support you on Monday with the media, and I promise that when our time is up, I will also get you to Malpensa on time on for your connecting flight. You are the only man for me. But, then you already know that. So, I'm just telling you…"

"Telling me what?" he interrupts very deliberately.

And, how do I answer that? It would be so much simpler right now to keep hold of those lapels and just kiss him. He's hiding a grin, I'm sure of it. He's breaking my train of thought. Only, me giving in too easily is not an option… "I'm challenging you," I start to say, nerves all a flutter again, "to let me show you how your worries about protecting me are not important. I challenge you to let me show you that… To, let someone try to protect *you* from all that stuff!"

Nathan again just stands there, gawping; no reaction.

"Well?" I persist.

"Okay," he says eventually. "Can I pour myself a glass of wine please?"

"Is that all you have to say?" I'm perplexed.

"Yes, Alice. I came back. I love you. We can try the next few days. But, I warn you, it could get complicated, so hang onto your hat."

I'm drained. I watch him as he crosses the room. I obviously thought it was going to be much harder than it actually is to make him want to stay with me, and I'm left holding my glass, feeling like my balloon just popped, when in fact, everything for now at least couldn't be any better, even in my wildest dreams…

Nathan

Until she uttered those four simple words, always loaded with foreboding, always spoken by women when they're worried something's getting out of control, I'd just assumed that '*talk*' is exactly what we'd do at breakfast.

"*We need to talk.*" I'm no stranger to that line. And, with me at least, the experience and the feeling, has never been good. I get up, disappointed, and walk away from her, ominous thoughts bubbling up. From as early as my sixth form days in Formby, I was quite popular with the girls. I was too shy to really take advantage, but I did get caught up with two or three of them before I left for university.

It always ended as quickly as it started and it was always my fault, apparently. "*We need to talk,*" is how every conversation I've ever had with an angry female has begun. Of course, looking back on my youth, each one of those girls was surely only doing what I think Alice is doing now; trying to get some assurances of feeling out of me before committing herself to the possibility of future heartache. And, I guess me treating the whole thing as a threat, basically gave girlfriends past the exact answers they'd been dreading, with the upshot always needing to be me getting the old heave-ho.

Being dumped hurt. So, I never spared a thought for how the girls must've felt. At seventeen, I just wasn't emotionally mature enough or ready for sex or falling in love with anyone…

Karen, at university, was two years older than me though, and she was also really wild; in some ways more adolescent than me. I loved that, and for a while I thought I loved her too.

At the time, I never thought I'd ever be with anyone else, ever. But life has a way of deciding what's going to be possible and what's not, even when, it turns out, there's no dumping involved.

…And, then there was Alice.

I stare into nothingness at the window knowing in my heart that I've got absolutely no choice but to listen to her. She knows nothing about the tempest she's about to throw herself into. And, there's Audrey to get past too.

This all feels so surreal. I mean, for starters, what am I even doing here? Who is she? How did this happen? What am I thinking?

Then, there's the problem. This *is* real. It's real and it's my life. And, I, Nathan Scott now understand what being in love with someone really feels like…

So, Alice is probably as shocked as I am at myself when I react so calmly, reasonably and lovingly to her *talk*. But then, I think I'm in love with her. And, isn't that just the way people in love behave with one another?

Alice

We take breakfast at one of my many local coffee shops. I take him to '*Iter*: *From Italy to the World*.' The owner once told me that the name refers to an itinerary of things world travellers might take. So, it seems appropriate to bring such a well-travelled Englishman here to kick-start my plan.

The bar is very light with huge bay windows. Montgolfier balloons and a model biplane hang over the service area and they always change the rest of the décor entirely each month with things the couple who run the bar had picked up on their travels when they were younger. This month it appears to be *Machu Pichu*, and I daydream about being in Peru with Nathan.

"Today, you'll shadow me," I tell him over croissants and small cafés. "You will see how I do Sundays in Milan."

"What, so, you always evict people from their hotel suites on Sundays?" he asks, his deadpan expression at last giving way to a broad toothy grin. The penny, as they say, takes a moment to drop before I laugh too. English humour, I guess.

We kiss, not for the first time this morning. It comes out of nowhere. Nathan's just sipped from his macchiato and his lips taste delicious. His eyes sparkle in the sunlight streaming in from outside as we part again. His affectionate touches this morning have left me in a state of ecstasy, though the full extent I shall keep under wraps for now. I'm also happier generally today as the ugly, bruised skies have cleared, bringing back our beautiful Italian blue.

I tell him that after breakfast, we'll stroll back to *Centrale* to pick up his things. And, the sunshine's calling us to see Milan in all its glory, I add. But, Nathan already knows that it's a long walk, and complains that the air's too cold for being out that long in just a suit jacket. I pat his cheek and kiss him again. Sundays in Milan are designed for relaxing, I say, and with the promise that we can hop in and out of as many bars all along the way as he wants to, he soon desists.

We leave *Iter* arm in arm, and ambling casually on the canal side, I ask him to talk. "What do you want to know?" he asks.

"Everything," I reply. "Start at the beginning. I want to know everything there is to know about Nathan Scott."

And so there, he began his story, as we started to make our way slowly across Milan. I only interrupt him briefly to point things out when we pass by something of cultural interest. But, just hearing his soft, melodic voice is enough for me to enjoy the rest of the walk...

...Nathaniel Rubén Scott was born on a very hot 1st August 1999 in the city of Liverpool, England. After a torturously humid day, clouds spread in from the west in the evening and thundery downpours covered much of the country.

I wonder how he knows all of that weird stuff about describing the weather to start his story off... I ask, and he says that his dad had written it in block capitals on the back of his birth certificate. Ok...

It seems Nathan was a happy child. His younger sister was born in late January 2001, and little Beck, Rebecca Lucie Scott, and he had always been close friends.

The pair grew up and were both educated in the English state school system in the small affluent town of Formby, about twelve miles north of the city and on the coast. They had two loving parents, Lucie from Troyes in the Champagne region of France and Rubén, of mixed English-Spanish heritage, though mainly feeling English despite his Christian name.

Nathan and Beck often played together with their friends in the pine forests and in the sand dunes by the beach. And, they enjoyed many a windy weekend walk, or missions of discovery and den making with their mum and dad too.

"My dad was mainly the wilder, creative parent. He was a well-known writer of children's fiction back in his day, and always brought his crazy imagination into all the games he taught us as kids," laughed Nathan. "Mum; we called her maman in French, dealt with all the practical stuff."

She took them to swimming lessons and tennis, football, dance, gymnastics and a whole range of other clubs. She also introduced them to the piano, trumpet, violin and guitar. But, neither Nathan nor Beck was *that* sporty *or* musical, as things panned out.

Nathan didn't have anything negative at all to say about his childhood except that it hurt when AC Milan won the Champions League in 2007, and Real Madrid in 2018. He quipped that football wasn't a priority to him growing up. He always had stimuli enough from home and from the local environment. But, football's a religion for many in Liverpool. And, when the teams are doing well, you can't help but be taken along for the ride.

Nathan had good parents, like Marco and I. "They spoke predominantly in French at home, so we called them maman and papa and not mum and dad," he explained. "English was the language of the outside world. French was the glue that held our family together."

In 2017, Nathan left Range High with four good *A levels* and headed south to university. He read Modern Foreign Languages, specialising in French and Spanish, and started to take a huge interest in film because of his girlfriend, Karen, a Film student in the year above with her sights set firmly on Hollywood. He says he missed her terribly when he started a gap year abroad and she went to America.

Karen took off to California with nothing but the clothes on her back *and* her father's credit card, at the end of

September 2019. Nathan left England a week later bound for Spain, where he attended the *Universitat de Girona* as an *ERASMUS* student, and just about preserved his funding in the wake of the whole Brexit thing...

But, while he was away, he fell into a completely different kind of love. For me, though I don't comment, it sounds like this was the first toxic relationship Nathan had ever experienced; a trap that he naively walked right into. Everywhere he went, whether for coffee, parties or just sitting in the park, locals found him easy prey to offload about the vassal state they saw themselves as being. "You're not in Spain. This is Catalonia," was the very well-rehearsed message he and I imagine other impressionable young foreigners had drilled into them on first arrival there.

As I listen, I feel that the Catalan problem's influence on the cynical Nathan of today can't be dismissed. I imagine from his tone, that it must've all been really exciting for him at the time. Yet, I sense we'll be back to talking Catalans again before long, and that's not a happy thought.

In only his first two months in Girona, Nathan was warmly invited to become involved with their thriving separatist movement. He loved hearing the passionate debates and arguments for self-rule away from Spain. His classmate and drinking partner, Sergi, a well-off local boy with big political ambitions took a keen interest in Nathan's Englishness but also in his passion for film and editing. According to Nathan, Sergi inspired him far more than his linguistics professors ever would. And, of that, I have no doubt. If it hadn't been for the Catalans, he may not be in the job he's in today. Yet, it also seems certain to me, if not to Nathan, that he'd been well used by the Independence Cause.

So, it was in Girona that Nathan really became inspired to start writing. Between Christmas 2019 and the end of February 2020, he wrote several short stories and almost completed editing a documentary film in English about the struggle of Carles Puigdemont and his followers.

The sudden threat of lockdowns, and rising panic about the rapid spread of the virus across all Spanish territories forced Nathan to cut his first stay over there short and return to Liverpool, though.

Waiting for things to calm down again lasted for the rest of 2020, and into the new year as well. But, with the help of *Zoom,* Nathan kept in close contact with his comrades in arms in Catalonia, his best friend's sister, Berta, and another girl, Mariona. He ended up translating his stories into Catalan and completed his film edit. Later, he enjoyed some acclaim for his *Homage to 'Contemporary' Catalonia* after, in 2021, he'd returned, if only briefly, to complete the overseas element of his degree course.

Though the content of Nathan's filmed work over there was highly contentious and seen by some in Spain as "*provocative, inflammatory lies,*" to quote a journalist from *El Pais,* it was the quality of his filming and editing all done on *mobile devices* and posted directly to his new commercial *YouTube* channel, that first attracted the attention of some more established professional film makers, initially in Belgium where Puigdemont was then living in exile.

In June 2021, Nathan managed to use the credits from his two stints in Girona to finish his degree back in England. He had missed the boat with Karen though. She graduated a year earlier, and with some help from the '*Bank of Mum and Dad*', she'd flown over to Hollywood to try to fulfil her dream.

She didn't spend long there. The bubble had quickly burst, and she soon flew back home to start work in regional television. She ended up working for BBC Hampshire & the Isle of Wight and never saw Nathan again. She eventually started a family with a man she met at work.

Meanwhile, Nathan had been networking all over Europe. The Catalans saw him as their unique chance to be heard by *'the many, not the few'* through the medium of documentary film in English. But Nathan was still young, ambitious and hadn't yet been burned for flying too close to the sun. After seeing his earliest work aired on Belgian TV in 2022, the BBC came asking after him. And, even if it was just to help create a new angle on an established hospital docu-drama in Liverpool, he headed home for the good, steady salary, and the chance to be near his parents and Beck, by then in her final year at Art College in Liverpool as well.

Nathan admits that the rest of it is something of a blur. While working on the documentary, he would return home in the evenings, emotionally tired, and would get bored all too easily. Ironically, he never liked watching television, and he wasn't really interested in socialising either. His sister took him out with the *Tate Modern* crowd from time to time, and she would've loved it if he'd been into one of her arty friends. But Nathan, for whatever reason, preferred to stay home alone of an evening. With just a bottle of whisky and a *chupito* glass for company, Nathan could sit up all night and just write and write and write…

Since early childhood, and very influenced by his dad, Nathan loved creating stories, often out of thin air. After his unanticipated career in the media had taken off, Nathan also taught himself to screen write, adapting short stories he'd made for his own amusement into miniature plays with speech. One of these efforts, *If I Can Make It There...*, a cathartic tale about a Film teacher with an annoying girlfriend, who goes to America on a wing and a prayer looking for peace and true love, was handed to someone at the BBC who handed it to someone they knew, who handed it to someone else they knew. Within a year, it was being made with a big budget in Hollywood and Nathan was invited by the director to assist him on set.

The film was a huge success all over the world, eventually ranking as the highest grossing *rom-com* of the 2020s, and by 2029, of the century. The entire crazy experience catapulted a boy from a small town in northern England into a world where only the people you read about in celebrity magazines mix. Strangely, Nathan had never been to Los Angeles, at the time of writing his screenplay, even though at least two thirds of the movie are set there. He puts that down to memorising details from a long descriptive phone conversation with Karen, but *I think* he's got an imagination and a way with words that clearly work well together. *Really well* as it turned out.

Still, Nathan believes otherwise, and we discuss this to death in one of the bars we stop in. He thinks that the opportunities he's had etc., have all just been down to complete luck. He says that *'If I Can Make It There...'* is a "shit" film (his own words). But, he says he's come to terms with that now, and as he ages, he slowly edges towards what he really wants to do.

"What really matters," he insists, "is love." In the last few years, he's lost his best friend. The whole affair was obviously big news what with Peter Allan-Ferris being a global superstar, and a new addition in death to the infamous *27-Club*... Nathan was an eyewitness to Pete's sorry end; he tears up just thinking about it. And then, there were the moments leading up to it, playing out, apparently, like some kind of horror remake of a '90s screen idol's early departure. There was the sidewalk in front of a well-known club in West Hollywood, the necessary narcotics overdose and the mysterious circumstances. Then, there was the twenty-first century twist; scores of unwelcome onlookers filming Pete's last movements on their cell-phones.

As Nathan tried to mourn his loss, he found it impossible to go out in public without the inevitable questions about Pete. And, still not over it, he'd then had to return to Liverpool to bury his father who died suddenly in his mid-sixties.

At this point, he starts to talk about how the French model and actress, Audrey Novel, also a good friend of Pete, helped him to get through a really long bad patch over in the States. But, I can see he's uncomfortable talking about her now. I get the feeling that he's holding something back. But, I don't pry.

Our last bar stop is just around the corner from the main entrance to the Excelsior. All the way over, Nathan's taken a mixture of coffees and bottled water. Here, he grabs a table in the window and asks an affable young waiter who's trying out his English, if we can have two empty water glasses and a bottle of their best red wine. I know what he's getting at, but need to repeat the request in Italian, and with a reason, before the boy heads off to get the order.

"I'm not used to talking about myself so much," he says. "After all that walking, I need a wee, a sit down in the sun, and some wine. Plus, I'm sure you're not done getting me to spill all either are you?"

"No, I'm not," I purr. "I've barely started yet."

The last bit of Nathan's story leading up to the 'here and now' in Milan this weekend, seems to start with when he sold the script of *'If I Can Make It There...'* nearly a decade ago. A production company in the U.S. paid him a cool sounding US$250,000 for his raw script. They'd then done what all such people do. After paying him off and promising he'd get the writing credits, they contracted a director who first bought himself a crew, then auditioned, and finally, hired some actors. Nathan had no say and no input in any of it. It was only later, when they were ready to start shooting, that Nathan got a break that nobody normally gets. In an unlikely sequence of events, luck really did, he vehemently insists, come along to shape his entire future in film...

The director, one James Roy, now most well-known for his apparently epic *Goonies* remake in '28, was not long off the start-blocks himself. Off the record, before filming began, he'd already asked Nathan for advice on a lot of stuff, mainly because he didn't know a whole lot about British culture. James seemed to like Nathan, and ended up inviting him to work with him on the film as chief advisor to the director. Nathan bit his hand off for the opportunity and this meant he got far more creative input than he was really meant to have on a film that he'd written but sold on. Then, even more crazily, before release, James had insisted that Nathan be credited as co-director. So,...

While on set, Nathan met Peter Allan-Ferris, a young Anglo-American actor who'd been selected to play the lead in *his* film. Pete had grown up living mainly with his English mother in Isleworth not far from Twickenham and Richmond-upon-Thames. They struck up a firm friendship. They shared digs for a while, and were often seen out and about together. Both were handsome, young and eligible English men, *"A Beatle and a Rolling Stone,"* as *Hollywood Reporter* once called them.

When *"If I can make it there..."* became a big hit, Allan-Ferris and Scott were much sought-after to direct and star in a variety of similar but mediocre scripts.

But, neither was really into the idea of being typecast to one genre, and particularly not rom-coms. Nathan started to write again. He wrote scripts and roles specifically for Allan-Ferris. And, Nathan's latest stories tended to reflect the kind of lifestyle the two friends were enjoying at the time.

Hollywood was not impressed and duly appeared to strike both boys off the A-list for a time. But, one of their vignettes did get funding from a commercial television network. It did well in the US and eventually got sold on to other parts of the world too. That's when the calls and offers from L.A. started to roll in again. Pete appeared in a couple of light-hearted films and Nathan gained kudos writing a handful of episodes for the T.V. comedy show *Chidi's World.*

The Dream was intended as the first of a trilogy of short films written and directed by Nathan and starring Pete. Funded by *Netflix,* it did really well on their streaming site, categorised as a postmodern thriller. Though the emphasis throughout seemed more to be about Pete's character looking cool than about developing his character's story along traditional lines, it quickly became cult viewing. I tell him I've seen *The Dream,* and really liked it. But Nathan disagrees again. "It's Pete," he says, "he was good eye-candy. But, the script sucked."

Set mainly in Gibraltar, it had cinematic airings on the arts scene all over Europe, which is how I saw it, here in Milan with Paolo. The other two movies in this loose trilogy, the second of which was set in Paris and the third in Buenos

Aires, were funded again by and aired exclusively on *Netflix*.

The first two films also both co-starred a well-known and popular French actress, Audrey Novel. She'd been modelling and acting since she was a child, mainly in France. But a foray into Hollywood to try her luck in English in the mid-2020s led to her meeting and later collaborating with Nathan and Pete.

And, for a short while, they were a real tight 'gang of three' in America. Nathan gave Audrey the chance to act in something artistic in a role designed specifically for her. She could show off in English without having to do anymore "homogenised garbage", as she apparently labelled Hollywood. Pete thought he'd found the beautiful girlfriend to save him from himself who'd settle down with him etc. And Audrey used her influence to bring the talents of both guys to the attention of *Cannes* and a coveted nomination for a *Palme d'Or* in 2025. They didn't win.

Pete got drunk at the after-show party and accused the French of being so traditional, they'd done their usual thing and shown favouritism to an old crusader. Yep, Tarantino won *again* that year for the umpteenth time and we never got nominated again.

There appeared to be little that Nathan or Audrey could argue to save face with the board. Nathan who says he's a huge fan of Tarantino reckons *The Dream* didn't win the *Palme* because "it's just pretentious shit" (again, his words). And, the mere fact that it was on the list at all was because, says Nathan, "*Audrey and Pete were in it*".

To the outside world, 'the band of three' had it all. "But, the outside world always think like that," comments Nathan, "because the outside world only see celebrity as meaning lots of money. And who doesn't think money will take away all their problems in life?"

"It helps," I chip-in. "But, I know what you mean."

Pete appeared to have the girl; oft sighted out and about with Audrey Novel on his arm. They were written about as '*the couple*' and I was the '*hanger-on.*'

But behind closed doors, Pete had confided to Nathan about how Aud, as they affectionately called her, would happily continue the charade of them being a couple for the press, but would never let him touch her in private. He thought she was teasing him and was convinced that if he stuck by her long enough, she'd realise she could trust him with her life and they'd *really* end up together.

Trouble was, he tended to obsess about her. And, the thought never once crossed his mind to ask her if she was ok. Pete wasn't aloof or arrogant. But, in respect of getting on with and understanding other people's feelings, he struggled, like a small child might.

Nathan says that Pete was a very talented actor, and in the right setting, he could also be highly charismatic. But, there was something amiss. He had real issues with his parents and one other sibling, and possibly found acting such an escape from reality, he ended up living and dying in his own made-up world that just revolved around him, trying in vain to impress Audrey, and at least on the night he died, achieving the ultimate high.

It'd taken Nathan a long time to get over seeing his friend die right in front of him. He tells me Pete's last words were, "**I'm less than zero**," also observing a possible irony or coincidence because of where it took place. I didn't really get the reference though, so nodded and hid behind my wine cup.

The movie they'd been working on when Pete died, *The Truth and the Light* (another *Netflix* Original) was a kind of amalgam of the *Dream* trilogy with some further chapters exploring the human condition. It was supposed to have action, romance, *some* fighting off bad guys in North Africa and lots of scope for Pete and Audrey to just be themselves. The very basic story arc saw the two main characters fight each other in love while being chased by circumstance across four continents, eventually ending up in Milan. It was meant to be art.

Sadly, all too often in the art world of the mid-2020s, drugs were used as fuel. Pete fell victim to a 5th generation *Punisher* pill on a night out with Nathan, Audrey and others at the start of February 2027. They'd been working on some interior scenes in a rented studio back in L.A. after lots of foreign travel, and were out on *Sunset* celebrating their efforts.

Back in 2029, due to advances in film technology, the star director of his age, James Roy expressed a very public wish to help an old friend finish what he thought had been his buddy's dream, to complete *The Truth and the Light*. Using advanced robotics and editing technologies he had at his disposal, his promise to both Nathan and Audrey and the film's original backers, was to allow Allan-Ferris to strut his stuff to the finish. Nathan says he had no intention at first to accept the offer. James and he had evolved into two completely different types of movie maker since *"If I can make it there..."* and part of the deal that James Roy wanted to cut, was that he would rewrite and refilm certain scenes and add a happy-ever-after for Audrey and Pete in Milan at the end. Just like their first project together, he wanted co-writer and co-director credits with Nathan, and no further questions asked. James Roy's ulterior motive was the 2032 Oscars. He'd never won one as a comedy and blockbuster film maker and Nathan's chances were even slimmer as an art film maker. But, James had viewed the raw footage of the shelved project and read the script. And, he felt there was enough in it for the *Academy* to praise a very daring, edgy, epic romance, if Nathan could compromise enough to allow it a commercial story arc and a happy ending.

Now, to me, a complete stranger still when all's said and done, this James Roy appears to be something of a guardian angel to Nathan. But, the way he talks about James, I sense a lot of animosity. So, I guess I'll just hang fire for now on commenting. I know an explanation can't be far away anyhow. If I've just learned almost everything there is to know about Nathan Scott, he's nearing the end point of his story, and tonight, James Roy's arriving here to see him. So, whenever Nathan accepted the Samaritan's offer, I guess I'm about to find out why…

"…I changed my mind after my dad died. I had no choice really. Maman and Beck told me to," he moans.

"And that's it." Nathan, James Roy and Audrey Novel will face the cameras in Milan tomorrow to launch their bid to win Best Film at the *Academy Awards* in Hollywood next February. They're coming here to officially announce the film's imminent release across America, Europe and the rest of the world. And, they've chosen Milan to start because that's where their story ends.

It turns out, after I ask, that Nathan's father died after suffering a stroke at home. He'd always been Nathan's biggest fan and most honest critic, and I can see in his eyes as he speaks, just how much he misses his dad.

Meanwhile, James Roy's arrival is imminent. Nathan's expected to greet him at the hotel later, but says he'd prefer to be AWOL when James arrives. I laugh politely hoping he doesn't pick up on it, yet pass the time searching up info on his colleague while Nathan uses the bathroom. And, as I suspected, he looks and sounds like a really charming guy. In a short *YouTube* clip, he interviews as someone who takes great pleasure in film making and sees it as his mission to make good, family entertainment carrying important messages about caring for one another and the planet.

I keep one eye on the door to the facilities and quickly slide my phone back into my anorak when Nathan returns.

He pays at the bar and we leave, turning towards the hotel. I ask him if he has anything else planned or if he's working on any other movies at the moment, but he just casts me a cursory glance and kind of sniffs and grins at the same time.

"What?" I ask, grinning back.

"Planned?" he quips. "I need some lunch and I want to get back to your flat and spend the rest of the day with you. Anything else beyond that can wait."

I suggest we eat in the *Excelsior,* and he agrees with a nod and a wry smile. It's convenient until…

…We are being led to our seats when the mood changes. A small wiry man inappropriately dressed for a five-star hotel restaurant takes a picture with a large camera. I notice immediately because of its loud flash from distance.

"I told you," he fumed, glaring at me across the table. Our otherwise very attentive waiter seats him without batting an eyelid.

We wait for the water and menus to arrive, and Nathan won't speak or look up at me. I stretch my leg out to touch his under the long white drape over the table; I even slip off my sneakers and start to rub his inner thigh provocatively with my stockinged toes. But, he won't take off his grumpy look.

"Come on Nathan," I tell him. "What's done is done."

He still doesn't respond, and we end up both ordering before I hear him mumble something inaudible behind his hand and feel the need to bare my teeth. "Nathan, this is nonsense," I snap at him. "It's stupid to worry about that camera guy."

"Look around you," I explain. "This is the Gallia Excelsior in Milan."

"And? Your point is?" he growls.

"Everyone in here is on the rich list. Lots of them way higher up it than you or I," I hiss back. "The paparazzi, if that's even what he was, could've been here for any one of them. There's a bloody football team in the far corner littered with stars!"

"Okay. You're right," he says. "But, they're probably…"

"…Here for *you*?" I complain sarcastically.

"What now?" he pleads. "I'm sorry."

"Yeh, well they filmed me too if they were here for you. Try thinking outside your own bubble Nathan. That photo has me in it, *with you,* and do you know what?"

"What?" he murmurs.

"I don't care, Nathan. I don't care what happens next with it because if we're a team, like those guys over there, we stick together. Everything'll be alright if we stick together."

Nathan quietly knocks back his entire glass of water and reaches to pour himself some more as he fires back. "Let's wait until tomorrow when you're famous, before we decide who cares and who doesn't shall we."

I shake my head and look away from him.

We sit in silence for what feels like too long. But my heart warms again the instant Nathan finally catches my eye and mumbles something about being sorry. He stretches a hand out to me over the table, and I take it, if only briefly. We are interrupted by the arrival of lunch.

We eat. I pick slowly at my food and hesitate before asking him again about his current work schedule. He looks over at me between quick mouthfuls of chicken and lettuce. "Sorry. I'm hungry," he grins. "And, it's not very interesting, *really.*"

I press though. I *am* interested. And, eventually, between his now customary sarcastic quips, I find he's actually working on two documentaries at the moment.

He's supposed to be following the fortunes of the USA Rugby team who are at the moment competing at the World Cup in Russia. The Americans always seem to produce winners in every sport, but they'd never been able to compete with the global giants of rugby until 2027 when against all odds, they reached the World Cup Semi Finals. Nathan's ESPN documentary apparently tracks the team's *From Zero to Hero* (also the name of the film) journey in a sport for which they've no pedigree. He moans though that he's no interest in rugby himself and finds it difficult to focus on anything anyone says to him about the job.

He's also working more discreetly for Belgian television again, about the ongoing and probably never-ending Catalan Troubles. "They're sliding quickly into civil war over there," he explains. "And, personally, I'm best off out of it. I'm only doing the film so Sergi Planas does think I've forgotten about them."

"Sergi Planas?" I ask.

"Sergi. He's just someone from my past who's making loud noises in Catalonia at the moment. Not someone I'd wish to upset though."

Nathan

Alice must've been planning this "next sixty hours" stuff all the while we were at Marco's. It's no wonder she was so quiet when we all started singing and dancing.

Of course, neither of us had any idea our weekends were going to turn out the way it has so far. But we can't wind the clock back to when I sat down in that bar on Friday night. And frankly, I wouldn't want to anyway. From the moment, Alice got up from that other guy's table and sat down opposite me, I'm sure something in me that was missing clicked into place. Like, my whole life up to then had just been some vast jigsaw puzzle with a lost piece. I'd never thought about any kind of eternity before now. I believed *that* was what happened to other people; people who weren't lucky in ways that I've been. People who lead normal, anonymous lives and just connect with others in public places, and love one another and have children and grow old together etc..

Yet, in the first thirty-six hours since we've met, I'm sure we've learned as much about one another, and experienced as much joy, pain and real love as those normal people with their normal lives only get through in the first thirty-six days of their own relationships.

Of course, this whirlwind has to slow down eventually. But right now, we've only really got Sunday all to ourselves. Today, I don't want to have to think about James, and especially not Aud and Monday.

It's not like any emotion I've ever felt before. With every fleeting glance she gives me, every breath she takes against my cheek, I'm both happy and scared out of my wits. It's like meeting her was the best thing that ever happened to me, but the fear of losing her again is always going to be there too.

I'm starting to think brave again though; to see future plans involving *us* and *we*. But, Alice for all her fearless talk, does need to understand that I'm not being paranoid. Far from it. My anxieties about her in my world *are* based on *real* dangers. And, as such, we need to be on our guard together as well as lost in each other, if such a thing is even possible...

We take breakfast outside. The café bar she shows me is cool, decorated for wanderers. I'd love to just don a backpack and take Alice around the world with me; no job calls, no commitments, just us and the road.

At first, I find the walk back across the city '*to get my stuff*' equally as cool. We stroll arm in arm, Alice asks lots of questions getting me to walk and talk about my life, and she points out places that interest her. I also insist on taking some photos, and we make multiple pitstops to shield from the fresh autumnal air.

I find myself kind of enjoying spilling the beans to her. I tell her lots of stuff and I can see she's really happy that I'm opening up. But, I do consciously avoid talking about my mum and Beck, and of course, Aud. Maman and Beck don't visit me in the States, and though I know especially Beck would love to, I really don't need those I love, especially those who have no choice, experiencing *my* daily routine. Audrey is another question entirely though. And, one that I'll need to address very soon; just not right now.

Back at the hotel is when I start to get that uncomfortable feeling I've been trying to warn Alice about. I'm hungry after the walk and she suggests we eat in the hotel. I don't really want to eat there, but for the sake of argument and the absence of a better idea, we do. Then, the inevitable happens...

There's a bright flash of white light, we look up, and the man in the fisherman green coloured mackintosh who looks like a twentieth century caricature of a flasher, is already heading for the door.

I watch Alice with interest. She saw the guy too. She knows he might've just photographed her. But, she doesn't react and this unnerves me all the more. I'm not sure if it's her lack of interest in him, or merely his presence in here that annoys me the most. Still, whatever it is, something about the situation makes my blood boil. This vermin is everywhere. They were in Pete's face as he lay dying in the road. I only want to protect her, yet she doesn't seem to care, let alone want to be protected…

I'm an idiot, I know. But I spark an argument. In between ordering and getting our food, I rant and rave and Alice just soaks it up, quietly. Then, probably as punishment, she maintains a prolonged silence as we wait for our order; just long enough for the *idiot-me* to cool down again and do something I'm really not accustomed to. Definitely, something I would probably never have done if I didn't really love her…

"I'm sorry," I say, gently.

She's been looking away from the table for a while now. But I guess the effect of the magic words is two-fold: I'm no longer a bad guy and she was right. I stretch my hand to her across the table, and she takes it back in hers if only for a few seconds as our lunch arrives.

As we eat, Alice is back again with her questions. She's doing a very good job of diverting me; "liberating me from myself" as she puts it. And, I'm glad that she skips over '*The Truth and the Light…*' looking to find out what else, if anything, I might have in my work pipeline.

Yes, if she and I can survive tonight and tomorrow, I could quite easily just cut out all of my ongoing jobs and dedicate all my time to building something with her here in Milan. But, as things stand, I start, between mouthfuls of chicken leg and potatoes, to honestly describe the two contracts I've got hanging over me right now.

"…At the moment, I have a documentary to make for the probably doped up US Rugby team," I scoff. I don't know. Rugby's a brutal sport that always seemed like a pretty closed shop. Five or six teams if that, had a chance of winning the world cup, three or four of them having already done so. Then suddenly one of the *shit* ones, *The USA* gets really, really good! It all sounds a bit *Lance Armstrong* to me. Still, it's money.

They thought that because I'm Anglo-French, both traditional rugby nations, and I'm a well-known director who can deal with romance, I'd be ideal for the job. But, following around a bunch of fat boys from the Deep South as they try to win the world cup, while claiming they're on some kind of spiritual journey, triumphing against all odds, isn't really doing it for me. I'm working on it now, and so far it looks like it might do okay. The yanks are in the semi-final in a week's time, for the second world cup in succession, and they're more hopeful this time of making it that one step further.

I'm no rugby fan, though. And, I did make that clear to them when they hired me. So, I'm praying they let me watch the match from my pad in L.A... I don't want to fly from Milan to L.A. and then back to Moscow inside a week, and certainly not for a rugby match.

Alice looks interested as I ramble on. This much I can easily make out. She, like me though, doesn't seem too bothered by the oval ball. If she was, she'd probably have said something about it being Italy that the U.S.A. knocked out in the quarters to set up their big match in Moscow next weekend.

It all goes wrong again when I mention that I might be making something else about Catalonia. I kind of feel as if I stabbed them in the back when I walked out on the struggle a second time to return to Liverpool a decade ago. And, a part of me still wants to help. Of course, if I did this, there would be some personal risk. I've got connections in Spain as well as knowing a lot of Catalan Nationalists, and

Spain has also been very kind, awarding me a GOYA in 2025 for *El Sueño* (The Dream). So, for starters, I'm not keen on upsetting them.

Then there's the current political situation between Spain and Catalonia. According to my sources *in country*, it has never been worse. There are daily stand offs involving weapons and shots exchanged, usually in the dark, between Spanish soldiers and Catalan militias. The guerrillas camp out in forests and hill villages near the border with Spain, in Girona and Lleida Province. And, though there've been no official casualties, both sides have dug their heels in. There's no EU presence to support Spain anymore. And, I've heard Catalan whispers of an aid package for Barcelona, strange though it may seem, from England. So, the war, if that's what it's descending into, could go on for some time.

Whatever happens to the place, *my* connections in Girona might be too dangerous for me to visit, if what I am hearing is true. But, I've promised an old friend I'll fly into Barcelona where I understand life goes on as normal for now. And there, we'll talk about making a new Belgian funded film in the region. Of course, we'd have guaranteed protection by the militia for me and my Belgian crew when working *in country*; that's everywhere north of Barcelona up to the French border.

Alice listens carefully throughout my explanation. But, if she furrowed her brow as soon as I started speaking about Catalonia again, the worry lines on her forehead were ocean deep when I asserted throwing myself and a film crew into hostile territory.

"Well, I don't think Sergi Planas sounds like someone I'd risk my life to help," objected Alice.

And, as I finish my plate, I think now is probably a very good time to get up and take my leave from the table. If I were Alice hearing me, I'd be concerned too. But, I'm not sure Catalonia should really be her concern, and I don't want another argument.

I stand without answering her and tuck my chair neatly under the table. "Maybe you could get coffees and a dessert if you want one, up at the bar. I'll go and clear my room, then if you don't mind, can we get a taxi back to yours?"

"Ours," she says, beaming as I walk away.

When I return to the lobby and to reception lugging my suitcase behind me, the guys on the desk are not expecting me to be checking out. They know that James Roy is checking in within the next few hours and that at least one more film person plus some foreign journalists will be in from Monday until Tuesday. They talk feverishly between themselves in Italian as I stand there feeling dumb. I want to lean over and ask what the problem is. I'll be back in the morning for my press commitments. I just won't need their bed. Christ! They could give it to James and not even clean the room. He's stayed at my place before and never complained. I gave him an expensive mattress. Did he really expect me to put a clean sheet on it as well?

They eventually turn around and a man not much older than I am, says to me in English that my restaurant lunch is paid so is not on the bill. They'd been discussing additional charges when he learned from his colleague in the restaurant that there were none. They don't care anymore than I do that I'm checking out and they don't seem at all interested in where I might be going, although the man does inform me that my *friend* is waiting over in the lounge bar and she has taken coffee and dessert for two. He says that they look forward to seeing me tomorrow and hope that I now have a restful stay in *the real Milano*. I tease him to watch out for the American arriving later and joke that they could say I'd left back to the States already. My humour appears lost on him though as he replies he won't be working when the American arrives but comments that he loves *The New Goonies* and would like to wish Mr. Roy a really pleasant stay in Italy too if I can pass that on for him. I nod politely and head over to Alice trundling my luggage noisily down a couple of steps and bumping past some tables and chairs en route.

She sits at the bar on a stool much like that in her apartment. She's alone, engrossed in some magazine article and doesn't notice me despite the racket. I take just a few moments to spy on her from afar, her head bent in deep concentration, so beautiful. Even from where I stand watching, everything looks easy for her; simplicity and style without any pretence. And, I'm learning. Sure, my Rome isn't gonna be rebuilt in just two days, but I am happier and more relaxed than I've been in a long time and it's all because of Alice.

As I approach, I see she's got herself another macchiato, and for me, an Irish coffee. Between us sits a boat of vanilla ice cream that looks like it's starting to melt. There's just one long spoon. As she looks up at me with those innocent, effervescent blue eyes again, I put one finger to my lips. I offer her some of her dessert on the spoon. She takes it seductively, and with her gaze firmly fixed on me, I too begin to melt.

We ride back to her apartment in a taxi from outside *Centrale*, and Alice declares that she's worn out and needs a siesta. While I was in my hotel room packing, she's remarkably got everything about our evening under control. We're returning later to meet James Roy. Assuming his flight arrives on time, we have reservations to eat at a good restaurant not far from the hotel. The reservation is set in her name and the reception staff will inform Mr. Roy where to find us. Alice's idea is that this intervention will soften the blow James will feel when he finds that I'm not in the hotel with him. Personally, I worry about what James will *say* more than what he might think. Right now, I couldn't care less what anyone from stateside thinks of me. I'm in the mood to get this film and the monkey that it carries off my back and out of my life for good. Then, I'll be free to come back to Europe and explore *new* possibilities…

Words often cut into me like knives. Words don't need to be thought out. They just come. I know Jim Roy is not a bad man. I know he'd never try to hurt me. But, he's brash and loud and shoots from the hip, and I'm just not in the right place to need that kind of company right now. Not today.

I don't want to go out and entertain James Roy tonight. In all honesty, I just don't want to go out tonight. I am tired of going out. But… Alice has it all set. She believes that it'll be a good idea for us to meet this way before Monday's event; something she also wants to come to. I still haven't the courage to explain to her why that most certainly *will not* be a very good idea.

For now, though, I don't put up any resistance beyond a nonchalant shrug when she asks if everything's okay with her plan. She gently nestles herself and then rests her head against my shoulder, reaching out for one of my hands as we pass *Il Duomo* again, about half way home. I don't want to think. So, I decide to try to get my head around Monday later, when she's asleep. In the cab, I squeeze her hand in mine and she lifts her head, still curled against my shoulder.

"How did you know I'd like Irish coffee?" I ask.

"I don't know. I just did," she says.

Alice

We've just arrived in my apartment block, standing next to all the mailboxes with his suitcase. Again, that '*click*' sound as the main door closes behind us sticks in my mind, for better or for worse. The elevator's small; only large enough for two people, yet he guides his big brown case on wheels in between us instead of manoeuvring it to one side. I lean against the wall and hit the button. He stands opposite me, suddenly with the look of an adversary.

I want to kiss him. I want to lay my head against his shoulder as I did in the taxi over here. But he's unnerved me. The old lift rattles skyward and I can sense panic in him again. I jab his belly with my index finger; being playful. He manages a tiny smile, starched on like a kid forced into a family photo. I prod him again, feeling for his Hollywood abs. But this time, Nathan just looks up at the ceiling. It's as if he's trying to understand where the sound of the pulley that's slowly dragging us up is actually coming from.

"Are you afraid of elevators?" I ask, in sudden realisation.

"I prefer the stairs," he says.

I shrug and give him a pitying smile. Personally, I always feel quite aroused in an elevator. I suppose you could call it a kind of fetish. I used to think I was odd, and never talked about it. Then, one time when I was in London, I chanced upon a newspaper article that said 31% of women feel the same way as me. When I came home, I told Paolo, but he just laughed. Still, it *was* a reaction. I remember that conversation fondly. We never made out in the lift, but it was one of the last few times I made Paolo smile.

And now, here I am again. I suppose on reflection that there must be more people out there who share Nathan's lift-phobia than my lift-lust. So, I guess that fantasising with the emergency button and Nathan will just have to stay in my dreams for the time being…

We arrive soon enough. A chill moves over my back as the doors slide cleanly open. Before I've time to catch my breath, Nathan's out, pulling his case along after him. And, only when the elevator closes again behind me does he turn around and smile.

"I'm sorry. I should have let you out first."

"Don't worry," I whisper reaching over the intrusive case and pulling him towards me. "Shall we go for a siesta?"

Several beads of sweat look as if they're glued onto his forehead. Otherwise, the panic lines have disappeared and that beautiful, interesting yet modest look that drew me to him in the first place has returned. I lean right in and kiss him deeply, feeling the smoothness of his cleanly shaven face and chin against my own before breaking the embrace and pulling both him and his bag quickly towards my door.

I turn my key. We enter quickly, me first this time. I usher him inside and close *us* in. I lean for a moment, my back against the door like yesterday, only now I want to look at what's in front of me. Fumbling, I turn the deadlock key until it *clicks*. Then I move into Nathan's personal space. He knows exactly what I want.

"What time do you make it?" he asks.

"We have time," I purr, taking him by the hand and leading him towards *our* bedroom.

Nathan

I've deliberately blocked her off to one side of the small lift space. I'm sober, so highly conscious of how noisily antiquated this contraption is. I don't want to fool around. I only need to get into her apartment and out of this hot, cramped box, quickly. I look across at Alice and try to steady myself, but it's not working. I'm sweating and I know she'll worry that I'm angry about something or that I'm afraid of my feelings for her again. I should just tell her, but I don't.

Some people fear aeroplanes. But not me. I've practically lived on the damned things for the last seven or eight years of my life. And, you do tend to feel a certain sense of invincibility after doing the Heathrow to LAX round trip over twenty times a year and in all weathers.

Up top, the champagne's always on ice, and there's usually the likes of Joey King or Brooklyn Beckham curled up with a fashion magazine in the next booth, oozing self-confidence. A few years ago, I once glanced over and caught Miley's eye as we hit turbulence over Canada. She smiled nervously, pretended to mop her brow, and I just remember thinking, *'if Miley's fine, we'll all be fine.'* Bad shit just doesn't happen to people like her…

But lifts…? If that big metal cord breaks for some reason; corrosion from leaky pipes, or just wear and tear, you're dead, dead, dead! And, there's no need to buy a coffin. You're already in one! Then, there's the electrics. It's one button! If my *E-car* button doesn't work, I call a cab to get to work. If the switch doesn't work in a lift mid-flight, you're trapped; suspended on a metal thread, possibly in the dark, until someone else realises and sends for help...

I swear, if this lift jams now, Alice will have a real job on her hands to stop me freaking out! Whether alone or with hundreds of other people like in those huge cargo lifts they have at big airports, I'm seldom happy in these things. Drunk, or distracted like Friday night, it can be ok. Otherwise, I just try my best to look stoic and hold my panic in.

Alice looks nervous too. I wonder for a second if she's claustrophobic in lifts like me. I doubt it though. She lives on a top floor! Then, out of the blue, she asks me if I'm afraid of lifts. She's worked me out again. And, if the tenderness of the kiss she gives me in her hallway is anything to go by, she's sympathetic to my pain.

"What time do you make it?" I ask her once inside her front door. I'm certainly relieved we're here.

"We have time," she replies. She's looking straight at me with fire lighting up her radiant blue eyes. I know exactly what she wants, and safely back in her apartment as she takes me by the hand, I'm happy to follow her lead.

Alice

I can't wait a second longer for him. Behind closed doors my animal instincts quickly take me over; my human, thinking brain is shutting down, leaving Nathan no choice but to let himself go and follow suit. In the blink of an eye, we're naked and moving against each other on *our* bed. Time is long forgotten. Every kiss deepens the passion I have for him now. There's nothing more either of us needs to say to communicate what we're about.

I moan pleasure in time to his every smooth action, breathing faster with each movement. I've seduced this man into my home twice now, yet every time we arrive, I love how he's so able to take back control. I surrender to him completely. He holds my hands down either side of my head and as I buck, pretending I want to escape, he pushes down soft and hard at the same time, maintaining focus lower down, and locking eyes as we so often do. I'm entranced by his. I know he loves mine, too. I try to stare back innocently and sweet for him: his damsel in distress, biting my bottom lip, knowing this will blow his mind. We move so naturally together; the perfect dance, neither wanting the end point that we're driving towards, yet holding each other so tight, smothered in kisses and smiles.

At some point we must've both drifted off into a blissful afternoon nap. Our bodies are still warmly entwined when we regain consciousness and not knowing who started what, we simply resume the last kiss without a single word spoken.

I'm feeling so good, I could just doze here in his arms for eternity. He's holding my hand in his and stroking my fingers; softly, slowly feeling the length of each one from the tip to the base. I like it. It tickles but it's nice. He observes me closely as his fingers glide over and over mine, as if probing for a reaction. I'm too busy to talk though; busy enjoying his warm, comforting touch, gradually waking up at my own pace until…

"This little piggy went to market…" he whispers, running thumb and forefinger up and down my thumb.

"What do you mean, 'Piggy'?" I ask him. He ignores me, grinning.

"This little piggy stays at home," he continues, this time playing the same way with my index finger.

"Why 'Piggy'?" I demand, definitely loud enough for him to hear me.

"This little piggy has roast beef," he states, again ignoring my question and now rubbing my middle finger up and down.

"Pigs don't eat roast beef," I object. "Nobody eats roast beef except the English."

"Oh?" he replies suddenly. "So?" He touches my ring finger. "Does this little piggy want *none*?"

"Oh, please Nathan. I don't know what you mean," I say.

He's staring at me. He continues to slide his thumb and index fingers up, and slowly down my ring finger, and I suddenly feel a bolt of nervous energy surge through me.

"Does this little piggy really want none?" he asks again. He copies me, biting his lip as he continues to glide his two fingers gently over mine. He knows that I don't want *none.*

"Does this little piggy really want none?" he cries, now bearing down on me with his large, expressive brown eyes.

"No! This little piggy wants *some*," I practically shout back at him, giggling, yet still anxious to see what he's going to say next…

At long last, "this little piggy goes…" He moves his attention onto my smallest finger, before completing the rhyme.

I won't fall for that trick again.

Nathan

We sit up together in bed, and reading our movement, Alice's ceiling lights come on brightly. She quickly says something in Italian and a dimmer starts to wind the lighting gradually down until she says "stop".

"I like your black nails," I remark looking down.

"Do you?" she replies. "I normally only wear black when I'm sad."

"And are you?" I ask.

"Am I what?" she says.

"Sad?"

"Should I be?" she questions. "I feel good right now."

"I feel good right now too," I say. "But…"

"Please don't," she replies. "I *just* …want this moment."

"**But**," I repeat, more forcefully this time. I feel her shudder a little next to me, and it's enough to command a quick sideways glance to check she's alright…

"If we have time right now, I'd really like to hear a little more about *you*," I continue. "You've told me a lot about your life here in Milan. But, you've only touched on where you and Marco actually come from."

"O-okay," she stutters. "What would you like to…"

We're interrupted by my mobile phone buzzing away to itself in my jeans on the floor; I never have the volume on for incomings, but it is set to vibrate what with Alice's plans and my co-director arriving in Milan later.

"Do you want to get your telephone?" she asks.

"No," I say bluntly. "You know I don't like technology."

"Oh yes, raging against the machine," quips Alice. "We're from a generation lost in pixels, I know. But, what if it's *him* and he needs you?"

"Ok," I grumble. "I know I need to get it, but I'd rather just sit here naked with you until we really have to move. Do you have the time?"

"No," she says. "We're fine though. We weren't asleep for very long and…, look, if you don't answer it, it'll only ring again."

I get up and go to use the toilet, grabbing my phone on the way. There are two messages from James. He already landed at Heathrow a while ago and is probably now in the air transferring to Milan. He's shattered, he comments, but happy to finally be off the jumbo and in Europe… Then there are six more nagging messages from Audrey, and I don't know what I'm gonna do about them… For now, I set the phone back onto 'silent' and leave it on top of the cistern.

"I really don't get along with smart tech either you know," declares Alice, as I hop back under the duvet and press my cold feet against her legs for warmth.

"Ouch…" she wails. "How did you get such cold feet? The floor's heated."

"I don't know," I reply, kissing her for her pains.

"And James?" she asks.

"Yeh, he'll be at Malpensa fairly soon, all ok."

"Good," says Alice. "I'm glad you checked. It was the right thing to do."

"Yeh," I reply, only half listening as I snuggle down against her warm body.

"You know, personal home technology is completely out of control don't you?" she remarks suddenly. "It's like, I've heard about people who were given a *Wii* for their seventh birthday, an *iPad* for their eleventh, had a new *iPhone* every year from the age of thirteen to thirty. You hear about them now living in those *Trance Domes*!"

"*Trance Domes?*" I ask.

"You know," she says. "Where they live in an alternate reality for work, and play online in character with a headset that transcends their whole being. They only ever get to see sunlight on the weekend, if they leave the dome at all..."

"*Transdom*!" I reply quickly as the penny drops on what she's trying to explain. "It's *Trans-**dom***. There are no domes. It's set out like a kingdom that transcends reality. You attach small metal detectors either side of your head. They stick to sweat or if you just give them a quick lick before... Anyway, they say the neck or just behind the ears is the best place, but never, ever the temples! But, I've never been into gaming, so..."

"Oh, I'm sorry," says Alice. "But you do get it don't you? *You're with the resistance like me. You* listen to the old music. *You* rarely touch that device."

"Unless I'm working," I chuckle.

"And are you?"

"Later," I reply.

We fall silent again. I'm completely at peace here with Alice, sharing her body heat, but so much more besides. Yet, it transpires she's still stuck on the *Transdom* concept a minute or so later.

"Nathan?" she asks hesitantly.

"Yes."

"These people; a lot of them *really do* live in the 'dome' or like you say, '*kingdom*' all the time. They work from home with their work-nodes either side of their heads, putting them into an office that could be anywhere from here to Tokyo. It's like they can attend meetings if they're junior managers or supervisors, and liaise on all matters everywhere at once, without the bad telephone feel of *Skype,* the distant screen-feel of *Zoom*, the air travel, or the risk of more pandemic diseases.

They maybe take them off when they go to eat; go shopping, I don't know. Then they're back on their sofas in the evenings with game-nodes on, playing rally racing in a real car. Isn't that just crazy? Don't you think it's wrong?"

"I don't know. I'm no expert...I only know it's not really for me," I reply. "I mean, we have no more global obesity than we did in 2021. There's less reported violent crime. And people *are* evidently going outside to grocery shop or to socialise still. We just walked across a big part of Milan this morning *on a Sunday* and saw lots of people outside in bars and just walking. I'm sure it's the same everywhere else… On Friday night, the bar where we met was full. So was the music bar. People connect. I think it's generally just different from you and me is all. I don't really think the real issues have changed in the last ten years, except the weather is getting more and more extreme and the threat of more pandemics won't go away. The nodes at least cut down on the need for people to physically travel as much as we *were* doing, so less emissions, less electrical waste too."

"You know," I keep on. "There's that, *the big environmental* plan, and then there's the social side too. We all know that the bad side effects of social media in its crudest early forms like chat rooms, then *Facebook1, Snapchat etc* totally outweighed the benefits of being able to send pictures of grandchildren and stuff right around the world to long lost love ones…But, with the nodes! They're easily replaced, cheap, work on all platforms, and if someone's feeling down or lonely they can just connect at work or over some action fantasy game in cyberspace. They can create what they look and feel like in the *Transdom* to suit whatever they'd like themselves to be. It's real first gen *Avatar* tech, Alice! I have no intention of using it. I'm happy with *Sergeant Pepper's* on an antique C.D. player or better still, vinyl. But shit! When we're in our fifties with the rate of change, unless the planet's overheated and killed us all by then, we may not have any choice. We might all be floating around in the atmosphere in big sleeper star-ships, nodes on, living out the rest of our lives through our avatars! And, anyway, why are you still travelling around for *your* bank when you could just wear a node and…?"

"Do you think node level workers own rooftop apartments in Downtown Milan?" she fumes. "Then,... I dare say they'll have to get one of those guys to go online to Prague for me this week because of you, so..."

"Are you sure you don't just want to go in? You seem pretty important."

"No," she replies. "I don't want to go to work tomorrow or go to Prague this week. And, I sincerely hope I don't end up living as an avatar in twenty years' time."

I get up, climbing over Alice and kissing her again as I roll in that direction. "I'm going to the toilet," I say.

"Again?"

"Sorry," I reply. I don't say so, but I'm actually going back to get my phone. Tomorrow, I need Alice and Audrey together like I need a hole in the head! And, I've had an idea that I'm going to text to Aud right away. I'll run it by Alice tonight if I get the response I'm hoping for.

Then, I flush, for effect, and open the door...

Alice

After the toilet, I hear Nathan wander over to the kitchen and the fridge door opens and quickly closes again.

"Why do you have no windows in your bedroom?" he asks.

"Isn't that obvious?"

I notice that he smiles wryly at my answer. Some men don't like the way that I often turn their questions back on them, but Nathan hasn't said anything *yet*. He jumps back over me into bed, followed by more deliberate cold feet and apologetic kisses…

"It's not so light as before," he informs me, unscrewing a small bottle of *San Pellegrino* for himself at the same time.

"Yes. It's nearly evening," I say. "And James?"

"He's probably landing now. He'll not be in the hotel for another couple of hours though yet. So, tell me all about Alice."

"Ok," I begin. "Why not."

Nathan hands me the water, nodding encouragement. Then, he reclines on his pillow, closes his eyes and waits. I watch him as I sit up to drink.

"Go on then," he urges, eyes still closed and cheeky grin stitched on to his face.

"I'm not quite sure where to start," I say. "But I'll give it a go, *for you*…"

And that's how I end up explaining my story to Nathan, who may or may not fall asleep as I drone on. Still,…

"I was born on 28th January 1999. I'm 32 years old just like you, and despite having done really quite well in my career, I'm not ambitious in the slightest, and I'm not really looking for much more in life than well, …*love*," I say.

I look down at Nathan. His grin has subsided into a contented smile. He's still resting his eyes though, so I turn back to my water and continue.

"I'm a dreamer, and always have been. I know I'm not the only one, and like the great John Lennon did before he was so cruelly taken from us, I believe that *love is* all you need. Sadly, unlike him, I've also got this annoying habit that's inbuilt. It's as if I'm a robot who's been hardwired needing to please *everyone* I meet *all* of the time.

I guess, that's not always a bad thing. It means I was never a rebellious teenager. I was really successful at school and now at work. But, being such a good girl has often gotten right in the way of my basic human needs. I don't know how to explain why…"

"I think I understand," he says. "Just keep going."

"…As far back as I can remember, I was always a good child. I grew up in a loving family. My parents are still very much alive, still healthy and still married too. I grew up in a big house on Lake Como, and then you know, I have one older brother, Marco who's about four and a half years older than me.

I was always very indulged as a child; we both were. But, I was always drawn towards my father, particularly when he was listening to music. Over time, he saw my interest and took to sharing all his music passions with me.

Marco always liked building things and drawing, and would spend hours happily alone in his room with *LEGO* and later *MECANO* or just a pad of plain paper and a pencil.

Our father's other passion's football! I remember him shouting *"goooooal!!!"* at the television screen most weekends when his team were doing well. Marco was never interested in sports though; he'd be skulking off to his room to play on some new graphics software he'd got our parents buy him. He even missed it when the rest of us, including my mum and some friends from the village sat around our huge screen to watch Italia win the World Cup in 2006. I remember this bit of my childhood very fondly. These were good times to be involved with the whole community, and I always felt very much part of something then, even if sometimes all the coming together was only inspired by football.

That night in 2006 though, I will always remember dancing with Papà. The entire neighbourhood seemed so happy, and there were all the car horns. They blared out all evening right across the lake, possibly even reaching Germany, or so we hoped.

Marco and I get along perfectly. He's very dramatic, but he loves me, and is always looking for a reason to see me or to show me how much he cares. Our lives are really busy these days and we don't get to see each other often enough, but he still calls me every week. We are also both really close to our parents, just as we always have been. Christmas down at the lake with all of us together is just magical..."

I look down in hope of a reaction. I'd love him to see what it's like at our Christmases. I glide a finger-tip gently down the bridge of his nose. He doesn't move, but I think he's still smiling. Then his arm comes up to scratch an itch on the back of his neck. That's good enough for now. He's not asleep, so I go on...

"My mum's an artist. I remember that when Marco was a boy, she would give him exhibitions of everything he ever painted or drew whenever anyone from outside of the family entered our house. This was all the time. She ran painting and sketch classes and clubs on the lake that were attended by anyone and everyone with artistic or intellectual leanings from nearby and beyond; sometimes we even received foreign guests!

I have so many fond memories from my early childhood. Like, there were always lots of interesting strangers in our home, either just painting, staying over for dinner and a debate, or sometimes… a German man and his Swedish girlfriend spent nearly a month in the summer of 2007! I was only eight years old. I remember I wanted to learn some words in Swedish, and the girl, Karin, she was very pretty; she taught me, "*Jag älskar dig.*" She repeated the words every time I asked her too, which was most nights before bedtime. And, I'll never forget them… It means, '*I love you.*'

As I grew older, into my teens, you'd expect me to have had boyfriends. But there weren't any. I just wasn't interested, and I didn't have time because, well, you've seen my *Fazioli*…"

"You're an amazing pianist," he interrupts, eyes still shut.

"Thanks." I wasn't expecting *that*.

"**I was a musician**," I continue. "From very early on, with my father, I took to music…and, I don't just mean 'I liked it' or that I took some lessons and could play an instrument or two…

People talk about *talent,* you know. I don't *generally* believe such a thing exists…"

I stutter at the end of making my point, and again deliberately pause and look down at Nathan. Here's where I'd have expected a comment or a question, what with the talent debate being one that's raged on throughout the twenty-first century, always sparking some really strong opinions. I'm looking at him, and I must've paused for long enough, as Nathan suddenly opens his eyes and stares back at me.

"So, you don't believe in the talent myth?" he says.

"N-no," I stammer. "And, did you just say, '*myth*'?"

"Yeh, it's nothing interesting though. I'm enjoying listening to you. No-one's born with magic in them, are they. It's all about, '*how much do you want it?*'"

"Thanks," I manage. "Most… Oh never mind… Growing up, I always had access to whatever musical instruments I wanted. If Marco or I said we wanted to learn *this or that*, our parents always supported us."

"That's good," he says. "So, you got obsessed by the piano?"

"Well, my dad was my main inspiration, but where we lived also played a huge part. I grew up with this large window in my bedroom, like the one in the rest of the flat. My room overlooked one of the world's most beautiful lakes and I was totally aware of how lucky I was, even as a little kid. Papa shared some amazing music, in Italian, English, and other languages with me; and the piano, I took to it like a duck to water. First, I spent hours learning to play all of my favourite tunes from classical through to pop. And later, I even wrote some of my own stuff too. I had a tutor up to the higher grades. But I'm mainly self-taught after that.

Music was my whole life. I worked hard at school because I had to. I was often catching up after having been away performing somewhere like Vienna, Munich or London, and Bratislava, Ljubljana or Rome.

In school, I absolutely loved Maths and Languages as a teenager. I found them easy. But, at home, all I ever did was play the piano at my window on the lake. All I did from when I was really small to when it was time to go away to university, was play the piano all the time; perfecting my art."

"And, you never wanted to be professional as an adult?" asks Nathan.

"No," I reply, cutting right across him.

"I think at college in Milan, when I first came here, some academic once told me that there was a specific link between music, maths and language acquisition. The suggestion *was* that I was born with some innate talent for all three. But, that's utter rubbish. Academics read and talk. I did and still do. That's how people get good at some things. They work at them, *very fucking hard* in my case.

So, I'm sorry for swearing in English. I rarely swear in any language. But, I think I've been trying to make a point about myself, that's hard for me to articulate, and now, I might have just done it without realising. Being such a good girl has often gotten right in the way of my basic human needs is what I told you before…"

"And, I said I understood you," says Nathan.

"But do you really?" I reply. "I've always been disciplined. I keep up with my work and I've kept my relationship with my ex-boyfriend under control. **Checked**. As a musician and a performer, I've lived a very self-disciplined lifestyle for more than twenty-five years. Now, this weekend, when I sat with Paolo, bored out of my mind, and I saw you, Nathan… I lost myself for a moment or two. I wanted to experience '*wild*.' I wanted to see if I could do something spontaneous at the sight of a handsome man, and I don't know? Have some fun for once!"

"And? What now?" he demands.

"And, now, I can't see myself ever turning back to how it was before. You see, you've awakened feelings in me this weekend…feelings I'm not sure I understand but…I want to explore more with you. I owe this to…"

"You don't owe anybody anything," he tells me. "In fact, by the sound of it, *life* owes you some free time and some *love*."

I recap the water bottle and put it down on the floor. I lie back down with him. I want to make love again, but I don't think we'll have time. I kiss him instead and then draw back and hold his face softly between my cupped hands, analysing his eyes, only seeing good intention.

"I reckon you've still got some regrets about your music career," Nathan guesses suddenly.

"Yep. I have one. I lost complete confidence in myself while performing at an international concert in England. I was so lucky, I'll only say now in hindsight, as I got to share the stage with a very young British prodigy called Alma Deutscher. She's one of the world's most accomplished classical composers now."

"I know, I've seen her," he says.

"I was still only young myself at the time …I'd only ever received praise all my life up until then, from my family, audiences all over Europe and my piano trainer. Despite the absolute fear I felt when Alma walked out of the wings to join me on stage with her little violin, I clapped her from my piano stool, and I didn't put a single foot wrong in the performance either. I accompanied her on *her own* violin piece. She was eight years old and had already composed on piano and violin as well as having completed a short opera, *The Sweeper of Dreams,* a year earlier.

I don't know how to explain to you how I felt as I sat there and watched her. She bowed and curtseyed and deserved all the applause she got at the end of our performance. So yes, I could have been a professional pianist. But, I'm not.

…I saw and I shared the stage with greatness. And, I was premier league too. I've played to packed houses in many great concert halls where the likes of Mozart, Schubert and Mendelssohn have played in the distant past. But,… Maybe it takes a trained ear like mine. Certainly, the audience couldn't see what was happening to me inside my head. I'd just finished playing a classical piece of piano that was so beautiful it brought a tear to my eye. Yet, it was written by a child barely out of kindergarten, standing right there next to me, smiling and mouthing 'thank you' up at me.

As an elite performer, when you see true greatness, you know you are beaten, and the only outward reaction that you can give because of the awe and fascination that you are feeling, is absolute respect for their superior dedication. I, of course, rose to my feet from the piano, but I did not bow to the audience alongside Alma. I bowed and curtseyed to *her*. This is how I parted company with the little English girl. And, it was probably the beginning of the end of my music career as well.

She will never realise, because she's far too lovely to ever think that, but like her mini opera, Alma Deutscher was *The Sweeper of Dreams* for me. I never played to such a large audience again after that date and I was only fourteen myself."

Nathan tries to speak, but I brush my hand gently over his mouth. I'm not quite finished what I wanted to say.

"So, neither you nor I believe in the talent myth as a general rule. But, if ever I've questioned my own reasoning or been asked by a higher power to try to accept faith, it was in Alma's company. Aside from all of the obvious passion and hard work, she's also got the spirit of Mozart in her."

"Either that or the poor girl just had really pushy parents," laughs Nathan. He presses his lips against mine before I can reply. The sadness and regret I just revisited is washed away in an instant by his touch. I don't know if he'd meant it to be a French kiss, but, as I feel my eyes start to bulge, I open my mouth to him, replacing one intense emotion with another newer, infinitely more exciting one.

I tell him all about my university career here in Milan. I studied Business and International Affairs. I followed the same ERASMUS program as he did, only in Lille; fortunately making it back to the lake just in time to be able to spend that awful, long Lockdown of 2020 with my family. I later did my postgraduate and Masters studies in Rotterdam and Dortmund. And, I've been working for *HSBC* in Milan ever since.

Nathan

As Alice talks about herself, I keep my eyes closed. It helps me focus on every last word she says. I learn all about the experiences that have shaped her, past and present. And, glimpse at perhaps why she is the way she is; a kind, loving, sincere, hard-working and intelligent woman.

If there's anything new that I've found out, something I perhaps didn't realise before, then it's got to be just how scared she is. Alice is a doer. She's humble about all her achievements, but she's also proud. Everything she has, she's worked hard to earn, and where her parents have supported her, she feels nothing but love and admiration for them. But, where she's always given everyone around her the impression she's strong and independent, she's actually not, and seems to have sacrificed the one thing she craves more than anything else in order to achieve the rest of it. And now, she looks to me, as if for approval that what we're doing here and how we're doing it and why, is all right and good, while fearing her emotions as they rob her of the control she's always believed she needed.

Alice and I are very different. Our experiences of the world and the ways we grapple with them set us apart straight away. She's honest and direct with people. I hide away from my problems, bury my head and hope they'll go away. Alice is a brilliant musician with a rare ability whose bad luck has set her on a completely different life path to the one she was surely designed for. I'm a brilliant nothing; a writer of sorts whose major successes have come from having had the good fortune to be in the right place at the right time and to have made friends with some important people along the way.

If there is one thing we have in common, besides *The Beatles*, it's that at heart, we're a pair of good natured, loving people. We also share some pretty fundamental beliefs. And, for whatever reason, whether it was written in the stars, ordained by God, or by an alien creed, we've had the chance to meet, talk, eat, drink, socialise and become intimate this weekend. And, to cut a long story very short, we've fallen in love…

A weird thought pops into my head. Two people are sitting in an old canoe with no oars. They're heading straight towards the rapids at break neck speed. They're clinging to each other for dear life, clueless, when they should probably both just dive overboard and take their chances alone to swim back to dry land. It's Alice and me in that canoe...

I don't know why I think that. I guess it's just fear of the unknown. In the past, Alice and I would both have opted to jump; no second thoughts. Right now, holding onto each other seems the best thing to do. But why? And, for how long before it becomes a bad idea?

"I'm sorry you lost confidence in your music," I say finally. "I'm sure you'd be selling out concerts all over Europe still now if you hadn't stopped."

"You don't have to say that."

"I do. I love the way you play."

She smiles sweetly before deliberately changing the subject. "How do I have to dress to meet a Hollywood film director?"

I sigh.

"What?" she asks.

I shake my head. "Look," I throw back the duvet to reveal our naked bodies on the bed. "I'm a Hollywood film director too."

"Wh.. You say we should go naked?" she asks.

"No!" I say. "Just try not to think of James in that way. All we're doing is having a light meal on a Sunday night with an aloof American who is highly likely to be suffering from jetlag and who won't be listening to anything we have to say anyway."

She goes to mouth something else but I cut her off. "And, besides, didn't *you* book the restaurant? Surely it should be me asking *you* how *I* should dress?"

At this, Alice gets up suddenly. "Open your suitcase," she smirks. "We can talk about *your look* for this evening in the shower."

We arrive back, right behind the Gallia Excelsior, at *The New York Lounge* looking like a team of sorts. She's made me go for my black suit trousers and shoes again with a slim fit black polo neck jumper I think I picked up off the *A&F* New Year Sale rack in Santa Monica. "Thick enough to keep out the evening chill, thin enough to give you some style," teases Alice.

She's also dressed all in black, going for trousers, flat soled shoes with a girlish looking little buckle at the side, "a coincidental" she remarks, black polo neck pullover and her ebony hair in a tight chignon with a wide black bandeau, she says because we don't have time for her to wash and dry her hair properly before we leave. She looks very cute and I tell her so. But she's not fooling me. She's so deliberately coordinated our dress tonight for James Roy's attention. She wants him to like her, and she wants him to acknowledge **us** as a couple. I just wonder what she's playing at.

He's already there when our taxi arrives out front. And, like I would have done in his place, he's taken the lone seat against the wall facing the rest of the room.

"Look," says Alice gripping my arm tightly as we enter. "I got us a table in the back, so you can face away from all your scary fans."

"Thanks," I say. "But James is more well-known than me and I can see him from here."

"So, he'll know to keep a better watch then. You just try to relax tonight okay?"
"Okay."

We pass directly by reception and Alice points over in James's general direction for the waitress to see that we're with him. They exchange a few words and the waitress nods and says something about menus. It's too late to escape. James has spotted us, takes his hand away from his phone screen and waves us over to join him.

"*Johnny English!*" he cries, as we draw nearer, getting up out of his seat and coming around the table to embrace me. I never liked the way he calls me that.

"What's with the black look dude?" he asks as he breaks away.

"Hangover," I reply.

"And a Milanese friend with a sense of style," interrupts Alice stealthily. She has to interrupt too. James has a tendency to struggle with having to focus on more than one person at once even when not severely jetlagged. I stand back to admire her sudden burst of courage. I'm guessing this is Alice the business woman coming to the fore.

"Yes," I say. "May I present Alice…"

"*D'Alessandro,*" he finishes for me in his best Italian accent. "Thank you so much for reserving in *your* name. And, a classy American joint for a tired American travelling man. Nice touch, and *Grazie.*" He leans across and kisses Alice on both cheeks so naturally anyone would think he was European.

"How was your trip?" asks Alice confidently.
"Oh, like merry hell!" he replies, gesturing for us all to sit down. I clock the waitress from the door hovering with menus a few metres away. "I don't do long haul too good, and it always sucks worse going east! But we're here now right?"

James sits back against the wall, making himself comfortable, takes a glass of still water in one hand and looks inquisitively across the table at where Alice and I sit together facing him.

"I'm gonna bet, looking at the state of you two that Nathan here has checked himself out of that hotel over the way there," he says finally, addressing Alice who just smiles and nods politely...

A broad grin like the Cheshire Cat breaks out across James's face and he tilts his head back towards me. "We can do press prep in the morning if you like."

"I like," I reply.

He pauses on my answer. Alice reaches out and takes my hand beneath the white table cloth just as the hovering waitress must've felt comfortable enough to stalk over with menus. I squeeze her hand for all I'm worth until she turns to face me. I kiss her gently on the lips, and the canoe image comes back into my head. Alice turns away from me smiling, and speaks to the waitress about drinks.

"Okay, so it doesn't take a genius…" says James. Where did you two find each other at?"

Alice

Nathan is only picking at his food this evening and really doesn't seem hungry. He drinks red wine like it's going out of fashion though, and holds onto my hand whenever he sees a possibility to do so, like right now. He's playing with my fingers again, sliding his thumb and forefinger up and down each one as he was in bed earlier. I love that he's so tactile, so affectionate. But my nerves are shot.

Every time he lets go, I suddenly feel light headed, like I'm hanging off the side of a plane about to do my first skydive. I want to turn back. I want him to hold my hand again and let me back inside the body of the plane! And, ... when he does... I sigh relief each time.

It's only Sunday evening. On Friday, I came home from work, got changed as usual, and then I walked down the canal side to *Bar UGO* to meet up with Paolo. Now, I'm sitting in a restaurant opposite perhaps the world's most well-known young film director and it's quite possible that next to me, another Hollywood director, definitely the far more handsome of the two, is my new boyfriend... *It's*... I want to say something else but I can't breathe. Then Nathan takes my hand again...It's okay.

...James Roy eats well, and seems generally charming in spite of his tiredness. He asks Nathan about his general impressions of Milan and they talk about films they've seen lately, checking out the competition before awards season perhaps. I sit in between the two of them, opposite James, and I watch him closely. If I focus on James's face, trying to study him, it helps me to keep a lid on the maelstrom of emotions that would otherwise carry me away or embarrass me beyond measure.

He seems much more self-assured than Nathan. He's got a laid-back style. He's not in the least bit brash or quite as loud as I thought he might be when we arrived and he called out, *"Johnny English!"* His choice of language is never rude or negative, though it is very informal.

I do notice however, that there's ever such a slight awkwardness every time I try to say something in *their* conversation. And, Nathan must have noticed this too as he squeezes my hand in his and glances a wry smile at me every time it happens.

So, when Nathan eventually excuses himself and heads quickly towards the toilets, James, without hesitation, initiates a conversation with me, and I'm completely taken by surprise...

"Can I tell you something discreet about Nathan Scott?" he asks me.

"That would have to depend?" I reply nervously.

"On what?"

"On whether it's nice, of course."

The American chuckles. "Look quick, before he comes back, gimme your cell," he says.

"Cell?"

"You know, your telephone," he replies quickly.

"Oh, okay," I mumble. He's caught me too off-guard to fire back at him with another question. I just blindly do as I'm told, on auto-pilot, unlocking and then handing him my mobile phone. He quickly keys in his number and writes

'*Jim*' in the contacts bar before phoning himself and then handing it back to me.

"There you go Alice," he says. "I've got your number now in case I need ya."

"And I've got yours *Jim*," I reply, trying and probably failing to sound as confident as I wanted to. "Now, what about Nathan?"

"Not now, I can see him coming back. You got *2030* or the older *WhatsApp*?"

"*2030*, why?" I reply.

"Excuse yourself when Nathan sits. I'll message you." He lowers his voice as Nathan nears the table, then alerts me to his arrival by crying out, "*Johnny English! Welcome back!*"

I get up before Nathan can sit back down. We kiss, and I fly. I glance down at James who's peering up at me while drinking from a glass of water. He stares in a way that suddenly gives me an ominous feeling in the pit of my stomach.

"Little girls' room," I say coyly, gathering up my phone in my handbag and scurrying away.

At a safe distance, I turn and look back towards the two of them. James glances over at me for just a split second. He seems to be explaining something to Nathan while clutching his 'cell.'

Nathan

I'm back from the toilet and kiss Alice who's stood up to greet me. Then she's gone herself. I guess she's politely waited.

James has his phone out and is busy texting. "I'm sorry man, you know how it is. The wife's asking where in the world I'm at. I'll just be a second."

"No problem." I just turn myself around in my seat and start to scan the room. In so much as I enjoy people watching, I really can't stand waiting, or looking at people on their mobile devices any more than I like playing with my own.

He looks up from his screen and remarks, "I haven't forgotten how you can't take your eyes off a packed diner man. I wouldn't mind betting it was those wandering eyes of yours that found the hot Italian girl, huh?"

"I guess," I say not really paying him much attention. He may be an old amigo who's in the process of saving my film career for me, single-handed, but I only want to be with Alice right now.

"There. All done, dude," says James. "You don't look too good this evening my man. You gonna tell me what's wrong before the girl gets back? I'm the one's meant to be jetlagged."

I sit there, half on the turn. I must look like shit to him. He'll assume I've been hitting the bottle all weekend, partying too hard with a local girl I've picked up as a tour guide with benefits. He's from Southern California, making him the kind of guy who'll refuse a glass of champagne at a wedding. I'm sure I saw him once at a benefit gala in

Beverley Hills surreptitiously tip the contents of his complementary glass onto a fake plastic tree in a massive ceramic pot by one of the exits, only for it to turn out it was non-alcoholic bubbly in the first place. James is a full-time fitness freak, and part-time yoga fanatic on account of his wife. He's also never known me to be regularly sober, or in love before. So, I don't need to be a smartass to see he doesn't approve of me tagging along a girl I just met to meet up with him.

I mumble something or other about being fine, then pour myself some more wine up to the rim of the little glass, and knock it all back in one go.

"Steady on dude," he says. "That stuff will kill ya if you let it."

"Don't mind me James," I reply. "I'll be ok. I'm just…"

Distractedly, I look around the room again over my shoulder, and he sees what I'm doing.

"Don't worry," he interrupts. "I can see when she's coming back. Now, you gonna tell ole Jim *what's eating Gilbert Grape* tonight or am I gonna have to drag it outta ya?"

Alice

I sit on the toilet at first with my pants up, waiting for Jim's *Whapp2030*. Everything always happens in slow motion when you're waiting around though… So, I roll down by trousers and knickers to relieve myself. I might as well do something useful while I'm in here.

I'm just finished when it arrives, and it starts off all friendly. 'He doesn't want to pop my bubble,' *he says*. 'He wants me to be able to walk into something that looks from the outside to be going great, but with my eyes wide open,' *he says*. 'He likes Nathan a lot,' *he says*, but…There's always a 'but.' …*He says* 'he's seen him at his worst in the last couple of years, and he thinks it's better I know what I'm walking into in the next twenty-four hours than not…'

'…Then, he's absolutely sure because of all of the above,' *he says*, that Nathan hasn't briefed me at all regarding tomorrow's press party at the hotel. 'Nathan's a complete coward,' *he says*. He stresses that Nathan is not a bad guy. 'He's known Nathan for a long time,' *he says*, and 'he's seen that Nathan never commits unless he's really *"all in!"* But… There *is* always a 'but'.

I flush. Then, I leave the cubicle not really knowing how to feel… I know I'm angry at myself for not doing more homework about Nathan online as I sat around waiting for him to call me on Saturday. I'm upset with Marco and Noah for not having done the same, especially with the amount of time those two usually dedicate to social media. I'm especially upset, and more than a little weirded out by the American. And, I'm both really puzzled with and angry at Nathan too.

The trouble is, the situation I now find myself in with those two out there. I just don't do public displays of upset very well, though at least one of them deserves my wrath. I've generally got everything I need figured out. But now, I'm on the verge of tears and I don't have the faintest idea what I should do next…

…This rollercoaster weekend continues to throw up things I did not expect. I stand by the mirror looking back at myself, eyes bulging, and decide: I need to walk.

At the reception desk I leave my card details, address and number and firmly request that they don't let either of the two English speakers in the corner pay when they're done. I know Jim can see me. We catch each other's eyes briefly. He doesn't say anything to Nathan. And why would he?

I quickly and quietly leave the restaurant and slip around the nearest corner. I just want to put my head down and power walk until I calm down and know what I want to do. Outside the *Milan Hilton* about a hundred metres up, I bump into two young men smoking cigarettes. "Ciao," one of them says, ever so politely, as I pass by.

I've only smoked maybe three or four cigarettes in my entire life. I've never disliked the smell; it's just that I was never in a social group with smokers before... *No. I tell a lie.* Paolo smokes marijuana. He always did. I suppose it's possible to get so used to something that you forget it's actually happening around you. I tried it one or two times too, but again like with the cigarettes, it wasn't that I disliked it. I was just always happier being his muse than his Lunar co-pilot.

The two guys giggle a little as I walk by them and I stop... They seem like gentlemen. I smile at the one who greeted me, introduce myself and ask him if I can maybe share one of his cigarettes with them.

He *is* a gentleman. He offers from his packet then cups his hand around the end for the night breeze and lights it for me. Both guys finish theirs and immediately spark up another, to keep me company.

Andrea, the gentleman with the *Marlboro Lights* and Lorenzo are young architects attending a conference on Monday. They came up on the train from Bologna this afternoon.

"There's a really nice tower in Bologna," I say, to which they both laugh. "Yes, seriously, *Asinelli*. I climbed it with my Papà when I was four years old."

"You look sad," says Lorenzo. "Are you okay?"

"Yes, can we help you get home maybe? You're from Milan?" says Andrea.

I tell them they're both wonderful, but that I will fine for getting home. "I just wonder," I say as I get to the end of my first cigarette in years, "if you could both give me a helpful answer to one very simple *'what would you do if…?'* question."

The two of them go back inside their hotel and offer me two more cigarettes for my route home. I send an SMS to Nathan before I march on. It reads:

 *"I'm sorry but I've been sick and
have had to take a walk to get fresh air."*

I know the American won't have told him what he did. But I surely will. I just hope he picks up.

Nathan

Alice has been gone for at least fifteen minutes, maybe more. Where can she be? I'm starting to worry and I want to ask the waitress to go look in the toilet and make sure she's okay… I'm getting really agitated without her here. I'm not in the slightest bit interested in speaking to James about anything other than 'shop.' And, he's already said we could do that in the morning.

Suddenly, my phone vibrates and buzzes in my pocket and I quickly reach down to grab it.

"Is it *Aud*?" asks James.

"*No!*" I bellow, glaring back at him, "*Why would it be?* I haven't seen her since like, February!"

"You mean she's not contacted you, not even about tomorrow?"

I don't answer him. The message is from Alice. She's been sick and has had to leave to get some air.

"Look man, I gotta go." I get up with only one thing on my mind. "Alice is sick. You okay to cover this one? I'll sort you out tomorrow, promise. I gotta go find her."

"Good luck," he calls as I head straight for the door.

I run in the direction of *Centrale*. I don't actually know anywhere else in this area. It's only when I arrive on the small square outside the station that it dawns on me… Alice didn't say in her text where she was.

Alice

I send a *Whapp2030* to the American from in front of *Centrale* where I'm fifth or sixth back in line for a taxi. I don't know what he deserved for making me feel like absolute shit this evening, but I guess he'd expect me to say something about his message.

I tell him I've paid for dinner and thank him for his '*brutal*' honesty. I don't want it to read 'cold', but I don't want to invite a longer conversation with him either. I finish off by saying I'll see him tomorrow morning, before the press arrive, and I hope he finds that sufficiently confusing for his pains…

I can see Nathan running across the street towards my taxi line. He looks worried. I don't wave him over. I wonder if it's me he's worried about, or just himself and where he's going stay tonight. He needn't fear on that score. I wouldn't stop him from coming back to the apartment, to my sofa. I watch as he looks frantically all about him. He's looking at everyone he sees and hoping to see me… He waves from maybe ten metres when he finally does and I make like I care by waving my hand weakly back.

He takes my hands in his. How can I now tell him it's probably over? As soon as his fingers touch mine, an electricity that I hadn't long missed, switches itself back on again. I'm looking down at my feet, gently shaking my head at my own inability to resist him, when he brings a gentle hand up under my chin and raises my head to look him in the eye.

"What's the matter?" he asks, concerned. "I was so worried about you."

Watching, analysing him, he really does seem worried. A taxi honks its horn and a Nigerian lady behind me in colourful traditional costume wants to know if she can take my cab.

"I was really scared when you took so long. I wanted to ask the waitress to go look for you in the toilet and then I saw your text."

I step out of the line and the lady shuffles on by and into the awaiting taxi followed by the next person, and the next after them.

"What can I get you? There's a newsstand in the station. D'you need water? Anything else?"

I keep studying him as he talks, and even when he stops, and he keeps looking, he's panting yet not out of breath. His genuine concern strikes right at my heart and I realise in this moment that I'd been right to ask Andrea and Lorenzo for advice. A woman picked at random would certainly have given me another very different answer. But, a woman's wisdom is not what I need right now. I'd needed to know how another man would make sense of our situation.

Nathan is still holding both my hands, yet he's started looking about, all around us, and he doesn't like what he sees. "C'mon," he starts, "You've been sick. You shouldn't be around here too long, you know. I already smell a lot of cigarette smoke, and it's a wild place here at night."

Two vagrants pass by swilling liquor from a bottle in a brown bag and staring at us. One of them makes a hissing sound and the other mutters, "*fanfarone*", I'm not sure at whom. It's not very polite though and the message to make us feel uncomfortable works.

"Come on, let's get you home," he says. "Shall we wait here, or go get on the metro?"

"I'm okay. But the metro sounds good. We'll get off at Porta Genova."

Nathan takes a firm grip on my hand and leads the way hurriedly towards the metro sign and the steps down, all the while telling me it'll all be okay. I wonder what this *"it"* really is though? My pretend sickness or my life with him? I want so badly to be able to trust him. Still, right now, I only need him to get me out of here, and back home.

In the metro station, away from the vagrants, he breaks down. "Jeez," he cries, rubbing tears away with his sleeve.

I did not see any of this coming.

"I was so scared when you weren't there," he says. "Then, I found you and you're okay and I was so relieved. But, I was scared up there. Those bums… How am I supposed to protect *you* from anything when I'm so afraid myself?"

I don't answer. It is instinctive in any good person I'm sure, to hug another when they show frailty as Nathan has, and I hug him straight away. I also do this because against my better judgment in this moment, I think I still want to love him.

I buy two tickets and we pass the barriers. On the short journey underground, I let him hold onto me and I rest my head on his shoulder throughout the ride. I sense this impossible dream affair may be about to abruptly come to an end. <u>But, there's always a *'But'*, right?</u>

…I love his smell. I love the fact that he's run away from the restaurant to look for me. I love the fact that he's found me and I love his concern But, he's still got a lot to answer for.

Outside Porta Genova Station, we cross the street together holding hands, fingers intertwined. I guide him away from the traffic and back down a quieter Via Casale, leading us back onto the canal front where we first walked together down the Alzaia Naviglio Grande. And, it's there where I decide to confront him, next to the bridge.

"Nathan," I say.

"Yes." He's much calmer in more peaceful surrounds.

"Nathan, I am not sick. I wasn't sick at the restaurant either. I'm just not happy with all of this. There are things… It's not going to work is it?"

He dips his head and says nothing.

I pause, stalling for a reaction. Anything will do. He looks at me, his eyes welling up with what look like genuine tears. He still says nothing though.

"I'm sorry," I say finally. "I thought I…we…could do this. I really wanted it to work out, but…"

"But?" snarls Nathan. He wipes away the first of his tears from his cheek.

"But, I just don't belong in your world. I realised when I was in the toilet. I just like being me really, here in Milan. This," I wave all about me as I speak. "This is my home. I don't want to be following you around all of the red carpets of the world. I'd miss my family too much. I was wrong to push you to accept me. I'm sorry."

Nathan stands there paying close attention. All the pent-up emotion of earlier looks for a moment like it's about to flood out of him when suddenly something just seems to snap. He dries his eyes again and makes himself tall. Then, staring down at me, his eyes narrow; it's as if he's looking right into my soul, searching for something that just doesn't add up from my little speech.

"I don't believe you," he says finally. "And, you know why?"

I don't know what to say. I hold his gaze and bite my lower lip nervously, gently shaking my head from side to side. I can feel tears rising up in my eyes now too. They're tears of frustration, yes, but also of knowing that he's right. Of course, I don't want to be standing here late at night having this conversation. But we can't go on. I know what's right. I know the difference between right and wrong!

"*You!...*" He can't get his words out. "*I...*" He still can't.

I so badly just want to grab him and hold him tightly right now. I want with every sinew in my body to take hold of this sweet, loving man standing right in front of me, and never, ever let him go. But...There *is* always a 'but'. I've learned *that* tonight if nothing else.

"Nathan," I say shortly. "When were you going to tell me that your *wife* was flying in tomorrow for the press conference?"

PART THREE – END GAMES

Nathan

I look down at the ground and wish it would just swallow me whole. My lead actress, flying into Milan tomorrow, from Paris, or wherever she is at the moment, *is* technically my wife.

The name, 'Audrey Novel', is a combination of her real middle name and her maiden surname; it's what she goes by for work. She's officially Louise Audrey Scott. She prefers if everyone but those closest to her to call her Aud, not Audrey; and Lou or Louise is reserved for close family. I call her Aud because that's just what Pete and I always called her from the beginning.

Despite a lot of what's written about her, Aud is a very private, peculiar person, and she's someone who cares about me. I care about her, too. I trust her. And *trust*, in our line of business usually only comes at a very high premium.

Then, aside from that, I really have nothing else I wish to say. I wish I'd been able to control this situation differently. I would have gotten around to telling Alice about Aud. It probably would have been tonight back at her place, or first thing in the morning after a good think. Of course, if Alice had continued to watch her visual history of me on *Wiki-gram* on Friday night, or if someone else like Marco or Noah had bothered to do a full web search on me after we left their place on Saturday, she would've known already but, she didn't, and they didn't. James Roy must have told her.

"Hey!" she cries, suddenly pressing her palm hard against me, pushing back against a railing. "Cat's got your tongue again has it?"

A passing couple arm in arm briefly turn and look at us, then move off quietly, crossing the bridge as Alice looks like she wants to scream at them.

"Can we go to your apartment? I'll explain everything there."

Alice looks hurriedly about her. "No," she says firmly. "My home. *Our home* with all your baggage in it, is a place of love. This is a conversation of shit; shit and problems I don't need. You can't dump all your shit in my apartment! There." She points at *Bar-a-vin, Alzaia 26*. "We're going there, on the terrace while there are still seats outside."

"Aren't you cold?"

"No. You're going to buy me a tea to keep me warm, and I need a cigarette. I'm sure someone's got a lighter over there."

"You smoke, Alice?"

"No! I do not! You, you make me smoke," she shouts stomping off. I shuffle on behind and then sit opposite her at a small metal table that doesn't feel too stable on the cobblestones. Alice summons the attention of someone inside even before we sit. A middle age woman comes outside fairly quickly. They exchange a few words and kiss on each cheek. The woman seems to be in hurry to tidy up indoors but isn't going to let Alice down for a late tea.

"What do you want?" barks Alice coldly. The woman looks at me waiting for a response. "Whisky," I say. "Anything. Just no ice. Make it a double."

"Yes, give him a treble. He's going to need it," sneers Alice.

Alice

...I won't let him crawl off the hook! Sure, he's charming, he's interesting to be around, and we've been intimate. We've been *really* intimate! But, it turns out he's having an affair. And I'm *the other woman!* That's awful! I feel awful for Audrey. And, I certainly do not want my photo used by that man in the flasher Mack now! I do not want to be implicated in some sordid celebrity divorce! That's disgusting! I would never knowingly put myself in such a position. He's a bastard!

'How could this get any worse?' I wonder. This is Audrey Novel! I've cuckolded Audrey Novel! I'll never live this down. I must be a bad person too. I'm still talking to him. Why am I still talking to him?

And, I actually admire *her*. She stands up for climate concerns, LGBT rights and animal welfare. She is the kind of icon I'd want to be if I were in her position. So, no. I most certainly do not want to be the woman who helps Nathan to end her marriage.

"Do you have children?" I ask while we wait for our drinks to arrive.

"No!" he mocks, like I should know he isn't a father.

He will not get away with this! It's not good for him. It's not good for me, and it's certainly not good for Audrey Novel. I can't believe I'm even thinking this! I've been sleeping with *The* Audrey Novel's husband this weekend! No. It's ten times fucking worse than that! I've fallen *in love* with Audrey Novel's fucking husband! At least, that must be what's happening here. If I hadn't already fallen for him, this conversation would've been two minutes, maximum! I would not be sitting here in the cold waiting for a bloody camomile!

Our drinks arrive shortly and I cup my hands either side of my tea to profit from its warmth. "Speak!" I demand, as I raise it to my mouth and blow across its surface.

"Okay," he replies, head bowed. I sit backwards carefully. The chairs are as wobbly as the table on the cobbles. But, as he will inevitably attempt to squirm as men do when caught out, I'm half expecting a monologue and I want to be as comfortable as I can be in the circumstances.

Then, he shocks me. Nathan suddenly explodes into life like a jack-in-the-box.

"Look! Pete and Aud and me… we were a team! We made American films together. Pete and Aud believed in me over there! I don't know if anyone else did! We all believed in each other and we knew they were just using us for…you know, whatever they use talent from Europe for…! This is America post 'The Anti-EU marches' of '23, remember? And Aud, she was in two of my most… She was in two of my films," he corrects himself, suddenly calmer. "Starting with *The Dream*."

"So, what," I contest sarcastically. "You blew each other's minds? Fell in love? Got married?… And look at you now!"

"I'm sorry Alice" he says. "We were always together in the mid '20s, if not writing and planning and filming, then travelling around the world promoting our movies for the cinema and *Netflix*."

He gets so animated when he talks about his time in Hollywood. It's kind of an insight for me. For him, Audrey and Pete were his friends and his colleagues. To them, the producers and other Americans they worked with were clearly some kind of enemy within, or in the very least, people to be carefully watched. Strong sentiments are written all over Nathan's face as he actively defends himself, and as he sees it, his two best friends, who for me and most other people around the world are no more than the faces of his stories…The two people taking all the credit for Nathan's imagination.

But why do I care? The bastard is married. He never told me *that* when he first entered my life, and he'd probably never have told me if I hadn't found out first. I give him a deliberately stony look. I'm not going to budge. I want to. But I won't.

He starts to ramble on again about himself, *her* (*his wife*) and his dead friend Peter. Audrey appeared in his third film, but only briefly and in flashback sequences that used outtakes from the second movie and *The Dream*. Allan-Ferris' love interest in the third film was an unknown Argentinian actress, and *bla, bla, bloody bla!*

I feel I'm being far too patient. I'm freezing cold in spite of my lovely infusion and only a few hours ago this man and I…

I don't want to think about that right now. I just have to stop him from waffling.

"What the *fuck* does any of this have to do with you being married to Audrey Novel?" I roar.

He raises his head to drink and glowers at me. I fix a stare straight back at him. He's ruined this weekend with his deceit. Why am I sitting here with feelings for a cheat?

All that was running through my head as he gave me the whole sad Hollywood script again was '*Vaffanculo Nathan, Vaffanculo!*' But, as he now sips from his *J&B* and watches my seething resentment from over the top of his glass, I don't see any remorse, regret or guilt in his eyes; only sadness.

"If I tell you why Aud and I got married, you'll listen to me right? I know you're angry. You have every right to be. But,…"

"What Nathan? What? You gave up your right to use 'buts' in our conversation when you left it to your colleague to remind me you were married to Audrey Novel!"

"Please," he begs, resting his glass back on the table and clapping his hands together in mid-air as if to pray. I just look at him in silence. It's no longer a glare. I just don't think I can believe what I'm sitting through this evening. It's been an information overload since we left my apartment.

"Do you even know what you're doing?" I ask him nodding in the direction of his hands. "I bet you don't even believe in God!"

"Namaste," he says dropping the hands. "I do yoga in L.A."

"Okay," I snap. "What's your problem?" Secretly, I like the idea of Nathan doing yoga; all the more reason why this explanation had better be a good one.

"Please," he says. "If I tell you the truth about me and Audrey, you will never, ever release this information, anywhere, to anyone. You have to promise me this. It is very sensitive, and very important".

"Okay." This is against my better judgment, but…

One of the young chefs from the bar comes to lean against the front door and smoke. I take out the two cigarettes Andrea and Lorenzo gave me and ask him if I can borrow his lighter.

"C'est toi qui me fait fumer Nathan!" I say. And I offer him one of the two crumpled *Marlboro Lights*.

He takes it.

Nathan

Louise Scott, *my Aud*, will be in Milan tomorrow from about 11am. She'll book into the Gallia Excelsior and she'll have her own private suite. She'll be there tomorrow with me and James for a round of interviews with the Italian media as Audrey Novel. Then, we start our European sales push for *The Truth and the Light* from Tuesday.

When the Italian party is over, James and Audrey have further tour dates and television interviews lined up in Paris as well as in London at the *EWBC* (formerly the BBC), before Germany, The Netherlands, Sweden, Spain, Portugal, Scotland and finally the Republic of Ireland. I did suggest I might do Edinburgh, but more likely Dublin with them both just for the crack. James won't drink, but Aud's always up for a night out, and an after-shoot party around Temple Bar in late-November could've been fun.

After Pete died, Aud and I were both hit hard. The media rumour mill in Hollywood always had the pair together. They weren't. I mean, they *were* in so much as *we* were three Europeans with a really special, strong bond, working hard with and for each other over there. But no one was sleeping with anyone. Pete slept with anyone else who'd put him up and put up with him so long as they were American and blonde. The reality was that he was in love with Aud and I think he did a lot of crazy stuff just to try to get her attention. It's just that the wilder he got, the less romantically interested in him that probably made her, or so I thought at the time. But there was no telling him. His ego wasn't up to it!

I'd had the odd girlfriend but nothing ever lasted more than five seconds. I was never someone who was into using my position to get girls to like me. Although, I will admit that I did take an active part in the recreational drugs culture, and so did Aud. At least, we did until that night on Sunset when everything changed...

"Oh, do tell," says Alice patronisingly. She's finishing her cigarette and as the lights go out inside the bar, there's little chance of more tea. "Did she love *you* all along? Were *you* her one and only?"

"Alice, Aud and I were married soon after my dad died. My mum and sister know all about it. I mean they know why we got married. But they're the only two other living souls who do."

"Go on," she says. "I am probably completely stupid, but..."

"I...I trust you," I interrupt. "I wouldn't be here otherwise, and I know you certainly wouldn't."

"I'm listening," she grumbles.

"Audrey is a very, very dear friend," I say, undeterred. "We got married in Vegas on 1st October 2029, so... We've been married just over two years now. But,... it's not real!"

"How's it not real?" asks Alice.

"The marriage has never been consummated," I reply, direct and to the point. "That and we don't live together. We don't even live in the same country as far as I'm aware."

"What does that even mean?"

"Audrey has a condition. It's a really odd one to explain. It's like, *the last taboo*," I tell her.

Alice

Nathan is increasingly embarrassed as he describes his wife's sexual orientation. The world-famous model and actress, Audrey Novel, aka Louise Scott's sexual orientation has no relation whatsoever to any of the millions of different images you can pull up on her in any simple web search. Typing her name into any search engine you'll find catwalks, aka runways, red carpets, holiday snaps of her in bikinis and never anything wholesome. The US media has made Audrey Novel, a woman to be gawped at…and I suppose, predominantly by heterosexual men.

> "Aud is neither male nor female, nor lesbian, nor bi, nor straight," he starts to explain. "She is simply…"

"I know what *asexual* is Nathan, I am not stupid," I snap again. "I just want to know where you come into all of this."

He's starting to shiver. He takes a dram and drains his glass. Setting it down softly, he asks if we can walk and talk. I don't see why not. We're both cold. But we're not going back to my apartment. He and I will freeze to death tonight by the side of the canal if I'm not satisfied with what he's saying. I'm not his mistress. And, I will not be used as such.

"Okay," I say. "We can cross the bridge but then turn left, not right like you know. We'll walk the *Ripa di Porta Ticinese*, in the opposite direction."

I enter the bar and pay for our drinks just as they're closing the till. I apologise and tip them for their trouble. I don't think Nathan's in any fit state. Then we walk, and he immediately starts talking again.

Nathan

"After my papa and Pete, and seven years living between Hollywood and Europe I, *we,* forgot to a large extent what normal lives looked like. Aud and I were the only two members of our three Musketeers left. We just wanted to protect one another from what we thought we'd seen happen to Pete."

"I see," says Alice.

"And Audrey is very attractive, right?" I ask.

"Yes. She is," says Alice.

"But Aud is often depressed. Every journalist's literally pairing her off with every guy she's snapped standing next to. Every interviewer wants to know who she's seeing. And, dumbass guys, minor celebrities from reality T.V., wanting her attention, often stop her in the street or say mean stuff about her on social media. It's all highly intrusive and more than a bit disgusting, especially when you consider…"

"…Her hidden sexual orientation?" offers Alice.

"That's right," I say. "It's not her choice. She's not celibate. And it's fucking crazy if you ask me. We supposedly live in the first true age of LGBT acceptance, but *asexuality* still doesn't exist for most men; especially if you're beautiful by default and happen to have female genitalia by default too!"

Alice stops walking.

"So, you stepped up and married the girl quickly in Las Vegas so that news would filter around, and she'd be left alone? Correct?"

"Yes. Correct," I reply. "I'd seen one friend die over there. I wasn't gonna…"

Alice touches my arm and I stop. She grips lightly at my elbow and begins to rub her hand slowly down my sleeve. I'm being absolutely honest with her. I want nothing more in this moment than to hold her hand in mine again and have her turn around and walk us back home on the *Ripa*. But,…

"There's just one thing that still doesn't add up," she says. "…What on Earth's in this deal for you?"

Alice

"At this precise moment in time Alice, nothing," he says.

"So, why?" I demand.

"Because I saw no reason not to at the time," he pleads. "Alice, Aud is asexual. But me… There'd been rumours flying around the media for years. They said I was gay, in love with Pete, and all sorts of other stuff. If I went on a *Tinder* date, they always '*kissed and told*' lies about what I was like… It was horrible. I basically stopped making public appearances. I got hooked on anti-depressants and

I've been so low at times I've thought about...you know... Then there were the *Tweets* and the *Instagram* attacks and other stuff on *Facebook* and other social media. It just wouldn't go away. So, after Pete left us, Aud and I went away too. We took an old *Mustang Mach-E* and just drove it into the desert. We were wasted when we married in Vegas. But I never regretted doing it, not 'till this weekend!"

"I don't know," I say releasing his arm. "Your little story there raises as many questions as it answers for me."

"Like what?" he begs. "What more do you want me to say?"

Nathan is starting to shiver in the cold night air. He hugs himself around his midriff and looks down at me, confused and possibly now frustrated, as I just give myself a moment. I sigh and see my breath. Then I add, "When we made love this weekend, each and every touch of your lips, your hands, every part of you, meant the world to me, but it also felt like it meant something for *you* too. When I look at you in my bed, you look so warm, so happy."

"I am," he replies.

"Good," I say. "Because, I will not be your mistress, Nathan. Do you understand what I'm saying?"

"Yes, I do," he insists.

Nathan

We don't talk on the way home along the *Ripa*. Alice doesn't want to. She moves quickly, while I just drag my heels along beside her, keeping up. In the lift, she bows her head and rests against the buttons on the side. She knows I'm scared stiff leaning against the opposite wall, not least now because of her mood. But, we're soon enough back in the apartment again where Alice shouts something in Italian and the air begins to heat up really quickly; the voice controlled central heating coming on with a vengeance to match her tone. At the same time, she's quickly off with the shoes and headband, and has gone over to the breakfast bar where she sets up two glasses and pours large measures of neat Scotch into each. Then she pulls up a stool and sits.

"It's *Talisker* they tell me. Do you like it? A man gave me the bottle in Edinburgh last year. I rarely touch it. But…"

I sit across from her and for just a few seconds, I look back at her eyes as they seem to be ablaze with a mixture of passion and resentment.

"Alice," I'm fighting back my emotions.

"Yes?" She's distracted, removing the pins holding her chignon, before finally tossing her head back and shaking her flowing black hair loose once more.

"Aud and I. It *was* romantic for a short time. She was always fine with me because I understood. We kissed, we held hands, we went to the movies and we were comfortable over in America for a while, just the two of us. It's like after we got married, the depressions that'd dogged us both just evaporated. We took a kind of year-long hiatus together where we took turns at making each other well again."

Alice is gently sipping her whiskey, not looking at me. She occasionally makes a strange face I hope because of the drink. But, eventually she nods, and I carry on.

"Look, my relationship with Aud, as was, is finished. The need for each other died as we both got back our respective rhythms. I've been doing what I do, she's been modelling, mainly in New York and Paris. She is very happy with who and what she is now. She doesn't do private interviews and neither do I. She has apartments that I've never seen in her two favourite cities, and I believe she likes looking after cats for her sins! Neither of us has any social media; that shit is designed to torture celebrities! But she sends me *Whapp2030s* all the time with *holo-vids* of her performances or of her petting some fur ball. But she left me in L.A. at the start of this year. She's never been back, and she never expects me to reply to her messages. She's just checking in really, like sending an old friend a postcard."

"Okay," says Alice.

"Look," I interrupt. "I **do** love Audrey. Just, not… She's like a sister, and a very dear friend."

"Okay," she says again. Her eyes now meet with mine. She even looks like she's trying to smile.

Alice

He raises his eyebrows, observing me. Then, he takes a deep breath and looks up to the heavens.

I'm exhausted. He wears me out. But I *am* smiling. He's not the bastard I thought he was. He's free to kiss me again, rescue me from this horrid burning drink. Why isn't he moving? Can't he take a hint? I surrender! Hello? I don't want to have to be the one who says it's ok to reach out to me. Only, if he doesn't get up soon, I'm fit to burst…

"Do you want to tell me anything else?" I ask. I hope he isn't going to think I need more answers from him. No, that came out all wrong…Think Alice, think.

I need his touch. I want to be able to hold him and kiss him again. I just need to turn the light out on this twisted, messed up end to the day.

"I don't know," replies Nathan.

I'm completely thrown. I probably need to give him a bigger clue. I gaze at him past my glass, and slowly lowering it to the bench top, I bite; just delicately, on the bottom corner of my lip.

Only then does Nathan realise. He chuckles to himself. Yet still, he doesn't move. I can feel a build-up inside me of all the emotion and frustration with him for everything that's happened this evening. I turn sidewards to avoid him noticing my tears. But, I'm too late. He notices.

I close my eyes, and hear him. He finally moves off his stool, and comes to me. My heart's racing. I dare not open my eyes. I just want him to lift me up off my stool into his arms again.

It's crazy. If he'd done this even ten minutes earlier, I might've pushed him away still.

Now, as Nathan holds my hands, guiding me softly up onto my feet, then wraps his arms tightly around me, I bite my lip again and blink back up at him. His kiss this time is not one that's full of lusty passion. It's soft like a sincere promise. This kiss tells me he's awake to me; that all his secrets are out, and *we* are all that matters to him from now on.

A couple of minutes later, I pull away. He looks sad; not in the least bit duplicitous. I get a sudden pang of guilt flash over me for even having thought that earlier. We continue to gaze at one another and his look changes to quizzical. I can't wait any longer. I need to say it. I need to confess I have something really important to tell him. I need to hear myself say it out loud. He raises his eyebrows and tilts his head gently to one side. I take a deep breath.

"I'm so in love with you it hurts," I suddenly blurt out, immediately turning my head away from him in shame.

Nathan

I act fast. I need to act fast. This terrible evening has to end happily. That's all I want in the here and now; tenderly placing a hand under Alice's chin and rotating her head back to face me again, I smile.

"I know," I say. "I love you too. I feel the same."

PART FOUR - CLOSURE

Alice & Nathan

"So, this is it," exclaims Alice with a wry grin. "Our big day with and without the media."

Beautiful autumn sunlight streams in through two large windows at the front of *Iter*, her favourite coffee shop just off the Ripa. Alice, forever putting others before herself, had thought she'd show Nathan somewhere new to kickstart their morning. But, it was him, to her surprise, who ended up choosing where they went.

"I really liked that place with the Machu Pichu pics; it's so bright and warm everywhere." He'd only meant it as a passing comment as they left the apartment by the stairwell that Alice hadn't seen for over a year since the lift was last serviced. But, she was more than happy to oblige him and go back to where she always felt at home.

As Nathan reclines on a low sofa, closing his eyes to the sun and absorbing its rays through his eye-lids in delicious orange, Alice sits up momentarily to sip her macchiato. She's soon back curled up under his protective arm, nestling against his shoulder though. Not a word is spoken. But communication is constant. He strokes and tucks several strands of her hair gently behind her ear and she softly plays *his game* with the fingers of his free hand.

Monika, the Polish owner, looks down at them both and smiles hopefully at Alice. Alice notices her and beams back, hopelessly in love.

After their Sunday of confessions, and the healing of old wounds, Alice and Nathan had shared the perfect end to a long and pivotal weekend. The simple touch of Nathan's hand leaves Alice spellbound. She'll follow him anywhere. His kiss and the way their bodies fuse together so gracefully, so naturally beneath the sheets, engulfs her senses and banishes all her earlier fears to an insignificant blur. Nathan has never felt so passionately about anyone or anything in his entire life. Every kiss from Alice leads him further away from everything he knew before. He's lost in time and space and doesn't ever want to return to Earth. When their bodies melt together again in bed, and their kisses deepen, Nathan becomes gentler towards his lover. He strokes her hair from her eyes, kisses her neck and whispers the words she wants to hear close to her ears.

And, after the gasping for air, the broad smiles and the untangling of bodies from their sweaty embrace, Alice had joked about trying smoking again.

"I read somewhere that it's 'really good' straight after…"

Nathan didn't disagree. "Yeh, true," he said. "But I don't want to get addicted to nicotine again."

Alice fell about in fits of laughter, and Nathan didn't know where to put himself. Sadly, the irony of what he'd said, didn't dawn on him for quite a while, and Alice felt really embarrassed when in the end she had to explain it to him.

Then, they talked and talked, and eventually came up with a plan for how they'd deal with James Roy on Monday. Nathan said he'd see *his Aud* privately, and promised Alice that everything would be ok come the evening.

"I'll be going now then," coos Alice, finally.

Nathan nods approval. "Give my regards to James won't you," he laughs.

She smirks backs at him before leaning over for one last kiss. "You're sure you're happy with this?" he says.

Alice stands and nods back down at Nathan. He isn't convinced. He knows she loves him but she's worried about how their meetings will go.

"Look, everything will be ok. It'll be perfect. Just wait and see." He gets to his feet and kisses Alice once more for luck.

"I love you, you know," says Nathan finally.

"And I love you too. *Ti amo tanto da morire!*" states Alice. "Now let's do this!"

She turns swiftly on her heel. "Ciao!" she calls, waving to Monika as she passes the till. Nathan rests back on the sofa again and watches her wave and blow a kiss back at him through the glass before disappearing around a corner.

Alice walks to the metro station deep in thought. It's the first time in over two years that she finds herself not dressed for the office on a Monday morning, and this feels strange for her. She's uncomfortable. It's not something she wanted to waste time trying to articulate to Nathan though. And anyway, she's tidily casual; not too dissimilar in style to Friday night in *UGO*.

In meetings, Alice knows that it's often all about striking the right image. She planned her outfit in her bathroom this morning, aiming to balance 'sure' and 'sweet' in a way that would hopefully charm James into backing off from her and Nathan for a while, without offending him.

Then, Alice's only other intention after visiting the Excelsior this morning, is to return home, eat lunch with Nathan, and take him back to bed for the rest of the day.

Nathan finishes his coffee and closes his eyes again. He's back to enjoying the sun's warmth on his face, when his phone buzzes in his pocket. He's expecting her *Whapp2030* message, but as he reads and replies to it, Nathan's a little surprised to see she's written to him in English:

> I'm outside a Porta Genova metro station?
> I don't know where to go... Can you come?

> No problem. Give me 5 minutes.
> Ciao x

Nathan

"I knew this day would come sooner or later," says Aud sipping an espresso on the pavement outside *Alzaia 26*. It's exactly where Alice and I sat the night before talking about her.

Audrey Novel has just stepped off her private jet from Brussels and has hastily checked a small overnight bag into the Gallia Excelsior while leaving her taxi outside on the meter. She sits before me bathed in sunlight now, looking as beautiful as anyone could, having been rushing around since before 6am and not having gone to sleep last night until after midnight. There are only a few people walking next to the Naviglio Grande this morning. It's maybe still an hour or so before the lunchtime toing and froing begins.

Aud has still taken her usual image precautions. She's dressed totally in black, from the long boots to the tights and the button-down winter dress that comes to just below her knees. An elegant leather jacket and matching gloves almost completes the look, save for the large black bug sunshades and French beret into which she has piled her shoulder length black hair.

"Jim told me everything I needed to know on the phone last night," she says.

"I wasn't aware you and he had such a good friendship that he'd know all of our business." I'm a little taken aback by his front, especially after the restaurant.

"Oh, please Nathan. Don't be so harsh on that man all the time. He's only ever tried to look out for you. It might all have ended at *If I can Make It There...* if he'd not helped you on your way."

"I often wish that that were true," I say.

"I know you do chéri. I know. You're like a big soft Lady Di," says Aud, pronouncing Diana's name in that delicate French way that I've always found touching. "The whole spotlight thing just wasn't for you, and…"

I try to speak but Aud's not one for listening this morning.

"Please don't interrupt chéri. It would have to be an ordinary girl, but an *exceptional* ordinary girl to bring you back from the brink, of that I am sure. You can be a lovely man when you want to be." She smiles with her lips. I can't see what's behind the shades and I doubt that here on this occasion she'll take them off to let me see. "Jim's told me who she is," she continues. "She impressed him."

"I love her," I say.

Aud takes out a cigarette from a pocket inside her leather jacket, and lights it quickly.

"I wasn't aware you smoked," I observe.

"There are lots of things about me you don't know Nathan. Besides, I am a catwalk model. All skinny models smoke, and I like it."

"What will you do, Aud?"

"Oh, don't you worry about me chéri," she says. "I suppose you'll want to annul our marriage?"

"Yes," I reply, straight off the bat.

"Ha-ha, look at *you*! Go Nathaniel Scott!"

"What's so funny?" I ask.

"Oh nothing. It's just how you can say 'yes' with no hesitation or emotion in your voice at all. That, for you, took more courage I bet, than I know you actually have. And, meeting me like this, I imagine was *her* idea as well, right?"

"Hers and mine," I reply. "As I said. I love her."

"Okay," she grins. "I believe you. Now, you have my number chéri. And, you know I'm a very understanding person. I hope you know I'll never let my phone ring off the hook if you call me. You understand that don't you? I love you like an annoying idiot brother Nathan Scott."

"Yes," I say. "You too."

"Me too what? An annoying idiot? Puah."

I rock back on my chair, satisfied with myself I guess. I watch her smoke just for a moment, and lose myself in thought.

In a short while, she'll get up and leave me here and it'll be the end. It's not been bitter like I'd always imagined it would be. But it's still a pretty definitive end to our acquaintance and the end of an era.

Right now, she's still my wife. Yet, when she walks away this time, I'm unlikely ever to see her more than a handful of times again, and probably only at formal events with Alice by my side. On that note, I actually feel really sad. Seeing her as she walked over the road from the metro to greet me with her usual three Parisian kisses, brought back a whole wealth of happy memories and emotions I evidently still have for her.

"I won't ever forget you Aud," I stammer. I'm conscious I probably sound like an embarrassed, sorry little boy to her.

Aud stubs her cigarette butt out into an ashtray and drains her coffee cup. "You just drop me a line when you need me to sign something and you will be free to go and tie yourself down to someone else, only with more real strings attached this time no doubt. Oh, and don't be so dramatic all the time. *I will never forget you?* Where are you going? I guess you're going to feign sickness today and let James and I carry the can for you? That's fine."

"I'm sorry," I mutter. But she ignores me and carries on.

"*You know*! We're going to win big in France, England and America with this one Nathan! I feel it more than I've ever felt it before! And, **you** co-wrote and co-directed it! **This** is your parting gift to Peter, *and* your parting gift to me. Thank you. Now,…"

She and I stand up together and as she does, she leans forward and kisses me softly, just a single peck on the lips. "We still have the red carpet, chéri. You let your new love get you fit for that. And, don't jump in there." She finishes off pointing at the canal.

I want to say something else, but I don't really know what… Aud waves me to sit down again or go and pay for her coffee. "I'll be fine," she says. "I know where that little station is. I'll find a taxi. I can probably speak more Italian than you anyway. *Allora, ciao. Ciao bello.*" And in an instant Audrey Novel is gone, clip clopping away from me over the cobblestones of the Via Casale.

Alice

I spot Jim from afar as I enter through the revolving doors. He's sitting alone staring at his cell phone screen in the back corner of the hotel bar. He looks relaxed in an easy chair positioned right next to a large bay window through which the sun deliciously pours in light as two distinct rays, set against the shadow of the room.

One of the concierges, an older man trying to look official, asks me if I have a reservation. It must be my clothes.

"No, I have an appointment with Mr. Roy," I say pointing over at him.

"Is Signora here as a member of the press?"

"No," I repeat. "We're friends."

"I will have to ask you to wait here," he huffs. "My manager won't allow anybody not with the registered press, past the door today."

"Okay."

As the jobsworth walks off, I get out my phone and send a simple *Whapp2030* over to Jim. I then stand on the spot as obediently as I've always been, watching him and glancing over at the concierge who's in deep conversation, I can only assume, with his boss, at the main reception desk.

The whole area is a hive of activity, with production crews and their roadies setting up a movie launch for *The Truth and the Light.* Billboard posters are being rolled and stretched out and attached to stands all around the lobby, each seeming to focus on either Peter Allan-Ferris, Audrey Novel, *Il Duomo,* or views along the canal close to where I live.

Eventually, I see Jim get up and start walking casually over towards me. I text him with quick fingers urging him to pace his arrival slowly. He stops, and looks at the screen, then smiles broadly up at me. I smirk cheekily back at him over the concierge's shoulder when he returns flanked by his reception manager. Both men look annoyed with me and probably with good reason.

"I'm really sorry madam," sniffs the manager. "But today, we are not permitted to allow you into the hotel without a formal press pass."

The light tap on his shoulder from behind takes him by complete surprise. "I'm the girl's passport to entry here," interrupts Jim. I've lowered my head, like a naughty school kid, but flash a glance and a grin upwards at my saviour.

The two employees, embarrassed, apologise to both of us and shuffle away back to the safety of their reception desk. Jim escorts me back to his table. "I didn't know you understood Italian Mr. Roy?" I ask, just kidding.

"I don't," he says. "I'm American. I can barely speak the King's English. I've just had so many situations like that over the course of my time in the business. My wife, Amanda teaches grade school. You won't find much about her on a *Google* search. We need a private life. Everybody needs a private life. But, she's still gotta be let in when I'm on set, you know."

"I completely agree," I say as he goes to pour me a cup of green tea from a large pot of the stuff he'd ordered with two cups before I arrived.

"I'm continuing my detox," he says. "I don't like liquor, but I always drink a lot of whisky on trans-Atlantic flights. I can't stand it when it gets all bumpy over Nova Scotia, so when they come round offerin'... and then as we start down over Scotland, it's the same all over again. Then, of course, there was that restaurant too, and thank you for paying by the way. You're too kind."

"You don't seem at all like Nathan describes you," I remark as I sip my tea.

"I bet he's pegged me for a real asshole, doesn't he?" he says.

"Well," I smile. "As a matter of fact,... I'm sorry."

"Don't worry. He's been tense and intense for as long as I've known him. He should have taken the money and ran. You know I asked him to help me film the script for *If I can make...*"

"Yes," I interrupt him. "I know. And look, you know why I'm here right now, don't you?"

"I'm guessing it's the old *Sliding Doors* routine. You don't want to bump into Audrey as she goes over to your part of town. That and a bit of closure with me."

"There is a bit of that," I reply. "But not entirely. I know I'm going to meet Audrey at some point. I just don't think that today's the right time for that do you?"

"No," he calmly agrees.

 "Look Jim, what you did in the restaurant was, you have to admit, more than a little bit strange, no?"

"Yeh, I suppose it was," he replies. "And, I'm guessing you wanna know why I did it right?"

I am direct and honest with Jim. In all of my dealings with American clients or business partners, I've never known them to be impolite. But, they are, more often than not very guarded, and they seem only to respect other people from other countries when they can see and sense directness. They like to shoot from the hip in my experience, and they like their competitors, adversaries and partners to do the exact same.

I tell him that though I was upset and angry with him at first, and I knew that he'd seen me leave the restaurant and not told Nathan, I soon figured out that his move was well intentioned. It made Nathan confront his issues, put me in the picture, and it certainly saved all of us a lot of problems today. I tell him he doesn't owe me any explanations from last night.

But, I also tell him I'd like to hear just how much he really knows about Nathan and Audrey's marriage.

Jim roars with laughter. "Does he know that's why you came here now?"

"Yes," I say.

"So, lemme get this straight. You're after some kind of a pre-nuptial understanding before you can let yourself proceed in an affair of the heart?" he asks, still looking really amused.

I hold the little tea cup and saucer to my mouth and sip as daintily as a princess. I want to keep my poker face, using the cup as a bit of a guard, especially as he finds my question so funny.

"Ok," I continue. "If you mean by that, 'have you fallen in love with someone else's husband?' Then you already know the answer is '*yes*.' If you mean, 'did he tell me a really plausible, if strange, story about his relationship with Audrey?' Then '*yes, he did.*' And, if you mean, 'am I just seeking reassurances from the same would-be friend of his who warned me about his marital status in the first place after you guessed he wouldn't have told me himself?' Then, '*yes, of course am.*' Wouldn't you?"

"Oh, I don't know. I don't think I'd ever have fallen for someone like Nathan in the first place," he replies, still chuckling. "You know, I liked you the minute I clapped eyes on you. You're a smart cookie."

"I know Jim. That's how I got in here today," I smile.

He sighs and looks at the clock on the front of his cell phone. "Okay, Alice. We don't have much time but you don't need to worry about Nathan being on the level. I'm sure he's been as honest with you as he's ever been with himself. I've never been too sure that he likes himself a whole bunch if you'll permit me to say something a bit 'off' about him. But, I know he's got a good heart deep down. His friend, Pete was a bit more 'rogue' if you see what I mean. I think that's why Nathan liked him so much. It was a kinda *Rebel* kinda thing they had going on for a time!"

"Then along came the girl. She never spoke about her sexuality to anyone at first. It was nobody's business. She was a professional from Europe with a big following in France, now making it Stateside. But, I'm guessing they were all about the same age. They were all a bit lost over in the States and Pete fell for her big time. It must've fucked him up big! And we all know what happened next, right? It only seemed natural to me at the time, when they hooked up and got married."

"But it wasn't though, was it? When did you find out?" I ask him.

"Their marriage was a game from the start. It was their little secret from the Americans. They even lived together in his place for over a year. But Nathan's traumas with himself and his place in the world were eventually too much even for her. He helped Aud to grieve for Pete but when she was ready to move on, and her husband was still all at sea, she came over to talk and she confided everything to me and Amanda before she eventually left him. If I can warn you of one thing Alice, Nathan can be a difficult guy when he's on a downer! Audrey is different. She's not messed up. She was sad because her friend Peter died, sure. And," he looks at the time on his phone again and shuffles slightly in his seat.

"She may well be sad right now this second too, as she heads back over here because, she'll realise she's finally losing Nathan forever. But she's not messed up like he's been. Oh no. Aud's just a very attractive woman with no sex drive. Can't be helped."

"Just so that I'm clear. I think I am, but…," I start to probe.

"But nothing signora," he interrupts. "There was Nathan sitting in front of me last night. He was his usual fucked up, shaky, nervous self. He was happily seeing out his weekend with someone he clearly enjoys the company of, knowing full well that come Tuesday he was gonna have to let her go, even though and I shit you not, he really does seem to like her this time. Then *he was gonna just fly, fly away back to another meltdown in good old L.A.!* Yep, that's it. Then, I looked at you with him and I saw that the carnage he creates for himself around about the place was going to have fall out on a really attractive, feisty, intelligent little gal from here too. The cycle needed stopping. Either that or some extreme testing. And, it worked out for you didn't it?"

"So, you attempted to play God, James?"

"Of course, I did Alice! I'm film director! I bring people to life, I dress them, I do their make-up and sometimes, get this,… I even kill them off too!"

"What did you hope would happen yesterday evening? I mean that *WhatsApp* was ambiguous, open to interpretation…" I reply.

"Yes, and like I said, you are an attractive, feisty and *intelligent* young woman Alice. I wanted you to stop and do something about what it was you really wanted before it got to be too late. Come on, it's only been two days, but true love hits us in a blinding flash! It doesn't grow over time. Just looking at the two of you together, it was obvious to me that either you were going to save Nathan, dump him quick or get dumped even quicker. Any option I gave you was designed to suit *you,* first. I've seen him hurt himself and those around him time and again. But,… and don't get me wrong, I don't deliberately want to see Nathan break down again, I'd just rather it be him than you. You needed to take back control of this one. And what do ya know? **You did it!**"

Nathan

I stand out in the middle of the street and watch as she walks away from me. She doesn't look back. When she rounds the corner onto Via Casale and out of sight, I stand for maybe just a few seconds more, listening out for the sound of her heels on the cobbles as it travels through the air.

I then go inside the bar for the first time and ask to pay for her coffee. A friendly older lady, maybe in her mid-fifties, tells me she owns the bar. She's got nearly no accent at all in English and I ask her where she's from. It turns out she's Dutch, originally from a small town close to Amsterdam. She tells me not to worry; I won't have heard of her village, "and that'll be four euros, please."

I pay and tell her that I've been to Amsterdam once or twice. But she just looks at me in my old jeans and sweater with hair falling into my eyes. And, as I push it back out of the way, I know what she's probably thinking.

"Last night with 'young Alice from along the Ripa', and this morning with the French woman. You move fast," she remarks suddenly. I'm not sure whether she's joking or not, but I try to keep it friendly. She clearly knows Alice.

"It's not quite like..." I try. But, she interrupts. "You've spent a long time on my terrace these days and you only manage a whisky, a coffee, a tea and a light for your cigarettes. Next time you come over, please bring one of your girlfriends inside and try my risotto. You won't regret it."

I smile broadly. I sometimes find with people whose first language isn't English, their nuances are that much harder to read. But, it appears, this lady *was* only joking.

"Your risotto? Is it good then?" I ask.

"I was only saying," she says. "But I stand by it."

"Good. Is tonight ok?" I reply. "I mean it's a Monday. Is that ok for you? I'm leaving for the States tomorrow."

"Oh! Ok. So, yes. Of course, it is. Would you like to pick a table? They're all available at the moment."

"Thank you. I'll have all of them!" I declare.

"I'm sorry, can you repeat, please," says the lady.

"No. I won't be repeating that. May I ask you what your name is Signora?"

"Y-yes. My name is Lotte," she stutters more quietly than at first.

"Well, I'm charmed to meet you Lotte," I say extending a hand to shake hers. "My name's Nathan. My girlfriend is 'young Alice from the Ripa' as you call her. She'll be my only guest tonight."

I quickly scan the small interior of her restaurant. It's quite rustic. All of the furniture is wooden and old looking. The walls are of a mahogany hue and the few decorations scattered around appear to be black and white framed paintings of canal boats from yesteryear working their way up or down the Naviglio Grande. It looks perfect. Intimate, dark, romantic, and clean.

"Okay Nathan?" says Lotte.

"Yes, thank you. Look, may I just say, the French lady with the beret and the shades just now, she is a dear colleague and very close friend. Her name is Audrey Novel. You may have seen or at least, heard of her."

"Oh my," replies Lotte. "Oh my…"

"Yes, and *she* was at *your* bar taking an espresso and a cigarette only this morning. Go figure, huh? …Now, how much would it cost me to hire out *your* restaurant this evening just for my girlfriend and I?"

"I don't know Nathan, I'm sorry. It's not a request I've ever had before," she replies.

"Well, I'm sure we'll figure something out," I suggest. "I would like a table for two in the far corner, right at the back." I point to the exact spot I want before explaining my need to sit with my back against the wall so that I can survey the room just like my dad would have done. I say I'd like romantic candles all around the table, and the best bottle of Italian red wine from her list, open and able to breathe a little just before we arrive at 8 o'clock. I also explain that I would like every other table in the place to be occupied with her family, friends or most loyal customers.

I apologise to her for the short notice and she says nothing. She appears to be fixed on who *I might be* that I can make all of these requests without a single care for cost, and take coffee with one of the world's most famous actresses and fashion models of the day.

"Lotte. My name is Nathaniel Scott," I say. "Some of the films that Audrey Novel stars in were written and directed by me. That's all. Now, where were we?"

"Oh my," repeats Lotte for a third time. "Thank you for…"

I interrupt *her* this time. I'm not normally this bold. But right now, spurred on by the thought of spending the rest of the day and evening pleasing myself in Milan with the girl I love, I tell Lotte quite succinctly that I haven't done anything to deserve her thanks. I merely want to close her restaurant for my use, and I'm very happy to pay her well for the privilege.

"And, can I make just two more very important requests please?"

I hope that my first one doesn't sound too strange for her. The last thing I want is to make it difficult for Lotte to find some discreet people who'd like a free *Monday* night out. But, it *is* important. I, and I know I speak for Alice here too, don't want to hear anyone's phone go off, nor even vibrate inside a pocket while she and I are there. I tell Lotte it's just a quirk of my personality. I only want people to come, eat well, and enjoy a good old-fashioned conversation, on me.

But, I needn't have worried. Lotte doesn't mind at all. In fact, she beams at the suggestion, remarking that it's becoming way too common these days for customers to turn up alone, then *Whapp2030* a friend in mini hologram to sit with them while they eat their meal. The little 3D images stand about ten centimetres off the table top from the diner's device laid flat. And, it particularly freaks her out when she needs to interrupt, and finds the hologram being invited to wave at her and say 'hi.'

After that, my other request is much simpler. And is, of course, also welcomed. I instruct Lotte that I don't want thanks, praise or publicity. I just want the chance to be intimate with Alice, and to make our last night here in Milan together a special one.

Lotte assures me that everything will be perfect and she'll expect us at 8pm.

I then walk happily back along the canal to Alice's apartment, when I get a text buzz on *my* mobile.

> Nathan, I hope you are okay. Are you in the apartment? I've got take-out pizza for lunch? Wine on the rack... Love xxx

> Hi Alice. I think these are our first ever texts to one another! Yes, to lunch and yes to everything! Luv u xxx

Alice

Before leaving the American, I insist that he gives Nathan some space in the run up to the first awards ceremonies in January. I make him agree that 'Nathan needs time to heal.' And, I solemnly promise him that cometh the hour, I'll get Nathan to where he needs to be, on time, sober and on good form.

Then, I get up to take my leave, glancing back towards the door as I do, to find my concierge friend still there glaring at us.

"Would you like me to escort you past the jobsworth?" asks James.

"No, I'll be just fine," I say.

"Oh, I know ya will Alice," he replies. "You're a far braver person than I am."

We shake hands on our deal, and he kisses me delicately on both cheeks. Then, I smile politely, wish him and Audrey well for the day ahead, and walk away with those last words of his still ringing in my ears.

Oh, and I know I'd have to be a complete fool not to at least pay some heed to Jim's advice. But, I also know for sure that I love Nathan. And, I'm going protect him from now on from all the things that he fears most, starting with his benefactor and tough love amigo, James Roy.

I walk back over to the metro, and ponder just for a minute. And, that's it. That's all the time it takes for me to realise. James will surely have gotten my message loud and clear too. So, now, it's just down to me again…

When I get home, he's already there. I want to kick off my *Converse* as soon as I come in and I've already undone the laces in the elevator. I'm thinking, 'this afternoon will be one, big, long siesta with the man I...'

...But his arms interrupt that train of thought around my middle. Nathan is there kissing me as soon as the door opens and I'm still trying to get inside. He grabs the hot pizza box I'm carrying and drops it to the floor, then whirls me about so fast it makes me wonder what's happened for him to be this excited.

"*Nathan!*" I say, "*stop!*" as I gather myself and lean forward into another tender kiss.

"Sofa or bar?" I ask him as we break apart, and I'm giddy, half jogging to the kitchen to get glasses and plates .

"How was James?" he replies.

"And how was *Aud?*" I volley back.

We sit huddled together on a fur rug right in front of what's perhaps the biggest window with the best panorama over Milan. And I take a bite from a slice of fresh, warm pizza looking forwards, both figuratively and literally.

I turn to watch him as we joyously share food with a view. And right now, I see Nathan still more magnificently than I did before. I'm acutely aware of the awful sadness hidden behind those beautiful brown eyes. But we'll fix that. As my love and admiration of him grows with every passing second, I know we'll be ok.

Right now, I'm reading his body language. As he stuffs pizza into his mouth uninhibited, occasionally scalding his tongue, he looks to me as if for approval while smiling playfully and puffing his cheeks out to cool down. He looks totally at peace with the world; genuinely happy. There is no sign whatsoever in this instant of the *Hollywood-Nathan*; the one who's lost and overwhelmed by seemingly everything and everyone. And, all I want to do is take him in my arms to feed off and devour his love.

Carefully, I remove the wine glass from his hand, and straddle him right there on the floor, easing him downwards and kissing him as he folds. I shush him with a forefinger to the lips. "Nathan Scott. You. Are. My. Dessert." I whisper, punctuating each word before I again part his lips with my tongue and bring both of his hands up either side of his head, fingers locked tightly in mine.

I tremble as he kisses back and I feel his tongue hungrily meet once more with mine. He opens his eyes briefly as I shift my weight over him and we catch each other's lustful stare. I bring my hands down to better feel his warmth, merging my billowing breath with his, tasting the floral scent of pinot noir. Then, I pull away from him and sit upright. Nathan eyes me closely, waiting. I bite my lower lip, seductively sweet.

We've already undressed each other with our eyes long enough for it to be quick and easy to lose and scatter our clothes. As he helps to slip my top over my head, Paolo's little headband clatters to the floor too, and with it, whatever was left of my innocence.

I gasp, giving way to moans of pleasure as we move, slowly, rhythmically, as one, there on soft carpet. And, I really do feel that we are now connected; bound together in body and soul. The sex is amazing. But, it's more than that. His look, his kisses and the way he softly caresses my hair, face and body are an expression of the love we now share. Jim's concerns have no meaning here. This intimacy is all ours, and I tell Nathan as we quicken. "I want to love you forever. Prends moi, je suis a toi." This is real love, *Made in Milan.*

Wearing only Nathan's t-shirt, long enough to almost brush against the tops of my knees and clutching a glass of wine in two hands, I go back to my lovely vista up at the window. The autumn afternoon blue is darkening. The lights from other apartments and businesses are coming on all across the city like dots on several distant battleship boards. I just stand, taking it all in, blissfully lost in the thoughts, hopes, dreams and wishes of a young woman in love.

Nathan went out just after four o'clock. He said he had a few things to do down the road, but that he'd be back by five. I didn't question him as he left, but I wouldn't be at all surprised if he came back through the door any second, carrying more wine.

I'm so lost in the depths of my imagination that I'm suddenly startled by the sound of the door when he does arrive back. I look at my watch and see it's ten past five. Nathan doesn't have any more wine. He does call over to me to ask if I'm ok though.

I'm not.

I'm suddenly the one who's panicking about the future. The dark thoughts hit me the second I hear the door and know it's him. By this time tomorrow, he'll be back on an aeroplane bound for the United States, but I'll still be here at this window, grieving his departure and pining for him to return.
I put my glass down on the coffee table and run over to him as he approaches me, pulling him close, begging with him to never let me go.

"I said I'd only be an hour. I'm here," he says, trying to reassure. But I'm at once inconsolably tearful. This is so not like me, the Alice of just a few days before.

Between sobs, I ask him why he can't stay in Milan for longer and then, why I can't come to the U.S. with him... Of course, I know the answers to my own questions as soon as, if not before they leave my mouth. But, rationality doesn't come into this equation.

Nathan hugs me tightly and I stay in his arms, feeling safely cocooned against the necessities of life and the world outside. "Don't worry," he whispers at last. And, there's a level of assurance in his voice that I've not yet seen or heard before when he says, "I'm coming back for you very, very soon."

I rub my tears on the back of my hand and rise up on tiptoes to gently kiss him.

"There are some things we need to figure out first, but we'll talk over dinner. I reserved for eight not far away. Is that ok?"

"Is that where you went just now?" I ask him.

"Maybe..." he replies.

Nathan

I tell Alice I have a few errands to run, and leave the flat before she can ask me anything. I take a short walk down the Ripa and over the first footbridge I come across onto the Alzaia Naviglio Grande. As I left the bar earlier, after paying Aud's coffee, a short Indian man was on the canal side, setting up to sell trinkets off a wooden contraption, shaped and coloured like an old gypsy caravan. As I passed,

I glanced over and saw that he had everything from hats and headscarves, to jumpers and jewellery on his stand.

I find the little fellow this afternoon, crouching low on the cobbles with coffee in a paper cup, seeming very cold. We exchange a few polite words, and after inspecting his stock and trying some things out for size, I find exactly what I'd come looking for. It's just a small romantic gesture really; something *real* Alice can keep, and that comes with a simple promise.

Later on, I'm sitting at her breakfast bar back in the apartment. She uncorks another bottle. I'm watching her busy herself, and getting a warm, fuzzy feeling inside. I'm by no means a perfect man. And I dare say, Alice probably has her faults too. But, together, this just feels perfect. I feel at home, and I think she feels that way too. Eventually, she pours me a glass, looks up and notices my eyes following her.

"What?" she asks. *Her* eyes are still tear stained and rounder after her little panic attack when I came back in from outside.

"Nothing," I reply calmly. "I just enjoy watching you. Do you even realise just how beautiful you are?"

She sits down next to me, shrugs off my comment with a tiny smile, and sniffles away the last of her sorrows for now. Next, she looks up and tilts her glass for me to clink; masking her sadness under a wry smile.

My idea, down in the street, had been to give Alice my gift in the restaurant later under candlelight. But, seeing her now, still upset, my only instinct is to love her; to make her know I love her. When words alone don't work…

...I reach into my pocket. The sound of paper rustling makes Alice look up. I hold the simple, round silver ring up to the light between my thumb and forefinger.

I have no clue which hand an Italian girl would wear a boyfriend's ring, and I'm not even sure she's going to like the idea. The only jewellery I've seen her wearing are her little pearl earrings and her big watch. But, it's too late to turn back now. My heart's beating like there's a storm in my chest, so much so that I momentarily lose sight of Alice.

She's put her glass back down and is welling up again. I smile, and a solitary tear makes it all the way down her left cheek. She immediately goes to wipe it and sort of giggles at the same time. I seize upon the moment. I don't know where the courage came from but, as I see it, the gesture is as important as the ring itself right now. I reach for her, and she offers me her left hand. And from there, the little silver band fits perfectly.

"Alice, I *will* be back for you," I promise.

Alice

The restaurant is surprisingly full for so early in the week, and Nathan is all smiles with Lotte, the owner. I won't say anything, but I know he's had a hand in filling the place for her this evening. *Alzaia 26* is always empty on a Monday night.

I stretch out my hand to admire the way Nathan's gift reflects the candle light of our table. I've already told him at home and on the walk over here just how beautiful it is; how happy I am to wear it for him. Yet, for me, the most special thing about it is not the ring itself, but what it symbolises to him and to us both. The part of the story that I have not shared with Nathan is the fact that I needed to know; to be sure that he really wanted to come back to me. This is the most important thing.

To have seen him back at the apartment, risk his pride to make such a gesture, was such an adorable moment. For him to have secretly gone out and planned something so simple yet so beautiful shows real care. And, yes I do love his choice. And, yes, I accept his promise with all my heart and soul...

Right here, right now in *Alzaia 26*, I'm happy. I'm happy to be with him. And I am feeling endlessly overwhelmed today, by the lengths he is going to show me his love.

When he reaches over and takes my outstretched hand back in his, I want to tell him just how great I feel right now. I want to shout out, 'you're coming back! You're coming back to me!' But I can't. I'm lost for words.

Nathan

The restaurant is quaint and rustic with a charm all of its own, harking back to simpler times here on the canal side. The old wood beams on the ceiling and the polished dark wood covered walls transport me far away from the large modern city that's now overtaken the old quarter where this fine building still stands.

Small oil burners on every table cast gorgeous dancing shadows in all the right places around the room. A number of tea lights surround our little corner, bringing with them their natural warm glow and ambient light. And *my* Alice, as radiant as the brightest candle, sits right across from me; her smile shining even brighter still.

Amid the general hubbub of the restaurant and some calm traditional music playing quietly in the background, we talk, or rather, I do. Holding hands across the table top, I play with her ring, spinning it round and round gently between my fingers while Alice watches on, speechless for the first time since we met.

I begin to explain the plan for after I arrive back in Los Angeles. I figure that by getting everything out in the open, Alice can better understand how long I'll need to finish all my current projects over there. We also agree that I'm going to look straight into getting an annulment of my marriage to Aud from the State of Nevada. And, though the airport on Tuesday afternoon is still going to be painful whatever we decide, we promise daily *Whapping* and a plan to holiday together for the whole of December. We'll spend time alone at the apartment and travel to see some of the best Christmas markets in Europe. Then, we'll visit my mum and Beck, and be back in Italy to spend *Natale* on the lake with Alice's family.

Alice

A wonderful evening is coming to an end. I've been swept off my feet by everything we've been through today. And, here at Lotte's, completely out of the blue, I find myself struck dumb; totally overcome by a mixture of joy and sadness that I can't control. I know Nathan understands. It's such a beautiful and rare thing when you can communicate as perfectly as we do, without uttering a word. I call it, *"La telepatia dell'amore."*

I enjoy watching him, and listening as he talks. He's so handsome, and with the added charm of not knowing it. From his high defined cheekbones, warm, inviting brown eyes and soft kissable lips, to the day's layer of dark stubble on his face, I could sit here for an eternity just gazing dreamily through the candlelight at him.

I love how he walks tall. And I can't get enough of his toned body, hidden beneath his sweater right now. But later on,…

When I muse on his achievements both in Europe and America, it's hard to see why he's so self-deprecating. His natural shyness, and the way he tilts his head to one side when he's embarrassed is so sweet. Yet, it also adds a certain mystique that's *oh so sexy* in him.

I observe from behind my little espresso cup as he runs a hand through his shiny brown hair and looks down at his whisky, as if deep in contemplation. He swirls the amber liquid around and around in the glass and I wonder what he's thinking about, hoping to catch his eye so that I can tell him how much I love him again by telepathy.

His eyes widen to meet mine as he draws his head back to sip whisky, and for the first time today, I see sadness in them. '*I feel the same,*' I say to him in my mind. '*I don't want to be apart from you either.*'

When it's time for us to leave, Nathan is so sweet with Lotte and the other people still in the restaurant. He's tactile, interested in the things people say to him, and generous in his praise, particularly of the *risotto* they pride themselves on.

I stand beside him at the door, holding his hand in a state of reverie. Nathan's chatting with another guest and I'm just wondering whether in the space of three days and three nights, I made him like this… I'm sure that I didn't. This *'love'* inside of him must've been there all along. Perhaps, he just needed someone to come along, shake him up and pop the cork? And, maybe, just maybe, that person was me?

We leave and make our way over the little stone bridge back onto the Ripa. We walk slowly, in silence, and Nathan holds me close to his chest against the cold night air.

At home, I want to make love again as soon as we arrive... In the gloom of our bedroom, the only light trickling through from the kitchen, we lie, entwined... Nathan, catching my mood perfectly, moves his fingers delicately over my skin. He traces the contours of my body from head to toe, generating electricity with every touch. I think my mind has been in a partial state of paralysis all evening. But, as his hands glide back upwards caressing my breasts, the curse is broken; I suddenly spark back to life, feeling *everything*.

Our lips meet once again, a perfect fit. His eyes search mine and find me, on fire. In the heat of passion, all my worries are banished from mind. Tomorrow, the memory of now will be what gets me through watching him leave. For the rest of tonight, after our bodies relax once more, I'll hold him in my arms, keep him warm and he'll know where his home is.

Nathan

Just in front of the lines of people readying themselves for airport security, we face one another.

"*Ça y est*. England first, and then on..." The words tumble out of my mouth quickly, and as little more than a dull murmur. "I really hate saying goodbye to you Alice."

"You're not leaving me," she declares. "I have you here." She pulls me close to her and holds out her left hand.

"And I have you in here." She gestures with the same hand, pressing her palm towards her heart. "We'll talk when you're safely home and rested, and when your work is done in Los Angeles… and Nevada, you'll be back. Now, turn around, walk away and do all that you have to. I'll do the same. Busy people, no tears."

And, she's right. Alice is always right. She only hesitated briefly before saying 'Nevada.' We talked about my necessary little detour last night. I need to make an application to the state department there to annul my marriage to Aud. It's apparently a simple enough procedure if the conditions are right, says the internet, and Aud already agreed to help if needed. Still,…

…Our time, this time, is almost up and my heart is racing as I pull her closer towards me one last time. When we kiss, I run my hand over her softly bunched up hair, releasing it down. Then, stepping back, I hold up her scrunchie. "A souvenir," I grin.

Alice nods tearily back at me and I gather my stuff.

It's time.

Alice

I finally turn away from Nathan at the gate. I don't want to cry in front of him again. I should save all of my tears for the tissues in my overcoat on the train home. The memory of all his kisses and his touch sends beautiful shock waves right through my entire body with every step I take. And, as I leave the main concourse at *Malpensa* back to the underground platform for my train to *Centrale*, I sit down on a bench and smile to myself.

Him & Her…

A decade earlier, Milan's Lockdowns were coming to an end. Talk of imminent vaccines for the first virus, meant some semblance of normality could return. Yet, for international businesses in *Porta Nuova* and their customers around the world, changes in how client services were managed, needed to be addressed. A lot of time and capital was spent reassessing how this would work at all levels of business. And, with new international laws meaning that world travel became highly restricted from 2022 onwards, so a new breed of hi-tech bank official was born.

Alice was fresh out of university at the time. With impressive credentials, the right look, and the ability to speak several languages, she seized her chance at one of Milan's biggest banks.

Most domestic business started to be done using video game inspired node-technology by the end of that year. And by 2025, with better tech then available, it became the norm for all standard level business meetings to be done without anyone needing to leave their own desk; their individual avatars getting together on the new *cyber conferences* app.

But, where decisive meetings and events were required overseas, larger firms still insisted on sending their top negotiators. At the time when Alice met Nathan, she was one of them.

The very next morning, she took an important assignment in Prague. But then, almost as soon as she returned to Milan, Alice tendered her resignation. She insisted it wasn't something she took lightly, but politely declined to give her reasons. Her employers were naturally not keen to let her go easily, and Alice had to promise them she had not been headhunted by a client or a rival firm.

She told colleagues she simply wanted a hiatus to consider her future. But, this only prompted concerns for her well-being and workload. Offers of extended holiday time to recharge her batteries soon followed. Though for Alice, her mind was already irreversibly made up. She knew exactly what she wanted to do next.

During her notice period, she worked abroad as often as she could. She found that keeping busy helped her mind to stay active and made the time pass quicker until her love would return. She visited some of her most valued clients in Edinburgh, Frankfurt and Paris, principally on business, but also to wish everyone she knew a fond farewell. Not unexpectedly, Alice received some lucrative job offers while on her travels. But, she always discreetly declined.

There was nothing, it appeared, that would divert Alice away from the course she'd plotted for herself. During their long month apart, Alice and Nathan had talked almost every day. Nathan had never asked Alice to give up her work for him, but when she spoke of having resigned, he set about building her confidence back up on piano with a view to a future comeback of sorts. And, with all this and more in mind, Alice worked her last day in banking on Friday 28th November 2031.

That evening, she sat at her grand piano with enough time to kill before Marco and Noah came around for a celebratory takeaway meal, and performed a piece of music that she'd not attempted since 2016. In *Cristofori's Dream,* she immersed herself, closing her eyes on the room and feeling absent love in each delicate note, safe in the knowledge that Nathan would be returning to her very soon...

When Nathan arrived back in California, the first thing he did was sign off on *The Truth and the Light,* definitely his best movie to date. James Roy's interventions both as co-director and co-writer had changed the film from out and out 'art-house' into a stylish modern love story with an open, yet positive ending.

All of his earlier anger and resentment towards James soon disappeared after he watched the finished product from start to finish alongside some of the cast and crew. And, buoyed by Alice's love and affection, even 10,000km apart, Nathan's general attitude around Tinseltown improved so much that *Hollywood Reporter* started sniffing around looking for gossip.

Despite many calls to respond, Nathan never did. He went out on two dinner dates with his compatriot, James Corden as well as members of his film's production crew on different days. He always smiled at any waiting cameras and replied confidently if asked about his imminent comeback.

Whenever he got the chance, Nathan also went for a decent home cooked meal at James Roy's house in *Malibu*. While James was still away in Europe, Mrs. Roy who enjoyed Nathan's dry English wit, liked having him over. And, after so many long months spent isolating himself in the Hollywood hills, Nathan just appreciated being invited.

With Mrs. Roy's help, Nathan managed to find an online company offering 'Joint Petition Annulments' of all Nevada marriages for as little as $1250 all in. Plus, he didn't even need to go back to Vegas!

After quickly receiving written consent from Aud in Europe, Nathan started the annulment process, specifically referencing as grounds, that '*the two had never engaged in sexual intercourse and had married each other while intoxicated with alcohol and possibly other stimulants and depressants while vacationing in Las Vegas.*'

'*Nevada Freedom*' who promised a thirty-year history of success and discretion in these matters, dealt with all the necessaries. And, after James Roy's lawyer made the company sign away all rights to inform the media of this particular case, Nathan and Aud were single again within as little as seven days of his original email.

Nathan gave the good news to Alice during a *3D Whapp* call on the evening of Monday 18th November 2031. It was still only early afternoon in Milan, but Alice was at home having just returned from Scotland the night before.

Two days later, Nathan left his house in Los Angeles and headed back to LAX, intending to fly direct to Barcelona. He'd completed his docusoap charting the rise of the U.S. Rugby team, and was on his way to do a voiceover in English for a Catalan *TV3* documentary and to discuss filming their Spanish Conflict for Belgian television.

Alice was well aware of Nathan's decision to honour his promises to the Catalans. She was excited that he'd soon be back in Europe and in the same time zone as her. But, she was worried for his safety and made that abundantly clear in conversation.

A short time before take-off in Los Angeles, and perhaps feeding off her concerns, Nathan was asked to comment by journalists unknown inside the baggage hall, about several unsubstantiated reports of a threat being made against him by a Spanish nationalist group, *Acción Contra la*

Separación (ACS). Nathan had frustratedly replied that ACS were *'no more than a bunch of little mierdas'* and the quote had gone viral immediately.

An international incident was sparked involving officials in Madrid saying that if he boarded his flight and was not killed in Barcelona, Spain would get to him and imprison him for incitement alongside his treasonous Catalan friends.

U.S. Immigration eventually pulled a bemused Nathan out of the line on the boarding ramp after apparently receiving some speedy safety advice from the English regarding their citizen.

Nathan stayed overnight down on the coast as Mrs. Roy's guest again. And, after some hasty and very lucky ticket changes, he flew to Manchester, England the very next afternoon. Everything at the airport had happened so quickly, Nathan didn't get chance to tell Alice what was going on until the next morning *en route* back to LAX in James' driverless car. Again, Alice advised Nathan against travelling on from England to Catalonia. The whole Iberian situation had given her a sleepless night worrying about him, and she hoped he'd reconsider taking the jobs he'd agreed to do over there, and just come back to her as soon as he'd seen his family.

Nathan reassured Alice that he'd be extra careful. Only, he wasn't. Soon after landing in England, he was asked to comment on his *'Catalan issues'* by reporters just beyond the gate. Nathan was jetlagged and simply wanted to get home. He ended up flicking his middle finger at the lens of a TV camera, and told journalists he'd thought were English to *'fuck off.'*

At his family home on Merseyside, Nathan had chance to reflect. What he'd done at the airport was wrong, and he wished he could take it back. The whole business had unnerved him, and served as a timely reminder of problems past, that deep down, he didn't want a repeat of. Alice had given Nathan the strength to look forwards again. And, conscious that she thought his involvement in Catalan politics too dangerous to pursue, he decided to put it to bed. As far as Nathan was concerned, the whole 'Catalan adventure' had run its course; his media commitments in Brussels and Barcelona could all just go to hell!

The next day, live on English radio, Nathan was asked over the telephone, to comment on his airport issues. He tried to explain that he'd been tired and made a half-hearted attempt at an apology. But, those asking the questions in Manchester had not been English as he'd suspected. They were Catalans from *TV3* in Barcelona.

"A very sad, very sad indeed and unwinnable war," said Nathan when pressed for an opinion during his interview. For the first time in his life, since he became involved with their issues, he refused to be drawn to one side or the other of the argument. "I simply can't help," he concluded.

Nathan refused all opportunities to explain his comments in greater depth. But when the journalist on *EWBC Radio 4's Today* Programme wouldn't let it lie, Nathan said that he had a family who needed him strong, and the Iberian Wars were none of his business. He then apologised again for any offence caused to both the Spanish and Catalan medias, but said that he wouldn't be back there again under any circumstance any time soon.

Threats of retribution against Nathaniel Scott particularly from Catalan separatist groups, grew and grew in the run up to Christmas 2031. Alice and Nathan had had strong words about this. She was of course trying to protect him. His comments on an English cable news channel later that same day after his *Today Show* interview, had gone viral. "I did what no one has ever been able to do in war or peace," he'd claimed. "I unified opinion in Spain and Catalonia!"

After a short break with his mum in Liverpool, Nathan flew back into Milan on a Sunday. He was public enemy number one in Catalonia. His comments had poured petrol on an already raging fire. And, his refusal to head back there to complete film work he'd promised was the least of his problems. Sergi Planas, the *de facto* leader of the new unofficial Catalan Republic declared publicly that Nathan would pay a heavy price for his actions. But he didn't care. Nathan only had his sights set on one thing…

It was the first day of advent, and one of the budget air passengers from Manchester on that day was a young man in shades, a low hanging baseball hat, jeans and a *Lakers* hoodie with hand luggage only. He flew discreetly on a French passport. He refused all offer of food or drinks on board the plane, speaking only in French, and passed through customs at the E.U. citizens electronic check in desks as opposed to joining the manned queue reserved for the English and other foreigners.

It had been his mum's idea: Low profile. New focus. Love.

Her

I can see him looking over at me from the table by the wall. I always clock everything in a crowded space. It's something I picked up from my boyfriend. He never sits in a bar or restaurant alone with his back to the rest of the room. He's talked to me a lot about this habit of his. He claims it's an Italian thing, though I very much doubt that. I'm Italian. He is not.

For the record, I have been sitting in the old aperitif bar, *UGO* on a side street just off *Alzaia Naviglio Grande* in Milan for the last hour waiting for him, praying for his safe return to me. Nathaniel Scott, or Nathan as I've come to call him, says this odd seating habit of his has something historical to do with Sicilian gangsters fearing a back stabbing if seated against the crowd. And, some might say that what with recent events in the media, Nathan himself has good cause to fear being stabbed in the back.

My Nathan is someone who has always enjoyed his own company over a party. And, this is kind of how we came to meet in the first place. You see, he's a secret people watcher. He reads stories in their gestures and postures, and he loves watching how folk interact. Above all though, Nathan enjoys gazing at me. In my eyes, he's found the meaning of true love. He loses his way when he can't see me, and right now he's been away from me for far too long.

His hair is longer than when he left me, yet still an amusing brown mop. I know his eyes are a gorgeous chestnut colour. He's hiding them from me behind sunglasses but I know it's him. His lightly tanned skin is typical of a man who's been living under the California sunshine. And, as the path taken by his gaze and mine briefly meets, I need to take a deep breath. Electricity. It's like he never left. I lower my eyes towards the top of my wine, and my fingers as they nervously spin the glass slowly round and round on the spot.

In that moment, he's got up and walked across the room, drawn up a chair and sat himself and his shades down right opposite me.

He says something about never having done anything like this before, grinning all the while.

"Ok?" I quip, trying to stifle a smile.

"You really look like my amazing girlfriend, Alice. And, I wondered if maybe you and I could spend this evening together, and maybe we'll find each other interesting, and never want to be apart ever again. May I sit?"

Him

She and I have been apart for quite some time. I worried before I arrived here about how it would be when we saw each other in the flesh again... There was no need. She is beautiful. She is amazing. She is everything.

Over the month or so that I've been away, we've met for coffee on 3D chat, usually in the morning for me, the evening for her. I talk about my work and how it's all going, and more recently she's pretty much known what I've been doing as I've been making headlines for all the wrong reasons in Spain and Catalonia.

Alice also talks about what she does. She's just quit her career in banking, which I know must've been a huge, huge step for her. I so admire her for the courage that must've taken. Though she's shy about it, she's also started taking the piano seriously again for the first time in more than a decade. I'm so proud of her for this too. And, I hope I can convince her to start playing professionally. She's so passionate and so talented, I just know she'll be a star.

But right now, looking straight at her across a small table for the first time in weeks, all I want to do is take her in my arms again. It's like nothing else matters when I'm with Alice, and the rest of this crazy world will just vanish into thin air around us, the second we touch...

I take off my sunglasses and our eyes meet once again. "I've never done anything like this before," I tease.

"Ok?" says Alice, trying and failing to sound all serious and sensual.

"It's just that you really look like my amazing girlfriend, Alice," I say. "And, I wondered if maybe you and I could spend this evening together, and maybe we'll find each other interesting, and never want to be apart ever again. May I sit?"

EPILOGUE – Friday 28th May 2032

"Do you take this man to be your lawfully wedded husband?" asked the master of ceremonies.

The sun, majestic against its prepossessing pale blue backdrop, rained down on *Aura Villa del Lago*. It was truly a palatial setting. With splendid manicured lawns and beautiful botanical gardens, right on the banks of Lake Como, this was a wedding venue perfectly fit for the new King of Hollywood and his beautiful young queen.

Nathan, also looked good. Yet, more importantly, he felt good too. For the last five months, he and Alice had toured the world attending awards ceremonies and premieres for his latest movie, *The Truth and the Light*.

In January 2032, the film had won big at both the *BAFTAs* in England, and *The Golden Globes* in Los Angeles. They'd also received awards and nominations in a host of other countries including Spain. And, the U.S. media was really starting to warm to Nathan as he relaxed and smiled more than he'd ever done before at media events. For her part, Alice loved the reception she got on what was only her first visit to California. And, she vowed publicly to go back for longer as soon as the chance came about.

Audrey Novel picked up the commendation for Best Foreign Language Film at the *César* Awards in Paris on behalf of the whole crew. But, the biggest prize of all, the *Academy Awards* or *Oscars*, in February, saw *The Truth and the Light* nominated in an amazing nine categories. They eventually won a fantastic four! And, James Roy with Nathan jointly took Best Director and Best Film, effectively cementing their names amongst the very best in the business.

Alice radiated beauty in traditional white. Her hair was braided elegantly with white flowers, and only the odd strand fell either side of her face in delicate rebellion.

Nathan, dashing in his black morning suit, beamed at Alice who smiled just as broadly back, facing him, both of her hands held delicately in his. Seconds earlier, he'd replied "yes", more convincingly than any 'yes' he'd ever uttered in his entire life.

For a moment, Alice stalled as she heard the same question asked of her. She looked over at her parents and at Marco and Noah. She glanced out over the lake towards the mountain range, noble and tall in the distance. Then, she turned again, and raised her head to look at her own man mountain. *"Sì,"* she grinned. *"Sì."*

The rings perfectly suited their minimalist style as a couple, simple bands in elegant white gold. And, as Nathan and Alice broke off from their first kiss as husband and wife, a grinning Mrs. Scott waved to their guests before turning to Mr. Scott and asking, "so, what now?"

"I don't know," he replied, smiling back at her. "But I'm sure it'll be an adventure."

Later that evening, after all of the festivities had died down, Alice and Nathan returned to their suite in the villa. Nathan stood at the window and looked out over the lake, illuminated by a clear night sky full of stars. Alice was in the shower.

As he listened to the night-critters chirping in the undergrowth down below, Nathan desperately fought an internal battle with himself. She'd be back with him any minute, and this was supposed to be the happiest night of their lives…

The terror just wouldn't go away though. Ever since the end of their reception dinner when Nathan had been called away, to take a call from overseas, the fear thoughts had played on continuous loop in Nathan's mind.

Alice approached so quietly she startled him. Looking up, she squeezed his hand. "Are you okay?" she cooed.

"I'm fine," he sighed.

Nathan glanced down at his bride, trying hard not to give himself away. Alice gazed back up at him, a picture of pure innocence with her neat, high ponytail, no makeup and dressed in a clean white bathrobe from the hotel.

"What would you think if we took the car tomorrow and just drove all day to somewhere else?" he asked suddenly. "Get away for a week… you and me, and peace and quiet."

"Where did you have in mind?" inquired Alice, intrigued.

"I don't know. I know a place in northern France. It's a bit remote but…"

"Okay." Alice spoke up before he'd even finished his sentence. "And will you write when we're there?"

"I will if you will," replied Nathan. "In fact, I already started scribbling something just the other day. It's just another romance but…"

"Tell me how it starts," she cried.

"Well," began Nathan. "It all takes place over a long weekend. A sad young man is sitting alone in a bar, when he is approached, completely out of the blue by the most beautiful girl he's ever seen in his life…"

Alice stopped him dead in his tracks. Then, she pulled Nathan gently towards her and rose up on her toes like she always did when she wanted to grab his full attention. Delicately, she bit her lower lip and continued to gaze up at her husband, sweetly seductive; waiting…

Nathan smiled knowingly, then kissed his wife. For Alice, his touch made the whole world fall away. She sensed his heart beat against her chest. She savoured his soft warm lips, and felt safe, loved and comforted. For Nathan, he didn't want to upset Alice with his worries. He promised himself he'd deal with them in the morning before they became bigger problems.

Outside, the water gently brushed back and forth against the shore, the night air was warm and still, and all was well for now, with Mr. and Mrs. Scott.

FIN

Please, please, please don't forget to rate this title at Amazon.co.uk or with Goodreads.

All of us new, upcoming authors rely on the reviews we receive from our beloved readers to help promote our work.

Thank you, for reading and thanks for your support.
Stephen J. Alexander
The Author, Made in Milan

MADE IN MILAN is the first title in a genre bending trilogy of novels tracking Nathan and Alice Scott's often troubled life together.

COMING SOON TO KDP:
BOOK 2 in the Series,
"FALLING STRONG"

FALLING STRONG

It's June 2032, and newly-wed bride Alice Scott has been kidnapped.

Bound, broken and transported far away, her first thought after Nathan, is to find out why she was taken.

But, while Alice thinks she's been snatched for ransom, there's much more to this dark romantic thriller than meets the eye...

Stephen J. Alexander is also the critically acclaimed author of:

Published by Olympia Pub., 2018.

"Join Peter and his daddy as they embark on a magical mission into the depths of outer space to explore the little known, dwarf planets.
Brought to life with stunning illustrations by Laura Coppolaro, this charming tale will both delight and educate young readers."

4.3 stars on Amazon.co.uk

4.8 stars on Goodreads

Please follow me at:

https://olympiapublishers.com/authors/stephen-j-alexander/

https://www.amazon.co.uk/Stephen-J-Alexander

https://www.goodreads.com/author/show/19074010.Stephen_J_Alexander

Twitter: @dwarfplanets5

Instagram: stephen_alexander_author

Facebook: www.facebook.com/dwarfplanets5